JOHN GODFREY'S FORTUNES;

RELATED BY HIMSELF.

A STORY OF AMERICAN LIFE.

BY

BAYARD TAYLOR.

NEW YORK:
G. P. PUTNAM; HURD AND HOUGHTON.
1864.

RIVERSIDE, CAMBRIDGE:
STEREOTYPED AND PRINTED BY
H. O. HOUGHTON AND COMPANY.

TO JAMES LORIMER GRAHAM, Jr., Esq.,

New York.

My dear Graham, — I owe it to your kindness that the mechanical labor of putting this book into words has been so greatly reduced as almost to become a pleasure. Hence you were much in my thoughts while I wrote, and I do not ask your permission to associate your name with the completed work.

I have found, from experience, that whatever the preliminary explanations an author may choose to give, they are practically useless. Those persons who insist — against my own express declaration — that "Hannah Thurston" was intended as a picture of the "Reformers" of this country, will be sure to make the discovery that this book represents the literary guild. Those, also, who imagine that they recognized the author in Maxwell Woodbury, will not fail to recognize him in John Godfrey, although there is no resemblance between the two characters. Finally, those sensitive readers who protest against any representation of "American Life," which is not an unmitigated glorification of the same, will repeat their dissatisfaction, and insist that a single work should contain every feature of that complex national being, which a thousand volumes could not exhaust.

I will only say (to you, who will believe me) of this book, that, like its predecessor, it is the result of observation. Not what ought to be, or might be, is the proper province of fiction, but what is. And so, throwing upon John Godfrey's head all the consequences of this declaration, I send him forth to try new fortunes.

Yours always,

BAYARD TAYLOR.

CEDARCROFT, *September*, 1864.

CONTENTS.

JOHN GODFREY'S FORTUNES;

RELATED BY HIMSELF.

CHAPTER I.

IN WHICH, AFTER THE VISIT OF NEIGHBOR NILES, MY CHILDHOOD SUDDENLY TERMINATES.

I WAS sitting at the front window, buried, chin-deep, in the perusal of "Sandford and Merton," when I heard the latch of the gate click. Looking up, I saw that it was only Neighbor Niles, coming, as usual, in her sun-bonnet, with her bare arms wrapped in her apron, for a chat with mother. I therefore resumed my reading, for Neighbor Niles always burst into the house without knocking, and mother was sure to know who it was by the manner in which the door opened. I had gotten as far into the book as the building of the Robinson-Crusoe hut, and one half of my mind speculated, as I read, whether a similar hut might not be constructed in our garden, in the corner between the snowball-bush and Muley's stable. Bob Simmons would help me, I was sure; only it was scarcely possible to finish it before winter, and then we could n't live in it without a fireplace and a chimney.

Mother was hard at work, making me a new jacket of gray satinet, lined with black chintz. My reading was interrupted by the necessity of jumping up every ten minutes, jerking off my old coat and trying on the new one, — sometimes the body without the sleeves, sometimes one of the sleeves alone. Somehow it would n't fit at the shoulders, and the front halves, instead of lying smoothly upon my breast as they should have done, continually turned and flew back against my arms, as if I had been running at full speed. A tailor would have done the work better, it can't be denied, but mother could not afford that. "You can keep it buttoned, Johnny dear," she would say, "and then I think it 'll look very nice."

Presently the door burst open, and there was Neighbor Niles, voice and figure all at once, loud, hearty, and bustling. Always hurried to "within an inch of her life," always working "like six yoke of oxen," (as she was accustomed to say,) she inveterately gossiped in the midst of her labor, and jumped up in sudden spirts of work when she might have rested. We knew her well and liked her. I believe, indeed, she was generally liked in the neighborhood; but when some of the farmers, deceived by her own chatter, spoke of her as "a smart, *doing* woman," their wives would remark, with a slight toss of the head, "Them that talks the most does n't always do the most."

On this occasion, her *voice* entered the room, as nearly as I can recollect, in the following style: —

"Good mornin', Neighbor Godfrey! Well, Johnny, how 's *he?* Still a-readin'? He 'll be gittin' too much in that head o' his'n. Jist put my bakin' into th' oven, — six punkin-pies, ten dried-apple, and eight loaves o' bread, besides a pan o' rusk. If I had nothin' else to do but bake, 't would be enough for one woman: things *goes* in our house. Got the jacket most done? Might ha' saved a little stuff if you 'd ha' cut that left arm more catercornered, — 't would ha' been full long, I guess, and there a'n't no nap, o' no account, on satinet. Jane Koffmann, she was over at Readin' last week, and got some for *her* boys, a fippenny-bit a yard cheaper 'n this. Don't know, though, as it 'll wear so well. Laws! are you sewin' with silk instead o' patent thread?"

"I find it saves me work," said my mother, as Neighbor Niles popped into the nearest chair, drew her hands from under her apron, leaned over, and picked up a spool from the lap-board. "Patent thread soon wears out at the elbows and shoulders, and then there are rips, you know. Besides, the color don't hold, and the seams soon look shabby."

I resumed my reading, while our visitor exhausted the small budget of gossip which had accumulated since her last visit, two days before. Her words fell upon my ears mechanically, but failed to make any impression upon my mind, which was wholly fixed upon the book. After a while, however, my mother called to me, —

"Johnny, I think there 's some clearing up to do in the garden."

I knew what that meant. Mother wished to have some talk with Neighbor Niles, which I was not to hear. Many a time had I been sent into the garden, on the pretence of "clearing up things," when I knew, and mother also knew, that the beds were weeded, the alleys clean scraped, the rubbish gathered together and thrown into the little stable-yard, and all other work done which a strong inventive faculty could suggest. It was a delicate way of getting me out of the room.

I laid down my book with a sigh, but brightened up as the idea occurred to me that I might now, at once, select the site of my possible Crusoe hut, and take an inventory of the material available for its construction. As I paused on the oblong strip of turf, spread like a rug before the garden-door, and glanced in at the back-window, I saw that mother had already dropped her sewing, and that she and Neighbor Niles had put their heads together, in a strictly literal sense, for a private consultation.

The garden was a long, narrow plot of ground, running back to the stable of our cow, and the adjoining yard, which she was obliged to share with two well-grown and voracious pigs. I walked along the main alley, peering into the beds right and left for something to "clear up," in order to satisfy my conscience before commencing my castle- or rather hut-building; but I found nothing more serious than three dry stalks of seed-radishes, which I pulled up and flung over the fence. Then I walked straight to the snow-ball-bush. I remember pacing off the length and breadth of the snug, grassy corner behind it, and discovering, to my grief, that, although there was room for a hut big enough for Bob and myself to sit in, it would be impossible to walk about, — much less swing a cat by the tail. In fact, we should have to take as model another small edifice, which, on the other side of the bush, already disturbed the needful solitude. Moreover, not a hand's-breadth of board or a stick of loose timber was to be found. "If I were only in Charley Rand's place!" I thought. His father had a piece of woodland in which you might lose your way for as much as a quarter of an hour at a time, with enough of dead boughs and refuse bark to build a whole encampment of huts. Charley, perhaps, might be willing to join in the sport; but he was not a favorite playfellow of mine, and would be certain to claim the hut as his exclusive property, after we other fellows had helped him to build it. He was that sort of a boy. Then my fancy wandered away to the real Crusoe on his island, and I repeated to myself Cowper's "Verses, supposed to be written by Alexander Selkirk." Somehow, the lines gave an unexpected turn to my thoughts. Where would be the great fun of playing Crusoe, or even his imitators, Sandford and Merton, in a back-garden, where a fellow's mother might call him away at any moment? I should not be out of humanity's reach, nor cease to hear the sweet music of speech; the beasts that roam over the plain (especially McAllister's bull, in the next field) would not behold my form with indifference, nor would they suddenly become shockingly tame. It would all be a make-believe, from beginning to end, requiring even greater efforts of imagination than I had perpetrated a few years earlier, in playing at the village school, —

> "Here come three lords, all out of Spain,
> A-courting of your daughter Jane,"

or in creating real terror by fancying a bear crouching behind the briers in the fence-corner.

A little ashamed of myself, I walked to the garden-paling, and looked over it, and across the rolling fields, to some low, hazy hills in the distance. I belong to that small class of men whose natures are not developed by a steady, gradual process of growth, but advance by sudden and seemingly arbitrary bounds, divided by intervals during which their faculties remain almost stationary. I had now reached one of those periods of growth, — the first, indeed, which clearly presented itself to my own consciousness. I had passed my sixteenth birthday, and the physical change which was imminent began to touch and give color to the operations of my mind. My vision did not pause at the farthest hill, but went on, eagerly, into the unknown landscape beyond. I had previously talked of the life that lay before me as I had talked of Sinbad and Gulliver, Robert Bruce and William Tell: all at once I became conscious that it was an earnest business.

What must I do? What should I become? The few occupations which found a place in our little village repelled me. My frame was slight, and I felt that, even if I liked it, I could never swing the blacksmith's hammer, or rip boards like Dick Brown, the carpenter. Moreover, I had an instinctive dislike to all kinds of manual labor, except the light gardening tasks in which I assisted my mother. Sometimes, in the harvest-season, I had earned a little pocket-money on the neighboring farms. It was pleasant enough to toss hay into cocks on the fragrant meadows, but I did n't like the smother of packing it in the steaming mows, and my fingers became painfully sore from binding sheaves. My ambition — at this time but a vague, formless desire — was to be a scholar, a man of learning. How this was to be attained, or what lay beyond it, I could not clearly see. I knew, without being able to explain why, that the Cross-Keys (as our village was called, from its tavern-sign) was no place for me. But, up to the afternoon I am describing, I had never given the subject a serious thought.

Many a boy of ten knows far more of the world than I then did. I doubt if any shepherd on the high Norwegian *fjelds* lives in greater seclusion than did we, — my mother and myself. The Cross-Keys lay aside from any of the main highways of the county, and the farmers around were mostly descendants of the original settlers of the soil, a hundred and fifty years before. Their lives were still as simple and primitive as in the last century. Few of them ever travelled farther than to the Philadelphia market, at the beginning of winter, to dispose of their pigs and poultry. A mixture of the German element, dating from the first emigration, tended still further to conserve the habits and modes of thought of the community. My maternal grandfather, Hatzfeld, was of this stock, and many of his peculiarities, passing over my mother, have reappeared in me, to play their part in the shaping of my fortunes.

My father had been a house- and sign-painter in the larger village of Honeybrook, four miles distant. Immediately after his death, which happened when I was eight years old, my mother removed to the Cross-Keys, principally because she had inherited the small cottage and garden from her spinster aunt, Christina Hatzfeld. There was nothing else, for my great-aunt had only a life-interest in the main estate, which — I do not know precisely how — had passed into the hands of the male heirs. My mother's means were scarcely sufficient to support us in the simplest way, and she was therefore in the habit of "taking in sewing" from the wives of the neighboring farmers. Her labor was often paid in produce, and she sometimes received, in addition, presents of fruit, potatoes, and fuel from the kindly-hearted people. Thus we never reached the verge of actual want, though there were times when our daily fare was plainer than she cared to let the neighbors see, and when the new coat or shawl had to be postponed to a more fortunate season. For at least half the year I attended the village school, and had already learned nearly as much as a teacher hired for twenty dollars a month was capable of imparting. The last one, indeed, was unable to help me through quadratic equations, and forced me, unwillingly, upon a course of Mensuration.

Between mother and myself there was the most entire confidence, except upon the single subject of my future. She was at once mother and elder sister, entering with heart and soul into all my childish plans of work or play, listening with equal interest to the stories I read, or relating to me the humble incidents of her own life, with a sweet, fresh simplicity of language, which never lost by repetition. Her large black eyes would sparkle, and her round face, to which the old-fashioned puffs of hair on the temples gave such an odd charm, became as youthful in expression, I am sure, as my own. Her past and her present were freely shared with me, but she drew back when I turned with any seriousness towards the future. At one time, I think, she would have willingly stopped the march of my years, and been content to keep me at her side, a boy forever. I was incapable of detecting this feeling at the time, and perhaps I wrong her memory in alluding to it now. God knows I have often wished it could have been so! Whatever of natural selfishness there may have been in the thought, she weighed it down, out of sight, by all those years of self-denial, and the final sacrifice, for my sake. No truer, tenderer, more single-hearted mother ever lived than Barbara Godfrey.

She was so cordially esteemed in our little community that no reproach, on my account, was allowed to reach her ears. A boy of my age, who had no settled occupation, was there considered to be in danger of becoming a useless member of society; antipathy to hard, coarse manual labor implied a moral deficiency; much schooling, for one without means, was a probable evil: but no one had the heart to unsettle the widow's comfort in her child. Now and then, perhaps, a visitor might ask, "What are you going to make of him, Barbara?" whereupon my mother would answer, "He must make himself," — with a confident smile which put the question aside.

These words came across my mind as I leaned against the palings, trying to summon some fleeting outline of my destiny from the vapory distance of the landscape. I was perplexed, but not discouraged. My trials, thus far, had been few. When I first went to school, the boys had called me "Bricktop," on account of the auburn tinge of my hair, which was a source of great sorrow until Sam Haskell, whose head was of fiery hue, relieved me of the epithet. Emily Rand, whose blue eyes and yellow ringlets confused my lessons, (I am not certain but her pink-spotted calico frock had something to do with it,) treated me scornfully, and even scratched my face when it was my turn to kiss her in playing "Love and War." The farmers' sons also laughed at my awkwardness and want of muscle; but this annoyance was counterbalanced in the winter, when they came to measure another sort of strength with me at school. I had an impression that my value in the neighborhood was not estimated very highly, and had periodical attacks of shyness which almost amounted to self-distrust. On the other hand, I had never experienced any marked unkindness or injustice; my mother spoke ill of no one, and I did not imagine the human race to be otherwise than honest, virtuous, and reciprocally helpful.

I soon grew tired of facing the sober aspect of reality,

so unexpectedly presented, and wandered off, as was the habit of my mind, into vague and splendid dreams. If I had the Wonderful Lamp, — if a great roc should come sailing out of the western sky, pick me up in his claws, and carry me to the peaks overlooking the Valley of Diamonds, — if there were still a country where a cat might be sold for a ship-load of gold, — if I might carry a loaf of bread under my arm, like Benjamin Franklin, and afterwards become rich and celebrated, (the latter circumstance being, of course, a result of the former,) — there would be no difficulty about my fate. It was hardly likely, however, that either of these things would happen to me; but why not something else, equally strange and fortunate?

A hard slap on a conspicuous, but luckily not a sensitive portion of my body caused me to spring almost over the paling. I whirled around, and with a swift instinct of retaliation, struck out violently with both fists.

"No, you don't!" cried Bob Simmons, (for he it was,) dodging the blows and then catching me by the wrists. "I did n't mean to strike so hard, John; don't be mad about it. I 'm going away soon, and came around to tell you."

Bob was my special crony, because I had found him to be the kindest-hearted of all the village boys. He was not bright at school, and was apt to be rough in his language and manners; but from the day he first walked home with me, with his arm around my neck, I had faith in his affection. He seemed to like me all the better from my lack of the hard strength which filled him from head to foot. He once carried me nearly a quarter of a mile in his arms, when I had sprained my ankle in jumping down out of an apple-tree. He had that rough male nature which loves what it has once protected or helped. Besides, he was the only companion to whom I dared confide my vague projects of life, with the certainty of being not only heard, but encouraged.

"Yes," said Bob, "I am going away, maybe in a few weeks."

"Where? Not going away for good, Bob?"

"Like as not. I 'm nearly eighteen, and Dad says it 's time to go to work on my own hook. The farm, you know, is n't big enough for him and me, and he can get along with Brewster now. So I must learn a trade; what do you think it is?"

"You said, Bob, that you 'd like to be a mason?"

"Would n't I, though! But it 's the next thing to it. Dad says there a'n't agoin' to be many more stone houses built, — bricks has got to be the fashion. But they 're so light, it 's no kind o' work. All square, too; you 've just to put one atop of t' other, and there 's your wall. Why, *you* could do it, John. Mort! Mort! hurry up with that 'ere hod!"

Here Bob imitated the professional cry of the bricklayer with startling exactness. There was not a fibre about him that shrank from contact with labor, or from the rough tussle by which a poor boy must win his foothold in the world. I would, at that moment, have given my grammar and algebra (in which branches he was lamentably deficient) for a quarter of his unconscious courage. A wild thought flashed across my mind: I might also be a bricklayer, and his fellow-apprentice! Then came the discouraging drawback.

"But, Bob," I said, "the bricks are so rough. I don't like to handle them."

"Should n't wonder if *you* did n't. Lookee there!" And Bob laid my right hand in his broad, hard palm, and placed his other hand beside it. "Look at them two hands! they 're made for different kinds o' work. There 's my thick fingers and broad nails, and your thin fingers and narrow nails. You can write a'most like copy-plate, and I make the roughest kind o' pot-hooks. The bones o' your fingers is no thicker than a girl's. I dunno what I 'd do if mine was like that."

I colored, from the sense of my own physical insignificance. "Oh, Bob," I cried, "I wish I was strong! I 'll have to get my own living, too, and I don't know how to begin."

"Oh, there 's time enough for you, John," said Bob, consolingly. "You need n't fret your gizzard yet awhile. There 's teachin' school is n't so bad to start with. You 'll soon be fit to do it, and that 's what I'd never be, I reckon."

We went into the little hay-mow over the stable, and sat down, side by side, in the dusky recess, where our only light came through the cracks between the shrunk clapboards. Bob had brought a horse to the smith to be shod all round, and there were two others in before him; so he could count on a good hour before his turn came. It might be our last chat together for a long time, and the thought of this made our intercourse more frank and tender than usual.

"Tell me, Bob," said I, "what you 'll do after you 've learned the trade."

"Why, do journey-work, to be sure. They get a dollar and a half a day, in Phildelphy."

"Well, — after that?"

"Dunno. P'raps I may be boss, and do business on the wholesale. Bosses make money hand-over-fist. I tell you what, John, I 'd like to build a house for myself like Rand's, — heavy stone, two foot thick, and just such big willy-trees before it, — a hundred acres o' land, and prime stock on 't,; would n't I king it, then! Dad 's had a hard time, he has, — only sixty acres, you know, and a morgidge on it. Don't you tell nobody, — I 'm agoin' to help him pay it off, afore I put by for myself."

I had not the least idea of the nature of a mortgage, but was ashamed to ask for information. Sometimes I had looked down on Bob from the heights of my superior learning, but now he seemed to overtop me in everything, — in strength, in courage, and in practical knowledge. For the first time, I would have been willing to change places with him, — ah, how many times afterwards!

When we went down out of the hay-mow it was nearly

evening, and I hurried back to our cottage. The fire which I was accustomed to make in the little back-kitchen was already kindled, and the table set for supper. Mother was unusually silent and preoccupied; she did not even ask me where I had been. After the simple meal — made richer by the addition of four of Neighbor Niles's rusks — was over, we took our places in the sitting-room, she with her lap-board, and I with "Sandford and Merton." She did not ask me to read aloud, as usual, but went on silently and steadily with her sewing. Now and then I caught the breath of a rising sigh, checked as soon as she became conscious of it. Nearly an hour passed, and my eyelids began to grow heavy, when she suddenly spoke.

"Put away the book, John. You 're getting tired, I see, and we can talk a little. I have something to say to you."

I shut the book and turned towards her.

"It 's time, John, to be thinking of making something of you. In four or five years — and the time will go by only too fast — you 'll be a man. I 'd like to keep you here always, but I know that can't be. I must n't think of myself: I must teach you to do without me."

"But I don't want to do without you, mother!" I cried.

"I know it, Johnny dear; but you must learn it, nevertheless. Who knows how soon I may be taken from you? I want to give you a chance of more and better schooling, because you 're scarcely strong enough for hard work, and I think you 're not so dull but you could manage to get your living out of your head. At least, it would n't be right for me not to help you what little I can. I 've looked forward to it, and laid by whatever I could, — dear me, it 's not what it ought to be, but we must be thankful for what 's allowed us. I only want you to make good use of your time while it lasts; you must always remember that every day is an expense, and that the money was not easy to get."

"What do you want me to do, mother?" I asked, after a pause.

"I have been talking with Neighbor Niles about it, and she seems to see it in the same light as I do. She 's a good neighbor, and a sensible woman. Charley Rand's father is going to send him this winter to Dr. Dymond's school, a mile the other side of Honeybrook. It 's the best in the neighborhood, and I would n't want you to be far away from me yet awhile. They ask seventy-five dollars for the session, but Charley goes for sixty, having his washing and Sunday's board at home. It seems like a heap of money, John, but I 've laid away, every year since we came here, twenty dollars out of the interest on the fifteen hundred your father left me, and that 's a hundred and sixty. Perhaps I could make out to let you have two years' schooling, if I find that you get on well with your studies. I 'm afraid that I could n't do more than that, because I don't want to touch the capital. It 's all we have. Not that you would n't be able to earn your living in a few years, but we never know what 's in store for us. You might become sickly and unable to follow any regular business, or I" ——

Here my mother suddenly stopped, clasped her hands tightly together, and turned pale. Her lips were closed, as if in pain, and I could see by the tension of the muscles of her jaws that the teeth were set hard upon each other. Of late, I had several times noticed the same action. I could not drive away the impression that she was endeavoring not to cry out under the violence of some mental or physical torture. After a minute or two, the rigidity of her face softened; she heaved a sigh, which, by a transition infinitely touching, resolved itself into a low, cheerful laugh, and said, —

"But there 's no use, after all, in worrying ourselves by imagining what may never happen. Only I think it best not to touch the capital; and now you know, Johnny, what you have to depend on. There 's the money that I 've been saving for you, and you shall have the benefit of it, every penny. Some folks would say it's not wisely spent, but it's *you* must decide that by the use you make of it. If I can see, every Saturday night when you come home, that you know a little more than you did the week before, I shall be satisfied."

I was already glowing and tingling with delight at the prospect held out to me. The sum my mother named seemed to me enormous. I had heard of Dr. Dymond's school as a paradise of instruction, unattainable to common mortals. The boys who went there were a lesser kind of seraphs, sitting in the shade of a perennial tree of knowledge. With such advantages, all things seemed suddenly possible to me; and had my mother remarked, "I expect you to write a book as good as 'The Children of the Abbey,' — to make a better speech than Colonel McAllister, — to tell the precise minute when the next eclipse of the sun takes place," — I should have answered, "Oh, of course."

"When am I to go?" I asked.

"It will be very soon, — too soon for me, for I shall find the house terribly lonely without you, John. Charley Rand will go in about three weeks, and I should like to have you ready at the same time."

"Three weeks!" I exclaimed, with a joyous excitement, which I checked, feeling a pang of penitence at my own delight, as I looked at mother.

She was bravely trying to smile, but there were tears in her black eyes. One of her puffs fell out of its place; I went to her and put it back nicely, as I had often done before, — I liked to touch and arrange her hair, when she would let me. Then she began to cry, turning away her head, and saying, "Don't mind me, Johnny; I did n't mean to."

It cost me a mighty effort to say it, but I did say, — "If you'd rather have me stay at home, mother, I don't want to go. The cow must be milked and the garden looked after, anyhow. I did n't think of that."

"But I did, my child," she said, wiping her eyes with her apron. "Neighbor Niles will take Muley, and give me half the milk every day. Then, you know, as you will not be here on week-days, I shall need less garden-stuff. It 's all fixed, and must n't be changed. I made up my mind to it years ago, and ought to be thankful that I 've lived to carry it out. Now, pull off your shoes and go to bed."

I stole up the narrow, creaking ladder of a staircase to my pigeon-hole under the roof. That night I turned over more than once before I fell asleep. I was not the same boy that got out of the little low bed the morning before, and never would be again.

CHAPTER II.

DESCRIBING MY INTRODUCTION INTO DR. DYMOND'S BOARDING-SCHOOL.

FROM that day the preparations for my departure went forward without interruption. Mother quite recovered her cheerfulness, both permitting and encouraging my glowing predictions of the amount of study I should perform and the progress I should make. The jacket was finished, still retaining its perverse tendency to fly open, which gave me trouble enough afterwards. I had also a pair of trousers of the same material; they might have been a little baggy in the hinder parts, but otherwise they fitted me very well. A new cap was needed, and mother had serious thoughts of undertaking its construction. My old seal-skin was worn bare, but even a new one of the same material would scarcely have answered. Somebody reported from Honeybrook that Dr. Dymond's scholars wore stylish caps of blue cloth, and our store-keeper was therefore commissioned to get me one of the same kind from Philadelphia. He took the measure of my head, to make sure of a fit; yet, when the wonderful cap came, it proved to be much too large. " 'T will all come right in the end, Mrs. Godfrey," said the store-keeper; "his head 'll begin to swell when he 's been at school a few weeks." Meanwhile, it was carefully accommodated to my present dimensions by a roll of paper inside the morocco lining. A pair of kip-skin boots — real top-boots, and the first I ever had — completed my outfit. Compared with my previous experience, I was gorgeously arrayed. It was fortunate that my Sundays were to be spent at home, as a second suit, much less a better one, was quite beyond my mother's means.

Mr. Rand, Charley's father, made all the necessary arrangements with Dr. Dymond, and kindly offered to take me over to the school in his "rockaway," on the first Monday of November. The days dragged on with double slowness to me, but I have no doubt they rushed past like a whirlwind to mother. I did everything I could to arrange for her comfort during my absence, — put the garden in winter trim, sawed wood and piled it away, sorted the supplies of potatoes and turnips in the cellar, and whatever else she suggested, — doing these tasks with a feverish haste and an unnecessary expenditure of energy. Whenever I had a chance, I slipped away to talk over my grand prospects with Dave Niles, or some other of the half-dozen village boys of my age. I felt for them a certain amount of commiseration, which was not lessened by their sneers at Dr. Dymond's school, and the damaging stories which they told about the principal himself. I knew that any of them — unless it was Jackson Reanor, the tavern-keeper's son — would have been glad to stand in my new boots.

"I know all about old Dymond," said Dave; "he licks awfully, and not always through your trousers, neither. Charley Rand 'd give his skin if *he* had n't to go. His father makes him."

"Now, that 's a lie, Dave," I retorted. (We boys used the simplest and strongest terms in our conversation.) "Old Rand would n't let Charley be licked; you know he took him away from our school when Mr. Kendall whacked his hands with the ruler."

"Then he 'll have to take him away from Dymond's too, I guess," said Dave. "Wait, and you 'll see. Maybe there 'll be two of you."

I turned away indignantly, and went to see Bob Simmons, whose hearty sympathy was always a healing-plaster for the moral bruises inflicted by the other boys. Bob was not very demonstrative, but he had a grave, common-sense way of looking at matters which sometimes brought me down from my venturesome flights of imagination, but left me standing on firmer ground than before. When I first told him of my mother's plan, he gave me a thundering slap on the back, and exclaimed, —

"She 's a brick! It 's the very thing for you, Johnny. Come, old fellow, you and me 'll take an even start, — your head aginst my hands. I would n't stop much to bet on your head, though I *do* count on my hands doin' a good deal for me."

Finally the appointed Monday arrived. I was to go in the afternoon, and mother had dinner ready by twelve o'clock, so that Mr. Rand would not be obliged to wait a minute when he called. Her plump little body was in constant motion, dodging back and forth between the kitchen and sitting-room, while she talked upon any and every subject, as if fearful of a moment's rest or silence. "It will only be until Saturday night," she repeated, over and over again. How little I understood all this intentional bustle at the time, yet how distinctly I recall it now.

After a while, there was a cry outside of "Hallo, the house!"— quite unnecessary, for I had seen Rand's rockaway ever since it turned out of the lane beyond Reanor's stables. I hastily opened the door, and shouted, "I 'm coming!" Mother locked the well-worn, diminutive carpet-bag which I was to take along, gave me a kiss, saying cheerfully, "Only till Saturday night!" and then followed me out to the gate. Mr. Rand and Charley occupied the only two seats in the vehicle, but there was a small wooden stool for me, where I sat, wedged between their legs, holding the carpet-bag between mine. Its contents consisted of one shirt, one pair of stockings, a comb, tooth-brush and piece of soap, a box of blacking and a brush. I had never heard of a night-shirt at that time. When I opened the bag, afterwards, I discovered two fall pippins and a paper of cakes snugly stowed away in one corner.

"Good-day, Mrs. Godfrey!" said Mr. Rand, squaring himself on his seat, and drawing up the reins for a start; "I 'll call on the way home, and tell you how I left 'em."

"I shall be *so* much obliged," my mother cried. "Do you hear, Johnny? I shall have word of you to-night; now, good-bye!"

Looking back as we drove away, I saw her entering the cottage-door. Then I looked forward, and my thoughts also went forward to the approaching school-life. I felt the joy and the fear of a bird that has just been tumbled out of the nest by its parent, and flutteringly sustains itself on its own wings. I did not see, as I now can, my mother glance pitifully around the lonely room after she closed the door; carefully put away a few displaced articles; go to the window and look up the road by which I had disappeared; and then sink into her quaint old rocking-chair, and cry without stint, until her heart recovers its patience. Then I see her take up the breadths of a merino skirt for Mrs. Reanor, and begin sewing them together. Her face is calm and pale; she has rearranged her disordered puffs, and seems to be awaiting somebody. She is not disappointed: the gate-latch clicks, the door opens, and good Neighbor Niles comes in with a half-knit stocking in her hand. This means *tea*, and so the afternoon passes cheerfully away. But when the fire is raked for the night on the kitchen-hearth, mother looks or listens, forgetting afresh every few minutes that there will be no sleeper in the little garret-room to-night; takes up her lamp with a sigh, and walks wearily into her chamber; looks long at the black silhouette of my father, hung over the mantel-piece; murmurs to herself, — is it a prayer to Our Father, or a whisper to the beloved Spirit? — and at last, still murmuring words whose import I may guess, and with tears, now sad, now grateful, lies down in her bed and gives her soul to the angels that protect the holy Sleep!

Let me return to my own thoughtless, visionary, confident self. Charley and I chattered pleasantly together, as we rode along, for, although he was no great favorite of mine, the resemblance in our destined lot for the next year or two brought us into closer relations. Being an only son, he had his own way too much, and sometimes showed himself selfish and overbearing towards the rest of us; but I never thought him really ill-willed, and I could not help liking any boy (or girl, either) who seemed to like me.

Mr. Rand now and then plied us with good advice, which Charley shook off as a duck sheds water, while I received it in all earnestness, and with a conscientious desire to remember and profit by it. He also enlarged upon our future places in the world, provided our "finishing" at the school was what it ought to be.

"I don't say what either o' you *will* be, mind," he said; "but there 's no tellin' what you *might n't* be. Member o' the Legislatur' — Congress — President: any man *may* be President under our institootions. If you turn out smart and sharp, Charley, I don't say but what I might n't let you be a lawyer or a doctor, — though law pays best. You, John, 'll have to hoe your own row; and I dunno what you 're cut out for, — maybe a minister. You 've got a sort o' mild face, like; not much hard grit about you, I guess, but 't a'n't wanted in that line."

The man's words made me feel uncomfortable — the more so as I had never felt the slightest ambition to become a clergyman. I did n't quite know what he meant by "hard grit," but I felt that his criticism was disparaging, contrasted with his estimate of Charley. My reflections were interrupted by the latter saying, —

"I 'm agoin' to be what I like best, Pop!"

I said nothing, but I recollect what my thoughts were: "I 'm going to be what I can; I don't know what; but it will be *something*."

From the crest of a long, rolling wave of farm-land we now saw the village of Honeybrook, straggling across the bottom of a shallow valley, in the centre of which, hard against the breast of a long, narrow pond, stood its flour- and saw-mills. I knew the place, as well from later visits as from my childish recollections; and I knew also that the heavy brick building, buried in trees, on a rise of ground off to the northeast, was the Honeybrook Boarding-School for Boys, kept by Dr. Dymond. A small tin cupola (to my boyish eyes a miracle of architectural beauty) rose above the trees, and sparkled in the sun. Under that magnificent star I was to dwell.

We passed through the eastern end of the village, and in another quarter of an hour halted in a lane, at one end of the imposing establishment. Mr. Rand led the way into the house, Charley and I following, carpet-bags in hand. An Irish servant-girl, with a face like the rising moon, answered the bell, and ushered us into a reception-room on the right hand of the passage. The appearance of this room gave me a mingled sensation of delight and awe. There was a bookcase, a small cabinet of minerals, two large maps on the walls, and a plaster bust of Franklin on the mantel-piece. The floor was covered with oil-cloth, checkered with black and white squares, and a piece of green oil-cloth, frayed at the edges, bedecked the table. The only ornament in the room was a large spittoon of brown earthen-ware. Charley and I took our seats behind the table, on a very slippery sofa of horse-hair, while Mr. Rand leaned solemnly against the mantel-piece, making frequent use of the spittoon. Through a side-door we heard the unmistakable humming of a school in full blast.

Presently this door opened, and Dr. Dymond entered. I looked with some curiosity at the Jupiter Tonans whose nod I was henceforth to obey. He was nothing like so large a man as I expected to see. He may have been fifty years old; his black hair was well streaked with gray, and he stooped slightly. His gray eyes were keen and clear, and shaded by bushy brows, his nose long and wedge-shaped, and his lips thin and firm. He was dressed in black broadcloth, considerably glazed by wear, and his black cravat was tied with great care under a very high and stiff shirt-collar. His voice was dry and distinct, his language precise, and the regular play of his lips, from the centre towards the corners, suggested to me the idea that he *peeled* his words of any roughness or inaccuracy as they issued from his mouth.

"Ah, Mr. Rand?" he said, bowing blandly and shaking hands. "And these are the boys? The classes are scarcely formed as yet, but we shall soon get them into the right places. How do you do? This is young Godfrey, I presume."

He shook hands with us, and then turned to Mr. Rand, who took out his pocket-book and produced two small rolls, one of which I recognized as that which mother had given to him when we left home. It was "half the pay in advance," in accordance with the terms of the institution. Dr. Dymond signed two pieces of paper and delivered them in return, after which he announced: —

"I must now attend to my school. The boys may remain in the family-parlor until tea, when they will join the other pupils. They will commence the regular course of study to-morrow morning."

He ushered us across the passage into the opposite room, bade good-bye to Mr. Rand, and disappeared. "Well, boys," said the latter, "I guess it 's all ship-shape now, and I can go. I want you to hold up your heads like men, and work like beavers." He shook hands with Charley, but only patted me on the head, which I did n't like; so, when Charley ran to the window to see him drive down the lane, I turned my back and began examining the books on the table.

There were "Dick's Works," and Dr. Lardner's "Scientific Lectures," and "Redfield's Meteorology," and I don't know what besides, for, stumbling on Mrs. Somerville's "Physical Geography," I opened that, and commenced reading. I had a ravenous hunger for knowledge, and my opportunities for getting books had been so few that scarcely anything came amiss. Many of the technical terms used in the book were new to me, but I leaped lightly over them, finding plenty of stuff to keep my interest alive.

"I say, Jack," Charley suddenly called, "here 's one of the boys!"

My curiosity got the better of me. I laid down the book, and went to the window. A lank youth of about my own age, with short brown hair and sallow face, was leaning against the sunny side of a poplar-tree, munching an apple. From the way in which he made the tree cover his body, and the furtive glances he now and then threw towards the house, it was evident that he was not pursuing the "regular course of study." We watched him until he had finished the apple and thrown away the core, when he darted across to the nearest corner of the house, and crept along the wall, under the very window at which we were standing. As he was passing it, he looked up, dodged down suddenly, looked again, and, becoming reassured, gave us an impudent wink as he stole away.

We were so interested in watching this performance that a sharp "Ahem!" in the room, behind us, caused us both to start and blush, with a sense of being accessories in the misdemeanor. I turned and saw an erect, sparely formed lady of thirty-five, whose clouded gray eyes looked upon me through a pair of gold-rimmed spectacles. Her hair was brown, and hung down each side of her face in three long curls. Her gown was of a black, rustling stuff, which did not seem to be silk, and she wore a broad linen collar, almost like a boy's, with a bit of maroon-colored ribbon in front. If I were an artist, I am sure I could draw her entire figure at this moment. It was Miss Hitchcock, as I discovered next day, — a distant relative, I believe, of Dr. Dymond, who assisted him in teaching the younger boys, and, indeed, some of the older ones. Her specialty was mathematics, though it was said that she was tolerably well versed in Latin also.

"You are new scholars, young gentlemen, I see," she remarked, in a voice notable, like Dr. Dymond's, for its precise enunciation. "May I ask your names?"

Charley gave his, and I followed his example.

"Indeed! Godfrey? A mathematical name! Do you inherit the peculiar talent of your famous ancestor?"

Her question was utterly incomprehensible to me. I had never even heard of Thomas Godfrey or his quadrant, and have found no reason, since, to claim relationship with him. I had a moderate liking for abstract mathematics, but not sufficient to be developed, by any possibility, into a talent. Consequently, after stammering and hesitating, I finally answered, "I don't know."

"We shall see," she said, with a patronizing, yet friendly air. "How far have you advanced in your mathematical studies?"

I gave her the full extent of my algebra.

"Do you know Logarithms?"

Again I was cruelly embarrassed. I was not sure whether she meant a person or a book. Not being able to apply the term to anything in my memory, I at last answered in the negative.

"You will come to them by the regular progressive path," she said. "Also the Differential Calculus. There I envy you! I think the sense of power which you feel when you have mastered the Differential Calculus never can come twice in the course of a mathematical curriculum. I would be willing to begin again, if I were certain that I should experience it a second time." Here she sighed, as if recalling some vanished joy.

For my part, I began to be afraid of Miss Hitchcock. I

had never encountered, much less imagined, such a prodigy of learning. I despaired of being able to understand her; how she would despise my ignorance when she discovered it! I afterwards found that, although she was very fond of expatiating upon mathematical regions into which few of the scholars ventured, she was a very clear and capital instructress when she descended to the simpler branches.

Turning from me, she now said to Charley, "Do you share your friend's taste?"

He appeared no less bewildered than myself; but he answered, boldly, "Can't say as I do."

"Come to me, both of you."

She took a seat, and we approached her awkwardly, and with not a little wonder. She stretched forth her hands and grasped each of us by the outer arm, stationed us side by side, and looked from one to another. "Quite a difference in the heads!" she remarked, after a full minute of silent inspection: "Number is not remarkably developed in either; Language good in both; more Ideality here," (touching me on one of the temples,) "also more of the Moral Sentiment," (placing a hand on each of our heads). Then she began rubbing Charley's head smartly, over the ears, and though he started back, coloring with anger, she composedly added, "I thought so, — Acquisitiveness six plus, if not seven."

We retired to our seats, not at all edified by these cabalistic sentences. She presently went to a bookcase, glanced along the titles, and, having selected two bulky volumes, approached us, saying, "I should think these works would severally interest you, young gentlemen, judging from your developments."

On opening mine, I found it to be "Blair's Rhetoric," while Charley's, as I saw on looking over his shoulder at the title, was the first volume of "McCulloch's Commercial Dictionary." For herself she chose a volume of equal size, containing diagrams, which, from their irregular form, I am now inclined to think must have been geological. Charley seemed to be greatly bored with this literary entertainment, and I should probably have been equally so, had I not found couplets and scraps of poetry on turning over the leaves. These kernels I picked out from the thick husks of prose in which they were wrapped, and relished.

The situation was nevertheless tedious, and we were greatly relieved, an hour later, when the dusk was already falling, to hear the loud sound of a bell echoing through the house. Miss Hitchcock rose and put away her book, and we were only too glad to do likewise. The regular tramp of feet sounded in the passage, and presently an immense noise of moving chairs came from the adjoining room on our left. The door of this room opened, and Dr. Dymond beckoned to us. On entering, we beheld two long tables, at each of which about twenty boys or young men, of all ages from twelve to twenty-four, were seated. Dr. Dymond, placing himself at the head of the first table, pointed out to us two vacant seats at the bottom of the second, which was presided over by Miss Hitchcock. All eyes were upon us as we walked down the room, and I know I was red to the roots of my hair; Charley took the scrutiny more easily. It was not merely the newness of the experience, though that of itself was sufficiently embarrassing, — the consciousness of my new clothes covered me awkwardly, from head to foot. I saw some of the boys wink stealthily at each other, or thrust their tongues into their cheeks, and envied the brazen stare with which my companion answered them.

No sooner had we taken our seats than Dr. Dymond rapped upon the table with the handle of his knife. The forty boys immediately fixed their eyes upon their plates, and a short grace was uttered in a loud tone. At its conclusion, the four Irish maids in waiting set up a loud rattling of cups and spoons, and commenced pitching measures of weak tea upon the table. I was so amazed at the rapidity and apparent recklessness with which they flung the cups down beside the boys, that I forgot to help myself to the plate of cold meat until all the best pieces were gone, and I was obliged to choose between a few fatty scraps. This dish, with some country-made cheese, and a moderate quantity of bread and butter, constituted the supper. When Dr. Dymond had finished, he clasped his hands over his stomach, twirling one thumb around the other, and now and then casting a sharp glance at such of the boys as were still eating. The latter seemed to have a consciousness of the fact, for they hastily crammed the last morsels of bread into their mouths and gulped down half a cup of tea at a time. In a few moments they also crossed their knives and forks upon their plates, and sat erect in their chairs. Thereupon Dr. Dymond nodded down his table, first to the row on his right hand, and then to the row on his left, both of whom rose and retired in the same order. Miss Hitchcock gave a corresponding signal to our table, and I found myself, almost before I knew it, in the school-room on the other side of the hall. Most of the boys jerked down their caps from the pegs and rushed out-of-doors, being allowed half an hour's recreation before commencing their evening studies. With them went Charley, leaving me to look out for myself. Some half-dozen youths, all of them older than I, gathered around the stove, and I sat down shyly upon a stool not far from them, and listened to their talk. Subjects of study, village news, the private scandal of the school, and "the girls," were strangely mingled in what I heard; and not a few things caused me to open my eyes and wonder what kind of fellows they were. I had one comfort, however: they were evidently superior to my former associates at the Cross-Keys.

As they did not seem to notice me, I got up after a while and looked out the window at the other boys playing. Charley Rand was already "hail-fellow well-met" with the most of them. I have never since seen his equal for making acquaintances.

It was not long before a few strokes of the bell hanging under the tin cupola called them all into the school-room. Lamps were lighted, and the Principal made his appearance. His first care was to assign desks to us, and I was a little disappointed that Charley and I were placed at different forms. I found myself sandwiched between a grave, plodding youth of two-and-twenty, and a boy somewhat younger than myself, who had a disagreeable habit of whispering his lessons. At the desk exactly opposite to me sat a boy of eighteen, whose face struck me as the most beautiful I had ever seen, yet the impression which it produced was not precisely agreeable. His head was nobly balanced and proudly carried, the hair black and crisply curling, the skin uniform as marble in its hue, which was a very pale olive, the lips full, short, and scornfully curved, and the eyes large and bright, but too defiant, for his years, in their expression. Beside him sat his physical opposite, — a red-cheeked, blue-eyed, laughing fellow of fourteen, as fresh and sweet as a girl, but with an imp of mischief dodging about his mouth, or lurking in the shadow of his light-brown locks. I had not been at my desk fifteen minutes before he stealthily threw over to me a folded slip of paper, on which he had written, "What is your name?"

I looked up, and was so charmed by the merry brightness of the eyes which met mine that I took a pen and wrote, "John Godfrey. What is yours?"

Back came the answer, — "Bill Caruthers."

It was several days before I discovered why he and all the other boys who heard me address him as Bill Caruthers laughed so immoderately. The little scamp had written the name of my grave right-hand neighbor, his own name being Oliver Thornton.

There was no recitation in the evening, so, after a few questions, Dr. Dymond ordered me to prepare for the grammar class in the morning. I attended to the task conscientiously, and had even gone beyond it when bedtime came. The Doctor himself mounted with us to the attic-story, which was divided into four rooms, containing six beds each. I had expected to sleep with Charley Rand, and was quite dismayed to see him go off to another room with one of his new playmates.

I stood, meanwhile, lonely and abashed, with my little carpet-bag in hand, in the centre of one of the rooms, with nine boys around me in various degrees of undress. Dr. Dymond finally perceived my forlorn plight.

"Boys," said he, "which beds here are not filled. You must make room for Godfrey."

"Whitaker's and Penrose's," answered one, who sat in his shirt on the edge of a bed, pulling off his stockings.

The Doctor looked at the beds indicated. "Where 's Penrose?" he said.

"Here, sir," replied Penrose, entering the room at that moment. It was my *vis-à-vis* of the school-room.

"Godfrey will sleep with you."

Penrose cast an indifferent glance towards me, and pulled off his coat. I commenced undressing, feeling that all the boys in the room, who were now comfortably in bed, were leisurely watching me. But Dr. Dymond stood waiting, lamp in hand, and I hurried, with numb fingers, to get off my clothes. "A slim chance of legs," I heard one of the boys whisper, as I crept along the further side of the bed and stole between the sheets. Penrose turned them down immediately afterwards, deliberately stretched himself out with his back towards me, and then drew up the covering. Dr. Dymond vanished with the lamp, and closed the door after him.

My situation was too novel, and — let me confess the exact truth — I was too frightened, to sleep. I had once or twice passed a night with Bob Simmons, at his father's house, but with this exception had always slept alone. The silence and indifference of my bedfellow troubled me. I envied the other pairs, who were whispering together, or stifling their laughter with the bedclothes, lest the Doctor might hear. I tucked the edges of the sheet and blankets under me, and lay perfectly still, lest I should annoy Penrose, who was equally motionless, — but whether he slept or not, I could not tell. My body finally began to ache from the fixed posture, but it was a long time before I dared to turn, moving an inch at a time. The glory of the school was already dimmed by the experience of the first evening, and I was too ignorant to foresee that my new surroundings would soon become not only familiar, but pleasant. The room was silent, except for a chorus of deep breathings, with now and then the mutterings of a boyish dream, before I fell asleep.

CHAPTER III.

IN WHICH I BEGIN TO LOOK FORWARD.

The bell in the cupola called us from our beds at the first streak of dawn. The clang awoke me with a start, my sleep having been all the more profound from its delay in coming. For a minute or two I could not imagine where or what I was, and even when the knowledge finally crept through my brain, and I had thrust my spare legs out from under the bedclothes, I mechanically kept my head bent down lest it should bump against the rafters in my garret at home. Penrose, who was already half dressed, seemed to notice this; there was a mocking smile on his handsome lips, but he said nothing. The other boys set up such a clatter that I was overlooked, and put on my clothes with less embarrassment than I had taken them off.

We then went down-stairs to a large shed — an appendage to the kitchen — at the back of the house. There was a pump in the corner, and some eight or ten tin wash-basins ranged side by side in a broad, shallow trough. Four endless towels, of coarse texture, revolved on rollers, and there was much pushing and hustling among the boys who came from the basins with bent, dripping faces, and extended, dripping hands. Towards the end of the ablutions, as the dry spots became rare, the revolution of the towels increased, and the last-comers painfully dried themselves along the edges.

There was a fire in the school-room, but the atmosphere was chilly, and the dust raised by the broom lay upon the desks. My neighbor Caruthers, however, had taken his seat, and was absorbed in the construction of a geometrical diagram. I made a covert examination of him as I took my place beside him. His features were plain, and by no means intellectual, and I saw that his hands were large and hard, showing that he was used to labor. I afterwards learned that he was actually a carpenter, and that he paid for his winter's instruction by the summer's earnings at his trade. He was patient, plodding, and conscientious in his studies. His progress, indeed, was slow, but what he once acquired was never lost. In the course of time a quiet, friendly understanding sprang up between us; perhaps we recognized a similar need of exertion and self-reliance.

After breakfast the business of the school commenced in earnest with me. Dr. Dymond, with some disqualifications, had nevertheless correctly chosen his vocation. Looking back to him now, I can see that his attainments were very superficial, but he had at least a smattering of every possible science, a clear and attractive way of presenting what he knew, and great skill in concealing his deficiencies. Though he was rather strict and exacting towards the school, in its collective character, his manner was usually friendly and encouraging towards the individual pupils. He thus preserved a creditable amount of discipline, without provoking impatience or insubordination. He was very fond of discoursing to us, sometimes for an hour at a time, upon any subject which happened temporarily to interest him; and if the regular order of study was thereby interrupted, I have no doubt we were gainers in the end. He had the knack of exciting a *desire* for knowledge, which is a still more important quality in a teacher than that of imparting it. In my own case, I know, what had before been a vague ambition took definite form and purpose under the stimulus of his encouragement.

With the exception of Miss Hitchcock, there was no regular assistant. One of the oldest pupils took charge of a dozen of the youngest scholars, in consideration (as was surmised in the school) of being received as a boarder without pay. Mrs. Dymond — or Mother Dymond, as the boys called her — was rarely seen, unless a scholar happened to fall sick, when she invariably made her appearance with a bowl of hot gruel or herb-tea. She was a mild, phlegmatic creature, with weak eyes, very little hair on week-days, and an elaborate cap and false front on Sundays. She had no children.

My first timidity on entering the school was considerably alleviated by the discovery that I was not behind any of the scholars of my age in the most important branches. Dr. Dymond commended my reading, chirography, and grammar, and gave me great delight by placing me in the "composition" class. I had a blank book for my exercises, which were first written on a slate and then carefully copied in black and white. The mysteries of amplification, condensation, and transposition fascinated me. I don't know in how many ways I recorded the fact that "Peter, the ploughman, ardently loved Mary, the beautiful shepherdess." I drew the stock comparisons between darkness and adversity, sunshine and prosperity, plunged into antithesis, and clipped away pleonasms with a boldness which astonished myself. Penrose was in the same class. I thought, but it may have been fancy, that his lip curled a little when I went forward with him to the recitation. He looked at me gravely and steadily when my turn came; I felt his eye, and my voice wavered at the commencement. It seemed that we should never become acquainted. I was too timid to make the least advance, though attracted, in spite of myself, by his proud beauty; and he retained the same air of haughty indifference. At night we lay down silently side by side, and it was not until the fourth morning that he addressed a single word to me. I heard the bell, but lingered for one sweet, warm minute longer. Perhaps he thought me asleep; for he leaned over the bed, took me by the shoulder, and said, "Get up!" I was so startled that I sprang out of bed at one bound.

I noticed that young Thornton, though a very imp of mischief towards the other boys, never dared to play the least prank upon Penrose. Something had happened between the two, during a previous term, but what it was, none except themselves knew. No one, I was told, could cope with Penrose in muscular strength, yet there was nothing of the bully about him. He was respected, without being popular; his isolation, unlike that of Caruthers, had something offensive about it. I was a little vexed with myself that he usurped so prominent a place in my thoughts: but so it was.

Charley Rand took on the ways of the school at the start, and was at home in every respect before two days were over. I could not so easily adapt myself to the new circumstances, but slowly and awkwardly put off my first painful feeling of embarrassment. Fortunately, before the week was over, another new scholar was introduced, and he served at least to turn the attention of the school away from me. I was older than he by three days' experience, — a fact which gave me a pleasant increase of confidence. Nevertheless, the time wore away very slowly; months seemed to have intervened since my parting with my mother, and I was quite excited with the prospect of returning, when the school was dismissed, early on Saturday afternoon.

"Oh, Charley!" I cried, as we passed over the ridge beyond Honeybrook, and Dr. Dymond's school sank out of sight, "only think! in an hour we shall be at home."

"If 't was n't for the better grub I shall get, Godfrey, I 'd as lief stay over Sunday with the boys," said he. He had already dropped the familiar "Jack," but this shocked me less than his indifference to the homestead, where, I knew, he was always petted and indulged. It was not long before I, in turn, learned to call him "Rand."

He continually detained me by stopping to search for chestnuts in the edges of the groves, or to throw stones at the squirrels scampering along the top-rails of the fences. Finally I grew impatient, and hurried forward alone, for the houses of our little village were in sight, and I knew mother would be expecting me every moment. I felt sure that I should see her face at the window, and considered a moment whether I should not jump into the next field and cross it to the rear of our garden, so as to take her by surprise. I gave up this plan, and entered by the front-door, but I still had my surprise, for she had not expected me so soon.

"Well, mother, have you been very lonely?" I asked, as soon as the first joyous greeting was over.

"No, Johnny, not more than I expected; but it 's nice to have you back again. I 'll just see to the kitchen, and then you must tell me everything."

She bustled out, but came back presently with red cheeks and sparkling eyes, moved her chair beside mine, and said, "Now" —

I gave the week's history, from beginning to end, my mother every now and then lifting up her hands and saying, "You don't say so!" I concealed only my own feelings of strangeness and embarrassment, which it was mortifying enough to confess to myself. The account I gave of the studies upon which I had entered was highly satisfactory to my poor mother, and I have no doubt that the pride she felt, or foresaw she should feel, in my advancement, helped her thenceforth to bear her self-imposed sacrifice. My description of Miss Hitchcock's singular questions and phrenological remarks seemed to afford her great pleasure, and I am sure that the picture which I drew of Dr. Dymond's erudition must have been overwhelming.

"I 'm glad I 've sent you, Johnny!" she exclaimed when I had finished. "It seems to be the right place, and I don't begrudge the money a bit, if it helps to make a man of you. I 've been more troubled this week on your account than my own. Some boarding-schools are rough places for a boy like you, that has n't been knocked about and made to fight his way. I was afraid I 'd kept you too long at home, maybe, but I guess you 're not spoiled yet, — are you ?"

"No, indeed, mother!" I cried, jumping up to smooth one of her puffs. How glad I was of the bit of boyish swagger which had so happily deceived her.

We had "short cakes" and currant-jam for supper that night. How cosy and delightful it was, to be sure! I had brought along the book in which my exercises in composition were written, and read them aloud, every one. Poor mother must have been bewildered by the transpositions; perhaps she wondered what upon earth it all meant; but she said, "And did you do all that yourself?" with an air of serious admiration which made my heart glow. After supper, Neighbor Niles came in, and I must read the exercises all over again for her benefit, my mother every now and then nodding to her and whispering, "All his own doing."

"It 's a deal for a boy o' his age," said Neighbor Niles; "though, for my part, I 've got so little book-larnin', that I can't make head nor tail of it. Neither my old man nor my boys takes to sich things. Brother Dan'l, — him that went out to the backwoods, you know, comin' ten year next spring, — he writ some verses once't on the death of 'Lijah Sykes, cousin by the mother's side, that was — but I disremember 'em, only the beginnin': —

> "Little did his parents think, and little did his parents know,
> That he should so soon be called for to go."

If Dan'l 'd ha' had proper schoolin', he might ha' been the schollard o' the fam'ly. When Johnny gits a little furder, I should n't wonder if he could write somethin' about my Becky Jane, — somethin' short and takin', that we could have cut on her tombstone. You know it costs three cents a letter."

"Think of that, Johnny!" cried my mother, triumphantly: "if you could do *that*, now! Why, people would read it long after you and I are dead and gone!"

My ambition was instantly kindled to produce, in the course of time, a "short and takin'" elegy on Becky Jane. This was my first glimpse of a possible immortality. I looked forward to the day when my fame should be established in every household of the Cross-Keys, to be freshly revived whenever there was a funeral, and the inscriptions on the tombstones were dutifully read. Perhaps, even, I might be heard of in Honeybrook, and down the Philadelphia road as far as Snedikersville! There was no end to the conceit in my abilities which took possession of me; I doubt whether it has ever since then been so powerful. When I went into the garden the next morning, I looked with contempt at the little corner behind the snowball-bush. What a boy I had been but a few weeks ago! — and now I was a man, or the next thing to it. I instinctively straightened myself in my new boots, and felt either cheek carefully, in the hope of finding a nascent down; but, alas! none was perceptible. Bob Simmons told me in confidence, the last time we met, that the hostler at the Cross-Keys had shaved both him and Jackson Reanor, and had predicted that he would soon have a beard. I must wait another year, I feared, for this evidence of approaching manhood.

Bob, I found, was not to commence his apprenticeship until early in the spring. I longed to see him and talk over my school experiences, but I was not thoughtless enough to leave mother during my first Sunday at home, especially as I saw that the dear little woman was becoming more and more reconciled to the change. The day was passed in a grateful quiet, and we went early to bed, in order that I might rise by daybreak, and be ready to join Charley Rand.

Thus week after week of the new life went by, until the pangs of change were conquered to both of us. I began to put forth new shoots, like a young tree that has been taken from a barren hill-side and set in the deep, mellow soil of a garden. My progress for a time was astonishing, for all the baffled desires of my later childhood became so many impelling forces. Mother soon ceased to be the oracle she had once been; but I think she felt this (if, indeed, she was aware of it) as one joy the more. Her hope was to look up to and be guided by me. She possessed simply the power of enduring adverse circumstances, not the energy necessary to transform them. In my advancement she saw her own release from a maternal responsibility, always oppressive, though so patiently and cheerfully borne.

The books I required were an item which had been overlooked in her estimate of the expenses, and we had many long and anxious consultations on this subject. I procured a second-hand geometry, at half-price, from Walton, the young man who taught for his board, and so got on with my mathematics; but there seemed no hope of my being able to join the Latin class, for which three new books were required, at the start. By Christmas, however, mother raised the necessary funds, having obtained, as I afterwards discovered, a small advance upon the annual interest of the fifteen hundred dollars, which was not due until April. This money had been placed in the hands of her brother-in-law, Mr. Amos Woolley, a grocer, in Reading, for investment. She had never before asked for any part of the sum in advance, and I suspect it was not obtained without some difficulty.

Dr. Dymond was too old a teacher to let his preferences be noticed by the scholars, but I knew that both he and Miss Hitchcock were kindly disposed towards me. He was fond of relating anecdotes of Franklin, Ledyard, Fulton, and other noted men who had risen from obscurity, and inciting his pupils to imitate them. Whatever fame the latter might achieve would of course be reflected upon him and his school. The older boys — who were mostly plodding youths of limited means, ambitious of culture — were also friendly and encouraging, and I associated almost exclusively with them. The pranks of the younger ones were no longer formidable, since there was so little opportunity of their practical application to me. I had spirit enough to resent imposition, and my standing as a scholar prevented me from becoming a butt suitable for torment: so, upon the whole, I was tolerably happy and satisfied, even without the existence of an intimate friendship. My childish faith in the truth and goodness of everybody had not yet been shaken.

Punctually, every Saturday afternoon, Charley and I returned to the Cross-Keys, on foot when the weather was good, and in Mr. Rand's "rockaway" when there was rain or mud. For three weeks in succession the sleighing was excellent, and then we had the delight of a ride both ways, — once (shall I ever forget it?) packed in with the entire Rand family, Emily, Charley, and myself on the front seat, with our arms around each other to keep from tumbling off. Emily was very gracious on this occasion; I suppose my blue cap and gray jacket made a difference. She wore a crimson merino dress, which I thought the loveliest thing I had ever seen, and the yellow ringlets gushed out on either side of her face, from under the warm woollen hood. We went home in the twinkling of an eye, and I forgot my carpet-bag, on reaching the front gate, but Charley flung it into Niles's yard.

I find myself lingering on these little incidents of my boyhood, — clinging to that free, careless, confident period, as if reluctant to march forward into the region of disenchantments. The experiences of boys differ perhaps as widely as those of men, but they float on a narrow stream, and, though some approach one bank and some the other, the same features are visible to all. How different from the open sea, where millions of keels pass and repass day and night, rarely touching the moving circles of each other's horizons, — some sailing in belts of prosperous wind, between the tracks of tempest, — some foundering alone, just out of sight of the barks that would have flown to their rescue! I must not forget that the details of my early history are naturally more interesting to myself than to the reader, and that he is no more likely to deduce the character of my later fortunes from them than I was at the time. Even in retrospect, we cannot always decipher the history of our lives. The Child is Father of the Man, it is true: but few sons are like their fathers.

The only circumstance which has left a marked impression upon my memory occurred towards the close of the winter. Both Dr. Dymond and Miss Hitchcock were obliged to leave the school one afternoon, on account of some important occurrence in Honeybrook, — I think a funeral, though it may have been a wedding. Walton was therefore placed at the central desk, on the platform, and we were severely enjoined to preserve order during the absence of the principal. We sat very quietly until the Doctor's carriage was seen to drive away from the door, whereupon Thornton, Rand, and a number of the other restless, mischievous spirits began to perk up their heads, exchange winks and grins, and betray other symptoms of revolt. Walton knew what was coming: he was a meek, amiable fellow, sweating under his responsibility, and evidently bewildered as to the course he ought to pursue. He knit his brows and tried to look very severe; but it was a pitiful sham, which deceived nobody. Thornton, who had been dodging about and whispering among his accomplices, immediately imitated poor Walton's expression. The corrugation of his brows was something preternatural. The others copied his example, and the aspect of the school was most ludicrous. Still, there had been no palpable violation of the rules, and Walton was puzzled what to do. To notice the caricature would be to acknowledge its correctness. He drew his left shoulder up against his ear and thrust his right hand into his back hair, — a habit which was known to the school. A dozen young scamps at once did the same thing, but with extravagant contortions and grimaces.

The effect was irresistible. There was a rustling and shaking of suppressed laughter from one end of the school-room to the other — the first throes of an approaching chaos. For the life of me, I could not help joining in it, though sympathizing keenly with Walton's painful position. His face flushed scarlet as he looked around the room; but the next instant he became very pale, stood up, and after one or two convulsive efforts to find a voice, — which was very unsteady when it came, — addressed us.

"Boys," said he, "you know this is n't right. I did n't take Dr. Dymond's place of my own choice. I have n't got his authority over you, but you 'd be orderly if he was here, and he 's asked you to be it while he 's away. It 's *his* rule you 're breaking, not mine. I can't force you to keep it, but I can say you 're wrong in not doing it. I 'm here to help any of you in your studies as far as I can, and I 'll attend to that part faithfully if you 'll all do your share in keeping order."

He delivered these sentences slowly, making a long pause between each. The scholars were profoundly silent and attentive. Thornton and some of the others tried a few additional winks and grimaces, but they met with no encouragement; we were waiting to see what would come next. When Walton finally sat down he had evidently little hope that his words would produce much effect; and indeed there was no certainty that the temporary quiet would be long preserved.

We were all, therefore, not a little startled when Penrose suddenly arose from his seat, and said, in a clear, firm voice, — "I am sure I speak the sentiments of all my fellow-scholars, Mr. Walton, when I say that we *will* keep order."

The older boys nodded their assent and resumed their studies. Thornton hung down his head, and seemed to have quite lost his spirits for the rest of the day. But the business of the school went on like clock-work. I don't think we ever had so quiet an afternoon.

CHAPTER IV.

CONTAINING FEATS IN THE CELLAR AND CONVERSATIONS UPON THE ROOF.

WITH the end of March the winter term of the school came to a close. I had established my position as an apt and rapidly advancing scholar; others had the start of me, but no one made better progress. I had mastered, among other things, Geometry and a Latin epitome of Sacred History. The mystic words — "*Deus creavit cœlum et terram*" — which I had approached with wonder and reverence, as if they had been thundered out of an unseen world, were now become as simple and familiar as anything in Peter Parley. Miss Hitchcock, with the air of a queen conferring the order of the Shower-Bath, promised me Cornelius Nepos and Fluxions for the summer term; and Dr. Dymond hinted to the composition-class that we might soon try our hands at original essays. Something was also said about a debating club. The perspective lengthened and brightened with every forward step.

The close of the term was signalized by a school exhibition, to which were invited the relatives of the pupils and the principal personages in Honeybrook, — two clergymen, the doctor, the "squire," the teacher of the common school, and six retired families of independent means. To most of us boys it was both a proud and solemn occasion. I was bent upon having mother to witness my performance, and hoped she could come with the Rands, but their biggest and best carriage would hold no more than themselves. At the last moment Neighbor Niles made the offer of an ancient horse and vehicle, which she used for her own occasional visits in the neighborhood. As the horse had frequently been known to stop in the road, but never, of his own will, to go faster than a creeping walk, it was considered safe for mother to drive him over alone and take me home with her for my month's vacation.

At the appointed time she made her appearance, dressed in the brown silk that dated from her wedded days, and the venerable crape shawl which had once covered the shoulders of Aunt Christina. She was quite overawed on being presented to Dr. Dymond and Miss Hitchcock, but made speedy acquaintance with Mother Dymond, and, indeed, took a seat beside her in the front row of spectators. The exercises were very simple. Specimens of our penmanship and geometrical diagrams (which few of the guests understood) were exhibited; we were drilled in mental arithmetic, and answered chemical, pneumatic, hydraulic, and astronomical questions. But the crowning pride and interest of the day was reserved for the declamations, in which at least half the pupils took part. From the classic contents of the "Columbian Orator," we selected passages from Robert Emmet, William Pitt, Patrick Henry, and Cicero; Byron, Joel Barlow, and Milton; Addison and Red Jacket. Dr. Dymond assigned to me the part of "David," from Hannah More's dramatic poem. I did n't quite like to be addressed as "girl!" by Bill Dawson, — the biggest boy in the school, who was Goliath, — or to be told to

"Go,
And hold fond dalliance with the Syrian maids:
To wanton measures dance; and let them braid
The bright luxuriance of thy golden hair," —

especially as Thornton and the younger fellows snickered when he came to the last line. My hair might still have had a reddish tinge where the sun struck across it, but it was growing darker from year to year. I gave it back to Goliath, however, when it came to my turn to say, —

"I do defy thee,
Thou foul idolater!"

or when, dilating into prophecy, I screamed, —

"Nor thee alone, —
The mangled carcasses of your thick hosts
Shall spread the plains of Elah!"

I think I produced an effect. I know that mother looked triumphant when I swung a piece of leather with nothing in it, and Bill Dawson tumbled full length on the platform, occasioning mild exclamations and shuddering among the female spectators; and I fancied that Emily Rand (in the crimson merino) must have been favorably impressed. I certainly made a better appearance than Charley, who rushed through his share of the debate in the Roman Senate, in this wise, —

"MythoughtsImustconfessareturnedonpeace."

The great, the auspicious day of Cato and of Rome came to an end. I said good-bye to the boys: Caruthers was going off to his carpenter-work, and would not return. I liked him and was sorry to lose him. We never met again, but I have since heard of him as State senator in a Western capital. Even the dark eyes of Penrose looked upon me kindly as he shook hands, bestowing a side-bow, as he did so, upon my mother. Miss Hitchcock gave me a parting injunction of "Remember, Godfrey!—Fluxions and Cornelius Nepos!" and so we climbed into the creaking vehicle and set off homewards.

We might have walked with much more speed and comfort. The horse took up and put down his feet as gently as if he were suffering from corns; at the least rise in the road he stopped, looked around at us, and seemed to expect us to alight, heaving a deep sigh when forced to resume his march. Then he had an insane desire of walking in the gutter on the left side of the road, and all my jerking of the reins and flourishing of a short dogwood switch produced not the slightest effect. He merely whisked his stumpy tail, as much as to say, "*That* for you!" We reached the Cross-Keys at last, long after sunset; but the abominable beast, who had been so ready to stop anywhere on the way, now utterly refused to be pulled up at our gate, and mother was obliged to ride on to the bars at the end of Niles's lane, before she could get down. Our good Neighbor thereupon sallied out and took us in to tea; so the end of the journey was pleasant.

The vacation came at a fortunate time. I succeeded in getting our garden into snug trim: the peas were stuck and the cabbages set out before my summer term commenced; nor were the studies neglected which I had purposed to continue at home. Bob Simmons had finally left, and I missed him sadly: Rand's great house, whither I was now privileged to go occasionally, with even the attraction of Emily, could not fill up the void left by his departure. I was not sorry when the month drew to an end. The little cottage seemed to have grown strangely quiet and lonely; my nest under the roof lost its charm, except when the April rains played a pattering lullaby upon the shingles; looking forward to Cornelius Nepos and Fluxions, I no longer heard my mother's antiquated stories with the same boyish relish, and something of this new unrest must have betrayed itself in my habits. I never, in fact, thought of concealing it — never dreamed that my mind, in breaking away from the government of home ideas and associations, could give a pang to the loving heart, for which I was all, but which, seemingly, was not all for me.

I returned to Dr. Dymond's with the assured, confident air of a boy who knows the ground upon which he stands. My relations with the principal had been agreeable from the commencement, and the contact with my fellow-students had long since ceased to inspire me with shyness or dread. I had many moderate friendships among them, but was strongly attracted towards none, except, perhaps, him whose haughty coldness repelled me. I was at a loss, then, to comprehend this magnetism: now it has ceased to be obscure. I was impressed, far more powerfully than I suspected, by his physical beauty. Had those short, full, clearly-cut lips smiled upon me, I should not have questioned whether the words that came from them were good or evil. His influence over me might have been boundless, if he had so willed it — but he did not. The tenderer shoots of feeling were nipped as fast as they put forth. He was always just and considerate, and perhaps as communicative towards myself as towards any of the other boys; but this was far from being a frank, cordial companionship. His reticence, however, occasionally impressed me as not being entirely natural; there was about him an air of some sad premature experience of life.

Few of the quiet, studious, older pupils remained during the summer, while there was an accession of younger ones, principally from Philadelphia. The tone of our society thus became gay and lively, even romping, at times. I was heartily fond of sport, and I now gave myself up to it wholly during play-hours. I was always ready for a game of ball on the green; for a swim in the shallow upper part of Honeybrook Pond; for an excursion to the clearings where wild strawberries grew; for — not at first, I honestly declare, and not without cowardly terrors and serious twinges of conscience — for a midnight descent into the cellar, a trembling groping in the dark until the pies were found, and then a rapid transfer of a brace of them to our attic. The perils of the latter exploit made it fearfully attractive. Had the pies been of the kind which we abominated, — dried-apple, — we should have stolen them all the same. Nay, such is the natural depravity of the human heart, that no pies were so good (or ever have been since) as those which we divided on the top of a trunk, and ate by moonlight, sitting in our shirts.

The empty dishes of course told the tale, and before many days a stout wooden grating was erected across the cellar, in front of the pastry shelves. This device merely stimulated our ingenuity. Various plans were suggested, and finally two of the boldest boys volunteered to descend and test a scheme of their own. They were absent half an hour, and we were beginning to be more amused than apprehensive at their stay, when they appeared with the coveted pies in their arms. They had secreted matches and a bit of candle, found the oven-shovel, and thrust it through the grating, after which it was an easy matter to reach the dish, withdraw the pie perpendicularly, and replace the dish on the shelf. I fancy Mother Dymond must have opened her silly eyes unusually wide the next morning.

The enemy now adopted a change of tactics which came near proving disastrous. Thornton and myself were chosen for the next night's foray. We had safely descended the stairs (which *would* creak tremendously, however lightly you stepped), and I, as the leader, commenced feeling my way in the dark across the dining-room, when I came unexpectedly upon a delicately piled pyramid of chairs. I no sooner touched the pile than down it crashed, with the noise of artillery. Thornton whisked out of the door and up-stairs like a cat, I following, completely panic-struck. I was none too quick, for another door suddenly opened into the passage and the light of a lamp struck vengefully up after us. By this time I had cleared the first flight, and all that Dr. Dymond could have seen of me was the end of a flag of truce fluttering across the landing-place. He gave chase very nimbly for his years, but I increased the advantage already gained, and was over head and ears in bed by the time he had reached the attic-floor. Thornton was already snoring. The Doctor presently made his appearance in his dressing-gown, evidently rather puzzled. He looked from bed to bed, and beheld only the innocent sleep, knitting up the ravelled sleave of care. If he had been familiar with Boccaccio (a thing not to be for a moment suspected), he might have tried the stratagem of King Agilulf with triumphant success. Even the test which Lady Derby applied to Fenella might have been sufficient. I fancy, however, that he felt silly in being foiled, and thought only of retreating with dignity.

He finally broke silence by exclaiming, in a stern voice, "Who was it?"

Bill Dawson, who had really been asleep, started, rubbed his eyes, and finally sat up in bed, looking red and flustered. The Doctor's face brightened; he moved a step nearer to Bill, and again asked: "Who made the disturbance?"

"I — I 'm sure I don't know," Bill stammered: "I did n't hear anything."

"You did not hear? There was a dreadful racket, sir. I thought the house was coming down. It roused me out of my sleep" (as if he had not been watching in the adjoining room!) "and then I heard somebody running up and down stairs. Take care, Dawson; this won't do."

Bill made a confused and incoherent protestation of innocence, which the Doctor cut short by exclaiming: "Don't let it happen again, sir!" and vanishing with his lamp. Whether he was really so little of a detective as to suspect the first boy whom his voice brought to life, or merely made use of Dawson as a telegraphic wire to transmit messages to the rest of us, I will not decide. At dinner the following day, and for several succeeding days, Bill was furnished, in accordance with private instructions to the waiting-maids, with an immense slice of pie, which he devoured in convulsive haste, Dr. Dymond's sharp eye on him all the time, and Dr. Dymond's thumbs revolving around each other at double speed. It was great fun for us, although it put a stop to our midnight excursions to the cellar.

A few weeks later, however, we found a substitute which was more innocent, although quite as irregular. The weather had become very hot, and our attic was so insufferably close and sultry that we not only kept the window open all night, but kicked off the bedclothes. Frequently one or the other of us, unable to sleep, would sit in the window and cool his heated body. And so it happened one night, when we were all tossing restlessly and exchanging lamentations, that Thornton's voice called in to us from the outer air, " I say, boys, come out here ; it 's grand."

The roof of the house was but slightly pitched, with a broad gutter at the bottom. Thornton had stepped into this and walked up to the comb, where he sat in his breezy drapery, leaning against a chimney. The prospect was so tempting that all of us who were awake followed him.

It was a glorious summer night. The moon, steeped in hazy warmth, swam languidly across the deep violet sky, in which only the largest stars faintly sparkled. The poplar-leaves rocked to and fro on their twisted stems and counterfeited a pleasant breeze, though but the merest breath of air was stirring. Stretching away to the south and southwest, the whole basin of the valley was visible, its features massed and balanced with a breadth and beauty which the sun could never give. The single spire of Honeybrook rose in darker blue above the shimmering pearly gray of the distance, and a streak of purest silver was drawn across the bosom of the pond. Those delicate, volatile perfumes of grass and leaves and earth which are only called forth by night and dew, filled the air. On such a night, our waste of beauty in the unconsciousness of slumber seems little less than sin.

We crowded together, sitting on the sharp comb (which, gradually cutting into the unprotected flesh, suggested the advantage of being a cherub) or lying at full length on the gentle slope of the roof, and unanimously declared that it was better than bed. Our young brains were warmed and our fancies stimulated by the poetic influences of the night. We wondered whether the moon was inhabited, and if so, what sort of people they were ; and finally, whether the lunar school-boys played ball, and bought pea-nuts with their pocket-money, and stole pies.

"By George!" exclaimed one of the composition-class, "that 's a good idea! Next week, the Doctor says, we may choose our own subjects to write about. Now I 'm going to write about the inhabitants of the moon, because, you know, a fellow can say just what he pleases, and who 's to prove it may n't be true?"

"I guess I 'll write a poem, or a tragedy, or something of that sort," said Brotherton, sticking up one leg into the air as he lay upon his back.

"What is a tragedy?" asked Jones.

"Pshaw! don't you know that?" broke in Thornton, with an air of contempt. "They 're played in the theatres. I 've seen 'em. Where the people get stabbed, or poisoned, and everything comes out dreadful at the end, it 's tragedy; and where they laugh all the time, and play tricks, and get married, and wind up comfortable, it 's comedy."

"But I was at the theatre once," said Brotherton, "and two of them were killed, and he and she got married for all that. I tell you, she was a beauty! Now, what would you call that sort of a play?"

"Why, a comic tragedy, to be sure," answered Thornton.

"Where do the theatres get them?"

"Oh, they have men hired to write them," Thornton continued, proud of a chance to show his superior knowledge. "My brother Eustace told me all about it. He 's a lawyer, and has an office of his own in Seventh Street. He knows one of the men, and I know him too, but I forget his name. I was in Eustace's office one afternoon when he came; he had a cigar in his mouth; he was a tragedician. A tragedician 's a man that writes only tragedies. Comedicians write comedies; it 's great fun to know them. They can mimic anybody they choose, and change their faces into a hundred different shapes."

"How much do they get paid for their tragedies?" asked the inquisitive Jones.

"Very likely a hundred dollars a piece," I suggested.

"A hundred dollars!" sneered Thornton; "tell that to the marines! Why, I suppose my brother Eustace could write one a day, — he writes like a book, I tell you, — and he 'd make tragedies quick enough, at that price. We had a boy, once, in father's store, that swept and made fires, and he went into the theatre for a soldier in the fighting-plays, for two dollars a week, — uniforms found. I should think if a regular tragedician got twenty dollars a week, he 'd be lucky."

"Why don't your brother write them?" I asked.

"He? Oh, he *could* do it easy, but I guess it is n't exactly respectable. A lawyer, you know, is as good as any man."

"Shut up, you little fool!" exclaimed a clear, deep voice, so good-humored in tone that we were slightly startled, not immediately recognizing Penrose, who had come up on the other side of the dormer-window, and was seated in the hip of the roof. His shirt was unbuttoned and the collar thrown back, revealing a noble neck and breast, and his slender, symmetrical legs shone in the moonlight like golden-tinted marble. His lips were parted in the sensuous delight of the balmy air-bath, and his eyes shone like dark fire in the shadow of his brows. I thought I had never seen any human being so beautiful.

"You forget, Oliver," he continued, in a kindly though patronizing tone, "that Shakspeare was a writer of tragedies."

"I know, Penrose," Thornton meekly answered, "that Shakspeare was a great man. His books are in my brother's library at the office in Seventh Street, but I 've never read any of 'em. Eustace says I could n't understand 'em yet."

"Nor he, either, I dare say," Penrose remarked.

"Boys," he added, after a pause, "Brotherton has had an idea, and now I 've got one. This is a good time and place for selecting our themes for composition. We are in the higher regions of the atmosphere, and where the air expands I should n't wonder if the brain expanded too. Moonlight brings out our thoughts. Who 'd have supposed that Thornton knew so much about 'tragedicians' and 'comedicians'?"

We all laughed, even Thornton himself, although he was n't sure but that Penrose might be "chaffing" him. The latter's suggestion was at once taken up, and the themes discussed and adopted. I believe mine was "The Influence of Nature," or something of the kind.

"Why could n't we get up a Fourth-of-July Celebration among ourselves? We have lots of talent," Penrose further suggested, in a mocking tone; but we took it seriously and responded with great enthusiasm. We appealed to him as an authority for the order of exercises, each one anxious for a prominent part.

"It might do, after all," he said, reflectively; "they usually arrange it so: — First, prayer; that 's Dr. Dymond, of course, always provided he 's willing. Then, reading the Declaration; we want a clear, straightforward reader for that."

"You 're the very fellow!" exclaimed Thornton. We all thought and said the same thing.

"Well — I should n't mind it for once, — so you don't ask me to spout and make pump-handles of my arms. That 's fixed, we 'll say. What 's next? Song — 'The Star-Spangled Banner,' of course; hard to sing, but four voices will do, if we can get no more. Then the Oration; don't all speak at once! I think, on the whole, Marsh would do tolerably."

"Marsh is n't here," Jones interrupted.

"What if he is n't! Are we to have a school celebration, or only a fi'penny-bit concern, got up by this bare-legged committee, holding a secret session on the Academy roof? Let me alone till I 've finished, and then say and do what you please. Oration — after that, recitation of

What-d'-you-call-him's 'Ode to the American Eagle'; one or two more addresses — short — to give the other Daniel Websters a chance; then, we ought to have an original poem, but who 'd write it?"

This seemed to us beyond the combined powers of the school. We were silent, and Penrose continued, —

"I don't know about that, I 'm sure. But it 's part of the regular programme, — no gentleman's Fourth of July complete without it. If Godfrey would try, perhaps he might grind out something."

"Godfrey?" and "Me?" were simultaneous exclamations, uttered by Jones, Brotherton, and myself.

"Yes, I can't think of anybody else. You could try your hand at the thing, Godfrey, and show it to Dr. Dymond. He 'll put a stopper on you if you don't do credit to the school. There 's nothing else that I know of, except a song to wind up with; 'Old Hundred' would do. But before anything more is done, we must let the rest of the boys know; that 's all I 've got to say."

While the others eagerly entered into a further discussion of the matter, I rolled over on the roof and gave myself up to a fascinating reverie about the proposed poem. How grand, how glorious, I thought, if I could really do such a thing! — if I could imitate, though at a vast distance, the majestic march of Barlow's "Vision of Columbus"! "Marco Bozzaris" I considered hopelessly beyond my powers. The temptation and the dread were about equally balanced; but the idea was like a tropical sand-flea. It had got under my skin, and the attempt to dislodge it opened the germs of a hundred others. I had never seriously tried my hand at rhyme, for the school-boy doggerel in which "Honeybrook" was coupled with "funny brook" and "Dymond" with "priming," was contemptible stuff. I am glad that the foregoing terminations are all that I remember of it.

It was long past midnight before the excitement subsided. Two boys, who had meanwhile gone to sleep on their backs, with their faces to the moon, were aroused, and we returned through the window. I got into bed, already linking "glory" with "story," though still tremblingly uncertain of my ability.

"Oh, Penrose," I whispered, as I lay down beside my bedfellow, "do you really think I can do it?"

"Don't bother me!" was all the encouragement he gave, then or afterwards.

Our airy conclaves were repeated nightly, as long as the warm weather lasted. The boys in the other rooms were let into the secret, and issued from their respective windows to join us. I remember as many as twenty-five, scattered about in various picturesque and sculpturesque attitudes. Dr. Dymond, apparently, did not suspect this new device: if we sometimes fell asleep over our books in the afternoon, the sultry weather, of course, was to blame. We afterwards learned, however, that we had been once or twice espied by late travellers on the neighboring highway.

The plan of our patriotic celebration matured and was finally carried out in a modified form. Our principal made no objection, and accepted our programme, with a few slight changes, such as the substitution of the Rev. Mr. Langworthy, of Honeybrook, for himself, in the matter of the prayer. There was some competition in regard to the orations, but Marsh justified Penrose's judgment by producing the best. No one competed with me, nor do I believe that any one supposed I would be successful. It was a terrible task. I had both ardor and ambition, but a very limited vocabulary, and, unfortunately, an ear for the cadences of poetry far in advance of my power to create them. After trying the heroic and failing utterly, I at last hit upon an easy Hemans-y form of verse, which I soon learned to manage. I was very well satisfied with the result. It was a glorification of the Revolutionary heroes, in eight-line stanzas, with a refrain, which is the only portion of it I can remember, —

> " Give honor to our fathers' name,
> Strike up the glorious lay:
> Sound high for them the trump of fame, —
> 'T is Freedom's natal day! "

" Not bad, not bad," said Dr. Dymond, when he had finished reading this effusion, and I stood waiting, with fast-beating heart, to hear his decision. " ' Great oaks from little acorns grow,' even if the acorn is not perfectly round. Ha!" he continued, smiling at the smartness of his own remark, " the Academy has never yet turned out a poet. We have two Members of Congress and several clergymen, but we are not yet represented in the world of letters. It is my rule to encourage native genius, not to suppress it; so I'll give you a chance this time, Godfrey. Mind, I don't say that you are, or can be, a genuine poet; if it 's in you, it will come out some day, and when that day comes, remember that I did n't crush it in the bud. These verses are fair, — very fair, indeed. They might be pruned to advantage, here and there, but you can very well repeat them as they are, only changing 'was' into 'were,' — subjunctive mood, you know, — and 'them' into 'they' — '*did*' understood. The line will read so: —

> " 'If 't were given to us to fight as they.'

And, of course, you must change the rhyme. 'Diadem' must come out: put '*ray*' ('of glory,' understood), or Americ*a* — poetic license of pronunciation. I could teach you the laws which govern literary performances, but it is not included in the design of my school."

Miss Hitchcock would have preferred one of the classic metres, only I was not far enough advanced to comprehend them. She repeated to me Coleridge's translation of Schiller's illustrations of hexameter and pentameter. I thought they must be very fine, because I had not the least idea of the meaning.

When I took the verses home to mother, she thought them almost as good as "Alcanzor and Zayda," the only poem she knew. I was obliged to make her an elegant copy, in my best hand, which she kept between the leaves of the family Bible, and read aloud in an old-fashioned chant to Neighbor Niles or any other female gossip.

When the celebration came off, the effect I produced was flattering. The excitement of the occasion made my declamation earnest and impassioned, and the verdict of the boys was that it was "prime." Penrose merely nodded to me when I sat down, as if confirming the wisdom of his own suggestion. I was obliged to be satisfied with whatever praise the gesture implied, for I got nothing else.

CHAPTER V.

WHICH BRINGS A STERNER CHANGE IN MY FORTUNES.

It is scarcely necessary to say that I was both proud and vain of the little distinction I had achieved. My pulse began to flutter with coy expectation whenever any of the boys mentioned the poem, — which happened several times during the two succeeding days. I was backward to say much about it myself, but I dearly liked to hear others talk, except when they declared, as Bill Dawson did, "Oh, he got it out of some book or other." It was the author's experience in miniature, — extravagant praise, conceit, censure, exasperation, indifference.

Of course, I made other and more ambitious essays. Several of the boys caught the infection, and for a fortnight the quantity of dislocated metre, imperfect rhyme, and perfect trash produced in the Honeybrook Academy was something fearful. Brotherton attempted an epic on the discovery of America, which he called "The Columbine"; Marsh wrote a long didactic and statistical poem on "The Wonders of Astronomy"; while Jones, in whom none of us had previously detected the least trace of sentiment, brought forth, with much labor, a lamentable effusion, entitled, "The Deserted Maiden," commencing, —

"He has left me: oh, what sadness,
What reflections fill my breast!"

Gradually, however, the malady, like measles or smallpox, ran its course and died out, except in my own case, which threatened to become chronic. My progress in the graver studies was somewhat interrupted thereby, but I prosecuted Latin with ardor, tempted by the promise of Virgil, and began to crave a higher literary culture. I am not sure but that it was a fortunate accident which turned my mind in this direction. The course of study at Honeybrook was neither thorough nor methodical. A piece of knowledge was hacked off this or that branch, and thrown to us in lumps. There was a lack of some solvent or assimilating element, to equalize our mental growth, and my new ambition, to a certain extent, supplied the need.

A week or so after the Fourth, three of us had permission to go to Honeybrook during the noon recess. My errand was to buy a lead-pencil for three cents, and Thornton's to spend his liberal supply of pocket-money in peanuts and candy, which he generously shared with us. As we were returning up the main street, we paused to look at a new brick house, — an unusual sight in the quiet village, — the walls of which had just reached the second story. A ringing cry of "Mort!" at the same moment came from an active workman, who was running up one of the corners. I recognized the voice, and cried out in great joy, "Bob! oh, Bob, is that you?"

He dropped his trowel, drew his dusty sleeve across his brow to clear his eyes from the streaming sweat, and looked down. The dear old fellow, — what a grin of genuine delight spread over his face! "Blast me if 't is n't John!" he cried. "Why, John, how 're you gettin' on?"

"Oh, finely, Bob," I answered; "may I come up there and shake hands with you?"

"No; I 'll come down."

He was down the gangway in three leaps, and gave me a crushing grip of his hard, brick-dusted hand. "I 've only got a minute," he said; "the boss is comin' up the street. How you 've growed! and I hear you 're a famous scholar already. Well — you 're at your trade, and I 'm at mine. I like it better 'n I thought I would. I can lay, and p'int, and run up corners, right smart. *That 's* my corner : is n't it pretty tolerable straight ? "

I looked at it with the eye of a connoisseur, and remarked, " It's very well done, indeed, Bob."

" Well, good-bye. I 've got another thousand to lay before I knock off. Take care of yourself ! "

He was back on the scaffold in no time. My two companions, standing beside me, had witnessed our interview with curiosity ; so I said, by way of explanation, as we moved on, " It 's Bob Simmons ; he 's a first-rate fellow."

" A relation of yours, Godfrey ? " asked Thornton, rather impertinently.

" Oh, no ! I wish he was. I have no relations except mother, and my uncle and aunt in Reading."

" I 've got lots," Thornton asserted. " Six — no, five uncles and six aunts, and no end of cousins. I don't think a fellow 's worth much that has n't got relations. Where are you going to get your money if they don't leave it to you ? "

" I must earn mine," I said, though, I am ashamed to say, with a secret feeling of humiliation, as I contrasted my dependence with Thornton's assured position.

" Earn ? " sneered Thornton. " You 'll be no better than that bricklayer. Catch me earning the money I spend ; I 'm going to be a gentleman ! "

I might here pause in the reminiscences of my school-days, and point a moral from poor Thornton's after-fate, — but to what end ? Some destinies are congenital, and cut their way straight through all the circumstances of life : their end is involved in their beginning. Let me remember only the blooming face, the laughing eyes, and the sunny locks, nor imagine that later picture, which, thank God ! *I* did not see.

Thornton did not fail to describe my interview with Bob, with his own embellishments, after our return ; and some of the boys, seeing that I was annoyed, tormented me with ironical references to my friend. The annoyance was less, however, than it would have been in a more aristocratic school, for we had not only the sons of farmers, but sometimes actual mechanics, among us. It was rumored, indeed, that Dr. Dymond, now an LL. D. of the Lackawanna University, had commenced life as a chair-maker in Connecticut.

So my school-life went on. The summer passed away, and the autumn, and the second winter. My mental growth was so evident, that, although the expenses of the school proved to be considerably more than had been estimated, my mother could not think of abridging the full time she had assigned to my studies. The money was forthcoming, and she refused to tell me whence it came. "You shall help me to pay it back, Johnny," was all she would say.

I believed, at least, that she was not overtasking her own strength in the effort to earn it. There was but limited employment for her needle in so insignificant a place as the Cross-Keys, and she was, moreover, unable at this time to do as much as formerly. The bright color, I could not help noticing, had faded from her face, and was replaced by a livid, waxen hue; thick streaks of gray appeared in her dark puffs, and her round forehead, once so smooth, began to show lines which hinted at concealed suffering. She confessed, indeed, that she had "spells of weakness" now and then; "but," she added, with a smile which reassured me, "it's nothing more than I've been expecting. We old people are subject to such things. There's Neighbor Niles, now, — to hear her talk, you would think she never had a well day in her life, yet what a deal of work she does!"

This was true. Our good neighbor was never free from some kind of "misery," as she expressively termed it. One day she would have it in the small of the back; then it would mount to a spot between the shoulder-blades; next, perhaps, she would find it in her legs, or elbows, or even on the top of her head. After a day of hard scrubbing, she would run over to our cottage, drop into mother's rocking-chair, and exclaim, "I feel powerful weak; the misery 's just got into every bone o' my body."

Thus, though at times I noticed with apprehension the change in my mother's appearance, the feeling was speedily dismissed. My own prospects were so secure, so glowing, that any shadow of unwelcome change took from them an illuminated edge as it approached. But there came, in the beginning of summer, one Sunday, when a strange, restless spirit seemed to have entered the cottage. Every incident of that day is burned upon my memory in characters so legible that to recall them brings back my own uncomprehended pain. The day was hot and cloudless: every plant, bush, and tree rejoiced in the perfect beauty of its new foliage. The air was filled, not with any distinct fragrance, but with a soft, all-pervading smell of life. Bees were everywhere, — in the locust-blossoms, in the starry tulip-trees, on the opening pinks and sweet-williams of the garden; and the cat-bird sang from a bursting throat, on his perch among the reddening mayduke cherries. The harmony of such a day is so exquisite that the discord of a mood which cannot receive and become a portion of it is a torture scarcely to be borne.

This torture I first endured on that day. What I feared — whether, in fact, I *did* fear — I could not tell. A vague, smothering weight lay upon my heart, and, though I could not doubt that mother shared the same intolerable anxiety, it offered no form sufficiently tangible for expression. She insisted on my reading from the Psalms, as usual when we did not go to church, but interrupted me every few minutes by rising from her seat and going into her own room, or the kitchen, or the garden, without any clear reason. Sometimes I caught her looking at me with eyes that so positively *spoke* that I asked, involuntarily, "Mother, did you say anything?" Then a faint color would come into her face, which had lost none of its roundness, so that she suddenly seemed to be her old, bright, cheerful self.

"I believe I *was* going to say something, Johnny," she would answer, "but it can't make much odds what it was, for I've forgotten it already."

As the day wore on, her restlessness increased. When it was necessary for her to leave the room, on some household errand, she would call to me, soon afterwards, "Johnny, are you there?" or come back to the room in flushed haste, as if fearful of some impending catastrophe. She prepared our tea with a feverish hurry, talking all the time of my hunger (though I had not the least) and my appetite, and how pleasant it was to have me there, and how she always looked forward to Sunday evening, and how fast the time had gone by, to be sure, since I first went to Dr. Dymond's school, and what progress I had made, and she wished she could send me to college, but it could n't be, no, there was no use in thinking of it — with such earnestness and so many repetitions that I became at last quite confused. Yet, when we sat down to the table she became silent, and her face resumed its waxen pallor.

During the evening she still talked about the school, and what I should do the following winter, after leaving it. "Perhaps Dr. Dymond might want an assistant," she said; "you 're young, John, it 's true, but I should think you could do as well as Walton, and then you could still study between whiles. I would n't have you mention it — the idea just came into my head, that 's all. If you were only two years older! I 'm sure I 'd keep you there longer if I could, but"——

"Don 't think of that, mother!" I interrupted; "we really can't afford it."

"No, we can't," she sighed, "not even if I was to give up the cottage and go somewhere as housekeeper. I did think of that, once, but it 's too late. Well, you 'll have the two years I promised you, Johnny."

Much more she said to the same purport, interrupting herself every now and then with, "Stop, there was something else I had to say!" — which, when recalled, generally proved to be something already mentioned.

When I went to bed, I lay awake for a long time, trying to explain the singular unrest which had come upon the house. It finally occurred to me that mother had probably gotten into some trouble on account of the expense of my schooling. I could hear her, in the room below me, walking about uneasily, opening and shutting drawers, talking to herself, it seemed. Once or twice something like a smothered groan reached my ear. I resolved that the following Sunday should not go by without my knowing to what extent she had drawn upon her resources for my sake, and that the drain should be stopped, even if I had to give up the remainder of my summer term. After congratulating myself on this heroic resolution, I fell asleep.

When I came down stairs in the morning, I found that breakfast was already prepared. Mother seemed to have recovered from her restless, excited condition, but her eyelids were heavy and red. She confessed that she had passed a sleepless night. When I heard Charley Rand's hail from the road, I kissed her and said good-bye. She returned my kiss silently, and went quietly into her bedroom as I passed out the door.

The vague weight at my heart left me that morning, to return and torment me during the next two days. It was but a formless shadow, — the very ghost of a phantom, — but it clung to and dulled every operation of my mind, muffled every beat of my heart.

Wednesday evening, I recollect, was heavy and overcast, with a dead, stifling hush in the atmosphere. The tension of my unnatural mood was scarcely to be endured any longer. Oh, if this be life, I thought, let me finish it now! There was not much talk in our attic that night: the other boys tumbled lazily into bed and soon slept. I closed my eyes, but no sleep came. The constriction about my heart crept up towards my throat and choked me. I clenched my hands and ground my teeth; the muscles of my face twitched, and with a spasm which shook me from head to foot and took away my breath, I burst into a passion of tears. I hid my head under the bedclothes, and strove to stifle the gasps that threatened to become cries — to subdue the violence of the crisis which had seized me. Penrose was such a quiet bedfellow that I forgot his presence until I felt that he was turning over towards me. Then, thoroughly alarmed, I endeavored to lie still and counterfeit sleep: but it was impossible. I could no longer control the sobs that shook my body.

Presently Penrose stirred again, thrust himself down in the bed, and I heard his voice under the clothes, almost at my ear.

"Godfrey," he whispered, with a tender earnestness, "what is the matter?"

"My mother!" was all the answer I could make.

"Is she sick — dangerous?" he whispered again, laying one arm gently over my shoulder. Its very touch was soothing and comforting.

"I don't know, Penrose," I said at last. "Something is the matter, and I don't know what it is. Mother has a hard time to raise money for my schooling: I am afraid it 's too hard for her. I did n't mean to cry, but it came all at once. I think I should have died if it had n't."

He drew me towards him as if I had been a little child, and laid my head against his shoulder. "Don't be afraid," he then whispered, "no one has heard you but myself. We are all so, at times. I recollect your mother; she is a good woman; she reminds me, somehow, of mine."

My right hand sought for Penrose's, which it held firmly clasped, and I lay thus until my agitation had subsided. A grateful sense of sympathy stole into my heart; the strange mist which seemed to have gathered, blotting out my future, began to lift before a breeze which blew from the stronger nature beside me. At last, with a final pressure, which was answered, I released his hand and turned to my own pillow. Next morning he was silent as ever, but his silence no longer repelled or annoyed me. I was beginning to learn that the heart lies much deeper than the lips.

In the afternoon Dr. Dymond was called into the reception-room. I paid no attention to this circumstance, for it was of frequent occurrence, but when he opened the door directly afterwards and called "Godfrey!" I started as if struck. Penrose darted a glance of keen, questioning interest across the intervening desk, and I felt that his eye was following me as I walked out of the school-room.

I was quite surprised to find "Old Dave," as we generally called him, — Neighbor Niles's husband, — waiting for me. He was standing awkwardly by the table, his battered beaver still upon his head.

"Well, Johnny," said he, giving me his hand, which felt like a piece of bark dried for tanning, "are you pretty well? I 've come for to fetch you home, because, you see — well, your mother — she 's ailin' some, that is, and so we thought the Doctor here 'd let you off for a day or two."

"Of course, sir," Dr. Dymond bowed. "Godfrey, this gentleman has explained to me the necessity of allowing you to be absent for a short time during the term. I sincerely regret the occasion which calls for it. You need not return to the school-room. Good-bye, for the present!"

I took his hand mechanically, ran up-stairs and brought my little carpet-bag, and was very soon seated at Niles's side, bouncing down the lane in a light, open wagon.

"I took the brown mare, you see," he said, as we turned into the highway. "She 's too free for the old woman to drive, but she knows my hand. This is Reanor's machine: he lent it to me at once't. Rolls easy, don't it?"

"But, Dave!" I cried, in an agony of anxiety, "you have not told me what has happened to mother!"

He fidgeted uneasily on his seat, addressed various remarks to the brown mare, and finally, when my patience was almost exhausted, said, in a confused way, "Well, you see, it has n't jist happened altogether now. 'Pears it 's been comin' on a good while, — a year or two, maybe more. The Doctor says it ought to ha' been done sooner, but I don't wonder much if she could n't make up her mind to it."

My distress increased with every one of these slowly drawled, incoherent sentences. "For God's sake," I exclaimed, "tell me what ails her!"

Dave started at my vehemence, and blurted out the dreadful truth at once. "Cancer!" said he: "they cut it out, yisterday — Dr. Rankin, and Dr. Lott, here, in Honeybrook. They say she bore it oncommon, but she 's mighty low, this mornin'."

I turned deathly sick and faint. I could not utter a word, but wrung my hands together and groaned. Dave pulled a small, flat bottle out of his breast-pocket, drew the cork with his teeth, and held the mouth to my lips, saying, "Take a swaller. You need n't say anything about it before the old woman."

The fluid fire which went down my throat partially restored me; but the truth was still too horrible to be fully comprehended. In spite of the glowing June-day, a chill struck to the marrow of my bones, as I thought of my poor, dear little mother, mangled by surgeons' knives, and perhaps at that very moment bleeding to death. Then a bitter feeling of rage and resistance took possession of my heart. "Why does God allow such things?" cried the inward voice: "why make her suffer such tortures, who was always so pure and pious, — who never did harm to a single creature?" The mystery of the past four days was now clear to me: but how blind the instinct that predicted misfortune and could not guess its nature! If mother had but told me, or I had not postponed the intended explanation! It was now too late: I dared not chide her who had endured so fearfully. If any such thought arose, I asked pardon for it of the same God I had accused a moment before. But the Recording Angel does not open his book for the blind words of the young.

Dave had been talking, I suppose, but I was unconscious of his words. Now that the truth had been told, he was ready enough to give all the particulars, and even attempt, in his rough way, to administer consolation.

"You must n't take on so," he said, patting me on the knee; "maybe she 'll git well, after all. While there 's life there 's hope, you know. Some has been cured that seemed jist about as bad as they *could* be. The wust of cancer is, it mostly comes back agin. It 's like Canada thistles: you may dig trenches round 'em, and burn 'em, and chop the roots into mince-meat, and like as not you 've got 'em next year, as thick as ever."

His words made me shudder. "Please go on fast, Dave," I entreated; "never mind telling me any more; I want to get home."

"So do I," he answered, urging the mare into a rapid trot. "I did n't much keer to come, but there was nobody else handy, and th' old woman said you *must* be fetched, right away."

As we approached the cottage, Neighbor Niles came out and waited for us at the gate. Her eyes were red, and they began to flow again when I got down from the wagon. She wiped them with her apron, took me by the hand, and said, in a whisper louder than the ordinary voice of most women, —

"I 'll go in and tell her you 're here. Wait outside until I come back. The Doctor 's with her."

It was not long before she returned, followed by Dr. Rankin. I knew him, from the days of my sprained ankle, and was passing him with a hasty greeting, when he seized me by the arm. "Control yourself, my boy!" said he; "she must not be excited."

I walked into the bedroom. It was very well to say, " Control yourself!" but the sight of my mother, with half-closed eyes, her face as white as the pillow beneath it, so unnerved me that I sank, trembling, upon the chair at the head of the bed, and wept long and bitterly. I felt her fingers upon my hair: " Poor boy!" she sighed.

" Oh, mother!" I cried, " why did n't you tell me?"

" 'T would have done no good, Johnny," she feebly answered. " I was glad to know that you were unconscious and happy all the time. Besides, it 's only this spring that I grew so much worse. I tried to bear up, my dear child, that I might see you started in life; but I am afraid it 's not to be."

" Don't say that, mother. I can't live without you."

" I have lived ten years without your father, child, — and they were not unhappy years. God does not allow us to grieve without ceasing. You will have some one to love, as I have had you. You will soon be a man, and if I should live, it would be to see some one nearer to you than I am. I pray that you may be happy, John; but you will not forget your old mother. When you have children of your own upon your knees, you will talk to them sometimes — will you not? — of the Grandmother Godfrey who died before she could kiss and bless them for your sake?"

Her own tears flowed freely as she ceased to speak, exhausted, and paused to recover a little strength. " I 've been blessed," she said at last, " and I must not complain. You 've been a good boy, Johnny; you 've been a dutiful and affectionate son to me. You 're my joy and my pride now, — it can't be wrong for me to take the comfort God sends. There would be light upon the way I must go, if I knew that you could feel some of the resignation which I have learned."

" Mother," I sobbed, " I can't be resigned to lose you. I will stay with you, and take care of you. I should never have gone away to school, — but I thought only of myself!"

Her face was suddenly touched with a solemn beauty, and her gentle voice had a sacred authority which I accepted as if it had truly spoken across the mysterious gulf which was soon to separate us. "My dear child," she said, "listen to me. I know how you feel in this moment. I can foresee that you may torture yourself after I am gone with the recollection of this or that duty omitted, of some hasty word spoken, perhaps some impatient thought which merely passed through your mind. After your father died, I called aloud, in anguish and prayer, for his spirit to speak down from heaven and forgive me all things wherein I had failed of my duty towards him. But I know now that the imperfections of our conduct here are not remembered against us, if the heart be faithful in its love. If you were ever undutiful in word or thought, the sun never went down and left you unforgiven. Remember this, and that all I have tried to do for you has been poor payment for the blessing you have always been to me!"

Blessed words, that fell like balm on my overwhelming sorrow! I took them to my heart and held them there, as if with a presentiment of the precious consolation they were thenceforth to contain. I pressed her pale hand tenderly, laid my cheek upon it, and was silent, for it seemed to me that an angel was indeed present in the little room.

After a while, Neighbor Niles softly opened the door, drew near, and whispered, "Mr. Woolley 's here — from Readin'; — shall I bring him in?"

My mother assented.

I had not seen my uncle for some years, and retained but an indistinct recollection of his appearance. He had been sent for, early in the morning, at my mother's urgent request, as I afterwards learned. When the door opened, I saw a portly figure advancing through the gathering dusk of the room, bend over my head towards my mother, and say, in a husky voice, "How do you feel, Barbara?"

"I am very weak," mother replied. "This is John,

Amos. John, shake hands with your uncle, and then leave me for a little while. I have something to say to him."

I rose. A fat hand closed upon mine, and again I heard the husky voice, " Well, really, as tall as this? I had no idea, Barbara."

I do not know whether he was aware of my mother's condition. Perhaps not; but it was impossible for me, at the moment, to credit him with the doubt. To my ear, his words expressed a cruel coldness and indifference; and I went forth from the room with a spark of resentment already kindled in the midst of my grief. I threw myself into my accustomed seat by the front window, and gave myself up to the gloomy chaos of my emotions.

Neighbor Niles was preparing the table for supper, stopping now and then to wipe her eyes, and "sniffling" with a loud, spasmodic noise, which drove me nearly to distraction. My excited nerves could not bear it. Once she put down a plate of something, crossed the room to my chair, and laid her hand on my shoulder. "Johnny," — she began —

"Let me be!" I cried, fiercely, turning away from her with a jerk.

The good woman burst into fresh tears, and instantly left me. "Them 's the worst," I heard her mutter to herself; "I 'd ruther he 'd half break his heart a-cryin'." And, indeed, I was presently sorry for the rude way in which I had repelled her sympathy, though I could not encourage her to renew it.

Supper was delayed, nearly an hour, waiting for my uncle. When he appeared, it was with a grave and solemn countenance. I took my seat beside him very reluctantly: it seemed dreadful to me to eat and drink while my mother might be dying in the next room. Neighbor Niles, however, would hear of nothing else. She had already lifted the tea-pot, in her haste to serve us, when my uncle suddenly bowed his head and commenced a grace. Neighbor Niles was so confused that she stood with the tea-pot suspended in the air until he had finished. I, who with difficulty swallowed a little tea, was shocked at the appetite he displayed, forgetting that he was human, and that it was a long drive from Reading.

"I am afraid, John," he finally said, "that the Lord is about to chasten you. It is some comfort to know that your mother seems to be in a proper frame of mind. Her ways were never the same as mine, but it is not too late, even at the eleventh hour, to accept the grace which is freely offered. It is not for me to judge, but I am hopeful that she will be saved. I trust that you will not delay to choose the safe and the narrow path. Do you love your Saviour?"

"Yes," I answered, — somewhat mechanically, I fear.

"Are you willing to give up everything and follow Him?"

"Uncle Amos," I said, "I wish you would n't ask me any more questions." I left the table, and stole quietly into mother's room. As I was passing out of the door I heard Neighbor Niles say, "This is no time to be preachin' at the poor boy."

That night my uncle took possession of my bed in the attic. I refused to sleep, and the considerate nurse allowed me to watch with her. Mother's condition seemed to be stupor rather than healthy slumber. There was no recuperative power left in her system, and the physician had already declared that she would not recover from the shock of the operation. He informed me, afterwards, that the strength of her system had been reduced, for years, by the lack of rich and nourishing food, — which circumstance, if it did not create the disease, had certainly very much accelerated its progress. "She was not a plant that would thrive on a poor soil," he said, in his quaint way; "she ought to have been planted in fowl and venison, and watered with Port."

The long, long night dragged away, and when the black mass of the lilac-bush at the window began to glimmer in dusky green, and some awakening birds cheeped in the branches of the plum-tree, mother seemed to revive. I was shocked to see, in the wan light, how her round cheeks had already fallen in, and what a ghastly dimness dwelt in her dark eyes. The nurse administered some stimulating mixture, smoothed the pillow, and, obeying some tender instinct, left us together. Mother's eyes called me to her; I stooped down and kissed her lips.

"John," she said, "I must tell you now, while I have strength, what your uncle and I have agreed upon. The money, you know, is in his hands, and it is better that he should keep it in trust until you are of age. You are to stay at school until the fall. I borrowed the money of Mr. Rand. There is a mortgage on the house and lot, and the doctors must be paid: so all will be sold, except some little things that you may keep for my sake. When you leave school, your uncle will take you. He says you can assist in his store and learn something about business. Your aunt Peggy is my sister, you know, and it will be a home for you. I could n't bear to think that you must go among strangers. When you 're of age, you 'll have a little something to start you in the world, and if my blessing can reach you, it will rest upon you day and night."

The prospect of living with my uncle was not pleasant, but it seemed natural and proper, and not for worlds would I have deprived the dear sufferer of the comfort which she drew from this disposition of my fortunes. She repeated her words of consolation, in a voice that grew fainter and more broken, and then lay for a long time silent, with her hand in mine. Once again she half opened her eyes, and, while a brief, shadowy smile flitted about her lips, whispered "Johnny!"

"I am here, with you, mother," I said, fondling the listless hand.

She did not reply: this was the last sign of consciousness she gave. The conquered life still lingered, hour after hour, as if from the mere mechanical habit of the bodily functions. But the delicate mechanism moved more and more slowly, and, before sunset, it had stopped forever.

CHAPTER VI.

IN WHICH I DISCOVER A NEW RELATIVE.

Why should I enter into all the dreary details of the funeral preparations, — of those black summer days, which still lie, an unfaded blot, in the soft and tender light of resignation now shining over my sorrow? I passed through the usual experience of one struck by sudden and bitter calamity: my heart was chilled and benumbed by its inability to comprehend the truth. My dull, silent, apathetic mood must have seemed, to the shallow-judging neighbors, a want of feeling; only Neighbor Niles and her husband guessed the truth. I saw men and women, as trees, come and go; some of them spoke to me, and when I was forced to speak in turn, it was with painful unwillingness. I heard my voice, as if it were something apart from myself; I even seemed, through some strange extraverted sense, to stand aside and contemplate my own part in the solemnities.

When I look back, now, I see a slender youth, dressed in an ill-fitting black suit, led through the gate in the low churchyard wall by my uncle Woolley. It is not myself; but I feel at my heart the numb, steady ache of his, which shall outlast a sharper grief. His eyes are fixed on the ground, but I know — for I have often been told so — that they are like my mother's. His hair cannot be described by any other color than dark auburn, and hangs, long and loose, over his ears; his skin is fair, but very much freckled, and his features, I fancy, would wear an earnest, eager expression in any happier mood. I see this boy as some mysterious double of mine, standing, cold and pale, beside the open grave; but the stupor of his grief is harder to bear, even in memory, than the keen reality to which I afterwards awoke.

I let things take their course, knowing that the circumstances of my immediate future were already arranged. My uncle Woolley, as my guardian and the executor of my mother's little estate, assumed, without consulting me, the disposal of the cottage and furniture. Mr. Rand purchased the former, as a convenient tenant-house for some of his farm-hands, and the latter, with the exception of mother's rocking-chair, which she bequeathed to Neighbor Niles, was sold at auction. This, however, took place after my return to the school, and I was spared the pain of seeing my home broken to pieces and its fragments scattered to the winds. My uncle probably gave me less credit for a practical comprehension of the matter than I really deserved. His first conversation with me had been unfortunate, both in point of time and subject, and neither of us, I suspect, felt inclined, just then, to renew the attempt at an intimacy befitting our mutual relation.

In a few days I found myself back again at Honeybrook Academy. The return was a relief, in every way. The knowledge of my bereavement had, of course, preceded me, and I was received with the half-reverential kindness which any pack of boys, however rough and thoughtless, will never fail to accord, in like circumstances. Miss Hitchcock, it is true, gave me a moment's exasperation by her awkward attempt at condolence, quoting the hackneyed "*pallida mors*," &c., but Mother Dymond actually dropped a few tears from her silly eyes as she said, "I 'm so sorry, Godfrey; I quite took to her that time she was here."

Penrose met me with a long, silent pressure of the hand, and the stolid calm with which I had heard the others melted for the first time. My eyes grew suddenly dim, and I turned away.

I had already profited by nearly two years' experience of human nature, or, rather, boy-nature, and was careful not to let my knowledge of his sympathy lead me into advances which might, notwithstanding all that had happened, be repelled. I had a presentiment that he esteemed me because I imitated his own reticence, and that he was suspicious of any intimacy which did not proceed from himself. In spite of his beauty, which seemed to be dimly felt and respected by the whole school, and the tender spot in my heart, kindling anew whenever I recalled the night he had taken me to his breast, I was not sure that I could wholly like and trust him — could ever feel for him the same open, unquestioning affection which I bestowed, for example, on Bob Simmons.

In my studies I obtained, at least, a temporary release from sorrow. The boys found it natural that I should not join in the sports of play-hours, or the wild, stolen expeditions in which I had formerly taken delight. When I closed my Lempriere and Leverett, I wandered off to the nearest bit of woodland, flung myself on the brown moss under some beech-tree, and listened idly to the tapping of the woodpecker, or the rustle of squirrels through the fallen leaves.

There was a little shaded dell, in particular, which was my favorite haunt. A branch of Cat Creek (as the stream in the valley was called) ran through it, murmuring gently over stones and dead tree-trunks. Here, in moist spots, the trillium hung its crimson, bell-like fruit under the horizontal roof of its three broad leaves, and the orange orchis shot up feathery spikes of flowers, bright as the breast of an oriole. In the thickest shade of this dell, a large tree had fallen across the stream from bank to bank, above a dark, glassy trout-pool. One crooked branch, rising in the middle, formed the back of a rough natural chair; and hither I came habitually, bringing some work borrowed from Dr. Dymond's library. I remember reading there Mrs. Hemans's "Forest Sanctuary," with a delight which, alas! the poem can never give again, even with such accessories.

One day I was startled from my book by hearing the dead twigs on the higher bank snap under the step of some one descending into the glen. I looked up and saw Penrose coming leisurely down, cutting now and then at a wood-moth or dragon-fly with a switch of leather-wood. Almost at the same moment he espied me.

"Hallo, Godfrey! Are you there?" he said, turning towards my perch. "You show a romantic taste, upon my word!"

The irony, if he meant it for such, went no further. The mocking smile vanished from his lips, and his face became grave as he sprang upon the log and took a seat carelessly against the roots. For a minute he bent forward and looked down into the glassy basin.

"Pshaw!" said he, suddenly, striking the water with his switch, so that it seemed to snap like the splitting of a real mirror, — "only my own face! I 'm no Narcissus."

"You could n't change into a flower, with your complexion, anyhow," I remarked.

"Curse my complexion!" he exclaimed; "it 's a kind that brings bad blood, — my father has it, too!"

I was rather startled at this outbreak, and said nothing. He, too, seemed to become conscious of his vehemence. "Godfrey," he asked, "do you remember your father? What kind of a man was he?"

"Yes," I answered, "I remember him very well. I was eight years old when he died. He was quiet and steady. I can't recall many things that he said; but as good and honest a man as ever lived, I believe. If he had n't been, mother could n't have loved him so, to the very end of her life."

"I have no doubt of it," he said, after a pause, as if speaking to himself; "there are such men. I 'm sorry you lost your mother, — no need to tell you that. You 're going to leave school at the end of the term. Where will you go? You have other relations, of course?"

Encouraged by the interest which Penrose showed in my condition, I related to him what had been decided upon by my mother and my uncle, without concealing the unfavorable impression which the latter had made upon me, or my distaste at the prospect before me.

"But you must have other aunts and uncles," he said, "or relatives a little further off. On your father's side, for instance?"

"I suppose so," I answered; "but they never visited mother, and I shall not hunt them up now. Aunt Peggy is mother's only living sister. Grandfather Hatzfeld had a son, — my uncle John, after whom I was named, — but he never married, and died long ago."

"Hatzfeld? Was your mother's name Hatzfeld?"

"Yes."

Penrose relapsed into a fit of silence. "It would be strange," he said to himself; then, lifting his head, asked:

"Had your grandfather Hatzfeld brothers and sisters?"

"Oh, yes. Aunt Christina was his sister: she left mother our little place at the Cross-Keys when she died. Now, I recollect, I have heard mother speak of another aunt, Anna, who married and settled somewhere in New Jersey; I forget her name, — it began with D. Grandfather had an older brother, too, but I think he went to Ohio. Mother never talked much about him: he did n't act fairly towards grandfather."

"D?" asked Penrose, with a curious interest. "Would you know the name if you were to hear it? Was it Denning?"

"Yes, that 's it!" I exclaimed; "why, how could you guess" —

"Because Anna Denning was *my* grandmother — my mother's mother! When you mentioned the name of Hatzfeld, it all came into my mind at once. Why, Godfrey, your mother and mine were first cousins, — *we* are cousins, therefore!"

He sat upright on the log and stretched out his hand, which I took and held. "Penrose!" I exclaimed, "can it be possible?"

"Plain as a pike-staff."

"Oh, are you serious, Penrose? I can hardly believe it."

I still held his hand, as if the newly-found relationship might slip away on releasing it. The old mocking light came into his eyes.

"Do you want me to show the strawberry-mark on my left arm?" he asked; "or a mole on my breast, with three long black hairs growing out of it? Cousins are plenty, and you may n't thank me for the discovery."

"I am so glad!" I cried; "I have no cousin: it is the next thing to a brother!"

His face softened again. "You 're a good fellow, Godfrey," said he, "or Cousin John, if you like that better. Call me Alexander, if you choose. Since it is so, I wish I had known it sooner."

"If my poor mother could have known it!" I sighed.

"That 's it!" he exclaimed, — "the family likeness between your mother and mine. It puzzled me when I saw her. My mother has been dead three years, and there 's a — I won't say what — in her place. As you 're one of the family now, Godfrey, you may as well learn it from me as from some one else, later. My father and mother did n't live happily together; but it was not *her* fault. While she lived, my sister and I had some comfort at home; she has it yet, for that matter, but I —— There 's no use in going over the story, except this much: it was n't six months after my mother's death before my father married again. Married whom, do you think? His cook! — a vulgar, brazen wench, who sits down to the table in the silks and laces of the dead! And worse than that, — the marriage brought shame with it, — if you can't guess what that means, now, you 'll find out after a while; don't ask me to say anything more! I am as proud as my mother was, and do you think I could forgive my father this, even if he had not always treated me like a brute?"

Penrose's eyes flashed through the indignant moisture which gathered in them. The warm olive of his skin had turned to a livid paleness, and his features were hard and cruel. I was almost afraid of him.

"He to demand of me that I should call *her* 'mother'!" he broke out again, his lip quivering, but not with tenderness, — "it was forbearance enough that I did not give her the name she deserved! And my sister, — but I suppose she is like most women, bent in any direction by anybody stronger than themselves. She stays at home, — no, not at home, but *with them*, — and writes me letters full of very good advice. Oh, yes, she 's a miracle of wisdom! She 's a young lady of twenty-one, and — and — The Cook finds it very convenient to learn fashionable airs of her, and how to eat, and to enter a room, and hold her fan, and talk without yelling as if at the house-maid, and all the rest of their damnable folly! There! How do you like being related to such a pleasant family as that?"

I tried to stay the flood of bitterness, which revealed to me a fate even more desolate than my own. "Penrose," I said, — "Cousin Alexander, you are so strong and brave, you can make your own way in the world, without their help. I 'm less able than you, yet I must do it. I don't know why God allows some things to happen, unless it 's to try us."

"None of that!" he cried, though less passionately; "I 've worried my brain enough, thinking of it. I 've come to the conclusion that most men are mean, contemptible creatures, and their good or bad opinion is n't worth a curse. If I take care of myself and don't sink down among the lowest, I shall be counted honest, and virtuous, and the Lord knows what; but I sometimes think that, if there are such things as honesty and virtue, we must look for them among the dregs of society. The top, I know, is nothing but a stinking scum."

I was both pained and shocked at the cynicism of these utterances, so harshly discordant with the youth and the glorious physical advantages of my cousin. Yes! the moment the new relation between us was discovered and accepted, it established the bond which I felt to be both natural and welcome. It interpreted the previous sensation which he had excited in my nature. Some secret sympathy had bent, like the hazel wand in the hand of the diviner, to the hidden rill of blood. But the kinship of blood is not always that of the heart. "A friend is closer than a brother," say the Proverbs; I did not feel sure that he could be the friend I needed and craved, but cousinship was a familiar and affectionate tie, existing without our volition, justifying a certain amount of reciprocal interest, and binding neither to duties which time and the changes of life might render embarrassing. The confidence which Penrose had reposed in me came, therefore, in some degree, as the right of my relationship. I had paid for it, in advance, by my own.

Hence I was saved, on the one hand, from being drawn, during the warm, confiding outset of life, into a sneering philosophy, which I might never have outgrown, and on the other hand, from judging too harshly of Penrose's inherent character. It would do no good at present, I saw, to protest against his expressions; so I merely said, —

"You know more of the world than I do, Alexander; but I don't like to hear you talk in that strain."

"Perhaps you 're right, old fellow," said he; "any way, I don't include *you* among the rabble. I might have held my tongue about my grandmother, if I had chosen; but I guess you and I are not nearly enough related to fall out. There goes the bell; pick up your Eclogues, and come along!"

We went back to the school, arm in arm, talking familiarly. From that time forward the recognized, mysterious circle of Family enclosed us, and Penrose's manner towards me was commensurate with the change. Never demonstrative, never even positively affectionate, he stood at least on level ground with me, and there was no wall between us. The other boys, of course, noticed the difference in our relations, and it was not long before the inquisitive Thornton said, —

"I say, Pen, how is it that you 've got to calling Godfrey 'John,' all at once?"

"Because he is my cousin."

Thornton's eyes opened very wide. "The devil he is!" he exclaimed. (Thornton was unnecessarily profane, because he thought it made him seem more important.) "When did you find that out?"

"It 's none of your business," said Penrose, turning on his heel. Thornton thereupon went off, and communicated the fact to the whole school in less than ten minutes.

After this, my cousin and I frequently walked out to the glen together. I was glad to see that the kinship, so inexpressibly welcome to myself, was also satisfactory to him. His first fragmentary confidence was completed by the details of his life, as he recalled them from time to time; but his bitter, disappointed, unbelieving mood always came to the surface, and I began to fear that it had already predetermined the character of his after-life.

One day, when he had been unusually gloomy in his utterances, he handed me a letter, saying, "Read that." It was from his sister, and ran, as nearly as I can recollect, as follows: —

"—— Street, Philadelphia.

"MY DEAR BROTHER, — Yours of the 10th is received. I am now so accustomed to your sarcastic style, that I always know what to expect when I open one of your epistles. I wish you joy of your — well, I must say *our* new cousin, though I am sorry you did not let me know of the discovery before telling *him*. He must be *gauche* and unpresentable in a degree; but then, I suppose, there 's no likelihood of his ever getting into *our set*. It is time your schooling was finished, so that I might have you for awhile as my *chevalier*. Between ourselves, I 'm rather tired of going about with" (here the word "Mamma" had evidently been written and then blotted out) "Mrs. Penrose. Not but what she continues to improve, — only, I am never certain of her not committing some *niaiserie*, which quite puts me out. However, she behaves well enough at home, and I hope you will overcome your prejudice in the end, for my sake. When you know as much about Society as I do, you will see that it 's always best to smooth over what 's irrevocable. People are beginning to forget the scandal, since that affair of Denbigh has given them something else to talk about. We were at Mrs. Delane's ball on Wednesday; I made her put on blue cut velvet, and she did not look so bad. Mrs. Vane nodded, and of course *she* was triumphant. I think Papa gives me the credit for all that has been done, — I 'm sure I deserve it. It 's a race between Mrs. P. and myself which shall have the new India shawl at Stokes's; but I shall get it, because Mrs. P. knows that I could teach her to blunder awfully as well as to behave correctly, and *would* do it, in spite of Papa's swearing, if she drives me to desperation. By the by, he has just come into the room, and says, 'You are writing to the cub, as usual, I suppose, Matilda.' So there you have him, to the life."

There was much more, in the same style. I must have colored, with offended pride, on reading the opening lines, for on looking up, involuntarily, I saw my cousin smile, but so frankly and pleasantly that it instantly healed the wound his sister made. I confess the letter disgusted me; but it was written by my own cousin also, and I did not dare to express to her brother what I felt. I handed the letter back to him in silence.

"Come now, John," said he, — "out with the truth! Would you not as lief be out of our family again?"

"Not while you are in it, Alexander," I replied.

CHAPTER VII.

IN WHICH UNCLE AND AUNT WOOLLEY TAKE CHARGE OF ME.

As the close of my last term at the Honeybrook Academy approached, I felt none of the eagerness for change, of the delight in coming release from study, which would have been natural to a boy of my age. On the contrary, I grew more and more reluctant to leave a spot which was now so familiar, and to give up the advantages of instruction at a time when I began to understand their importance. Both Miss Hitchcock and Dr. Dymond were sorry to lose me, — the former because there was no other Latin pupil far enough advanced to read her expurgated Horace, and the latter because my original dialogues and speeches were beginning to constitute a feature in the semi-annual exhibitions. If, among the boys, I had contracted no strong, permanent friendship, I had at least encountered no more than transient enmities; besides, I was getting to be one of the older and more conspicuous scholars, and thus enjoyed a certain amount of authority.

It was hardest of all to part with Penrose. I could talk with him of my mother, — could ask his counsel, as a relative, in regard to my proposed plans of life. The latter were still indefinite, it is true; but they pointed towards teaching as a preliminary employment. Behind that crowded a host of ambitious dreams, upon which I secretly fed my mind. Penrose, however, was to leave the school in the spring, and I should therefore have lost him six months later, in any case.

On the last Sabbath before my departure, I walked over to the Cross-Keys, and spent the day with the Niles family. The shutters of the little cottage were still closed; I was glad of it. If strange faces had gazed from the windows, I should have passed with averted head; but I could now stop and look over the paling, and peer under the boughs of the plum-tree for a glimpse of the garden in the rear. Weeds were growing apace, and in the narrow strip of the "front yard" I missed a dainty little rose-bush — mother's pet — which used to be covered with diminutive double crimson blossoms. Neighbor Niles always called it the "fi'penny-bit rose." I afterwards found it in the church-yard, so carefully transplanted that it was already blooming on mother's grave. It was not necessary to ask whose pious hand had placed it there.

The good Neighbor and "Dave" gave me an honest and hearty welcome. She insisted on opening the best room, though I would have preferred the kitchen, where I could hear her cheery voice alternately from the vicinity of cook-stove, cupboard, and table. For dinner we had the plain, yet most bountiful fare of the country, and she heaped my plate far beyond my powers of eating, saying, with every added spoonful, "I expect you 're half starved at the school."

"Dr. Dymond does n't look as if *he* ett much, anyhow," Dave remarked, with a chuckle.

"It seems quite nateral to have you here ag'in, Johnny," said the Neighbor. "Dear me! to think how things has changed in the last two year. Poor Neighbor Godfrey! — as good a woman as ever lived, though I say it to your face, — dead and gone, and you movin' away to Readin', like as not never to come back ag'in. Well, you must n't forgit your old neighbors, them that 's always wished you well. Out of sight out of mind, they say; but I guess it don't hold true with everybody, — leastways not with me. I can't git over thinkin' about Becky Jane yit: it comes on to me powerful hard sometimes. She 'd ha' been sixteen last August, if she 'd ha' lived. I often go up and scrub off her tombstone, and scrape the rust out o' the letters."

"Oh, Neighbor Niles!" I cried, "you asked me once to write a few lines to put on the stone. I'll do it yet, before I leave."

The good woman's face glowed with gratitude. "I 'll see that it 's put on — whatever you write," she said, "if it takes the vally of every turkey I 've raised!"

I kept my promise. Four lines, containing a simile about a broken flower being laid beneath this sod, to bloom above in the garden of God, were sent to Neighbor Niles, and whoever takes the trouble to visit Cross-Keys churchyard will find them on Becky Jane's tombstone to this day.

It was some twenty miles to Reading, and accordingly, on the day after the closing exhibition at the academy, a horse and light vehicle, despatched by my uncle, arrived to convey me to my new home. Nearly all the scholars were leaving for the autumn vacation, and my departure lost its solemnity in the hurry and confusion that prevailed. Penrose promised to correspond with me, and Charley Rand said, "Don't be astonished if you find me in Reading next summer." Mother Dymond gave me something wrapped up in a newspaper, saying, "Take it, now; you 'll want them before you get there." "Them" proved to be six large and very hard ginger-cakes. My trunk — an old one, which had once belonged to my father — was tilted up on end in front of the seat, occasioning much misery both to my legs and the driver's; and so I left Honeybrook, the magnificent tin cupola sparkling a final farewell as we dashed up the "Reading pike."

The inevitable step having been taken, — the fibres I had put out during the second stage of my boyhood torn loose, — I began to speculate, with some curiosity, on the coming phase of my life. I found this attraction at least: I should live in a much larger and more important town than I had ever visited — a town with a river, a canal, and a new railroad. At the Cross-Keys, people always spoke of Reading as being inferior only to Philadelphia, and one of the Honeybrook boys, Detweiler, hotly and constantly proclaimed its glories, to the discomfiture of Marsh, who was from Lancaster. As the afternoon wore away, and the long miles slowly diminished down the teens, and then more slowly down the units, and the unsocial driver fell asleep every ten minutes, of which fact the horse took base advantage, I grew weary and impatient. My uncle's house became a less unwelcome terminus to the journey.

At last we approached some bold hills — wonderful, astonishing mountains, I thought them. Our road stretched forward through a hollow between; a scattering village came into view, and a toll-gate barred the road. The driver awoke with a start. "Here 's Gibraltar!" he said; "we 'll soon be there, now!"

"Are those the Alleghany Mountains?" I asked.

"Guess you 're green in these parts," said he: "them a'n't mountains."

"Well, what are their names?" I asked again, in much humiliation.

"This'n ha'n't no proper name, — 'Penn's Mount' some call it. T' other, on the left, is Neversink. You 'll see Readin' in two minutes."

We presently emerged upon a slope, whence a glorious landscape opened upon my eyes. Never had I seen or imagined anything so beautiful. The stately old town lay below, stretched at full length on an inclined plane, rising from the Schuylkill to the base of the mountain; the river, winding in abrupt curves, disclosed itself here and there through the landscape; hills of superb undulation rose and fell, in interlinking lines, through the middle distance, Scull's Hill boldly detaching itself in front, and far in the north the Blue Ridge lifted its dim wall against the sky.

The sinking sun turned the smokes of the town and the vapors of the river to golden dust, athwart which faintly gleamed the autumn coloring of distant woods. The noises of the scene were softened and mellowed, and above them all, clear, sweet, and faint, sounded the bugle of a boatman on the canal. It was not ignorant admiration on my part; for one familiar with the grandest aspects of Nature must still confess that few towns on this side of the Atlantic are so nobly environed.

As we entered the place I could scarcely turn my head rapidly enough to the right and left, in my inspection of signs, houses, and people. The brick sidewalks seemed to be thronged, but nobody paid any particular attention to us. In Honeybrook every one would have stopped and looked at us, so long as we were in sight. The driver turned into the broad main avenue of Penn Street, with its central line of markets, then downward towards the river, and drew up, a few blocks further, at a corner. It was a low, old-fashioned brick house, with a signboard over the front door and window, upon which was inscribed, in faded letters, "A. Woolley's Grocery Store." There were boxes of candles, some bottles, a rope of onions, half a dozen withered lemons, and a few other articles in the window; a woman was issuing from the door with a basket full of brown paper parcels on her arm. On the other side of the portly window a narrow door was squeezed into the wall. The driver, having alighted, jerked my trunk out of the wagon, brought it down with a crash on the upper step, and rang the bell. The door was opened by Aunt Peggy, in person: she had been one of the shadows which had haunted my mother's funeral, and I therefore recognized her.

My trunk was brought in and stood on end in the narrow passage, which it almost blocked up. "You won't want it before bedtime, I reckon," said my aunt; "so leave it there, and Bolty will help you carry it up. Come into the settin'-room."

Following her I found myself presently in a small room behind the store. It was comfortably furnished, but somewhat chill and unfriendly in its atmosphere, — stiff, almost, although nothing could have been less so than my aunt's appearance. She wore a limp calico dress, of some dark pattern, and a cap, the strings of which were untied and hung over her breast. Her face was long and thin, and her hair, many shades lighter than my mother's, fell in straight, lank lines over her ears. There was usually a tuft of it sticking out somewhere about the back of her neck. Her eyes were small and gray, her nose long and pointed, and her lips thin and sunken at the corners, from the loss of most of her back teeth. Add to this a weak, lamenting voice, — rather, indeed, a whine, — and it will readily be conceived that my aunt Peggy was not a person to inspire a young man with enthusiasm for the female sex. Never were two sisters more unlike than she and mother. I presume there must have been a family likeness somewhere, but I was really unable to discover it.

In a few minutes Uncle Amos came in from the store. He shook hands with me with more cordiality than I had anticipated. "We 'll have things fixed, in the course of a day or two," he said. "Now, Peggy, I guess you had better get tea ready: John will be hungry, after his ride. Will you come into the store, John, and look around a little?"

I preferred that to sitting alone in the back room. After stumbling over some coffee-bags, — for it was getting dusky, and the lamps were not yet lighted, — I came forth into the open space behind the counter, where a boy of my own age was very busily engaged in weighing and "doing up" various materials. Uncle Amos stepped forward to assist him, leaving me to play the spectator. For a little while, both were actively employed; then, the rush of custom having suddenly subsided, my uncle said, "Here, Bolty, this is my nephew, John Godfrey. John, this is my assistant, Bolty Himpel."

Bolty grinned and nodded, but said nothing. He was larger in every way than myself, but looked younger. His hair, so blond as to be almost white, was cut close to his head; his forehead was low, his eyes large, wide apart, and pale blue; his nose short, thick, and flattened in the middle, and his mouth large and partly open. He was of the pure peasant-blood of Southern Germany, his name, Bolty, being simply a contraction of Leopold, with a little confusion of kindred consonants. I was a good deal surprised at my uncle's choice of an assistant, but I afterwards found that Bolty understood the business, and nothing else. His round, unmeaning face was a perpetual advertisement of simple honesty to the customers. He knew it, and profited thereby. Besides, he spoke fluently that remarkable language, the Pennsylvania German, — a useful accomplishment in a town where many native families were almost wholly ignorant of English.

In a quarter of an hour my aunt whined out of the gloom at the back of the store, "Tea, Amos!" and we obeyed the melancholy summons. The table was set in the kitchen behind the sitting-room, and so near the stove that Aunt Peggy could reach the hot water with her right hand, without rising from her chair. The board looked very scantily supplied, to my eyes, accustomed to country profuseness, but there proved to be enough.

After we were seated, Uncle Amos bent, or rather plunged forward, over his plate, waving his hands with the palms outward, before bringing them together in the attitude of prayer. There was a certain ostentation in this gesture, which struck me at once. It seemed to say, "Take notice, Lord: I am about to ask Thy blessing." This was a very irreverent fancy of mine, I confess; but there it was: I could n't help it.

Most people — as we find them — would have considered Uncle Amos a man of imposing presence. He was both tall and stout, and the squareness in his outlines, both of head and body, suggested a rough, massive strength. His head was bald from the forehead to the crown, but the side-hair was combed upwards so as to overlap and partially conceal it. His eyes were hard, and shot forth a steely twinkle from under their fat lids; the corners were channelled with a multitude of short, sly wrinkles. The skin of his cheeks was unpleasantly threaded here and there by fine, dark-purple veins, and always had a gloss like varnish when he was freshly shaven. I half suspect, now, that part of my instinctive dislike to him arose from the jar which his appearance occasioned to my sense of beauty. As a matter of conscience, I tried to like him; but I am afraid the exertion was not very severe.

After tea, I went back to the sitting-room, while my uncle took Bolty's place and allowed the latter to get his meal in turn. Then it was necessary to wait until the store should be closed for the night, and, to divert the time, Aunt Peggy brought me the "Life of Henry Martyn," which I read with hearty interest. "A good model," said my uncle, looking over my shoulder, as he came in, after the shutters had been duly fastened and bolted.

"Shut it up now," he continued. "We go early to bed, and get up early, in this house. Bolty, come here, and help John up-stairs with his trunk."

Bolty seized one end of the unwieldy box, and we slowly bumped and stumbled up two flights of stairs, into a large room under the roof, with a single window in the gable. I remarked, with a disagreeable sensation, that there was only one bed, and that one not remarkably broad. The big, coarse fellow would be sure to usurp the most of it, and his broad nose and open mouth indicated an immense capacity for snoring. Besides, I was always, from a very child, exceedingly sensitive to what I may call, for want of a better term, human electricity; that is to say, certain persons attract me, or impart a sense of comfort, by their physical nearness, while others repel or convey an impression of vague discomfort. This feeling seems to have no connection with beauty or ugliness, health or disease, or even affection or enmity. It arises from some subtle affinity of physical temperament, like that which we occasionally notice in the vegetable world. There are certain plants which flourish or droop in the neighborhood of certain others. I think this delicate, intangible sense is general among cultivated persons, but I have never found it developed to the same extent as in my own case.

I could not justly class Bolty Himpel among those strongly repellant natures whose approach to me was like that of a poisonous wind, but there was sufficient of the feeling to make the necessity of lying all night in his "atmosphere" very distasteful. However, there was no help for it; he had already asked me, —

"Which side 'll you take?"

I chose that nearest the window, and soon fell asleep, wearied with the changing excitements of the day. It was not long, apparently, before the bedstead creaked and shook, and a loud voice yelled, "Tumble out!"

The dawn was glimmering through the window. Bolty was already hauling on his trousers, and I rose and looked out. To my delight I could see the long, majestic outline of Penn's Mount above the houses, its topmost trees making a dark fringe against the morning sky. The view became a part of my garret-furniture, and changed the aspect of the room at once.

"Boss is pretty sharp," said Bolty to me, as I commenced dressing; "he opens half an hour sooner and keeps open half an hour later than any other grocery in the town. 'T a'n't a bad plan. People get to know it, and they come to us when they can't go nowhere else. It keeps us on the go, though. You ha'n't done nothin' at business, ha'n't you?"

"No," I answered; "I 've been at school. 'T was Uncle Amos's plan that I should come here, and I don't know how I 'll like it."

"Oh, you 'll soon git the hang of it. I don't s'pose he 'll put you to rollin' o' bar'ls and openin' o' boxes. Y' a'n't built for that."

Whereupon Bolty deliberately squeezed and twisted the muscles of my upper arm, in such wise that they were sore for the rest of the day. "That 's the crow-bar," said he, bending and stiffening his own right arm, until the flexor rose like an arch; "and them 's the death-mauls," shaking his clenched fists. These expressions he had evidently picked up from some canal boatman. Their force and fierceness contrasted comically with the vacant good-humor written on his face.

We went down to the shop and opened the shutters. There was little custom before breakfast, so I lounged about behind the counter, pulling open drawers of spices and reading the labels on bottles and jars. After all, I thought, there are more disagreeable avocations in the world than that of a grocer, — bricklaying, for instance. I determined to do my share of the work faithfully, whether I liked it or not. I was in my nineteenth year, and, at the worst, would be my own master at twenty-one.

Bolty was right in his conjecture. He had not only more strength than myself, but greater mechanical dexterity, and consequently the heavy work fell to his share. My uncle, finding that I wrote a neat hand and was a good arithmetician, gradually initiated me into the mysteries of day-book and ledger. I also assisted in waiting upon the customers, and in a few days became sufficiently expert at sliding sugar or coffee out of the scoop, so as to turn the scale by the weight of a grain or single bean, settling the contents in paper bags, and tying them squarely and compactly. My uncle was too shrewd a business-man to let me learn at the expense of customers: I was required to cover the counter with packages of various weights, the contents of which were afterwards returned to the appropriate bins or barrels. Thus, while I was working off my awkwardness, the grocery presented an air of unusual patronage to its innocent visitors.

Many of our customers were farmers of the vicinity, who brought their eggs, butter, and cheese, to exchange for groceries. This was a profitable part of the business, as we gained both in buying and selling. There was a great demand among these people for patent medicines, which formed a very important branch of my uncle's stock, and he could have found no better salesman than Bolty Himpel. The latter discovered, in an incredibly short time, from what neighborhood a new customer came, and immediately gave an account of the relief which somebody, living in an opposite direction, had derived from the use of certain pills or plasters.

"Weakness o' the back, eh?" he would say to some melancholy-faced countrywoman; "our Balm of Gilead 's the stuff for that. Only three levies a bottle; rub it in with flannel, night and mornin'. Mr. Hempson—you know him, p'r'aps, down on Poplar Neck?—was bent double with the rheumatiz, and two bottles made him as straight as I am. Better take some o' the Peruvian Preventative, while you 're about it, ma'am,—keeps off chills and fevers. Deacon Dingey sent all the way down from Port Clinton t' other day for some: they don't keep it there. Lives in a ma'shy place, right on to the river, and they ha'n't had a chill in the family since they use 'em. I reckon we 've sold wheelbarra loads."

I noticed, in the course of time, that Uncle Amos never interfered with Bolty's loquacity, unless (which happened very rarely) his recommendation was overdone and the customer became suspicious. Sometimes, indeed, he said, with a gravity not wholly natural, "Rather too strong. Don't tell more than you know."

"Oh," Bolty would answer, "'t won't kill if it don't cure."

This youth had an astonishing memory of names and faces,—a faculty in which, probably from want of practice,

I was deficient. His German also made him indispensable to many of the country people. My uncle possessed a tolerable smattering of the language, and insisted that I should endeavor to learn it. "It 's more use than the heathenish Latin you learned in school," said he.

"Why, Uncle Amos," I retorted, "I read Sacred History in Latin."

"Then it was n't the Word of God, which was inspired in Hebrew," he answered.

I had determined to go on alone with my Latin studies, and his disapprobation of the language troubled me. I could not, as I proposed, bring the books down to the desk behind the counter, and devote the end of the evening to them, without incurring his pious censure. Against German he would have no such scruples, and I decided, though with regret, to take that language instead. I remembered that Grandfather Hatzfeld, who had been educated in Bethlehem, spoke it habitually, and that my mother retained her knowledge of it to the last. Among her books was an old edition of Herder and Liebeskind's "Palmblätter," which she had often read to me, as a child, and I had then understood. This early knowledge, however, had long since faded to a blank, but it left the desire to be renewed, and perhaps unconsciously smoothed the first difficulties of the study.

I saw little of Aunt Peggy, except at meals and on Sundays. Having never had any children of her own, she would scarcely have been able to assume a motherly attitude towards me; but I do not think she tried. Her share in the conversation was generally of a discouraging cast, and the subject which most seemed to excite her interest was a case of backsliding which had recently occurred in my uncle's church. For several days the latter added to his tri-daily grace a prayer "that them which have forsaken the light may be brought back to it, and that them which wander in darkness may be led to seek it!" He was undoubtedly sincere in this prayer, and I could have joined in it, had I not been suspicious enough to guess that the latter clause must be aimed at myself.

On Sundays, Bolty and I went twice to church with my uncle and aunt, dutifully joining in the hymns, as I had been accustomed to do with my mother. I declined taking a class in the Sunday-school, much to my uncle's displeasure; but, after being confined to the store all the week, I felt an urgent craving for a mouthful of fresh air and the freedom of the landscape. Sometimes I climbed high up the sides of Mount Penn, whence the brown tints of the coming winter vanished far off in delicious blue; but more frequently I walked northward to the knoll now covered by the Cemetery, and enjoyed the luxury of a wide lookout on all sides. In the evening, Bolty was allowed to visit his father, an honest, hard-working shoemaker, living on the eastern edge of the town, and I occasionally accompanied him. The family conversation was entirely in German, so that these visits were not much of a recreation, after all.

I soon saw that the literary performances which had been my pride and delight at school must be given up, at least for the winter. There was no fire in the garret bedroom, and I was not likely to be left in possession of the sitting-room behind the store more than once a month.

CHAPTER VIII.

DESCRIBING CERTAIN INCIDENTS OF MY LIFE IN READING.

The winter, having fairly set in, dragged on its monotonous round. During the cold weather there was less to do in the store, and I had frequent hours of leisure, which I passed on my high stool at the desk, reading such books as I could procure, and a few which I bought. The sale of the cottage and furniture left a surplus of sixty-seven dollars, after paying the expenses of my mother's funeral and my last term at Dr. Dymond's. On making this statement, as my guardian, my uncle said, —

"You don't need any more clothes this winter, and you 'd better let me put this out for you. You 'll have no expenses here, as I count that what you do in the store will about balance your board."

I greatly longed to have the whole sum in my hands, but offered to let him "put out" fifty dollars and give me the remainder. He consented, though with an ill grace, saying, "It is n't good to give boys the means of temptation."

I had never before had one tenth part as much money in my pocket, and it gave me a wonderfully comfortable feeling of wealth and independence. My first step was to buy an octavo volume, containing the poems of Milton, Young, Gray, Beattie, and Collins, every word of which I faithfully read. (I wonder whether anybody else ever did the same thing.) I also purchased a blank diary, with headings for every day in the year, and kept it in the breast-pocket of my coat, with fear and trembling lest it should be left lying where my uncle might find and read it. For a month or two the entries were very regular, then more and more fragmentary, and before summer they ceased altogether. The little volume, with its well-worn cover and embrowned paper, is now lying before me. I turn its pages with a smile at its extravagant sentiment and immature reflections. Can it be that I really wrote such stuff as this? —

"*Jan.* 28. — Cold and cloudy — emblematic of my life. In the afternoon, gleams of sunshine, flashing like the *wings of angels*. Would I too could *soar* above these sublunary cares! Read 'Childe Harold' while uncle was out. Is it wrong to *steal* one's intellectual food? No; the *famishing* soul must have nourishment!"

As I became familiar with the routine of my duties, and Uncle Amos found that the accounts could be safely intrusted to my care, he frequently left the store to Bolty and myself, and made short trips into the country for the purpose of procuring supplies and perfecting his system of exchange. In this way he snapped up many a pound of butter and dozen of eggs, which would have found their way to other groceries; and during the season when those articles were rather scarce he was always well supplied, — a fact which soon became known and brought a notable increase of custom. He also went to Philadelphia, to make his purchases of the wholesale dealers in person, instead of ordering them by letter. We, of course, felt a greater responsibility during his absence, and were very closely confined to our duties. Bolty had no other ambition than to set up in business for himself, some day; it was an aim he never lost sight of, and I was sure he would reach it. For my part, having been forced into my present position, I longed for the coming of the day which would release me, but I was too conscientious either to break loose from it or to slight my share of the labor.

About the beginning of April, either from the close confinement within-doors to which I had been subjected, or to some change in my system, — for I was still growing, and had now attained the average height of men, — I was attacked with fever. The malady was not severe nor dangerous, but stubborn; and though, after a week's confinement to the spare bedroom on the second story, I was able to sit up and move about again, the physician prescribed rest for a fortnight longer, with moderate exercise when the weather was fine. Aunt Peggy waited upon me as well as she was able: that is, when her household duties had been performed, she brought her knitting and sat by the stove at the foot of my bed, asking occasionally, in a tearful voice, "How do you feel, John?" Fortunately, I required no watching at night, for there was no element of tenderness in the house to make it endurable. My uncle took my place in the store, though it must have been a serious interruption to his outside plans. He acquiesced, without apparent impatience, in the doctor's prescription of further rest.

During those days of convalescence I experienced a delicious relief and lightness of heart. Spring had burst suddenly upon the land with a balmy brightness and warmth which lingered, day after day, belying the fickle fame of the month. Walking down Penn Street and crossing the bridge, I would find a sunny seat on the top of the gray cliff beyond, and bask in the soft awakening of the landscape around. The bluebird sang like the voice of the season; below me, in gardens and fields, I saw how the dark brown of the mellow earth increased for the planting, and how sheets or cloudy wafts of green settled over the barrenness of winter. Again I became hopeful, joyous, confident of the future. Time and the tenderness of memory had softened my grief: I often recalled mother's words on her death-bed, and allowed no unavailing sting of remorse for neglected duties to cloud the serenity of my resignation. It was thus, I felt, that she would have me to feel, and her sainted spirit must rejoice in the returning buoyancy of mine.

On one of those lovely April afternoons, as I was musing on the cliff, — my thoughts taking a vague, wandering rhythm from the sound of a boatman's horn down the river, — the idea of writing something for publication came into my mind. A poem, of course, — for "Childe Harold," "Manfred," and "The Corsair" had turned the whole drift of my ideas into a channel of imagined song. To write some verses and have them printed would be joy — triumph — glory. The idea took possession of me with irresistible force. Two dollars out of my seventeen had gone for a subscription to the *Saturday Evening Post*, — an expense at which Uncle Amos had grumbled, until he found that Aunt Peggy took stealthy delight in perusing the paper. In its columns I found charming poetry by Bessie Bulfinch and Adeliza Choate, besides republications from contemporary English literature, especially Dickens. B. Simmons, T. K. Hervey, and Charles Swain became, for me, demigods of song: I could only conceive of them as superior beings, of lofty stature and majestic beauty. I had never seen a man who had written a book. Even the editors of the *Gazette* and *Adler*, in Reading, were personages whose acquaintance I did not dare to seek. There was always a half-column in the *Post*, addressed "To Correspondents," containing such messages as, — "Ivanhoe's story contains some sweet passages, but lacks incident: declined with thanks;" or, "The 'Fairy's Bower,' by 'Cecilia,' is a poem of much promise, and will appear next week." I invariably read the articles thus accepted, and, while I recognized their great merit, (for were they not printed?) it seemed to me that, by much exertion, I might one day achieve the right to appear in their ranks.

After having given hospitality to the idea, I carried pencil and paper with me, and devoted several afternoons to the poem. It was entitled, "The Unknown Bard" (meaning myself, of course), written in heroic lines, after I had vainly attempted the Spenserian stanza. As nearly as I can recollect, there were fifty or sixty lines of it, describing my intellectual isolation, and how I must stifle the burning thoughts that filled my bosom, lest the cold world should crush me with its envenomed scorn! I signed myself "Selim," a name which I found in Collins's First Eclogue, and particularly admired. How I used to wish that some good genius had inspired my mother to give me the name of "Selim," or "Secander," instead of "John"! However, as "Selim" I would be known in the world of letters and on the tablets of fame — Selim, the Unknown Bard!

Finished, at last, and copied in my distinctest hand, there came the question — how should I send it? The clerk at the post-office knew me, because I went there for my uncle's letters, and also, weekly, for my beloved newspaper. Perhaps he also read the paper, and would be sure to find a connection between my letter and the editorial answer to Selim of Reading. Not for the world would I have intrusted the awful secret to a single soul, — not even to Penrose or Bob Simmons. Perhaps I should still have run the risk, as I fancied it to be, of using the post, but for a most lucky and unexpected chance. Uncle Amos suggested that I should go to Philadelphia in his stead, on some business relating to sugar, with the details of which I was acquainted. I was almost too demonstrative in my delight; for my suspicious uncle shook his head, and made it a condition that I should go down in the morning-train, accomplish my mission at once, and return the same evening.

On reaching the right-angled city, I found my way with little difficulty to "Simpson & Brother," Market Street, near Second, and, after very faithfully transacting the business, had still two hours to spare before the departure of the return-train. The newspaper office was near at hand, — Chestnut, above Third, — and thither I repaired, with flushed face and beating heart, the precious epistle held fast in my hand, yet carefully concealed under my sleeve, lest any one, in passing by, should read the superscription and guess the contents. I do not smile at myself, as I recall this experience. The brain, like the heart, has its virginity, and its first earnest utterance is often as tremulously shy as the first confession of love.

My intention had been to deliver the letter at the office of the paper, as if I had been simply its bearer and not its author. But after I had mounted two dark, steep flights of steps, and found myself before the door, my courage failed me. I heard voices within: there were several persons, then. They would be certain to look at me sharply — to notice my agitation — perhaps to question me about the letter. While I was standing thus, twisting and turning it in my hand, in a veritable perspiration from excitement, I heard footsteps descending from an upper story. Desperate and panic-stricken, I laid the letter hastily on the floor, at the door of the office, and rushed down to the street as rapidly and silently as possible. Without looking around, I walked up Chestnut Street with a fearful impression that somebody was following me, and turning the corner of Fourth, began to read the titles of the books in Hart's window. Five minutes having elapsed, I knew that I was not discovered, and recovered my composure; though, now that the poem had gone out of my hands, I would have given anything to get it back again.

When the next number of the paper arrived, I tore off the wrapper with trembling fingers and turned to the fateful column on the second page. But I might as well have postponed my excitement: there was no notice of the poem. Perhaps they never received the letter, — perhaps it had been trodden upon and defaced, and swept down-stairs by the office-boy! These were, at least, consoling possibilities, — better that than to be contemptuously ignored. By the following week my fever was nearly over, and I opened the paper with but a faint expectation of finding anything; but lo! there it was, — "Selim" at the very head of the announcements! These were the precious words: "We are obliged to 'Selim' for his poem, which we shall publish shortly. It shows the hand of youth, but evinces a flattering promise. Let him trim the midnight lamp with diligence."

If the sinking sun had wheeled about and gone up the western sky, or the budding trees had snapped into full leaf in five minutes, I don't believe it would have astonished me. I was on my way home from the post-office when I read the lines, and I remember turning out of Penn Street to go by a more secluded and circuitous way, lest I should be tempted to cut a pigeon-wing on the pavement, in the sight of the multitude. I passed a little brick building, with a tin sign on the shutter, — "D. J. Mulford, Attorney-at-Law." "Pooh!" I said to myself; "what 's D. J. Mulford? *He* never published a poem in his life!" As I caught a glimpse of his head, silhouetted against the back window, I found myself, nevertheless, rather inclined to pity him for being unconscious that the author of "The Unknown Bard" was at that moment passing his door.

This disproportionate exultation, the reader will say, betrayed shallow waters. Why should I not admit the fact?

My mind *was* exceedingly shallow, at that time, but, thank Heaven! it was limpid as a mountain brook. It could have floated no craft heavier than a child's toy-sloop, but the sun struck through it and filled its bed with light. If it is expected that we should feel ashamed of our intellectual follies, we must needs regret that we were ever young.

When the poem at last appeared, after a miserably weary interval of two or three weeks, I was a little mortified to find that some liberty had been taken with the language. Where I had written "hath" I found "has" substituted, and, what was worse, "Fame's *eternal* brow," which I thought so grand, was changed into "Fame's resplendent brow." The poem did n't seem quite mine, with these alterations: they took the keen edge off my pride and my happiness.

However, Selim was at last the companion, if not the equal, of Bessie Bulfinch and Adeliza Choate, — that was a great point gained. I determined that he should not relapse into silence.

My next essay was a tale, called "Envy; or, the Maiden of Ravenna." I am ashamed to say that I placed the city upon the summit of a frightful precipice, the base of which was washed by the river Arno! Laurelia, the maiden of the story, fell from the awful steep, but fortunately alighted on the branch of a weeping willow, which gently transferred her to the water, whence she was rescued by the Knight Grimaldi. But this story proved too much even for the kindly editor, whose refusal was so gentle and courteous that it neither wounded my pride nor checked my ambition.

One day in early summer I happened to pass again by the office of D. J. Mulford. I glanced at the sign mechanically, and was going on, when a terrible thumping on the window-panes startled and arrested me. I stopped: the window was suddenly raised, and who but Charley Rand poked his head out!

"I say, Godfrey!" he cried; "come in here a minute! Mulford 's out, and I have the office to myself."

"Why, Rand," said I, as he opened the door for me, "how did you get here?"

"Sit down, and I 'll tell you all about it. Father said, you know, that I might be a lawyer, if I had a mind. Well, this spring, when he found I had Latin enough to tell him what *posse comitatus* meant, and *scire facias*, and *venditioni exponas*, and so on, — such as you see in the sheriff's advertisements, — he thought I was ready to begin the study. I had no objections, for I knew that the school would be dull, with Penrose, Marsh, Brotherton, and most of the older boys gone, and, besides, it 's time I was seeing a little more life. Many fellows set up in business for themselves at my age. Mulford 's father's lawyer, whenever he 's obliged to have one; I suppose he 'll be *my* first client, after I pass. I 've been here ten days, and was just thinking I must find you out, when I saw you go by the window. Have a cigar?"

I declined the offer, and politely, considering my abhorrence of the custom.

"You 've grown, Godfrey," Rand continued, hauling a second chair towards him and hoisting his feet upon the arms, "and I see you 're getting some fuzz on your chin. You 'll be a man soon, and I should n't wonder if you 'd make your mark some day."

I overlooked the patronizing manner of this remark in its agreeable substance. And here I should explain that Charley Rand was now by no means the same youth as on the day when we were together intrusted to Dr. Dymond's care. Until then he had been petted and humored in every possible way, and was selfish and overbearing in his manner. A few months among forty or fifty boys, however, taught him to moderate his claims. He was brought down to the common level, and with that flexibility of nature which was his peculiar talent, or faculty, leaped over to the opposite extreme of smooth-tongued subservience. What he had ceased to gain by impudence, he now endeavored to obtain by coaxing, flattering, and wheedling. In the latter art he soon became an adept. Many a time have I worked out for him some knotty problem, in violation of the rules of the school, and in violation, also, of my own sense of right, cajoled by his soft, admiring, affectionate accents. I do not describe his character as I understood it then, but as I afterwards learned it. I was still his dupe.

In the space of half an hour he managed to extract from me the particulars of my life and occupation in Reading. He already knew, in ten days, much more about the principal families of the place than I had learned in eight months. After this interview, I soon got the habit of walking around to Mulford's office on Sunday afternoons and spending an hour or two with him. We sat in the backroom, which opened on a little yard covered with weeds, boards, and broken bottles, so that the proprieties of the street-side of the building were carefully respected. I felt less lonely, now that there was a schoolmate within hail.

In my uncle's house things went on very much as usual. Bolty and I had scarcely any taste in common, (unless it was a fondness for pea-nuts, which I retain to this day,) but we never quarrelled. As we were strictly attentive to our respective duties, my uncle seemed to be satisfied with us, and was, for this reason perhaps, forbearing in other respects. Aunt Peggy adhered to her monotonous household round, and made no attempt to control my actions, except when I bought white linen instead of nankeen, for summer wear. "There 'll be no end to the washin' of it," she said, in a voice so suggestive of tears that I expected to see her take out her handkerchief.

It was plain to me that Uncle Amos intended to enlarge his business as rapidly as was consistent with his prudent and cautious habits. I had good reason to believe that my services were included in his plans; yet, though I was more firmly fixed than ever in my determination to leave when his legal guardianship should cease, I judged it best to be silent on this point. It would only lead to tedious sermons, — discussions in which neither could have the least sympathy with the other's views, and possibly a permanent and very disagreeable disturbance in our relations towards each other. I do not think he recognized, as I did, that I had quietly established an armistice, which I could at any time annul.

In one sense, Bolty was my aid. He never mentioned the subject, but I understood then as well as I do now that he knew my want of liking for the business, and was satisfied that it should be so. After the weather grew warm enough, I resumed my Latin studies in the garret; thither also I took prohibited books, and filled quires of paper with extracts and comments, feeling, instinctively, that my companion would never betray me.

This sort of life was not what I would have chosen. It was far from satisfying the cravings of heart and brain; but I bore it with patience, looking forward to the day of release.

CHAPTER IX.

IN WHICH I OUGHT TO BE A SHEEP, BUT PROVE TO BE A GOAT.

THERE was one point upon which I was always apprehensive that Uncle Amos would assail me. It dated from that first evening in the little cottage at the Cross-Keys, the previous summer. What I have said of my shrinking delicacy of feeling with regard to my poetic attempts will equally apply to the religious sentiment. A dear and tender friend might have found me willing to open my heart to him concerning sacred things; but I could not, dared not, admit a less privileged person to the sanctuary. I had not the courage or the independence necessary to arrest my uncle's approach to the subject, and was therefore preternaturally watchful and alert in retreating. Very often, I suspect, I fancied an ambush where none existed. My uncle probably saw that he must tread cautiously, and feel his way by degrees, for I only remember one conversation in the course of the summer which really disturbed me.

My poor mother had been an earnest Lutheran, of the hearty, cheerful, warm-blooded German sort. She always preferred thanksgiving for God's mercies to fear of His wrath, and had brought me up in the faith that the beauties and blessings of this life might be enjoyed without forfeiting one's title as a Christian. At the age of fourteen I had been confirmed, and was therefore to be considered as a member of the Church. At least, I supposed that the principal religious duty thenceforth required of me was to follow God's commandments as nearly as my imperfect human nature would allow. I never closed my eyes in sleep without invoking the protection of my only Father, with a grateful feeling in my heart of hearts that He did indeed hear and heed me. I did not fear damnation, because I had not the slightest liking for the Devil.

I knew little or nothing of the slight partitions which divide the multitudinous sects of the Christian world, and was not the least troubled in conscience at attending my uncle's church instead of my own. Whatever was doctrinal in the latter I had forgotten since my confirmation, — probably because it had then made very little impression on my mind. My uncle's clergyman was a mild, amiable man, whose goodness it was impossible to doubt, and I listened to his sermons with proper reverence.

Something, I know not what, — possibly some memory of my mother, — led me, one Sunday in summer, to attend the Lutheran church. The well-known hymns fell on my ear with a home-like sound, and the powerful tones of the organ seemed to lift me to new devotional heights. In the sermon I felt the influence of a strong, massive intellect, the movements of which I could not always follow, but which stimulated and strengthened me. After this, I divided my Sundays nearly equally between the two churches. On informing my uncle and aunt, at dinner, where I had been, the former was at first silent; but, after some grave reflection, asked me, —

"Are you a member of that persuasion?"

"Oh, yes," I answered, "just the same as mother and Aunt Peggy."

I struck a blow without intending it. Aunt Peggy looked startled and uneasy; a strong color came into her face; then, after a quick glance at uncle, she lifted her hands and exclaimed, "No! Praise and Glory, not now!"

"Hem!" coughed Uncle Amos; "never mind, Peggy; blessed are them that see!" Then, turning to me, he added, "Do you mean that you have professed faith and been baptized?"

"I was baptized when I was a baby," I answered, "and confirmed when I was fourteen."

"Have you experienced a change of heart?"

"No," I boldly said, thinking that he meant to indicate infidelity, or some kind of backsliding, by this term.

Uncle Amos, to my surprise, uttered a loud groan, and Aunt Peggy made that peculiar clucking noise with her tongue against her teeth, which some women employ to signify disaster or lamentation.

"You feel, then," said Uncle Amos, after a long pause, "that your nature is utterly corrupt and sinful. Do you not see what a mockery it is to claim that you are a follower of the Lamb?"

"No, uncle!" I cried, indignantly; "I am *not* corrupt and sinful. I don't pretend to be a saint, but no one has a right to call me a sinner. I have kept all the commandments, except the tenth, and I never broke that without repenting of it afterwards. Mother belonged to the Lutheran Church, and I won't hear anything said against it!"

For a moment an equally earnest reply seemed to be hovering on my uncle's tongue; but he checked himself with a strong effort, groaned in a subdued way, and remarked with unusual gravity, "Darkness! darkness!" His manner towards me, for a day or two afterwards, was unusually solemn. The exigencies of business, however, soon restored our ordinary relations.

In the autumn, my uncle's church was visited by a noted "revival" preacher, whose coming had been announced some time in advance. He was a Kentuckian, of considerable fame in his own sect, and even beyond its borders, so that his appearance never failed to draw crowds together. As this was his first visit to Reading, it was an event which could not, of course, be allowed to go by without giving the church the full benefit of the impression he should produce, and a large increase of the congregation was counted upon as a sure result.

Finally, Mr. Brandreth, the resident clergyman, announced with unusual unction that "on the next Sabbath, Brother Mellowby would occupy the pulpit." The news immediately spread through the town, and was duly announced in the papers. When the day and hour arrived, the church was so crowded that extra benches were brought and placed lengthwise along the aisles. Expectation was on tiptoe, when, after the hymn had been sung and Mr. Brandreth had made a prayer in which the distinguished brother was not forgotten, a tall form arose and stood in the pulpit. Brother Mellowby was over six feet in height, and rather lank, but with broad, square shoulders and massive face. His eyes were large and dark, and his black hair, growing straight upward from his forehead, turned and fell on either side in long locks, which tossed and waved in the wind of his eloquence. His cheek-bones were prominent, his mouth large and expressive (that of Michael Angelo's "Moses" still reminds me of it), and his chin square and strong. Altogether, evidently a man of power and of purpose, but with more iron than gold in his composition. He looked, to me, as if he had at one time been near enough to Hell to feel the scorch of its flames, and had thence fought his way to Heaven by sheer force of a will stronger than the Devil's.

The commencement of his sermon was grave, earnest, and deliberate. It held the attention of the congregation rather by the clear, full, varied music of his voice than by any peculiar force of expression. Towards the close, however, as he touched upon the glories of the Christian's future reward, the wonderful power of his voice and the warmth of his personal magnetism developed themselves. Looking upwards, with rapt ecstatic gaze, he seemed verily to behold what he described, — the clouds opening, the glory breaking through, the waving of golden palms in the hands of the congregated angels, the towers of the New Jerusalem, shining far off, in deeps of infinite lustre, the green Eden of Heaven, watered by the River of Life, —

and then, glory surpassing all these glories, the unimaginable radiance of the Throne. Still pointing upwards, as he approached the awful light, he suddenly stopped, covered his eyes, and in a voice of tremulous awe, exclaimed, "The Seraphs veil their brows before Him, — the eyes of the redeemed souls dare not look upon His countenance, — the mind clothed in corrupting flesh cannot imagine His glory!"

The speaker sat down. I had scarcely breathed during this remarkable peroration, and, when his voice ceased, seemed to drop through leagues of illuminated air, to find myself, with a shock, in my uncle's pew. For a few seconds the silence endured; then a singular, convulsive sound, which was not a cry, yet could scarcely be called a groan, ran through the church. Some voices exclaimed "Glory!" the women raised their handkerchiefs to their faces, and an unaccustomed light shone from the eyes of the men. The hymn commencing, "*Turn to the Lord and seek salvation*," then arose from the congregation with a fervor which made it seem the very trumpet-call and battle-charge of the armies of the Cross.

I did not go to church in the evening, but I heard that the impression produced by Mr. Mellowby's first sermon was still further increased by his second. Several "hopeful" cases were already reported, and the services were announced to continue through the week. My uncle proposed that Bolty and I should relieve each other alternately, in the evenings, so that we might both attend. I was prevented, however, from going again until Wednesday, by which time he had decided to put up the shutters an hour earlier, even at the loss of some little custom.

On this occasion, Bolty and I went together. When we entered the church, we found it well filled, and the atmosphere almost stifling. Brother Mellowby was "exhorting," but, from a broad cross-aisle in front of the pews, up and down which he walked, pausing now and then to turn and hurl impassioned appeals to his auditors. Whenever he stopped a moment to recover breath, a wild chorus of cries and groans arose, mingled with exclamations of "Amen!" "Glory!" "Go on, Brother!" Speaker and hearers were evidently strung to the same pitch of excitement, and mutually inspired each other. Mr. Brandreth, Uncle Amos, and several prominent members of the congregation walked up and down the aisles, seizing upon the timid or hesitating, placing their arms about the necks of the latter, gently coaxing them to kneel, or, when wholly successful, leading them, sobbing and howling, to the "anxious seat" in front of the pulpit. These intermediate agents were radiant with satisfaction; the atmosphere of the place seemed to exhilarate and agreeably excite them. For my part, I looked on the scene with wonder, not unmixed with a sense of pain.

Brother Mellowby had been apparently engaged in persuasive efforts up to the time of my entrance. Some twelve or fifteen persons had been moved, and were kneeling in various attitudes — some prostrate and silent, some crying and flinging up their arms convulsively — at the anxious seat. Others were weeping or groaning in their seats in the pews, but still hung back from the step which proclaimed them confessed sinners, seeking for mercy. It was to these latter that the speaker now addressed himself with a new and more powerful effort.

I can only attempt to describe it. To my sensitive, beauty-loving nature, it was awful, yet pervaded with a wonderful fascination which held me to listen. He painted the future condition of the unconverted with an imagination as terrible as his vision of the Christian's Heaven had been dazzling and lovely. It was a feat of word-painting, accompanied with dramatic gestures which brought the white-hot sulphur of Hell to one's very feet, and with intonations of voice which suggested the eternal despair of the damned.

"There!" he cried, lifting his long arms high above his head, and then bringing them down with a rushing swoop until his hands nearly touched the floor, — "Sinners, there is your bed! In the burning lake — in the bottomless seas of fire, — where the Evil that now flatters you with honeyed kisses shall sting and gnaw and torture forever, — where the fallen angels themselves shall laugh at your agonies, and the burning remorse of millions of ages shall not avail to open the gates of the pit! For you will be forever sinking down — *down* — DOWN — DOWN, in the eternity of Hell!"

He shouted out the last words as if crying from the depths of anguish he had depicted. His face was like that of a lost angel, grand and awful in its gloomy light. Exclamations of "Lord, have mercy!" "Lord, save me!" arose all over the church, and some of the mourners in front became frantic in their despairing appeals. Bolty, at my side, was sobbing violently. For myself, I felt oppressed and bewildered; my mind seemed to be narcotized by some weird influence, though I was not conscious of any terror on my soul's account.

Brother Mellowby's tone suddenly changed again. Stretching forth his hands imploringly, he called, in accents of piercing entreaty, "Why do ye delay? See, the Redeemer stands ready to receive you! Now is the accepted time, and now is the day of salvation. Kneel down at His feet, acknowledge Him, lay your burden into His willing hands. Oh, were your sins redder than scarlet, they shall be washed white; oh, were the gates now yawning to receive you, He would snatch you as a brand from the burning; oh, if your hearts are bruised and bleeding, they will be healed; oh, the tears will be wiped from your eyes; oh, your souls will rejoice and will sing aloud in gratitude and triumph, and you will feel the blessed assurance of salvation which the world cannot take away!"

Tears rolled down his cheeks as he uttered these words: a softer yet not less powerful influence swayed the doubtful mourners. They shook as reeds in the wind, and one by one, amid shouts of "Glory! glory!" tottered forward and sank down among the other suppliants.

I could not doubt the solemn reality of the scene. The preacher felt, with every fibre of his body, that he was announcing God's truth, and the "mourners," as they were called, were, for the hour at least, sincere in their self-accusations and their cry for some evidence of pardon. I comprehended also, from what I saw and heard, that there was indeed a crisis or turning-point of the excitement, beyond which the cries of penitence and supplication became joyful hosannas. There, before me, human souls seemed to be hovering in the balance, each fighting for itself the dread battle of Armageddon, the issue of which was to fix its eternal fate. Some were crouching in guilty fear of the Wrath they had invoked, while others sprang upward with radiant faces, as if to grasp the garments of the invisible herald of mercy. The tragedy of our spiritual nature, in all its extremes of agony and joy, was there dimly enacted.

It was impossible to stand still and behold all this unmoved. I was not conscious of being touched, either by the Terror or the Promise; but a human sympathy with the passion of the fluctuating, torn, and shattered spirits around me — drifted here and there like the eddies of ghosts in the circles of Dante's "Purgatorio" — filled me with boundless pity. The tears were running down my face before I knew it. Yet I could not repress a feeling of astonishment when I saw the impassive Bolty led forward weeping and roaring for mercy, and bend down his bullet-head in the midst of the mourners.

Presently Uncle Amos came towards me. He laid his hand affectionately upon my shoulder, and said, with a tone in which there was triumph as well as persuasion, "Ah, I see you are touched at last, John. Now you will know what it is to experience Religion. The gates are opened this night, and there is joy and glory enough for all. Come forward, and let us pray together."

He took hold of my arm, but I drew back. I could not plunge into that chaos of shrieks and sobbing, around the "anxious seat."

"How?" said my uncle, in grave surprise: "with all this testimony of the saving power of Grace, you are not willing to pray?"

"Oh, yes," I answered, "I am willing to pray."

"Come, then."

"I need not go there to do it. I can pray, in my heart, here, just as well."

"Ah!" he exclaimed, "it was thus that the Pharisee prayed; but the poor publican, who threw himself on the ground and cried, 'God, be merciful to me a sinner!' made the prayer which was accepted."

"No, Uncle Amos," I retorted, "the publican did not throw himself upon the ground. The Bible says he *stood* afar off, and smote upon his breast."

I was perfectly earnest and sincere in what I said, but I verily believe that my uncle suspected a hidden sarcasm in my words. He left me abruptly, and I soon saw him in conversation with the Rev. Mr. Brandreth, in the forward part of the aisle. It was not long before the latter, stopping by the way to stoop and whisper encouragement into the ears of some who were kneeling in the pews, approached the place where I stood. I knew, immediately, that he had been sent, but I did not shrink from the encounter, because, so far as I knew him, I had found him to be an amiable and kindhearted man. My tears of sympathy were already dry, but I felt that I was trembling and excited.

"Brother Godfrey," said the clergyman, "are you ready, to-night, to acknowledge your Saviour?"

"I have always done it," I answered; "I belong to the Lutheran Church."

"You are a professing Christian, then?"

I did not precisely know what meaning he attached to the word "professing," but I answered, "Yes."

"We accept all such to free communion with us. Come and unite with us in prayer for these perishing souls!"

I again declined, giving him the same reason as I had given to my uncle. But the clergyman's reply to this plea was not so easy to evade.

"In the hearing of God," said he, "your prayer may be just as fervent; but, so far as your fellow-mortals are concerned, it is lost. While you stand here, you are counted among the cold and the indifferent. Give a visible sign of your pious interest, my brother; think that some poor, timorous soul, almost ready to acknowledge its sin and cry aloud for pardon, may be helped to eternal salvation by your example. Come forward and pray for and with them who are just learning to pray. If you feel the blessed security in your own heart, oh, come and help to pour it into the hearts of others!"

He said much more to the same effect, and I found it very difficult to answer him. I was bewildered and distressed, and my only distinct sensation was that of pain. The religious sentiment in my nature seemed to be raked and tortured, not serenely and healthfully elevated. But I was too young to clearly comprehend either myself or others, and I saw no way out of the dilemma except to kneel, as Mr. Brandreth insisted, and pray silently for the rest of the evening.

I therefore allowed him to lead me forward. The congregation, of course, supposed that I came as another mourner, — another treasure-trove, cast up from the raging deeps, — and greeted my movement with fresh shouts and hosannas. Uncle Amos gave a triumphant exclamation of "Glory!" or, rather, "GULLOW-RY!" as he pronounced it, in the effort to make as much as possible out of the word. Brother Mellowby tossed back his floating hair, threw out his long arms, and cried, "Another — still another! Oh, come all! this night there is rejoicing in Heaven! This night the throne of Hell totters!"

The "anxious seat" was painful to contemplate at a distance, but there was something terrifying in a nearer view. A girl of twenty, whose comb had been broken in tearing off her bonnet, leaped up and down, with streaming hair, clapping her hands, and shouting, or rather chanting, "Praise the Lord, praise the Lord, O my soul!" Another lay upon her back on the floor, screaming, while Aunt Peggy, leaning over the back of the next pew, fanned her face with a palm-leaf fan. The men were less violent in their convulsions, but their terrible weeping and sobbing was almost more than I could bear to hear.

I was glad to sink into some vacant place, and bury my face in my hands, that I might escape, in a measure, from the curious eyes of the unconverted spectators and the mistaken rejoicings of the church-members. On either side of me was a strong, full-grown man, — one motionless, and groaning heavily from time to time, while the other, after spasms during which he threw up his head and arms, and literally howled, fell down again, and confessed his secret sins audibly at my very ear. He was either unconscious of the proximity of others, or carried too far in his excitement to care for it. I could not avoid hearing the man's acknowledged record of guilt, — let not the reader imagine that I ever betrayed him, — and I remember thinking, even in the midst of my own bewilderment, that he was a very venial sinner, at the worst, and his distress was altogether out of proportion to his offences. God would certainly pardon him. This thought led me to an examination of my own life. To Uncle Amos I had rather indignantly repelled the epithet of "sinner," but might I not, after all, be more culpable than I had supposed? Was there nothing on account of which I might not plead for the Divine pardon?

But I was not allowed to proceed far in this silent survey of my life. Supposing, after my conversation with Mr. Brandreth, that the attitude and fact of prayer was all that was required of me, as an evidence of sympathy and a possible help to some hesitating soul, I made no further demonstrations, but knelt, with my arms upon the bench and my forehead bowed upon them. I was beginning to collect my confused thoughts, when a lamenting female voice was heard at my ear, " How do you feel, John ? "

If a feeling of exasperation at such a place and time was sinful, I sinned. " Aunt Peggy," I said, somewhat sternly, — (for I knew that unless I made answer the question would be repeated,) — " Aunt Peggy, I am trying to pray."

She left me, but I was not long alone. As soon as I heard a combined creaking of boot-soles and knee-joints behind me, I knew whose voice would follow. I was patted on the back by a large, dumpy hand, and Uncle Amos said, in a hollow undertone, " That 's right; John, pray on ! shall I help you to throw down your burden ? "

My nerves twitched and drew back, as his heavy arm stole across my neck. This was the climax of my distress, and I plucked up a desperate courage to meet it. " Uncle Amos," said I, " I can neither pray nor think here, among these people. Let me go home to my room, and I promise you that, before I sleep to-night, I will know what is in my heart and what are its relations to God ! "

Mr. Brandreth was standing near, and heard my words. At least, some voice which I took to be his, whispered, " I think it will be best." I have a dim recollection of getting out of the church by the door in the rear of the pulpit ; of my aunt walking home beside me, under the starry sky, uttering lamentations to which I paid no heed ; of rushing breathlessly up the staircase to my garret, opening the window, drawing a chair beside it, resting my chin on the window-sill, and shedding tears of pure joy and relief on finding myself alone in the holy peace and silence of the night. The presence of God came swiftly down to me from the starry deeps. " Here is my heart ! " cried a voice in my breast ; " look at it, Father, and tell me what I am ! "

Then I seemed to behold it myself, and strove to disentangle the roots of Self from the memory of my boyish life, that I might stand apart and judge it. I found pride, impatience, folly; but they were as light surface-waves which disappeared with their cause. I found childish likes and dislikes; silly little enmities, which had left no sting; pranks, instigated by the spirit of Fun rather than that of Evil; and later, secret protests against the sorrows and trials of my life. But all these things gave me less trouble than one little incident which perversely clung to my memory, and still does, with a sense of shame which I shall never be able to overcome. Several of us boys were playing about the tavern at the Cross-Keys, one afternoon in August, when a dealer in water-melons came by with a cart-load of them for sale. We looked on, with longing eyes and watery mouths, while he disposed of several; and at last the dealer generously gave us one which had been several times "plugged," and was cracked at one end. We hurried under the barn-bridge with our treasure, and agreed to take "slice about," so as to have an equal division. The crack, however, divided the solid, sweet, crimson centre from the seedy strip next the rind — so we commenced with the latter, leaving a tower of delicious aspect standing in the midst of the melon. I looked at it until I became charmed, entranced, insane with desire to crush its cool, sugared filigree upon my tongue, and when my next turn came, stretched forth a daring hand and cut off the tower! The other boys looked at each other: one gave a long whistle; one exclaimed "Goy!" and the third added the climax by the sentence, "What a hog!" Before I had finished eating the tower it had turned to gall and wormwood in my mouth. I choked it down, however, and went home, without touching the melon again.

That night, as I leaned upon the window-sill, and recalled my faults and frailties, this incident came back and placed itself in the front rank of my offences. I could look calmly, or with a scarcely felt remainder of penitence, upon all else, but my humiliation for this act burned as keenly as on the first day. It so wearied me, finally, that I gave up the retrospect. I was satisfied that God's omnipotent love, not his wrath, overhung and embraced me; that my heart, though often erring and clouded, never consciously lusted after Evil. I longed for its purification, not for its change. I should not shrink from Death, if he approached, through fear of the Hereafter; I might receive a low seat in Paradise, but I certainly had done nothing — and would not, with God's help — to deserve the awful punishment which Brother Mellowby had described.

In relating this portion of my life, I trust that I shall not be misunderstood. I owe reverence to the spirit of Devotion, in whatever form it is manifested, and have no intention of assailing, or even undervaluing, that which I have just described. There are, undoubtedly, natures which can only be reached by brandishing the menace of retribution, — perhaps, also, by the agency of strong physical excitement. I do not belong to such. Religion enters my heart through the gateway of Love and not that of Fear. The latter entrance was locked and the key thrown away, almost before I can remember it. Brother Mellowby's revival had an influence upon my after-fortunes, as will be seen presently, and I therefore relate it precisely as it occurred.

Two hours passed away while I sat at the open window. I cannot now reproduce all the movements of my mind, nor follow the devious ways by which, at the last, I reached the important result — peace. When it was over, I felt languid in body, but at heart immensely cheered and strengthened. I foresaw that trouble awaited me, but I was better armed to meet it.

I had scarcely gone to bed, before Bolty made his appearance. From the suppressed shouts of "Glory! Glory!" as he was ascending the last flight of stairs, I knew that he had "got through," — to use Uncle Amos's expression. I therefore counterfeited sleep, and was regaled with snatches of triumphant hymns, and a very long and hoarsely audible prayer, delivered at the foot of the bed, before he became subdued enough to sleep. The powers of his big body must have been severely taxed, for, when I arose in the morning, he still lay locked in a slumber as heavy and motionless as death. In fact, he did not awake until nearly noon, Uncle Amos not allowing him to be disturbed. The latter looked at me sharply and frequently during the day, but he had no opportunity for reference to my spiritual condition, except in the course of the unusually prolonged grace at dinner. He prayed with unction both for Bolty and myself.

In the evening, when he announced that we might again put up the shutters at eight o'clock, in order to attend the services, I quietly said, —

"It is n't necessary, Uncle Amos. I am not going to your church this evening."

He grew very red about the jaws, and the veins on his forehead swelled. "What did you promise me last evening?" he asked.

"I have kept my promise," I answered. "It would be a mockery if I should go forward with the rest to repent of sins which have been already forgiven. I understand, now, what you mean by a change of heart, but I do not need it."

Uncle Amos threw up his hands and exclaimed, "Lord, deliver me from vanity of heart!" Aunt Peggy, in her dingy bombazine bonnet, fell into spasms of clucking, and this time did really shed a few tears as she cried, "To think that one o' *my* family should be so hardened!"

"I should like to know where the Pharisees are now!" I cried, hot with anger.

"Come, wife, — let us pray to-night for the obdoorate sinner!" said my uncle, taking her by the arm. Bolty followed, and they all went to church, leaving me in the store.

After I had closed for the night, I resumed my post at

the bedroom-window, and reflected upon my probable position in the house. It had hitherto been barely endurable to a youth of my tastes and my ambition, but now I foresaw that it would become insupportable. Neither uncle nor aunt, I was sure, would ever look upon me with favor; and even Bolty, who had thus far tacitly befriended me, might think it his duty to turn informer and persecutor. I much more than earned my board by my services, and therefore recognized no moral obligation towards my uncle. The legal one still existed, but it could not force me to lead a slavish and unhappy life against my will. I should not get possession of my little property for a year and a half; but I could certainly trust to my own resources of hand or brain, in the meantime. The matter was soon settled in my mind: I would leave "A. Woolley's Grocery Store" forever.

CHAPTER X.

CONCERNING MY ESTABLISHMENT IN UPPER SAMARIA.

I DEVOTED my first leisure hour to a confidential visit to Charley Rand. His smooth, amiable ways had done much to make our intercourse closer than it ever had been at school, though there was still something in his face which led me occasionally to distrust him. His mottled gray eyes, which *could* look at one steadily and sweetly, were generally restless, and the mellowness of his voice sometimes showed its want of perfect training by slipping into a harsher natural tone. Besides, he was a little too demonstrative. His habit of putting his hand on my shoulder and commencing a remark with (emphasizing every word) "MY — DEAR — FRIEND," made me feel uncomfortable. Nevertheless, his presence in Reading was a satisfaction to me, and I bestowed a great deal of friendly affection upon him for the reason that there was no one else to whom I could give it.

To him, then, I related all that had happened. The habit of the future lawyer seemed to be already creeping over him. He interrupted my narrative with an occasional question, in order to make certain points clearer, and, when I had finished, meditated a while in silence. "It 's a pity," he said at last, "that I 'm not already admitted to practice, and sporting my own shingle. I should like to know your uncle, anyhow: can't you introduce me?"

I felt a great repugnance to this proposal, and urged Rand not to insist upon it.

"Oh, well," said he, carelessly, "it 's of no consequence,

except on *your* account. I 'm sure I have no inclination to meet the old porpoise. But I 'd advise you to work along, the best way you can, until you can get a better hook on him than you have now."

"No, Rand!" I interrupted, "my mind is made up. I shall leave his house."

In the course of the conversation Rand had managed to extract from me the amount of my own little property, and the disposition of the interest due the previous spring, the greater part of which I had allowed my uncle to reinvest. He also questioned me concerning the latter's fortune, and seemed desirous to know a great many particulars which had no apparent bearing on the present crisis in my fortunes. Our talk ended, however, in my repeating my determination to leave.

"I hoped, Rand," I added, "that you could advise me what to do. I can only think of two things, — teaching a country school, or getting a situation in another store. Of course, I should rather teach."

"Then, if you are bent upon it, Godfrey, I think I can help you. One of Mulford's clients, from Upper Samaria township, — not far from Cardiff, you know, — was talking about a teacher for their school, three or four days ago. He 's a director, and has the most say, as he 's a rich old fellow. I 'll tell Mulford to recommend you, if you 've a mind to try it, and meanwhile you can write to Dr. Dymond for a certificate of your fitness. If the plan succeeds — and I don't see why it should n't — you may say good-bye to the old porpoise in less than ten days."

I seized Rand's hand and poured out my gratitude; here was a way opened at once! I should have pleasant employment for the winter, at least, and a little capital in the spring to pursue my fortune further. The same evening I wrote to Dr. Dymond, and in four days received a stiffly-worded but very flattering testimony of my capacities. In the beginning of the next week, Mulford's client, a Mr.

Bratton, came again to Reading, and Rand was as good as his word. He recommended me so strongly that Mr. B. requested an interview, which was at once arranged. Rand came for me, and we met in Mulford's back-office.

The director, upon whom my success mainly depended, was a bluff, hearty man, with a pompous and patronizing manner. "Ah, you are the young man," he said, stretching out his hand, and surveying me the while from head to foot, — "should have liked a little more signs of authority, — very necessary where there are big boys in the school. However, Mine is not a rough neighborhood, — very much in advance of Lower Samaria."

I handed him Dr. Dymond's letter, which he ran through, with audible comments; — "'promising scholar' — good, but hardly enough for Me; — 'thorough acquaintance with grammar' — ah, very good — My own idee; — 'talent for composition,' 'Latin,' — rather ornamental, *ra-a-ther;* — hem, 'all branches of arithmetic' — that 's more like business. A very good recommendation, upon the whole. How much do you expect to be paid?"

I replied that I wanted no more than the usual remuneration, admitting that I had never yet taught school, but that I should make every effort to give satisfaction.

"We pay from twenty to twenty-five dollars a month," said he; "but you could n't expect more than twenty at the start. You 're a pig in a poke, you know."

This was not very flattering; but as I saw that no offence was intended, I took none. Nay, I even smiled good-humoredly at Mr. Bratton's remark, and thereby won his good-will. When we parted, the engagement was almost made.

"For form's sake," said he, "I must consult the other directors; but I venture to say that My recommendation will be sufficient. If you come, I shall depend upon you to justify My selection."

I now judged it necessary to inform my uncle of the contemplated step. I presume the idea of it had never entered his head; his surprise was so great that he seemed at a loss what course to take. When he found that both opposition and ridicule were of no avail, he tried persuasion, and even went so far as to promise me immunity from persecution in religious matters.

"We will let that rest for the present," said he. "My ways a'n't your'n, though I 've tried to bring you to a proper knowledge of your soul, for your own good. I promised your mother I 'd do my dooty by you, but you don't seem to take it in a numble spirit. But now you 're acquainted with business, in a measure, and likely to turn out well if you stick to it. I 'd always reckoned on paying you a selery after you come of age; it 's a sort of apprenticeship till then. And you 've a little capital, and can make it more. I don't say but what I could n't take you, in the course of time, as a pardner in the concern."

I tried to explain that my taste and ambition lay in a totally opposite direction, — that I neither could nor would devote my life to the mysteries of the grocery business. It required some time to make my uncle comprehend my sincerity. He looked upon the matter as the temporary whim of a boy. When, at last, he saw that my determination was inflexible, his anger returned, more violently than at first.

"Go, then!" he cried; "I wash my hands of you! But this let me tell you — look out for yourself till you 're twenty-one! Not a penny of your money will I advance till the law tells me, — and more, not a penny of *mine* will you get when I die!"

These words roused an equal anger in my heart. I felt myself turning white, and my voice trembled in spite of myself as I exclaimed, "Keep your accursed money! Do you think I would soil my fingers with it? Holy as you are, and sinful as I am, I look down upon you and thank God no mean thoughts ever entered my heart!"

The breach was now impassable. I had cut off the last bridge to reconciliation. Nothing more was said, and I quietly and speedily made my preparations for leaving the house. Bolty, whose manner had become exceedingly mild and subdued since his conversion, did not seem much surprised by the catastrophe. Perhaps he regretted the loss of a companion, but his personal emotions were too shallow to give him much uneasiness. I watched, with some curiosity, to see whether he would still recommend his patent-medicines in the accustomed style; but even here he was changed. With an air of quiet gravity, he affirmed, "The pills is reckoned to be very good; we sell a great many, ma'am. Them that cares for their perishin' bodies is relieved by 'em."

This mode of recommendation seemed to be just as effectual as the former.

Two days afterwards a note arrived from Mr. Bratton and I left my uncle's house. There were no touching farewells, and no tears shed except Aunt Peggy's, as she exclaimed, "I would n't have believed it of you; but you'll rue it! — *ts, ts, ts, ts,* — you 'll rue it, too late!" In spite of this evil prediction, I think she must have felt a little shame at seeing her sister's child leave her doors in the way I did.

A rude mail-coach took me as far as Cardiff, where I left my trunk at the tavern, and set out on foot for the residence of Mr. Bratton. It was Friday; I was to be presented to the directors on Saturday, and to open school on Monday. Upper Samaria was only three miles from Cardiff, — the latter place, a village of some four hundred inhabitants, being the post-office for the region round about.

It was a bright, cheery day. A bracing wind blew from the northwest, shaking the chestnuts from their burrs and the shell-barks from their split hulls. The farmers and their men sat in the fields, each before his overturned shock, and husked the long, yellow ears of corn. I passed a load of apples on their way to the cider-press, and the sunburnt driver grinned with simple good-will as he tossed me a ruddy " wine-sap." Never before had I breathed so exquisite an atmosphere of freedom. I stood at last on my own independent feet, in the midst of the bright autumnal world. Wind and sun, the rustling trees and the hastening waters, the laborers looking up as I passed, and somewhere, deep in the blue overhead, the Spirit that orders and upholds every form of life, seemed to recognize me as a creature competent to take charge of his own destiny. On the hilltops I paused and stretched forth my arms like a discoverer taking possession of new lands. The old continent of dependence and subjection lay behind me, and I saw the green shores of the free, virgin world.

Happy ignorance of youth that grasps life as a golden bounty, not as a charge to be guarded with sleepless eyes and weary heart! Surely some movement of Divine Pity granted us that blindness of vision in which we only see the bloom of blood on cheek and lip, not the dark roots that branch below — the garlanded mask of joy hiding the tragic mystery!

After a while the rolling upland over which I had been wandering, sank gently towards the southeast into a broad, softly outlined valley, watered by a considerable stream. The landlord at Cardiff had given me minute directions, so that when I saw a large mill-pond before me, with a race leading to an old stone-mill, a white house behind two immense weeping-willows on the left, and a massive brick house on the right, across the stream, I knew that the latter edifice must be the residence of Mr. (or " Squire ") Septimus Bratton. The main highway followed the base of some low, gradual hills on the left bank, and a furlong beyond " Yule's Mill," as the place was called, I noticed a square, one-story hut, with pyramidal roof, which I was sure must be the school-house. A little further, another road came across the hills from the eastward, and at the junction there were a dozen buildings, comprising, as I afterwards discovered, the store, blacksmith's and shoemaker's shops, and the "Buck" Tavern, where, on election-days, the polls for Upper Samaria were held. Down the stream, the view extended for two or three miles over rich and admirably cultivated farm-land, interspersed with noble tracts of wood, and with clumps of buttonwood- and ash-trees along the course of the stream.

Mr. Bratton's house stood upon a knoll, commanding a very agreeable view of the valley. It was a large cube of red brick, with high double chimneys at each end, and a veranda in front supported by white Ionic columns of wood. A dense environment of Athenian poplars and silver-maples buried the place in shade, while the enclosure sloping down to the road was dotted with balsam-fir and arbor-vitæ. The fact that this lawn — if it could be so called — covered an acre of ground, and was grown with irregular tufts of natural grass, instead of being devoted to potatoes, indicated wealth. In the rear rose a huge barn, with a stable-yard large enough to hold a hundred cattle.

I walked up a straight central path, trodden in the grass, and ungravelled, to the front-door, and knocked. Footsteps sounded somewhere within and then died away again. After waiting ten minutes, I repeated the knocking, and presently the door was opened. I beheld a lovely girl of seventeen, in a pale green dress, which brought a faint rose-tint to a face naturally colorless. Her light gray eyes rested gently on mine, and I know that I blushed with surprise and confusion. She did not seem to be in the least embarrassed, but stood silently waiting for me to speak.

"Is Mr. Bratton at home?" I finally stammered.

"Pa and Ma have gone to Carterstown this afternoon," said she, in the smoothest, evenest, most delicious voice I had ever heard. "They will be back soon; will you walk in and wait?"

"Yes, if you please," I answered. "I think Mr. Bratton expects me; my name is Godfrey."

I am sure she had already guessed who I was. She betrayed no sign of the fact, however, but demurely led the way to a comfortable sitting-room, asked me to take a seat, and retired, leaving me alone. I stole across the carpet to a small mirror between the windows, straitened the bow of my cravat, ran my fingers through my hair to give it a graceful disposition, and examined my features one by one, imagining how they would appear to a stranger's eye.

I had scarcely resumed my seat before Miss Bratton returned, with a blue pitcher in one hand and a tumbler in the other.

"Will you have a glass of new cider, Mr. Godfrey?" she asked, dropping her eyes an instant. "It's sweet," she added; "you can take it without breaking the pledge."

"Oh, of course," I answered; for, although I was not a member of a Temperance Society, I thought *she* might be. She stood near me, holding the pitcher while I drank, and it seemed to me that there was a noise of deglutition in my throat which might be heard all over the house.

She took a seat near the opposite window, with some sort of net-work in her hand. I felt that it was incumbent on me to commence the conversation, which I did awkwardly enough, I suppose, her slow, even, liquid words forming a remarkable contrast to my rapid and random utterances. At length, however, I got so far as to inform her that I hoped to teach in the neighboring school-house during the coming winter.

"Ind-e-e-ed!" she exclaimed, in an accent of polite, subdued interest. "Then we shall be neighbors; for I suppose you will board at Yule's. All the schoolmasters do."

"The white house with the willows?"

"Yes. Mr. Yule is Pa's miller. He has been there twenty years, I think Pa said. I'm sure it was long before

I was born. They are very respectable people, and it 's nicer there than to board at 'The Buck.'"

I was about to reply that the choice of the directors must be made before I could engage board anywhere, when she interrupted me with, "Oh, there 's Pa's carriage just turning the corner. Excuse me!" and walked from the room with a swift, graceful step.

In a few minutes I heard a heavy foot, followed by a rustling, along the veranda, and Mr. and Mrs. Septimus Bratton entered the room. The former greeted me with stately cordiality. "I see," said he, "that you have already made my daughter's acquaintance. My dear, this is Mr. Godfrey, whom *I* have recommended as our teacher this winter."

Mrs. Bratton, a sharp-featured little woman, swathed in an immense white crape shawl, advanced and gave me her hand. "How d' ye do, sir?" she piped, in a shrill voice; "hope you 've not been kept long a-waiting?"

Then she and the daughter retired, and Mr. Bratton flung his hat upon the table and sat down. "I guess there 'll be no difficulty to-morrow," he remarked; "I 've seen Bailey, one of the directors, and he 's willing to abide by Me. As for Carter, he thinks something of his learning, and always has a few questions to ask; but we had a poor shoat last winter, of his choosing, and so you 'll have the better chance. You 'll board at Yule's, but you may as well stay here till to-morrow, after we meet. 'T is n't good luck to give a baby its name before it 's christened. You can send up to Cardiff for your things when the matter is settled."

We were presently summoned to the early tea-table of the country. When Mrs. Bratton was about to take her seat, her daughter murmured — oh, so musically! — "Let me pour out, Ma — you must be tired."

"Well, have your own way, 'Manda," said the mother; "you 'll be getting your hand in, betimes."

I was first served, the lovely Amanda kindly asking me, "Shall I season your tea for you, Mr. Godfrey?"

It was the sweetest cup I had ever tasted.

"Where 's Sep?" suddenly asked Mr. Bratton.

"I 've sent out to the barn and down to the mill, but they don't seem to find him," his wife remarked.

"I 'll go to 'The Buck,' then; but I won't go much oftener."

I saw wife and daughter suddenly glance at him, and he said no more. But he was in a visible ill-humor. There was a lack of lively conversation during the evening, yet to me the time passed delightfully. Miss Bratton, I discovered, had just returned from the celebrated School for Young Ladies at Bethlehem, and was considered, in Upper Samaria, as a model of female accomplishment. She had learned to write Italian hand, to paint tulips and roses on white velvet, to make wax-flowers, and even to play the piano; and an instrument ordered by her father, at the immense price of two hundred dollars, was then on its way from Philadelphia. These particulars I learned afterwards from Mrs. Yule. During that evening, however, I saw and admired the brilliant bouquets in mahogany frames which adorned the parlor-walls.

At nine o'clock, Mr. Bratton, who had already several times yawned with a loud, bellowing noise, rose, took a candle, and showed me to a large and very gorgeous chamber. The bedstead had pillars of carved mahogany, supporting a canopy with curtains, and I sank into the huge mass of feathers as into a sun-warmed cloud. I stretched myself out in all directions, with the luxurious certainty of not encountering Bolty Himpel's legs, composed my mind to an unspoken prayer, and floated into dreams where Aunt Peggy and Miss Amanda Bratton had provokingly changed voices.

The next morning, at ten o'clock, the directors met at the school-house. Mr. Bratton, who had charge of the key, opened the shutters and let out the peculiar musty smell, suggestive of mould, bread and butter, and greasy spelling-books, which had accumulated. He then took his seat at the master's desk, and laid the proposal before Messrs. Bailey and Carter. He read Dr. Dymond's letter of recommendation, and finished by saying, "Mr. Godfrey, I believe, is ready for any examination you may wish to make."

Mr. Bailey remarked, in a sleepy voice, "I guess that 'll do;" but Mr. Carter, a wiry, nervous little man, pricked up his ears, stroked his chin, and said, "I 've got a few questions to put. Spell '*inooendo*.'"

I spelled in succession the words "innuendo," "exhilarate," "peddler," and "pony," to the gentleman's satisfaction, and gave, moreover, the case of the noun "disobedience," in the first line of "Paradise Lost," and the verb which governed it. Then I calculated the number of boards ten feet long, thirteen inches wide, and one inch thick, which could be sawed out of a pine log three feet in diameter and seventy feet long; then the value of a hundred dollars, at compound interest, six per cent., for twenty years; and, finally, the length of time it would take a man to walk a mile, supposing he made ten steps, two feet long, in a minute, and for every two steps forward took one step, one foot long, backwards. I think Mr. Carter would have been vexed if I had not made a mistake of three cents on the compound interest question. Furthermore, I wrote on a sheet of paper, "*Avoid haughtiness of behavior and affectation of manners*," as a specimen of my penmanship, and read aloud parts of a speech of Patrick Henry, from the "Columbian Orator." Geography and the various branches of natural philosophy were passed over in silence, and I was a little surprised that the fact of my never having taught school before was not brought forward in objection. After Mr. Carter had exhausted his budget of questions, I was requested to step outside for a few minutes while the directors consulted.

When Mr. Bratton called me, I saw by his slightly increased pomposity that I was accepted. His choice was confirmed; and as the "poor shoat" of the previous winter had been taken on Carter's recommendation, it was now my patron's turn to triumph. My salary was fixed at twenty-five dollars a month, and I was gratified to find that my board and washing at Yule's would cost me but a dollar and a half per week. This secured me the prospect of a capital of some fifty or sixty dollars in the spring.

Mr. Bratton completed his patronage by presenting me to the Yule family. The plain, honest face of the old miller made a fatherly impression upon me, and Mrs. Yule, a bustling, talkative woman, — a chronicle of all the past and present gossip of the neighborhood, — accepted me as a predestined member of the family. She had already put "the master's room" in order, she said; it never went by any other name in the house, and she allowed a fire in cold weather, only "the master" always carried up his own wood, and kindled it, and raked the ashes carefully before going to bed; and Daniel was going to Cardiff that very night for the paper, and he should take the light cart and bring my trunk, — so I could stop then and there, while I was about it. Which I did.

"Daniel" was the older son, — a tall, lusty fellow of twenty-four. There was a younger, Isaac, about my own age, and a daughter, Susan, between the two. I met the whole family at dinner, and, before the meal was over, felt that I was fast becoming an Upper Samaritan.

CHAPTER XI.

CONTAINING BRATTON'S PARTY AND THE EPISODE OF THE LIME-KILN.

When I opened school on Monday morning, I had some twenty pupils, mostly the younger children of the neighboring farmers. The late autumn was unusually clear and mild, and the larger boys were still needed in the fields. I was glad of this chance, as it enabled me the more easily to get the machinery of the school in motion and familiarize myself with my duties. I recollected enough of our commencement-days at the Cross-Keys to form my pupils into classes and arrange the order of exercises. So far as the giving of instruction was concerned, I had no misgivings, but I feared the natural and universal rebellion of children against rules which impose quiet and application of mind. Accordingly, I took the master's seat at my desk on a small raised platform, with stern gravity of countenance, and instantly checked the least tendency to whisper or giggle among my subjects. The process was exhausting, and I should like to know which side felt the greatest relief when the first day came to an end.

In a short time, however, as I came to know the faces and dispositions of the children, I found it necessary to relax something of this assumed strictness. Dr. Dymond's method, which I had found so pleasant, seemed to me better adapted to their needs, also, and I frequently interrupted the regular sequence of the lessons in order to communicate general intelligence, especially of a geographical or historical character, wherein they were all lamentably deficient.

I had a great liking for oral narrative, and perhaps some talent in constructing it, for I always found these breaks more efficient to preserve order than my sternest scolding.

I soon saw that the children enjoyed my method of instruction. Many a bell-flower and fall pippin was laid upon my desk in the morning, and some of the girls, noticing that I gathered gentians and late asters in the meadows during their nooning, brought me bunches of chrysanthemums from their mothers' flower-beds. I should have soon found my place insupportable, had I been surrounded by hostile hearts, children's though they were, and was therefore made happy by seeing that my secret favorites returned my affection in their own shy way. Mrs. Yule, who had a magnetic ear for hearing everything that was said within a radius of two miles, informed me that I was much better liked by the pupils than last winter's master, though some of the parents thought that I told them too many "fancy things."

This was the sunny side of the business, so far as it had one. On the other hand I grew weary to death of enlightening the stupidity of some of the boys, and disgusted with their primitive habits. I shuddered when I was obliged to touch their dirty, sprawling, warty hands, or when my eyes fell upon the glazed streaks on their sleeves. They surrounded me with unwashed smells, and scratched their heads more than was pleasant to behold. Physical beauty was scarce among them, and natural refinement, in any sensible degree, entirely absent. A few had frank, warm hearts, and hints of undeveloped nobility in their natures, but coarseness and selfishness were predominant. My experience convinced me that I should never become a benefactor of the human race. It was not the moral sentiment in the abstract, but that of certain individuals, which inspired me with interest.

My home at the white house behind the willows was a very agreeable one. There was a grand old kitchen, paved with flag-stones, and with a chimney large enough to contain a high-backed wooden settle, on either side of the fire. Here the old miller and Dan smoked their pipes after supper, while Mrs. Yule and Susan pared apples, or set the bread to rise, or mixed buckwheat-batter for next morning's cakes. I could place my tallow-candle in a little niche, or pocket, of the jamb, and read undisturbed, until some quaint lore of the neighborhood drew me from the book. The windows of my room in the southeastern corner of the house were wrapped about with the trailing willow-boughs; but, as their leaves began to fall, I discovered that I should have a fine winter view down the valley.

The miller was one of those quiet, unmarked natures, which, like certain grays in painting, are agreeable through their very lack of positive character. He suggested health — nothing else; and his son Dan was made in his likeness. I did not know, then, why I liked Dan, but I suspect now it must have been because he had not an over-sensitive nerve in his body. His satisfied repose was the farthest vibration from my restless, excitable temperament. Susan was a bright, cheerful, self-possessed girl, in whose presence the shyest youth would have felt at ease. She was not cultivated, but neither was she ashamed of her ignorance. Her only æsthetic taste was for flowers; there were no such pot gillyflowers and geraniums as hers in all Upper Samaria. She sewed buttons on my shirts and darned the heels of my stockings before my very eyes. It was rumored that she was engaged to Ben Hannaford, a young farmer over the hill to the north; but she spoke of him in so straightforward and unembarrassed a way that I judged it could not be possible. Still, it was a fact that a fire was made in the best sitting-room every Sunday night, and that both Ben and Susan somehow disappeared from the kitchen.

The ways of the neighborhood were exceedingly social. There were frequent "gatherings" ("getherin's" was the popular term) of the younger people, generally on Saturday evenings. The first which I attended was given by Miss Amanda Bratton, about three weeks after my arrival. The impulse thereto was furnished, I imagine, by the arrival of the new piano from Philadelphia. Everybody on the main road, from Carterstown up to the Buck Tavern, had seen the wagon with the great box lying on trusses of straw, as it passed along, and the news had gone far to right and left before it was announced that "Squire Bratton's" house would be open. Pianos were not common in Upper Samaria; indeed there were none nearer than Carterstown, and the young men and women were unaccustomed to other music than the flute and violin. Miss Amanda, on her father's hint, was profuse in her invitations; he knew that the party would be much talked about, both before and after its occurrence.

I walked over with Dan and Susan Yule, at dusk, and found the company already arriving. The hall-door was open, and we were received at the entrance to the parlor by Miss Amanda, who looked lovely in a pale-violet silk. She gave me her hand with the composure of an old acquaintance, and I took it with a thrill of foolish happiness.

"*He* 's not come yet, Sue," said she. "Mr. Godfrey, let me introduce you to the gentlemen."

I was presented to five or six sturdy fellows, each of whom gave me a tremendous grip of a large, hard hand, and then sat down in silence. They were ranged along one side of the parlor-wall, while the ladies formed a row on the opposite side, occasionally whispering to each other below their breath. I took my seat at one end of the male column, and entered into conversation with my neighbor, which he accepted in a friendly and subdued manner. No one, I think, quite ventured to use his natural volume of voice except young Septimus, or Sep Bratton, who dodged back and forth with loud explosions of shallow wit and unjustifiable laughter. Many eyes were directed to the piano, which stood open at the end of the room, and it was evident that the tone of the company would be solemn expectation until the instrument had been heard.

Squire Bratton, in a high stock and sharp, standing collar, moved majestically about, greeting each fresh arrival with a mixture of urbanity and condescension. When all the chairs which could be comfortably placed were filled and the gentlemen were obliged to stand, the company began to break into groups and grow more animated. Then Miss Amanda was importuned to play.

"Oh, I 'm really afraid, before so many!" she exclaimed, with a modesty which charmed me; "besides, the piano is hardly fit to be played on, is it, Pa?"

"Hm — well," said her father, "I believe it is a little out of chune, from being jolted on the road, but I guess our friends would make allowance for that."

"Oh, yes!" "We sha'n't notice it!" eagerly burst from a dozen voices.

After some further solicitation, Miss Amanda took her seat, and a breathless silence filled the room. She struck two or three chords, then suddenly ceased, saying, "Oh, I can't! I shall shock you; the G is *so* flat!"

"Go on!" "It 's splendid!" and various other encouraging cries again arose.

I happened to be standing near the piano, and she caught my eye, expressing its share of the general expectancy.

"*Must* I, indeed, Mr. Godfrey?" she asked, in a helpless, appealing tone. "What shall it be?"

"*Your* favorite air, Miss Bratton," I answered.

She turned to the keys again, and, after a short prelude, played the Druids' March from "Norma," boldly and with a strongly accented rhythm. I was astonished at the delicacy of her ear, for I should not have known but that the instrument was in very good tune.

When she had finished, the expressions of delight were loud and long, and "more" was imperiously demanded, coupled with a request for a song.

This time she gave us "Oh, come o'er the Moonlit Sea, Love," and "The Dream is Past"; and I knew not which most to admire, — the airy, dancing, tinkling brilliancy of the first, or the passion and sorrow of the second. No one, I thought, could sing that song without feeling the words in their tragic intensity: Miss Bratton must have a heart like Zuleika or Gulnare.

I believe I made a good appearance, as contrasted with the other young men present. I had fastened my cravat with a small coral pin which had belonged to my mother, and this constituted a distinguishing mark which drew many eyes upon me. Little by little, I was introduced to all the company, and was drawn into the lively chatter which, in such communities, takes the place of wit and sentiment. Among others, Susan Yule presented me to Miss Verbena Cuff, a plump, rattling girl, who was not afraid to poke a fellow in the ribs with her forefinger, and say, "Oh, go 'long, now!" when anything funny was said. She had the fullest, ripest lips, the largest and whitest teeth, and the roundest chin, of any girl there.

After the refreshments — consisting of lemonade, new cider, and four kinds of cakes — were handed around, we all became entirely merry and unconstrained. I had never before "assisted" at a party of the kind, except as a juvenile spectator, and my enjoyment was therefore immense. Nothing more was needed to convince me that I was a full-grown man. Whenever I put my hand to my chin I was conscious of a delightful, sand-papery feeling, which showed that the down I so carefully scraped off was beginning to acquire strength, and would soon display masculine substance and color. My freckles were all gone, and, as Neighbor Niles had always prophesied, left a smooth, fair skin behind them. I was greatly delighted on hearing one of the girls whisper, "He 's quite good-looking." Of course she referred to me.

Miss Amanda's album, gilt-edged and gorgeously bound

in red morocco, lay upon a side-table under the mirror. I picked it up and looked over its contents, in company with Miss Verbena Cuff. The leaves were softly tinted with pink, green, buff, and blue, and there were both steel engravings and bunches of flowers lithographed in colors. Miss Verbena stayed my hand at one of the pictures, representing a youth in Glengarry bonnet and knee-breeches, with one arm round a maiden, whose waist came just under her shoulders, while he waved the other arm over a wheat-field. In the air above them two large birds were flying.

The title of the picture was, "Now Westlin' Win's."

"Mr. Godfrey," said Miss Verbena, "I want you to tell me what this picture means; *she* won't. *I* say 'Westlin'' is the name of one o' the birds; they 're flyin' a race, and he thinks 'Westlin'' will win it. What do *you* say?"

I looked up, and saw that "*she*" was standing near us, listening. I smiled significantly, with a side-glance at Miss Verbena. My smile was returned, yet with an expression of tender deprecation, which I interpreted as saying, "Don't expose her ignorance." I accordingly answered, with horrid hypocrisy, —

"You may be right, Miss Cuff. I never saw the picture before." Again we exchanged delicious glances.

I turned over the leaves, and presently stumbled on the name of "Susan Yule." She had written —

"Oh, Amanda, when I 'm far away,
To taste the scenes of other climes,
And when fond Memory claims its sway,
And tells thee then of happier times, —
Oh, let a Tear of Sorrow blend
With memory of thy absent Friend."

I was greatly diverted with the idea of good, plain, simple-hearted Susan Yule, whose thoughts never crossed the township-line of Upper Samaria, going away to taste the scenes of other climes, but I did my best, for her sake, to preserve a serious countenance. I was rather surprised to find, on looking further, that both Mattie McElroy and Jemima Ann Hutchins had written precisely the same lines.

"Why," I exclaimed, "here it is again! I thought the verse was original. There must be a great scarcity of album poetry, Miss Bratton."

"Ye-e-es," she answered, in a gentle drawl. "We all found it so at school. I'm sure I went over the 'Elegant Extracts' ever so many times, but there was so little that would suit. I think it 's *so* much nicer to have original poetry! don't you?"

I assented most enthusiastically.

"Perhaps *you* write poetry, Mr. Godfrey?" she continued.

I blushed and stammered, longing, yet shy to confess the blissful truth.

"He, he!" giggled Miss Verbena Cuff, giving me a poke with her forefinger; "he does! he does! I'll bet anything on it. Make him write something in your book, 'Manda!"

"*Won't* you?" murmured Miss Amanda, fixing her soft, pale eyes full upon mine.

I blushed all over, this time. The red flushed my skin down to my very toes. My eyelids fell before the angelic gaze, and I muttered something about being very happy, and I would try, but I was afraid she would n't be satisfied with it afterwards.

"But it must be right out of your own head, mind," Miss Cuff insisted.

"*Of* course," said Miss Bratton, with slight but very becoming *hauteur*.

"And then you must write something for me. We won't say anything about it to the other girls, 'Manda, till they 're finished."

I was n't very well pleased with this proposition, and it

seemed to me, also, that the merest gossamer of a shade flitted across Miss Bratton's smooth brow. Still, it was impossible to refuse, and I endeavored to promise with a good grace.

"Mine has the language of flowers," said Verbena; "I'm so sorry that the Rose is already writ. I'd have liked you to take that. There 's Pink and Honeysuckle left, and something else that I disremember. I'll show you the book first."

Later in the evening it happened that Miss Bratton and I came together again, with nobody very near us. I made instant use of the opportunity, to confirm the confidential relation which I imagined was already established between us. "I understood you," I said; "did you ever hear such an absurd idea as she had?"

She was evidently puzzled, but not startled. Nothing, in fact, seemed to agitate her serene, self-poised, maidenly nature. "Oh, the picture?" she said, at last; "very absurd, indeed."

"You know the poem, of course?" I continued.

"Yes," (slightly smiling,) "I read it, long ago, but I've forgotten how it goes. Won't you write it down for me?"

I assented at once, though to do so implied the purchase of a copy of Burns, which I did not possess. How grateful it was to find *one* in that material crowd who knew and reverenced the immortal bards among whom I hoped to inscribe my name!

"I'll bring it over to you, some evening!" I exclaimed.

She smiled sweetly, but said nothing.

"I am so glad you are fond of poetry! Do you ever see the *Saturday Evening Post?*"

"Yes; Pa takes it for me. There are such *sweet* poems in it, — and the tales, too!"

Here we were interrupted, but I had heard enough to turn my head. She had certainly read "The Unknown Bard" and all the other productions of "Selim"! They were among the poems, and, of course, they too were "sweet."

The party broke up at midnight, and I had the pleasure of escorting Miss Verbena Cuff across the stream to Yule's Mill, where her brother Tom had left his horse and vehicle. We started with Dan and Susan Yule, but had scarcely left Bratton's veranda, before Miss Verbena took my arm and whispered, "Let's hang back a little; I want to tell you something."

I hung back, as desired, and we were soon alone under the dark, starry sky. I was wrapped in dreams of Miss Amanda Bratton, the touch of whose slender fingers still burned on my right palm. Hence I did not manifest the curiosity which my companion no doubt awaited, for after walking a few rods in silence, she said, giving me a jog of her elbow, —

"Well — what do you think it is?"

Thus admonished, I confessed my inability to guess.

"I'll tell you, but don't *you* tell nobody. Tom's going to set the last kiln a-burning, Friday morning, and there'll be a bully blaze by Saturday night. You know our house, don't you? — stands on the left, a mile and a half this side of Carterstown, — stone, with brick chimbleys, and the barn t' other side of the road: you can't miss it. Now, I want you to come, and we'll have some fun. There won't be many, and I don't want it to get out, — I'd rather it would seem accidental like. We *had* a getherin' three weeks ago, but, you know, when the kiln's afire, it seems to 'liven people up. Some say, the more the merrier, but it a'n't always so."

Here she gave my arm an interrogative clutch; and I, thinking of Milton's "fit audience, though few," answered, "No, indeed, Miss Cuff; it's also true that the fewer the nearer in heart."

"Then you'll come? You'll be sure and keep your word?"

I had not yet given my word, but the prospect of a select few assembled around the burning lime-kiln was weird, poetic, and by no means unwelcome. Of course Amanda Bratton would be one of the few, and I already speculated how wonderfully her calm face would appear in the blue gleam of the fire, against a background of night. I therefore exclaimed, —

"Oh, I shall be delighted!"

"And you won't say anything?"

"Not a word!"

"Don't even tell Yules. I like Susan very much, but her fortune 's made, they say, and I only want them that can take an interest in each other. You understand, don't you?"

Again I felt the powerful squeeze of her arm, and involuntarily returned it. She hung upon and leaned against me quite alarmingly after that, but a few more steps brought us around the mill to the hitching-post at Yule's gate, where Tom Cuff, whip in hand, stood awaiting her.

"It 's late, Sis, and we must be off. Finish your sparkin', quick," he growled, in a coarse voice.

He thereupon turned his back, and Miss Verbena, giving me her hand, looked into my face in a momentary attitude of expectation which I did not understand. She jerked away her hand again rather hastily, whispered — "Don't forget — next Saturday night!" and then added, aloud, "Good night, Mr. Godfrey!"

"Good night, Miss Cuff!" I replied, and they drove away as I was mounting the projecting steps in the stone wall.

That week I made use of "the master's" privilege, and, beside a fire in my bedroom, devoted myself to the composition of a poem for Miss Bratton's album. I wrote four, and was then uncertain which to choose, or whether any one of them was worthy of its destined place. I finally fixed upon one entitled "A Parable," which represented a wandering bird of sweet song in a cold, dark forest where the trees paid no heed to his lays. But just as he was becoming silent forever, from despair of a listener, he saw a *lovely flower lift* up its head, open the lips of its blushing petals, and ask him to sing; so he built his nest at her feet, and piped his sweetest song in the fragrance of her being.

"*She* will understand it!" I said to myself, in triumph; "and to the obscure, unpoetic minds around her it will simply be a bit of fancy. What a godlike art is the Poet's!" Then I sang, to a tune of my own invention, —

"Drink to her who long
  Has waked the Poet's sigh,
The girl who gave to song
  What Gold could never buy!"

Meanwhile, the week drew to an end, and as Saturday afternoon was always a holiday for the school, I had ample time to prepare myself for the visit to Cuff's. Inasmuch as the Yule family was ignorant of the proposed calcareous party, I was a little puzzled how to get away without being observed. Also, how to get into the house, if I should not return before midnight. I made up my mind, at last, to inform Dan, upon whose silence I knew I could rely. I found him in the mill, white with the dust of floating meal, and the hopper made such a clatter that I was forced to put my mouth to his ear, and half scream the fact that I expected to be away from home in the evening. He nodded and smiled, remarking the sheepish expression of my face, and, coming close to me, said, "Shall I leave the back-entry door open?"

"And don't say anything about it, please?" I added.

His simple grin was as good as anybody else's oath; so, completely assured, I made myself ready during the afternoon, in every respect but the coat, which I whipped on after supper. Stealing out by the back door, I jumped over the garden-wall and took my way down the valley.

It was a sharp, frosty night in the beginning of December, and I walked briskly forward, busy with imaginary scenes and conversations, in which Amanda Bratton had an important share. It was a habit of my mind — and still is — to create all presumed situations in advance, and prepare myself for the part I expected to play in them. I must frankly confess to the reader, however, that the interference of some avenging Nemesis always darkens this voluntary clairvoyance, and spoils my tags and cues. Hence all my best remarks have never been uttered, my most brilliant humor has rusted in its sheath, and with undoubted capacity to sparkle in conversation (if the occasions would only arise as I project them in advance), I have never achieved more than an average reputation as a talker. How my anticipations on this particular evening were fulfilled, I shall now proceed to relate.

As the distance to Carterstown was four miles, Cuff's house and lime-kiln must therefore be two and a half miles from Yule's Mill, a walk of three quarters of an hour. I had not been down the road before, but I supposed that the burning kiln would be as a banner hung out, afar off, to guide my steps. On I went, passing many houses on one side of the road, with their barns on the other, but no blue blaze showed itself, and I began to suspect that I was on the wrong road. A wide stream, coming down through the hills on the left, arrested my way, until I discovered a high log and hand-rail on one side, and felt my way over in the dark. Just beyond this stream stood another house on the left, on a bold knoll, through which the road was cut. The shrubs in the front yard rustled darkly over the top of a lofty stone wall.

As I approached this point, a huge dog sprang down from above and commenced barking furiously. Having no means of defence, I stood still, and the animal planted himself in the middle of the road as if determined to bar my advance. Presently I heard a whistle from the top of the wall, and a stern female voice exclaimed, "Be quiet, Roger!"

I started. It was surely the voice of Miss Verbena Cuff. The next moment she herself suddenly appeared in the road at my side, and I heard a whisper, " Is it you ? "

" Yes," I said ; " do you live here ? I was afraid I should not find the house."

Taking my hand, she led me to a break in the wall, up which ran a steep flight of stone steps. When I had gained the top, I found myself on the knoll in front of the house, and saw a flickering cone of blue and scarlet fire at the foot of the slope beyond.

"A'n't that a blaze ? " said Miss Verbena ; " I never get tired a-looking at it. It 's Tom's turn to tend the fire to-night, so he won't be in the way. Tom 's rather rough, he is."

" ' Men scarcely know how beautiful fire is,' " I said, quoting Shelley. " It looks as if a little volcano had broken up out of the earth. See, that 's the crater, at the top. Are you not afraid of the lava bursting out ? "

" Go along, you ! " was her answer, as she gave me a poke in the ribs. " Come in the side-door, into the setting-room. I did n't make a fire in the parlor, because I was n't quite sure you 'd come. But I 'll bring in some wood, right away, and then run up-stairs and fix myself in no time."

She ushered me into the sitting-room, which was dimly lighted by a single tallow-candle. An old woman, with a curious cap and no upper teeth, sat in a high-backed rocking-chair, knitting. She must have been very deaf, for Miss Verbena stooped down and shouted in her ear, " Mother, this is Mr. Godfrey, the schoolmaster at Yule's Mill ! "

The old woman looked at me with a silly smile, nodded, and murmured to herself as she resumed her knitting, " Yes, yes ; young people will be young people. I s'pose I 'm in the way now."

In a few minutes she rose and retired to the kitchen, and Miss Verbena, following her, soon reappeared with an armful of sticks and chips, and a piece of candle which she managed to hold between two of her fingers. I ought to have gone and opened the parlor-door for her, but I was struck dumb at my reception, and sat like a fool while she pressed down the handle of the lock with her elbow and pushed the door open with her foot. Good heavens! I thought, what does it all mean? There is nobody else here, and it looks as if nobody was expected! She is making a fire in the parlor and she is going to "fix herself in no time" — only for me? Why, when the old woman goes into the kitchen, and the big brother stays at the lime-kiln, and the young man and the young woman sit by themselves in the best parlor, it's "keeping company" — it's "courting"!

Instead of trembling with delight, I shivered with fear. Miss Verbena Cuff was no longer a buxom, rollicking damsel, but a young ogress, who had lured me into her den and would tear me with relentless claws until I purchased my deliverance with sweet words and caresses. I knew that "courting" implied such familiarities; I had often heard that even candles were not necessary to its performance; and in my boyish ignorance I had always supposed that the sentiment of love, upon one side at least, must precede the custom. I did not know that in many parts of the country it was a common expedient, indifferently practised, to determine whether the parties were likely to love each other. A kiss or a hug, now and then, was not looked upon as a committal of the heart to a serious attachment; such things were cheap coins, used publicly in forfeits and other games, and might be exchanged privately without loss to either's emotional property.

No; I was haunted by a softer and sweeter image than that of Verbena Cuff, — a pure, ideal flame, which her lips, red and full as they were, seemed pursed to blow out. Every fibre of my heart tingled and trembled with alarm.

When she returned from the parlor, she brought her album and gave it to me. The back was covered with green and brown calico, to preserve the morocco binding. "That 's the flower I could n't remember," said she, opening the book at a lithographed ranunculus; "it looks just like our butter-ball in the garden."

On turning over the leaves, my eye caught the name of Amanda Bratton. Ah, I said to myself, let me read her selection. It commenced, —

"Verbena, when I 'm far away," &c.

"What exquisite irony!" I thought. "*She* is too cultivated to cast pearls before swine."

All at once Tom Cuff came in, with a black jug in one hand. He twisted his mouth when he saw me, but gave me his hand and said, "How are you, Master Godfrey?"

I returned his greeting with a dignified air.

"Sis!" he called, "more cider! It 's mortal hot work, and makes a fellow dry. Bring Godfrey a swig, while you 're about it."

The cider was soon forthcoming, and so sharp and hard that it made me wink. Tom took up his jug and started, but halted at the door and said to me, "When you 're tired talking to Sis, you may come down and look at the kiln. I 've put in some big chunks, and it 's burnin' like all hell!"

"I 'll come!" I answered; "I want to see it."

Here was a chance of escape, and I recovered my courage. I informed Miss Verbena that I would write something for her which would suit the lily of the valley. I should have preferred the verbena, but I saw that somebody had been before me, — somebody, I added, who no doubt had a better right.

"Oh, go along, now! shut up! it a'n't so!" cried the energetic maiden, giving me a poke which took away my breath.

She bustled about a little more, arranging some household matters, and then came and stood before me, saying, "Now I 'm done work; don't I look like a fright?"

"No: you could n't do that if you were to try," I gallantly answered.

"None of your soft soap so soon in the evening!" she retorted. "Now I 'm going up-stairs to fix. You 'd better sneak into the parlor; it 's nice and warm."

"I guess I 'll step down and call on Tom. I want to have a look at the kiln."

"Well — don't stay more than ten minutes."

This I promised, solemnly intending to keep my word. I went out the opposite door, opened a gate in the paling, and found myself in a sloping field. The top of the kiln glimmered in wreaths of colored flame, just below me, and I could see Tom's brawny form moving about in the light which streamed from the mouth, at the foot of the knoll. I walked first to the top, inhaled the pungent gas which arose from the calcining stones, and meditated how I should escape. The big dog had followed me, and was walking about, sniffing suspiciously and occasionally uttering a low growl. To quiet him, first of all, I went down to Tom, took a pull at his jug, and commented on the grandeur of the fire.

"Yes, it 's good now for half an hour," he said. "I 'm agoin' to take a snooze. You 'd better go back to the house — Sis 'll be expectin' you."

"I will go *back*," I answered.

He lay down on a warm heap of sand and slaked lime, and I climbed again to the burning crest of the kiln. The big dog was there still! but I saw a fence before me, and knew that the road was beyond. I walked rapidly away, and had my hand on the topmost rail, when the beast gave a howl and bounded after me. Over I sprang, and started to run, but I had totally forgotten that the road had been cut into the side of the knoll, leaving a bank some fifteen or twenty feet deep. My first step, therefore, touched air instead of earth: over and over I went, crashing through briers and mullein-stalks, and loosening stones, which rattled after me, until I brought up, with a thundering shock, in the gutter below. I was on my feet in an instant, and tearing at full speed past the wall in front of the house, on the top of which I saw the dusky outline of the dog, springing towards the steps. There was a light at an upper window, and I fancied that I heard the sash raised. In less time than it has taken to write these lines, I had reached the creek and splashed through it, without taking time to find the log. The water, fortunately, was only mid-leg deep. Then I rushed forward again, stopping neither to think nor take breath, until the fainter barking of the dog showed that he had given up the chase.

How I had escaped cuts, bruises, or broken bones seemed a miracle, but I was sound in every limb. I cannot now pretend to unravel the confusion of thought in which I walked slowly homewards. Was my fine-strung, excitable nature a blessing or a curse? Had I acted as a wise man or a fool? I strongly suspected the latter; I had, at least, betrayed a weakness at utter variance with my pretensions to manhood, and which would render it impossible for me ever again to meet either Verbena or Tom Cuff without feeling abashed and humiliated. I had run away, like a coward, from the possibility of a situation which, in itself, would have been, at the worst, a harmless diversion in the eyes of the world. I was not forced to bestow the kisses and hugs I foreboded; a little self-possession on my part was all that was necessary to give the visit a cool, Platonic character, and I should have carried home my unprofaned ideal. I imagined what Dan Yule would do in a similar case, and admitted to myself that he would get out of the scrape in a much more sensible way than I had done.

On the other hand, the aforementioned ideal was flattered. I had saved it from even the suspicion of danger, — had braved ridicule, worse than hostility, for the sake of keeping it pure. I was made of better clay than the men around me, and ought to be proud of it.

When I reached home, the family had not yet gone to bed. Nevertheless, I entered by the back-entry door, which I found unlocked, stole to my room, kindled a fire, and changed my coat, — my best coat, alas! which was much soiled, and torn in two or three places. When I had become composed, I went down to the kitchen, on the pretence of getting a glass of water, but in reality to make the family suppose that I had been spending the evening in my own room.

Dan looked at me with a very queer expression, but he asked me no questions, and it was many days before I confided to him my adventure.

CHAPTER XII.

IN WHICH LOVE AND LITERATURE STIMULATE EACH OTHER.

It must not be supposed that my literary ambition had slumbered during all this time. Some four or five of my poems had been published, — the last two, to my great satisfaction, without editorial correction; and moreover, a story of the Colonial days, entitled "The Wizard of Perkiomen," was announced as accepted. My first timidity to be known as an author was rapidly wearing away. I began to wish that somebody would suspect me of being "Selim," but alas! who was there of sufficient taste and penetration to make the discovery? Would not Miss Amanda Bratton, at least, recognize in the "Parable" I had written for her album the same strings which vibrated in the "Unknown Bard?" To make assurance doubly sure, however, I attached to the next poem I forwarded to Philadelphia, after the signature of "Selim," the local address, "Yule's Mill, Berks County, Pa." This would settle the matter forever.

My mind the more easily habituated itself to literary expression from the isolation, whether real or imagined, in which I lived. I learned to confide to paper the thoughts which I judged no one around me (except, perhaps, *one* whom I dared not approach) was worthy to share. My treasures accumulated much more rapidly than I could dispose of them; but I looked upon them as so much available capital, to be used at the proper time. I had no further doubt of my true vocation, but what rank I should attain in it was a question which sometimes troubled me. I lacked patience to toil for years in obscurity, looking forward to the distant day when recognition *must* come, because it had been fairly earned. My energy was of that kind which flags without immediate praise.

There was now, as the reader may have suspected, an additional spur to my impatience. My heart was pitched to the key of a certain sweet, subdued, even-toned voice. I was jubilant with the consciousness that the one passion which is not only permitted to authors, but is considered actually necessary to their development, had come at last to quicken and inspire me. It was a vague, misty, delicious sensation, scorning to be put into tangible form, or to clothe its yearnings with the material aspects of life. There was poison in the thought of settlements, income, housekeeping details; I turned away with an inward shudder, if such things were accidentally suggested to my mind. My love nourished itself upon dew, odors, and flute-like melodies.

I took the album back to Miss Amanda with a tremor of mingled doubt and hope. She read the lines slowly, and as she approached the bottom of the page I turned away my eyes and waited, with my heart in my mouth, for her voice.

"Oh, it is *so* pretty!" she said; "there is nothing so nice in the book. You *do* write beautifully, Mr. Godfrey. Have you composed anything for Verbena Cuff?"

She put the question in a careless way, which satisfied me that there was not the least jealousy or selfishness in her nature. So far as my hopes were concerned, I should have been better satisfied if she had betrayed a slight tinge of the former emotion; but, on after-reflection, I decided that I liked her all the better for the unsuspicious truth and frankness of her nature.

"I could n't avoid it, you know, after promising," I said.

"I wish you would let me see it."

"I have no copy with me," I replied; "but I have the

lines in my head. I wrote them for the lily of the valley, which, you know, means 'Humility': —

"'My dwelling is the forest shade,
Beside the streamlet wandering free;
'T is there, in modest green arrayed,
I hide my blossoms from the bee.

"'But thou dost make the garden fair,
Where noonday sunbeams round thee fall;
How should the shrinking Lily dare
To hear the gay Verbena's call?'

You notice the irony?"

"Yes," she answered, after a pause. "It 's a shame." But she smiled sweetly, as she said so.

"Oh, you don't know," I cried, in transport, — "you don't know, Miss Bratton, how grateful it is to find a mind that can understand you! To find intelligence, and poetic feeling, and — and — "

I paused, not knowing how to make the climax.

"Yes," she replied, casting down her eyes, and with a mournful inflection of voice which went to my soul, "I understand it, from my own experience."

What more I should have said, with this encouragement, I know not, for Mrs. Bratton put her head into the room, announcing, "Tea, 'Manda. Mr. Godfrey, will you *set by?*"

This was one of her peculiar phrases, which would have provoked my mirth, had she not been the mother of her daughter. But, as she was, I thought it quaint and original. Another expression was, "*Take off* some o' the butter," or whatever dish it might be. I accepted the invitation, although my pleasure at having my tea "seasoned" by Miss Amanda was greatly lessened by the presence of young Sep, in a state of exhilaration. He had just come up from the Buck Tavern, and was in a humor for any devilment. It pleased him, in addressing me, to abbreviate my family-name in a way which made his remarks seem shockingly profane. This he thought the perfection of wit, and he roared every time he uttered it.

Miss Amanda looked pained, as well she might be, and over and over again exclaimed, "Don't, Sep!" — but to no purpose. I thought this was bad enough, but worse was to come.

"I say, ——," (I will not write the syllable he used), "I saw Tom Cuff at the Buck to-day. He says the lime-kiln 's done burning." Then he winked at me, and burst into a hoarse laugh.

I sat, frozen with horror.

"Lime-kiln?" was all I could say, hoping my confusion might pass for ignorance in the pale, steady eyes which must certainly be fixed on my face.

"You did n't know they had one, I reckon!" he continued. "Well, — I won't tell tales out of school, even against the schoolmaster."

I caught Miss Amanda's look, which asked, "What does he mean?" Explanation, however, was impossible at the time, and I said nothing. Sep's thoughts presently turned into another channel, and my torment ceased, though not my apprehensions as to the impression he had produced on somebody else.

I did not dare to call too frequently, and several days elapsed before I could make an explanation. I approached the subject clumsily enough, feeling that my allusion to it was a half-confession of misdemeanor, yet too disturbed to take the opposite course, and ignore it. Of course, I omitted the catastrophe of the evening, making the album account for my visit, and hinting, as delicately as possible, that I had expected to meet Miss Bratton at Cuff's. How I was relieved to find that I had misinterpreted the latter's glance at the tea-table! She had attached no meaning to her brother's remark, — had, in fact, forgotten all about it! Now that I mentioned the matter, she had an indistinct recollection of something about Tom Cuff and a lime-kiln;

but Sep had such a way of blurting out everything that came into his head! She knew, moreover, how "people" always talked, making mountains out of mole-hills, — but Verbena Cuff was reckoned to be quite a nice girl, and I need not object to have it known that I visited her now and then.

I affirmed, with great earnestness, that I hoped I should never see her again.

"Why, you seem to have quite a prejudice against her, Mr. Godfrey," said Miss Amanda. "She is a good-hearted creature, I assure you, with, perhaps, a little — though it may be wrong in me to say it — a *little* want of polish. That is a common want in Upper Samaria, however, and maybe we *all* have it in *your* eyes."

"Oh, Miss Amanda — Miss Bratton!" I remonstrated, "not *all!* You are unjust to yourself, and to me, if you imagine I could think so. Your generosity will not allow you to admit Verbena Cuff's coarseness and boldness of manner; you cannot feel the contrast as *I* do. It is just because *some others* are cultivated, and refined, and pure-spirited, that her ignorance is so repulsive to me!"

She cast down her eyes, and was silent for a minute. Then she spoke in that gentle, deliberate way which so charmed me: "Ye-es, there are others who have risen above those who surround them. You will find them here and there."

This was taking up my words altogether too literally. I had spoken, it is true, in the plural, but my heart meant a singular. In her perfect modesty, — her ignorance of her own spiritual value, — she had misunderstood me. I did not admire her the less for this quality, though I felt that all my indirect professions, hitherto, must have failed to reach her maidenly consciousness.

While I was uneasily shifting my cap from one hand to another, uncertain whether to continue the subject, or give our conversation another direction, she took up a paper which lay on the table beside her, unfolded it, and asked, with a bewitching air of pleasantry, —

"Mr. Godfrey, do you know who 'Selim' is?"

I had not yet received my copy from the post-office at Cardiff, and was therefore ignorant that my poem, entitled "The Lament of Hero, after the Drowning of Leander," commencing, —

"Ay, howl ye Hellespontic waves!"

had been printed in the number for that week; but a glance at the first page, as she held it towards me, showed the success of my stratagem. I was discovered at last. There, under "Selim," was the address, "Yule's Mill, Berks County." I will not describe my sensations at that moment. I have understood ever since how a young girl must feel when the man her heart has chosen unexpectedly declares his own attachment.

"Have you read it? Do you like it?" I breathlessly asked.

"Yes, indeed, — it is *lovely!* I knew you must be a poet, Mr. Godfrey. I saw the Belvidere Bard at Bethlehem. He visited our school; and he had eyes with the same expression as you have. There 's something about poets that distinguishes them from common people."

My own thought! Was I not, like Byron, not altogether made of such mean clay as rots into the souls of those whom I survey? And she, who stood as far above the rest of her sex in that secluded valley as I stood above mine, was the first — the only one — to recognize my nobility. Only the exiled Princess knew, under his rags, the lofty bearing of the exiled Prince! Oh, could I but woo her to return my sprouting love, I would immortalize her in future song, — she should be my Hinda, my Medora, my Astarte, my Ellen of the Lake! After Burns and his Highland Mary, should be written the names of Godfrey and his Amanda.

There was no end, that night, to my preposterous dreams. As I recall them, I know not whether to weep or laugh. The puny lily of my imaginative faculty seemed destined to fill the world with its fragrance, and I could not see that it was rooted, no less than the pig-weed, in the common mud. I had yet to learn that the finer clay, upon which I congratulated myself, is more easily soiled by the Devil's fingers than one of coarser grit, — that neither do such natures as mine monopolize the beauty, the romance, and the tragedy of life, nor are they exempt from the temptations which assail the ignorant, the excesses committed by the vulgar.

The tidings that "the schoolmaster wrote verses for the papers" were soon spread through the neighborhood. I cannot, to this day, decide whether it was an advantage to my reputation among the people, or the reverse. On the one hand, they had little respect for any talent which did not take a practical direction; on the other, they vaguely felt that it was a certain sort of distinction. The Yules, and others, borrowed my copy of the paper, and, I am bound to believe, dutifully read the poem. Dan was honest enough to confess to me: "It's a pretty jingle, but I can't say as I know what it all means." The girls, I did not fail to observe, were much more impressed by the discovery than the young men.

By degrees, however, I received encouraging notices of one kind or another. The shoemaker at the Buck, an old Scotchman, who knew Burns by heart and sneered at Homer and Shakspeare, was one of my very first admirers; but he used to say, "Ye ha'n't got the *lilt*, lad," — which was very true, only I did n't believe him at the time. Squire Bratton, being one day at Carterstown, brought me a message from the Rev. Mr. Perego, to the effect that I would find sublime subjects for my muse in the Scriptures: he suggested Moses on Pisgah, and the visit of Naaman to Elisha. I did, indeed, commence a poem on the former subject, out of pure gratitude for the clergyman's interest, — but this was an insufficient inspiration, and the work was never finished. Then I received many applications to write obituary verses, made from so evident a piety towards the dead, and with such sincere good faith in my powers, that I had not the heart to refuse. I have no doubt that some of my manuscripts are still preserved between the leaves of old Family Bibles, in Upper Samaria. The applications for album poetry, at first so agreeable, became at last a positive annoyance, because my poetic apostrophes to Youth and Beauty were always taken in a literal and personal sense. One day, in sheer desperation, I wrote in a volume sent to me, through Susan Yule, by a young lady of Cardiff, —

> "Oh, fair Unknown! believe my simple rhyme:
> Procrastination is the thief of time."

The lady, of whose age and circumstances I was utterly ignorant, happened to be verging on ancient maidenhood, much to her own disgust, and immediately suspected me of a malicious insinuation. She tore out and burned the leaf, and within three days Mrs. Yule picked up a report that I had written something unmentionably coarse and profane. It must have been generally believed, for I received very few albums afterwards.

During this time the number of my pupils had been gradually increasing, until there were frequently between forty and fifty present at once, and all my youthful authority was required to preserve even tolerable order. I had little trouble with the oldest and the youngest, but the cubs between twelve and sixteen sometimes drove me nearly to distraction. Keeping them in after school-hours, was more of an annoyance to myself than to them; I had a dislike to bodily punishment, although it was well merited, and allowed by the custom of the country; and, moreover, to confess the truth, I did not feel sure of my ability to suppress a well-organized plan of rebellion. Towards the end of the winter, I had reason to believe that a "barring out" was really contemplated, and communicated my suspicions to Dan Yule, who was my confidant in all external matters.

Dan took the matter much more coolly than I did. "Boys will be boys," said he; "they do it every winter;—fact is, I 've had a hand in it myself. But if you want to fix 'em, I 'll put you up to a trick worth two o' their'n."

This struck me as better than resistance; so, prompted by Dan, I procured some large iron spikes, and prepared oblique holes in the window-frames to receive them. The window-shutters consisted of a single piece, bolted on the inside. I also went into the loft and bored a small hole through the plaster of the ceiling, just over the stove. Then, with tranquillity of soul, I waited for the event.

On Saturday morning, the closed shutters of the school-house announced to me that the barring-out had commenced. I tried to open the door, but found it firmly fastened on the inner side. Then I went to each of the four windows, pretending to examine them, but really inserting my spikes. When this was done, I locked the door from without, and, with a stone, drove the spikes home. The boys thought I was attempting to force an entrance: I could hear their malicious laughter. When all was secure, I took a rail from the fence and placed it against the gable. It reached so near the little garret-window that I easily effected an entrance, and stole quietly along the middle joist to the hole in the ceiling. The boys were at the windows, trying to catch a glimpse of me through the cracks under the shutters. It was a favorable moment. I hastily poured the contents of a small paper of ground cayenne pepper down through the hole upon the stove, slipped back again, replaced the rail, and gave a few more thumps on the window-shutters by way of farewell.

Dan could not resist the temptation to lurk and listen after I reported that the work was done, and his description, that evening, of the sneezes and cries of distress; the swagger of some boys and the penitence of others; the consultations and the final determination to surrender; the bewilderment and dumb dismay at finding that they had not only barred the master out, but the master had barred them in, — occasioned more laughter in the family than I had heard since I came to live with them. The efforts of the boys to get out lasted for some time, and was only accomplished at last by wrenching one of the shutters off its hinges. Then they scattered to their several homes, very sheepish and crestfallen.

On the following Monday I opened school as usual. There was a curious expectancy among the pupils, but I made not the slightest allusion, then or afterwards, to the Saturday's performance. Dan told the whole story at the Buck, and it was some time before the boys heard the last of it. I had much less difficulty, thenceforth, in preserving order.

As week after week of the winter passed away, and my thoughts turned from the memory of autumn to the hope of spring, the temporary character of my occupation forced itself more and more upon my attention. In a short time my engagement would be at an end, and I was less than ever in the humor to renew it. What the next step should be, was yet undecided, except that it must be forward and upward into a wider sphere of action.

CHAPTER XIII.

IN WHICH I DECLARE, DECIDE, AND VENTURE.

I HAVE already spoken of the exceptional way in which my nature developed itself — by sudden bounds, which, in a very short time, carried me quite out of my former self. The two, or three, or possibly twenty inherited elements were not smoothly blended in my composition; the blood of my father's and mother's lines seemed only to run side by side, not mingle in a new result, in my veins. It was a long time — very long after the period of which I am now writing — before I could comprehend my own laws of growth and being, and reconcile their apparent inconsistencies. As yet, my power of introversion was of the shallowest kind. I floated along, with closed eyes, on the current of my sensations and my fancies.

My growing attachment to Miss Amanda Bratton, however, was the means of pushing me a long stride forwards. It thoroughly penetrated me with a soft, ideal warmth, far enough removed from the strong flame of ripe masculine passion, and gently stimulated all my mental and moral energies. My ambition began to find its proper soil of self-reliance, and to put forth its roots. A new force was at work in my frame, giving strength and elasticity to the muscles, "keying up" many a slack fibre, lifting the drooping lid of the eye and steadying its gaze, and correcting, with a clearer outline, the boyish softness of the face. I no longer shrank from the coming encounter with the world, but longed for the test of courage and the measure of strength.

Yet, in one respect, I felt myself still a coward. Although convinced of the eternal devotion of my heart to the beloved object, I had not dared to declare it. I saw her frequently, and our relation became more and more sweetly intimate and confidential; but I never surprised a blush when I came, nor detected a tender tremor of voice when I left. Her nature was as calm, and apparently as limpid, as a shaded pool in the heart of a forest. When I looked in her clear, unchanging eyes, as they steadily rested on mine, I felt the presence of a pure, unsuspecting, virgin soul. It seemed to me that my ever-present consciousness of love was met by as profound an unconsciousness. I longed, yet dreaded to arouse her from her peaceful and innocent dream.

The solution of my two uncertainties was hastened by an unexpected occurrence. Early in March I was surprised by a visit from Rand, who came, as he said, on some business in which D. J. Mulford and Squire Bratton were both concerned. Of course he was the guest of the latter during the two or three days of his stay. He came over to the mill on the evening of his arrival, and almost embraced me in a gush of affectionate ardor when we met. I was equally delighted, and took him at once up to my room for a chat, as on our Sunday afternoons in Reading.

"Why, Godfrey, old boy," said he, lighting a cigar without ceremony, "what a snug little den you have! And Bratton tells me you 're a good hand at the school, and do credit to his choice. I must say I 'm glad it has turned out so, for I took a little of the responsibility upon myself in the beginning, you remember. Bratton 's a keen, long-headed man — something of a swell, between ourselves; but so is your affectionate old uncle, for that matter. By the way, I 've made Woolley's acquaintance, in the way of professional business; — oh, you need n't be alarmed; your little legacy had nothing to do with it. I 'm sorry I can't explain myself more particularly, but these matters are confidential, you know. I 'm posted up about all the business in Mulford's hands, and he finds it convenient to let me help him now and then. I say, though, Godfrey, — no, 'Selim,' I mean, — you are getting famous. That Hero and Leander article was copied into the *Gazette*, the other day. Of course, when I saw "Yule's Mill" at the bottom, I knew what bird had whistled. I congratulate you, — upon my soul I do!"

I was not proof against such hearty, outspoken sympathy. Before Rand left I had confided to him my most cherished literary hopes and desires, had read to him the best of my treasures in manuscript, and asked his advice as to the next step I ought to take.

"Leave here, by all means," he said. "Go to Philadelphia, or, still better, to New York, where you 'll find the right sort of work. You may come to write novels or tragedies, in the course of time, and make as much in a month as you would in a year with such a school as this. I should advise you, though, Selim," (he persisted in addressing me so,) "to get into some newspaper or book business; it 's more solid and respectable. Poets, you know, are always dissipated, and finish with the poor-house."

I resented this statement with great warmth.

"Oh, well," he continued, "I did n't mean that that would be *your* fate, Selim. Besides, it may work off after a while. Lots of fellows catch poetry, and have it a year or two, and it don't seem to do them any harm. Mulford wrote a song for the last Presidential campaign, to the tune of '*Tullahgorum*,' and it does n't sound so bad, when he sings it. But, to come to the point, the city 's the place for you, or any man that wants to live by his wits. Only keep your eyes skinned, and don't let the hair grow on your tongue. You must either have gold in your pocket, or brass in your face. Most people can't tell one from t' other."

Rand's expressions jarred harshly on my more delicate nature; but then, I knew precisely what he was, — good-hearted, I believed, but thoroughly unideal. The main thing was, his judgment coincided with my own; he, too, recognized that I was fitted for a more important field of action. The very materialism of his views gave them greater practical value in my eyes. Not that I paid much regard to this side of the question; but it is always more comfortable to have the conclusions of Selfishness with you than against you.

My first plan had been to select Philadelphia as my future residence. My poetical pseudonym was known to at least one literary paper there, and I might make the acquaintance of Saxon, author of the series of "Moral Novels," and Brightaxe, who wrote the dramatic poem of the "Traitor of Talladega." On the other hand, the *dii majores* had their seats in New York; and I fancied Irving, Cooper, Percival, and poets whose names I will not mention because they are still living, seated day by day around the same Olympian board, and talking in splendid tropes and cadences. Even if they only asked for potatoes, there must be a certain rhythmic grace in the words, with cæsural pauses falling at classic intervals. Ye gods! what a fool I still was!

There was at that time a monthly magazine, called "The Hesperian," published in New York. It was devoted to Literature and Fashion, and was illustrated both with colored figures copied from *Le Follet*, and mezzotints of mushy texture, representing such subjects as "The Mother's Blessing," or "He Comes Too Late." I looked upon the latter as miracles of art, and imbibed the contributions as the very cream of literature. The names of the writers were printed in capitals on the last page of the cover, and my heart throbbed when I saw Adeliza Choate among them. I wondered whether I could not keep step with her on the Parnassian steep; to have *my* name so printed was a downright assurance of immortality. Accordingly, I picked out my choicest manuscript and forwarded it with a note, signed with my proper name. By a happy coincidence, the very day after Rand's arrival I received a note from " G. Jenks, Publisher, per W. Timms," stating that my poem would appear in the May number, — further, that it was not G. Jenks's habit to pay a *nom de plume*, but that he would send me the Magazine gratuitously for six months.

This piece of good fortune decided me. True, it opened no prospect of remunerative employment, but then I should not be obliged to pay for " The Hesperian."

As I was walking home from school, reading the letter over again, Rand and Squire Bratton, coming up from the direction of the Buck, overtook me. The latter was unusually cordial and condescending, insisting that I should take tea at his house that evening, as my friend Rand was to return to Reading the next morning. Of course, I was only too willing to comply.

After tea, Miss Amanda opened her piano and sang for us. My enjoyment of her talent, however, was a little disturbed by Rand's prosaic whispers of, " She 's been put through the regular paces at school, and no mistake. That style of thing was n't meant for Upper Samaria."

At the close of the song, tears of feeling swam in my eyes, but Rand loudly clapped his hands. " You have an exquisite touch, Miss Bratton," he called across the room; " it 's rare to find so much musical talent."

" I have no doubt you hear much better music in Reading, Mr. Rand," she modestly replied.

" No, I assure you ! " he exclaimed, in his most earnest voice, starting from his seat and approaching her. " The Miss Clevengers are called fine performers, but I prefer your style. They bang and hammer so, you can hardly make out what it is they 're playing. It does n't touch your feelings."

Hang the fellow ! I thought. If I had but half his assurance, I should know my fate before twenty-four hours are over. I did not hear the conversation which ensued, for

Squire Bratton turned towards me with some question about the school; but I could mark the honeyed softness of his voice, as he hung over her music-stool. I did not know why I should feel disturbed. He was a chance visitor — had never seen her before, and might never come again. She was bound to treat him with proper courtesy, and her manner was not such as to invite an immediate familiarity. There was nothing wrong anywhere, yet a foolish, feverish unrest took possession of me.

Later in the evening, the album was produced. Miss Amanda immediately turned to *my* page, and said, "Oh, Mr. Rand, you must read what Mr. Godfrey has written."

"Capital!" he exclaimed, after he had perused the lines. "What a nice touch of fancy! Godfrey, you must really have been inspired. But *such* a flower would make almost any bird sing — even a kill-deer like myself."

He looked full in her face as he uttered the words. Involuntarily, I did the same thing, to note how she would receive the brazen compliment.

"You shall have a chance, then," she quietly said; "I will bring you pen and ink directly."

"Oh, by Jove, that 's taking me up with a vengeance!" Rand exclaimed. "I could n't do such a thing to save my life. Godfrey, you must help me."

"I 'm not a mocking-bird. I can only sing my own song."

She smiled, but without looking at me.

"Well, then," said Rand, "I must get something out of my memory. How will this do?

"'My pen is bad, my ink is pale,
My love to you shall never fail.'"

"No," said she, taking the book from his hand, "I will not have anything of the kind. You are making fun of my album, and I 'll put it away."

"Aw, now," groaned Rand, assuming an expression of penitence. But it was too late. The book was already removed, and Miss Bratton came back with an arch air of reproof, saying to him, "You must behave better another time."

"Oh, I shall always be afraid of you."

I went home that night with an increase of hope, and a growing determination to declare my sentiments. I scarcely slept, so busily was my mind occupied in creating possible situations, and enacting the tender drama in advance. I succeeded in everything but her answers, which I could not — through sympathy with myself — make rejective, yet did not dare to make consentive.

I had hoped, all along, that some happy accident might disclose the truth, — that some mutually felt warmth of longing might bring us naturally to the brink where my confession would be the first step beyond; but no such came. I must either seek or make the opportunity. After much painful uncertainty of mind, I hit upon what I suppose must be a very general device of young lovers, — to announce my approaching departure, and be guided by the manner in which she should receive it.

The month of March drew to a close, and I had but one week more of the school before the coveted chance arrived. It was Saturday afternoon, and one of those delicious days of windless and cloudless sunshine when the sad-hued earth sleeps, and sleeping, dreams of summer. I walked up the creek, in order to look for arbutus-blossoms on a wooded knoll above the mill-dam. We had been talking of them a few days before, and she had told me where they grew. I found the plants, indeed, pushing forth from under the fallen leaves, but the flowers were not yet developed. I gathered, instead, a bunch of club-moss, and took my seat upon an old stump, to listen to a bluebird that sang from the willow-thicket below. Something in the indolent quiet of the air reminded me of the shady glen at Honeybrook, and I thought of my cousin Penrose. How far away it seemed!

After a while I heard the sound of wheels approaching on the road from Cardiff, and a light open wagon came into sight around the head of the knoll. I recognized Sep Bratton by his voice before I could distinguish his figure through the trees; and the dark-blue drapery beside him — could it be? — yes, it really was — Amanda! The road passed some thirty or forty feet below me, but neither of them looked up in my direction.

"I'm going down to the Buck," I heard Sep say, "but I'll let you off at the turning. Or, do you want to stop and see Sue Yule?"

"Not to-day," she answered. "But don't stay long, Sep. You know, Pa don't like it."

I listened no more, for a wild idea shot through my brain: I would cross the stream above the dam, hurry down on the opposite side, and intercept her! As soon as the vehicle disappeared, I bounded down the knoll, leaped the narrow channel, and stole as rapidly as possible, under cover of the thickets, towards the path she must take. I had plenty of time to recover my breath, for she was still standing beside the wagon, talking to Sep, who seemed excited. I could hear the sound of his voice, but not the words.

At last, the sweet suspense terminated. Sep drove off, and I saw her gradually approach. Assuming a careless, sauntering air, which belied my inward perturbation, I emerged into view, walked a few steps, paused and looked around, seemed suddenly to perceive her, and then went forward to meet her.

Never had she looked so lovely. Her eyes expressed the same unchanging calm, harmonizing, as I thought, with the peaceful sky over us, but the air had brought a faint tinge to her cheek and ruffled a little the smoothness of her light-brown hair. I noticed, also, the steady even measure of her step: if there had been harebells in her path, they would have risen up from it, elastic, as from the foot of the Lady of the Lake. She carried a dainty parasol, closed, and occasionally twirled it on her forefinger by an ivory ring at the end of the handle.

By the time we had exchanged greetings, and I had spoken of the arbutus and given her the club-moss, we passed the dam, and the road would soon bring us to Bratton's gate. What I had to say must be said speedily.

"I am going to leave here, Miss Bratton."

"Inde-e-d! *So* soon?" she exclaimed, pausing in her walk, as I had done.

"Yes, I am going to New York. This may be my last walk with you. Let us go down the bank, as far as the old hemlock."

She seemed to hesitate. "I don't know," she said, at last. "Ma expects me." But while she spoke her steps had turned unconsciously, with mine, into the footpath.

"I want to tell you why I go," I continued. "Not because I have not been very happy here, but this is not the life for me. I must be an author, if I can, — *something*, at any rate, to make my name honorable. I feel that I have some little talent, and if I am ambitious it is not for myself alone. I want to be worthy of my — friends."

"Oh, you are that already, Mr. Godfrey," said she.

"Do *you* think so, Miss Amanda?"

"Certainly."

Her voice expressed a positiveness of belief which was grateful, but, somehow, it did not encourage me to the final avowal. I had reached the brink, however, and must plunge now or never.

"If I should make myself a name, Miss Amanda," I went on, with broken, trembling voice, "it will be for your sake. Do you hope, now, that I shall succeed?"

She did not answer.

"I *must* tell you, before I go, that I love you — have loved you since we first met. I am presumptuous, I know, to ask for a return, but my heart craves it."

I paused. She had partly turned away her head, and seemed to be weeping.

"Tell me, you are not offended by what I have said," I entreated.

"No," she murmured, in a scarcely audible voice.

A wild hope sprang up in my heart. "You do not command me to forget you?"

"No," said she, as faintly as before.

"Then may I go and labor in the blessed knowledge that you think of me, — that you will be faithful as I am faithful, — that, — O Amanda! is it really true? Do you return my love?"

She had buried her face in her handkerchief. I gently put one arm around her waist and drew her towards me. Her head sank on my shoulder. "Speak, darling!" I entreated.

"I cannot," she whispered, hiding her face on my breast.

It was enough. A pulse of immeasurable joy throbbed in my heart, chimed wonderful music in my ears, and overflowed in waves of light upon the barren earth. The hilltops were touched with a nimbus of glory, and far beyond them stretched a shining world, wherein the thorns burst into muffling roses, and the sharp flints of the highway became as softest moss. I loved, and I was beloved!

My arms closed around her. My face bent over her, and my lips sealed on hers the silent compact. I would not torture her pure, virginal timidity of heart. Her sweet and natural surrender spoke the words which her voice could not yet utter. I repeated my own declaration, with broken expressions of rapture, now that my tongue was loosed and the courage of love had replaced its cowardice.

We reached the old hemlock, I knew not how, and sat down on the bank, side by side. I took and tenderly held her hand, which trembled a little as it lay in mine. Measuring her agitation, as woman, by mine, as man, I could readily make allowance for all that was passive in her attitude and words. I had burst upon her suddenly with my declaration, startling the innocent repose of her heart with the consciousness of love, and she must have time to become familiar with the immortal guest.

I explained to her my plans, so far as they possessed a definite shape. My success in literature I spoke of as a thing assured; one year, or, at most, two, would be sufficient to give me a sure position. *Then* I could boldly return and claim her as my precious reward, — now, I must be satisfied with my blissful knowledge of her love, upon which I should rely as upon my own. My trust in her was boundless, — if it were not so, I could not possibly bear the pangs of absence.

"We shall write to each other, shall we not, Amanda?" I asked. "Our hearts can still hold communion, and impart reciprocal courage and consolation. Promise me this, and I have nothing more to ask."

"If we can arrange it so that no one shall know," she answered. "I would n't have Pa or Ma find it out for *anything*. I 'm sure they would n't hear of such a thing yet awhile. But we are both young, Mr. Godfrey" —

"Call me 'John,'" I murmured, in tender reproach.

She beamed upon me a sweet, frank smile, and continued: "We are so young, John, and we can wait and hope. I am sure if ever anybody was constant, you are. You must write, but not *very* often. If you could only send your letters so that Pa or Sep should not see them! Sep would soon notice them, and you know how he talks!"

I was equally convinced of the propriety of keeping our attachment secret for the present. The difficulty in relation to correspondence had not occurred to me before. It was a new proof of the interest she felt in the successful issue of our love.

"How can it be done?" said I. "We might send our letters through somebody else. There 's Dan Yule, as honest a fellow as ever lived!"

"Oh!" she exclaimed, "nobody must know what — what you have said to me!"

"He shall not know!" I protested. "I'll make up some story to explain the letters to Dan, and he's so simple-minded, he never suspects anything. Or, is there anybody else?"

No, she could think of no one, and she finally consented, though with reluctance, to the proposal. She now insisted on returning home, and I must, perforce, be satisfied with one more kiss before we emerged from the screen of the brook-trees. On reaching the road, we parted with a long clasp of hands, which said to me that her heart now recognized the presence of love, and would be faithful forever.

I saw her twice again before my departure, but could only exchange a few stolen words, hot with compressed emotion. Sorrow for the parting, and a joyous impatience to be away and at work for her sake, were strangely mingled in my heart; yet joy was most natural to my temperament, and it now poured through my days like a freshet, flooding over and drowning every lingering barrier of doubt or self-distrust.

When my school closed and my account with the directors was settled, I found myself in possession of nearly seventy dollars, as the net result of my winter's labors. I was also, had I known it, entitled to receive the annual interest on the sum in my uncle's hands; but I was too little alive to mere material matters to make any inquiry about it, and supposed that, in breaking away from his guardianship, I had debarred myself from all claims of the kind, until I should be my own master.

The arrangement with Dan Yule, with regard to my correspondence with Amanda, was easily made. My repeated declaration that it was mere friendly interchange of letters would have made any one else suspicious, but Dan merely nodded his head, and said, "All right, — I'll 'tend to it."

The day of departure came, and, with many a hearty farewell and promise to revisit them, I took leave of the kind Yules, and commenced my journey into the world.

CHAPTER XIV.

IN WHICH I GO TO MARKET, BUT CANNOT SELL MY WARES.

On a cloudy afternoon, in the early part of April, behold me stepping ashore on the Courtlandt Street pier, from the Jersey City ferry-boat. Everything was new and bewildering. The rush of my fellow-passengers; the cries of the hackmen, brandishing their long whips; the crowd of carts, drays, and carriages, and the surge and swirl of one chaotic whirlpool of Noise, in the vortex of which I seemed to stand, stunned and confused my perceptions. After nearly losing the trunk in which my inestimable manuscripts were stowed, and paying an enormous price for its transfer to a thick-necked porter, who, I feared, would knock me down before I could hand him the money, I succeeded in finding quarters at Lovejoy's Hotel, an establishment which Sep Bratton had recommended to me. The officiating clerk, who struck me as a fellow of very obliging manners, gave me a front room on the fourth story, on learning that I should probably remain a week or two. I had neither an acquaintance nor a recommendatory letter to any person in the great city; but my funds, I supposed, were sufficient to support me for two or three months, and it was quite impossible that I should not find employment by that time.

I spent the remainder of my first day in wandering around the Park and up and down Broadway, feasting my eyes on the grandeur and novelty of everything I saw. I knew not which was most remarkable — the never-ending crowd that filled the chief thoroughfare, the irregular splendor of the shops, or the filthiness of the pavement. With the recollection of the undeviating Philadelphian squares of brick bound in white marble in my mind, I could with difficulty comprehend that I had not passed into some foreign country. I was also favorably impressed with the apparent friendliness of the inhabitants. Although the most of them passed me without even a glance, I was accosted in the Park by several gentlemen, who, probably recognizing the stranger in my air, asked me if I did not wish to see the city. Indeed, they were so importunate that I had some difficulty in declining their proffered services. Then, as evening came down on Broadway, I was quite surprised at receiving now and then a greeting from a superbly dressed lady, who certainly could never have seen me before. Some of them, in fact, seemed to be on the point of speaking to me; but as I feared they had mistaken me for some one else, I hurried away, slightly embarrassed.

I was so impatient to explore the field which I intended thenceforth to cultivate, that, as soon as I had taken breakfast next morning in the subterranean restaurant of the hotel, I set out for the office of "The Hesperian," which was near at hand, in Beekman Street. A small boy was just taking down the shutters. On my inquiring for Mr. Jenks, he informed me that that individual would be in at eleven o'clock, when I might call again, if I wanted to see him. During the intervening three or four hours I wandered about, from the Battery to Canal Street, purchased and read two or three literary papers I had never heard of before, and supplied myself with several manuscripts, for Mr. Jenks's inspection.

On returning to "The Hesperian" office, I found a tall, thin-faced young man, with a black moustache, behind the counter. He was making up bundles of the magazine, and the number of copies on the shelves behind him excited my amazement. If this was Jenks, I thought, no doubt he was a young author like myself, and would receive me with the open arms of fraternal sympathy.

"Are you Mr. Jenks?" I asked.

"No: wish to see him particular?"

It was, therefore, only W. Timms, the "per."

"Anything *I* can do for you?" he repeated.

"Thank you," said I, "I should like to see Mr. Jenks himself, a moment, if he 's in."

By way of answer, he twirled his left thumb towards the back of the office, giving a jerk of his head in the same direction, as he tied another bundle.

Looking that way, I saw that one corner of the office was partitioned off from the rest, monopolizing more than half the light of the back-window. The door to this enclosure was open, and I could distinguish a large head, mounted on a square body, within.

Mr. Jenks was absorbed in the perusal of a newspaper, which he held before him, firmly grasped in both hands, as if about to tear it in twain. Before he looked up, I had time to take a rapid survey of his appearance. He was a man of forty-five, short, stout, gray, and partly bald; features keen, rigidly marked, and with a hard, material stamp — no gleam of taste or imagination anywhere. He evidently noticed my entrance, but finished his sentence or paragraph before consenting to be interrupted.

"Well?" said he, suddenly, tossing the paper to one side: "what is it?"

"Perhaps you remember," I mildly suggested, "writing to me about my poem of 'Leonora's Dream,' which will be in 'The Hesperian' for May."

"What 's your name?" he asked.

"Godfrey."

"What 's the handle to your 'Godfrey'?"

This question was not only rude but incomprehensible. I supposed, after a moment's reflection, that he must mean my business or vocation, and was about to explain, when he repeated, —

"Your *given* name?"

I gave it.

He stretched forth his arm, took a folio volume from its upright niche over his desk, looked at its index, turned over the pages until he found what was probably a copy of the letter, and read, jerking out these words as he did so:

"Yes — Godfrey — May number — magazine for six months gratuitously." Here he slapped the volume shut, replaced it, and reiterated, "Well?"

"I have brought some other poems," I said. "Perhaps you might like some of them. I have come to New York to make literature my profession, and should therefore expect to be paid for my articles. Here is a long narrative poem, which I think my best; it is a romantic subject — 'Ossian on the Hill of Morven.' Would you like to look at it?"

He took the proffered manuscript, tossed over leaf after leaf to see its length, and then addressed me with unnecessary energy: "Young man, this may be apples of gold in pictures of silver, for anything I know, — but it won't do for me. It would make ten pages of the magazine, and four a month is as much as I can allow for poetry. I have a bushel-basket full of contributions which I can't use. The public want variety. It's a good thing to encourage young writers, and we reckon to do our share, — but business is business."

Very much discouraged, yet unwilling to give up all hope of literary occupation, I asked whether it would not be possible for me to furnish articles of another character.

"You're hardly up to what I want," said Mr. Jenks. "I'd like to have a few short, sentimental stories, to piece out with now and then, — something light and airy," (here he made a spiral upward movement with his forefinger,) "such as women like to read, — with a good deal of Millinery in them. It takes practice just to hit the mark in these things."

"I might try, Mr. Jenks," I suggested.

"As you please. But I make no engagements beforehand, except with standard authors. What have you there?"

I handed him the remaining sheets, which contained various brief lyrics, mostly of an amatory character. He whirled them over in the same rapid way, reading a line here and there, and then returned them, together with my "Ossian."

"One or two things there might do, if I was n't overstocked," he said. "Besides, you 're not known, and your name would be no advantage to the Magazine. Get a little reputation, young man, before you try to make your living by literature. Write a sonnet on a railroad accident, or something else that everybody will read, or have one of your singable poems set to music and made fashionable, and then I 'll talk to you. You can't expect me to pay, while there 's a young and rising genius on every bush, and to be had for the picking."

As he said this, he turned short around to his desk, and began opening a pile of letters. Nothing was left to me but to retreat, in rather a disordered manner. W. Timms gave a significant glance at the manuscripts in my hand as I passed out through the store, and I hastened to hide them in the breast-pocket of my coat. I will not conceal the fact that I was deeply humiliated, not so much because my poems were refused, as because I had voluntarily come down to the plane where I must submit to be tested by coarse, material standards. I felt now for the first time that there is an Anteros, as well as an Eros, in literature, and the transition from one to the other was too sudden to be made without a shock. I began to fear that what I believed to be Inspiration would accomplish little towards the furtherance of my plans, unless it were allied to what I knew to be Policy; — in other words, that my only chance of success with "The Hesperian" lay in writing one of the short, airy, *millinery* tales, which Mr. Jenks could use "to piece out with."

The idea grew less repulsive, as I brooded over it. I found my mind spontaneously at work, contriving characters and situations, almost before I knew it. By night, I had wellnigh decided to make the attempt. Meanwhile, I recognized that there was a grain of truth amid the harshness of Mr. Jenks's concluding words. I should certainly have but little chance of obtaining employment unless my name were known to some extent. "Selim," of course, must be dropped, and "John Godfrey" stand forth boldly as the father of his own angelic progeny; but even then, I was not sure that the reputation would immediately follow. I might plunge into the golden flood as soon as I was able to swim, but how could I learn the art on the dry land of poverty and obscurity? One of the suggestions struck me as being plausible. I knew how eagerly songs are passed from voice to voice through the country, and music seemed a fitting adjunct to some of my shorter lyrics. If, for instance, that commencing "I pine for thee at night and morn" were wedded to some fair and tender melody, it alone might raise me in a short time from the darkness of my estate.

In the afternoon, therefore, I made another venture. Not deterred by the crossed banjos in the window of a music-store, and the lithograph of Christy's Minstrels, in costume, on the title-page of a publication, I entered and offered my finer wares. I was received with more courtesy than at "The Hesperian" office, but the result was the same. The publisher dealt rather in quadrilles, polkas, and Ethiopian melodies, than songs of a sentimental character. He read my poems, which he pronounced very sweet and tender, and thought they might be popular, — but more depended on the air than on the words, and it was rather out of his line. His politeness encouraged me to use a little persuasion, yet without effect. He was sorry, etc., — under other circumstances, etc., — and I felt, finally, that his smooth manner covered a fixed decision. I went home towards evening, with the manuscripts still in my pocket.

It is useless to deny that my hopes were somewhat dashed by the day's experience. Already the fragrance of life began to drift away, and the purple bloom to fade. Even a poet, I saw, (and whether I were one or not, this was the only character in which I had presented myself,) met with a cold and questioning reception from the world. Whatever I might achieve must be the spoil, not the gift, of Fate: I must clench for a blow the hand which I had stretched out with an open palm. All my petty local triumphs, my narrow distinctions, my honest friendships, were become absolutely nothing. I wore no badge that could be recognized, but stood naked before a world that would test every thew of my frame before it clothed me with its mantle of honor.

Physical fatigue and the reaction from my first causeless yet inevitable excitement added to the gloom of the mood that fell upon me. Let no one tell me that there are natures so steeled and strung to their purpose that they never know discouragement. Some, indeed, may always turn a brave face to their fellow-beings; a few, perhaps, might sooner die than betray a flagging courage; but no high prize was ever reached by a brain unacquainted with doubt.

I read something — I forget what — to escape from myself, and went early to bed. There, I knew, I should find a certain balm for all moral abrasions. With each article of clothing I laid aside a heavy thought, and when my body dipped into the air as into some delicate, ethereal fluid, every material aspect of life drifted away like fragments of a wreck and left me the pure sensation of existence. Then I sank into my bed, as some wandering spirit might sink to rest for a while, upon a denser cloud, cool with dew, yet warm with rosy sunshine. Every joint and muscle fell into slack, exquisite repose, or, if sometimes a limb stretched itself forth with an exploring impulse, it was simply to enjoy more fully the consciousness of its freedom. My breast grew light and my heart beat with an even, velvety throb; the restless thoughts laid themselves, one by one, to sleep, and gentle, radiant fancies whispered from the pillow. In that sensation lay for me almost the only pure and perfect blending of body and spirit; — their natural enmity forgotten, their wavering bounds of rule softly obliterated, they clasped each other in a brief embrace of love.

Wretched, thrice wretched is the man whose bed has ceased to be a blessing — whose pillow no longer seems, while his eyes close with a murmured word of prayer, the arm of God, tenderly upholding his head during the helplessness of Sleep!

In the morning, I put on a portion of my trouble with my clothes. I was yet without a moral disinfectant, and the rustling of the manuscripts in my pocket brought back some of yesterday's disappointment. I had no intention, however, of giving up the struggle; it had become a sort of conscience with me to perform what I had once decided upon. The obligation was not measured by the importance of the act. I had half made up my mind to attempt a short "millinery" story for "The Hesperian"; but, even if this should fail, there were other literary papers and periodicals in the city. My interview with the music-dealer had left a more agreeable impression than that with Mr. Jenks. Generalizing from single experiences, as a young man is apt to do, I suspected that publishers of songs were a more courteous and refined class of men than publishers of magazines. I would therefore first exhaust this class of chances.

After some search, I discovered another music-store, in the lower part of Broadway. There was a guitar in the window, instead of banjos, and the title-pages represented young ladies gazing on the moon, bunches of forget-me-nots, and affectionate pairs in crimson gondolas. This looked promising, and I entered with a bold step. On either side ran a counter, heaped with squares of music-sheets, but nobody was in attendance. Beyond this, an open space, in which pianos stood, and there I saw two gentlemen, one seated and playing a lively air, the other standing near him. As I advanced towards them, the former looked up from his performance, addressed me in a sharp, shrill voice, with — "Wait a minute, sir!" and went on playing.

I leaned against the end of the counter, and heard what followed.

"This is the way it should be played," said the performer, — "quite a different movement, you see, from yours. I 'll sing two or three lines, to show you what I mean."

Thereupon, clearing his throat, he sang, with a voice somewhat cracked and husky, —

> "When — I-ee am dying, the angels will come
> On swift wings a-flying, to carry me home."

"There!" he continued, "that 's about the time I want, but I see you have n't enough syllables for the notes. I had to say '*a*-flying' to stretch the line out. There 's another wanted in the first, after 'when.' I 'll put in another 'when,' and you 'll see how much better it will go, and faster.

> "'Whenwhen I am dying, the angels will come'" —

"If you please," said the other gentleman, who, I now saw, was a young, fresh-faced, attractive person, "I will show how I meant the song to be sung."

He took his seat at the piano, and, with a weak but clear and tuneful voice, sang the same lines, but much more slowly and with a different accentuation.

"Oh, that won't do, that will *never* do!" exclaimed the first, almost pushing him from the stool. "It would n't be popular at all; it 's quite doleful. More spirit, Mr. Swansford! Listen again, — you *must* see that my idea is the best, only you should change the words, and have just as many syllables as notes." Thereupon he sang, to a galloping accompaniment, faster than ever, —

"Whenwhen I am dying, the angelswillcome
On swift wingswings flying, to carrymehome."

The young man looked dejected, and I could see that he was not in the least convinced. "If you insist upon having it so, Mr. Kettlewell," said he, "I must rewrite the music."

"I have nothing against the music, Mr. Swansford," said the publisher, as I now conjectured him to be; "it 's only the *time*. You might, perhaps, put a little more brilliant fingering in the accompaniment, — it would be more popular. The more showy music is, the better it sells. Think over the matter, while I attend to this gentleman."

He rose from the piano and came towards me. He was a small man, with lively gray eyes, a hooked nose, and a shrivelled throat. "Business" was written upon his face no less distinctly than on that of Mr. Jenks, though in different hieroglyphics. He was easier to encounter, but, I feared, more difficult to move. I told him in a few words what I wanted, and offered him my lyrics for inspection. They began already to seem a little battered in my eyes; they were no longer wild-flowers, fresh with dew, but wilted vegetables in a market-basket.

"Hm — hm," said he, "the words are good in their way, though it is n't much matter about *them*, if the subject is popular and the air is taking. I don't often do this sort of thing, Mr. — ?"

"Godfrey," I remarked.

"Ah, Mr. Godfrey. The name seems familiar. What songs of yours are in circulation?"

I was obliged to confess that none of my effusions had yet been sung. Always detected as a beginner! It is very likely that, for a single second, I may have felt a temptation to lie.

"That makes a difference," he said. "It 's risky. But

if you 'll leave them, I 'll show them to my composer, and see what he thinks. How much a piece do you want for them? I always like to know terms in advance."

Thankful not to have received a downright rebuff, I informed him that I was ignorant of the usual remuneration, but would be satisfied with whatever he should think them worth.

"Well," he observed, "I mostly get common, sentimental songs for a dollar. There 's Spenser G. Bryan, to be sure, *he* has five dollars, but then his songs are always fashionable, and the sale makes up the difference to me. You could n't expect to compete with a Spenser G. Bryan, so I suppose a dollar would be about the right thing."

As he paused, awaiting an answer, I modestly signified my assent, although the sum seemed to me terribly insignificant. At that rate I should have to write three hundred and sixty-five songs in a year, in order barely to live! After being notified that I might call again in eight or ten days, to learn the composer's decision, I took leave of Mr. Kettlewell.

This transaction gave me at least a momentary courage. It promised to be a stepping-stone, if of the smallest and most slippery character. There was also this pitiful consolation, — that I was not the only aspiring young author, struggling to rise out of obscurity. I could not doubt that the young man — Mr. Swansford — had come on an errand similar to mine. He was perhaps a little further advanced — had commenced his career, but not as yet emerged from its first obstructions. I longed to make his acquaintance, and therefore lingered near the place. In a few minutes he issued from the store, with a roll of paper in his hand. His head was bent, and his whole air expressed discouragement: one hand crushed the paper it grasped, while the other was clenched, as it hung by his side.

Presently he seemed to become magnetically aware of my gaze, and looked up. I noticed now, that his skin was quite transparent, and there were dark shades under his eyes. He wore a very silky moustache, and had a soft, straggling tuft on his chin; yet, even with these masculine indications, his face was delicate as a young girl's. I recognized a kinship of some sort between us, and, fancying that I read a similar recognition in his eyes, I said to him, without further prelude, —

"*You* sang the song correctly."

"Did I not?" he exclaimed. "You heard how he butchered it; — was ever anything so stupid and so profane? But he won't hear of anything else; I must change it. You offered him songs, too, I noticed. Do you compose?"

"Only words — not music."

"Then you can only half understand what I must put up with. You see I always write the melody first: it 's more to me than the poetry. If I knew a poet who understood music, and could give its sentiment truly in words, I should not try to write them myself."

"I wish you had seen the songs I just left with your publisher!" I eagerly exclaimed. "But I have others in my trunk. Will you come to my room and look over them, Mr. Swansford?"

He accepted the invitation, and in the course of an hour or two we became very well acquainted indeed. We interchanged biographies, and were delighted to find here and there a point of resemblance. He was a native of a small town in Connecticut, where his parents — persons of limited means — still lived. He had already been a year in the city, studying music on a fund derived from his moderate savings as teacher of a singing-class at home. He was four or five years older than myself, and thus possessed a little more experience of the ways of the world; but he never had, and never would, overcome his distaste for the hard, practical materialism which he encountered on every side. A few of his songs had been published, and had attained a moderate success, without bringing him much remuneration. He was now far enough advanced in his musical studies, however, to give lessons, and should rely upon them for support while elaborating his great musical designs. I dimly felt, in the course of our conversation, the presence of a purer and loftier ideal than my own. The first half-unconscious contrast of our natures presented him sublimed and etherealized beside the sensuous love of Beauty which was my strongest characteristic.

We parted on good terms with each other — almost as friends. That evening I returned his visit, at his boarding-house in the triangular region between the Bowery and East Broadway. He had an attic room, with a dormer-window looking out on a realm of narrow back-yards, divided by board-walls, which had received such a nap from the weather that they resembled felt rather than wood. A bed, cottage-piano, and chest of drawers so filled up the room that there was barely space for a little table squeezed into the hollow of the window, and two chairs. He had no stove, and could only obtain a partial warmth in winter by leaving his door open to catch the atmosphere from below. Above his bed hung lithographic heads of Mendelssohn and Beethoven. Poor and starved as was the aspect of the room, there was nevertheless something attractive in its atmosphere. It was not beautiful by day, but was admirably adapted to the midnight isolation of genius.

CHAPTER XV.

CONCERNING MY ENTRANCE INTO MRS. VERY'S BOARDING-HOUSE, AND VARIOUS OTHER MATTERS.

My acquaintance with Swansford, at that period of my fortunes, was a piece of good luck for which I have ever since been thankful. I derived a certain sort of consolation — selfish, no doubt, but very natural — from the knowledge that his circumstances were scarcely better than my own, his future equally uncertain. Without a friendly acquaintance, whose respect I desired to retain, I should probably have succumbed to the repeated rebuffs I experienced, and given up my chosen career in despair. The thought of Amanda was a powerful stimulant, it was true, but the breadth of New Jersey divided her from me. Here, however, was an ever-present eye which must not be allowed to discover my flagging courage. I must make good to him my first boast, and counterfeit a certain amount of energy, until the force of habit transformed it into the genuine article. The efforts I made were not without their results in my nature, and, since I have come to understand myself better, I am reconciled to that mixture of pride and vanity to which I can now trace so many of my actions.

During the succeeding week I made many additional trials, persevering after each failure, finally, from a curiosity to assure myself that my original plans were indeed futile. One or two literary editors accepted a poem from me as an unpaid contribution, but no one was willing to purchase. My only prospect of earning a trifle dwindled down to the short "millinery" story, which I completed and carried to Mr. Jenks, who promised to read it "in the course of the week." Mr. Kettlewell's composer had no objections to make in regard to the songs submitted to his inspection; they were smooth and sentimental, he said, and if he had time, he might marry some of them to his immortal music; but he was now busily engaged in preparing two new quadrilles and a polka.

I confided these experiences to Swansford, who did not seem to be in the least surprised; so I, also, pretended to take them as a matter of course. Meanwhile, my little stock of money was beginning to go, and prudence advised me to enter upon a more economical mode of living. About this time the front attic in Swansford's boarding-house became vacant, and I considered myself fortunate in being able to secure it, with board, for three dollars and a half per week. Swansford took me down to a dark parlor on the first floor, and summoned Mrs. Very, who kept the establishment. It was a splendid apartment; the carpet-pattern was of immense size, and the furniture real mahogany and horse-hair. I was obliged to wait some time before the appearance of Mrs. Very,—a tall, middle-aged lady with an aquiline nose. A cap with crimson ribbons and streamers was thrown upon her head, concealing to some extent the frowziness of her hair, and a heavy velvet cape on her shoulders was so confused in its fastenings that one side was an inch higher than the other. In the dim atmosphere, nevertheless, she was rather an imposing presence and suggested to me at once the idea of an unfortunate duchess.

Swansford performed the ceremony of introduction, stating my wish to become the occupant of the vacant room. The lady bent her piercing eyes upon me and took a silent survey of my form.

"I have not given out the room yet," she remarked. "Miss Dunlap spoke to me of her cousin wanting it, but I did n't promise positive. I wish to form an agreeable family, and would rather be vacant for a week or two than have them that don't seem rightly to belong to our domestic circle. There are now three ladies and two gentlemen, you know, Mr. Swansford; so it would seem proper for me to take another gentleman. Mr. Godfrey, I suppose, would not be likely to have lots of visitors till midnight or two o'clock in the morning?"

"Oh, no!" I exclaimed. "I scarcely know anybody in New York except Mr. Swansford."

"*That* would be a recommendation," Mrs. Very reflectingly observed. "Mr. and Mrs. Mortimer having the room under you; they 're the oldest members of my family and stand by me faithful. Them that know me generally do. Our circle is the best in Hester Street, and I often have competition for my vacancies. I 'm mostly full, all summer, when other people, who are not particular as to genteel boarders, are half empty."

Mrs. Very finally informed me that she would make up her mind that evening, and dismissed us with a stately salutation. I should have gone away in great doubt, had not Swansford whispered to me, at the door, "That 's always her way of talking. She has taken you already."

This proved to be the case. The next morning one of Lovejoy's porters followed me up Chatham Street with my trunk, and I took possession of the coveted attic. Mrs. Very's residence was a narrow three-story house of brick, with wooden steps and a small platform before the door. This was called "the stoop." The house was two or three blocks removed from the noise of the Bowery, and its neighborhood wore an aspect both of quiet and decay. The street was rarely cleaned, and its atmosphere was generally flavored with the smells arising from boxes of ashes and kitchen-refuse which stood on the sidewalks awaiting removal. Most of the houses were only of two stories, some of them of wood, and Mrs. Very's thus received a certain distinction. Whether or not the hall was swept, the brass plate on the door, with her name, was always brightly scoured. Not far off, on the opposite side of the street, there was a blind alley, leading to some hidden cluster of tenements, whence issued swarms of dirty, ragged, and savage children.

The room to which I was conducted was almost a facsimile of Swanford's. It commanded a view of the opposite side of the street, and overlooked the mysteries of several second floors. The absence of a piano made it seem more spacious; its appointments, such as they were, were complete; and, indeed, I was not so accustomed to luxury as to find the least fault with them. The wall was papered gray, with a large blue pattern, and there was a faded and frayed ingrain carpet on the floor. A very small stand of pine-wood, with a drawer for soap, held the washbowl and pitcher; the thin little towel was suspended from a nail. I had, further, an old chest with three drawers, surmounted by a square foot of mirror, and, as Swansford had dropped a hint that I was a young man of literary habits, Mrs. Very considerately added a little table, with one shrunk leg, which I steadied by means of folded newspapers. The bed was smaller and harder than any I had before occupied. The change from the spacious beds of Berks County was like that from a pond to a bath-tub, and I could no longer stretch myself in all directions with impunity. It was symbolic of the contraction which my hopes and my plans had suffered.

Swansford had obtained two or three pupils, at moderate terms, in the vicinity, and these, with his own studies, kept him employed the greater part of the day; but I had nothing to do except write and keep my eyes open for any chance that might turn up. When we met for dinner at five o'clock, — which hour had been chosen by Mrs. Very, as she informed me, on account of Mr. Mortimer, who was assistant teller in one of the Bowery Banks, — I was formally presented to my fellow-boarders. Mr. Mortimer was a grave, middle-sized man of forty, whose authority in that genteel circle was evidently only less than the landlady's. The outward projection of his right ear-flap, and a horizontal groove in his short hair, showed that the pen had grown to be a member of his body. His wife, a lady some five years younger, was taller than himself, though in dignity of deportment she harmonized fully. Her neck was a very stiff prolongation of her spine, and she had a way of bending her head the least in the world when she spoke to you, as much as to say, "I will subdue my feelings and condescend to speak." She was always dressed in dark silk, and her skirts rustled a great deal. Even in my attic, whenever I heard a shrill, sweeping noise, like the wind through a dead thorn-bush, I knew that Mrs. Mortimer was passing up or down-stairs.

The two remaining ladies were Miss Tatting, and her niece, Miss Dunlap. The former kept a trimming-store in Grand Street, in which the latter officiated as her assistant. There was less difference between the ages of the ladies than their relationship would indicate. It was difficult, in fact, to decide upon this question, especially in the case of the former; she might have been twenty-five and old-looking, or carrying forty summers with an air of youth. The necessity of unbending to her customers had given her an easy, familiar manner, which seemed occasionally to shock the delicate sensibilities of Mrs. Mortimer. Though comparatively uncultivated, she had a good deal of natural shrewdness, and was well skilled in the use of her tongue. Her niece was cast in a similar yet softer mould. A vein of sentiment, somewhat weak and faded now, to be sure, ran through her composition. But she was an amiable creature, and I have not the heart to dwell upon this little weakness, even if it had been more grotesquely developed.

When Mrs. Very took her seat at the head of the table (Mr. Mortimer facing her at the foot), her face was still flushed from her superintendence in the kitchen, but her hair had been rapidly compelled to order, a silk cape was substituted for the velvet one, and correctly fastened. A small black girl stood at her elbow.

No grace was said, although the landlady waited until Mr. and Mrs. Mortimer had lifted their eyes from their plates. Then she questioned each of us in turn, "Shall I send you some of the soup to-day?" After the soup, Mr. Mortimer carved a piece of roast-beef, while Mrs. Very addressed herself to a diminutive remainder of cold ham. Potatoes, turnips, and spinage boiled in an uncut, tangled mass, completed the repast.

Conversation rose as appetite declined, and after various commonplaces had been discussed, Mrs. Very suddenly exclaimed, "Who do you think I met, coming home from market, Mrs. Mortimer?"

The lady addressed slightly curved her neck and answered, in the mild voice of propriety, "I 'm sure I don't know."

"Her!"

"Indeed!" said Mrs. Mortimer.

"You don't mean Mrs. Gamble, now, do you?" asked Miss Tatting, suspending her fork in the air.

"Mrs. Gamble!" echoed Mrs. Very, with an air of triumph. "They were walking together, and there was no mistaking *her* at once. She seems to carry her head high enough, for all the trouble, and I should n't wonder if they 'd cave in, though they *have* said he should never darken their doors. I 've asked them to come around to tea some evening."

"Will they come?" all three of the ladies exclaimed at once.

"They promised positive they would, but could n't name the day certain. He does n't look a bit down about it, I must say. Perhaps *they* 'll come round when they find it only hurts themselves. I was in such a hurry that I could n't ask many questions."

This theme was pursued by Mrs. Very's domestic circle with lively interest. I gradually discovered that Mr. Gamble was my own predecessor in the attic room, and at the genteel board where I now sat.

The occasion of his leaving was his marriage with the daughter of a prosperous shoe-dealer, who was opposed to the match on account of Mr. Gamble being only clerk for a soap-boiling firm. The young lady, however, had a will of her own, and boldly married, in defiance of her parents. She had not returned home after the ceremony, but sent for her wardrobe, which the angry father refused to give up. The happy couple made a short wedding-trip to the bridegroom's relatives in the country, and were just returning to the city when Mrs. Very was so fortunate as to intercept them. Of course, everybody at the table espoused the cause of Mr. and Mrs. Gamble, the former being still claimed as a member of the family. It was well known that he would have remained, but for the lack of proper accommodations, and I fancy Mrs. Mortimer would have willingly seen a vacancy made for the romantic pair, by the removal of Miss Tatting and her niece.

By the time our dessert of rice-pudding was reached, this topic had been quite exhausted, and the conversation became mixed and lively. I talked across the table to Swansford about a story which had just appeared in one of the Philadelphia magazines, while Mrs. Very's and Mr. Mortimer's remarks crossed ours at right angles. Miss Dunlap listened to us, and her aunt was occupied with the stately Mrs. Mortimer, apparently on the mysteries of dress, for I caught such phrases as "a great demand for chenilles," "corn-color coming up again," etc. etc.

The same scene repeated itself every day — with slight variations. We had veal sometimes, instead of beef, and tapioca instead of rice. Mrs. Mortimer walked in Broadway, and often found subjects for short, decorous, condescending narratives. Swansford was questioned about his musical compositions, and variously advised, — Miss Dunlap hoping that he would write an opera, while Mrs. Mortimer thought an oratorio would be much more elevated. The boarding-houses of Bevins and Applegate, in the same street, were discussed with acrid satire, in which Mrs. Very heartily joined. In short, the latter's effort to create a harmonious domestic circle was entirely successful, so far as the satisfaction of the members with themselves was concerned.

I had been an inmate of the house about a week when I achieved my first success. Mr. Jenks, after postponing his decision and keeping me on thorns for three days longer, finally made up his mind to accept my millinery story, with the proviso that I changed the denouement, and instead of an elopement reconciled Ianthe's parents to the match. "The Hesperian," he said, was a family magazine, and designed to contain nothing which could plant an unconventional or rebellious thought in the breast of infancy. There had been several elopements in the previous stories, and he had already heard complaints. The article was pleasantly written, and he thought I might succeed in that line, provided I took care to "give a moral turn" to my sketches. What could I do? Swansford's experience with Kettlewell now came home to me with a vengeance, but I grinned (I am afraid I came very near cursing) and endured. For the story thus mutilated I was to receive five dollars after its appearance. I immediately commenced another story, in which the characters were absolute angels and devils, winding up by assigning the former to Paradise and the latter to Hades. The moral of that, I thought, would be plain enough.

I now wrote a page to Dan Yule, stating that I was well, and hoped he was, with a few little particulars of my life, which I thought would interest him. Inclosed was a letter of sixteen pages for Amanda, in which the joys of love, the sorrows of absence, and the longings for that assured future which would bring us together again, were mixed in equal proportions. I know that my mind, released from the restraints imposed by publishers of moral and millinery tales, poured itself out freely and delightedly to the one ear which would hear me aright. It was my first letter, and I doubt whether her joy in receiving it was greater than mine in writing it.

Swansford knew nothing, as yet, of my attachment. Although we had become earnest friends, I could not open to him this chamber of my heart. Our talk was mostly upon our "kindred arts," as we styled them. I was even more desirous than he to supply the words for his own melodies, and we made, one day, a double experiment. I gave him my last and, of course, sweetest song, taking in return a pensive, plaintive air which he had just written, and set myself to express it in words as he mine in music. The result was only partially satisfactory. I reproduced, tolerably, the sentiment of the air, but I was ignorant of the delicate affinity between certain vowel sounds and certain musical notes — whence, though my lines were better than Swansford's, they were not half so easy to sing. This discovery led to a long conversation and an examination of the productions of various popular song-writers, the result of which was an astonishing conviction of my own ignorance.

I should have enjoyed this vagabond life thoroughly, nevertheless, but for the necessity which impelled me to secure some sort of provision for the future. I saw no way of reaching the Olympian society of the celebrated authors, or in otherwise dragging myself out of the double insignificance (compared with my position in Upper Samaria) into which I had fallen. Week after week went by, yielding me nothing but an accumulation of manuscripts. I was obliged to procure a few better articles of clothing than I had brought with me, and this made a great hole in my funds. Indeed, with strict economy, they would barely last another month. Many a night I lay awake, revolving plans which brightened and grew rosy with the excitement of my brain; but, when morning came, the color had faded out of them, and they seemed the essence of absurdity.

I was not devoid of practical faculties, but they had hitherto lain dormant, or been suppressed by the activity of the tastes and desires first awakened. I now began to find a wide vibration in my nature, between the moods of night and day; but their reciprocal action hastened my development. Still, I was at heart a boy, and troubled with a boy's restless impatience. I had no suspicion of the many and the inevitable throes which men as well as planets must endure, before chaos is resolved into form.

CHAPTER XVI.

DESCRIBING MR. WINCH'S RECONCILIATION BALL AND ITS TWO FORTUNATE CONSEQUENCES.

A FORTNIGHT after my introduction into Mrs. Very's domestic circle, Mr. and Mrs. Gamble redeemed their promise of coming to tea. The important event was announced at dinner on the previous day, and little else was spoken of until the appointed evening came. Mrs. Very informed us, with a solemn air, that we should assemble in the parlor instead of the basement dining-room: Mr. Gamble, as a member of her family, should be treated just as well as if he were her own brother (" son," I thought, would have been more appropriate), and the Winches should see what *her* behavior was, as compared with theirs. They might hurt her, if they liked: thank Fortune, her house was well-known, and her boarders stood by her faithful.

" Yes," said Mr. Mortimer, with becoming gravity, " we must give Gamble a lift, now he 's in trouble. Old Winch keeps his deposits in our bank, but I won't let that stand between me and what 's right."

Mrs. Mortimer bent her stiff neck assentingly.

We were all seated in the parlor when the bell rang. Mrs. Very triumphantly issued into the hall and received the interesting couple, while we waited in silent expectation until the usual rustling up and down stairs should announce that the bride had adjusted her toilette. Then she entered, dark, full, and voluptuous in her form, and resplendent in a dead golden-colored silk. Mr. Gamble, beside her, dwindled into a very commonplace individual, as he no doubt was. He was cordially, if somewhat stiffly, congratulated — for the Very idea of gentility was too conscious of itself to be easy — by his old friends, and the bride received the same with an added tint of gracious deference. She, however, understood the interest of her position, and determined to enjoy it.

"Oh, I have heard of you all, from Harry!" she exclaimed, shaking hands with everybody, even myself, to whom she said, — "So, *you* have fallen heir to his room! Don't you let him in, if he ever repents of his bargain and wants to come back!"

Then she cast a loving, mischievous glance at her husband, who was radiant with pride at the gay fascination of her manner. "Now you see, Laura, from what company you have taken me away," he said, with a semicircular bow which embraced Mrs. Very, Mrs. Mortimer, and Miss Tatting. "It was a hard struggle, I assure you." And he heaved a mock sigh.

"You can't make us believe that," said Miss Tatting, tapping him on the arm with a large green fan.

This is a fair specimen of the conversation during tea. It was not very intellectual, I admit, but it was quite a pleasant and entertaining change from our usual routine, and I enjoyed it amazingly. Mrs. Gamble was the life of the company. Being privileged to give the tone of the evening, she did so with a will, and it was astonishing how much fun and laughter we produced from the most trifling themes. After her departure we were all loud in our expressions of admiration. It was decided, without a dissenting voice, that Mrs. Very's family circle would henceforth espouse the cause of the Gambles against the Winches.

About the middle of May, however, we were surprised by a rumor that the unnatural father had been led, either by policy or penitence, to relent, and that Mr. Gamble would shortly give up his situation in the soap-boiling establishment, to take an important post in Winch & Son's shoe-store. I know not whether Mrs. Very or the Mortimers were most flattered by this news: either party was sure that their countenance of the match had something to do with it. The climax to the general satisfaction was given by a package of notes which came, a few days afterwards, stating that Mr. and Mrs. Franklin Winch requested the pleasure of our company, on Thursday evening, at their residence, No. 322 Columbia Street.

There was no difficulty in comprehending the nature of this event. Mr. Winch, having made up his mind to do the proper thing, intended to do it in the proper way, crushing gossip and family estrangement with the same blow. The temptation to attend the ball was too great to be resisted, and our inveterate hostility to the Winches came therefore to a sudden end.

When the evening arrived, we marched across the Grand-Street region, like a well-ordered family, Mrs. Very taking Mr. Mortimer's other arm, Miss Tatting Swansford's, and Miss Dunlap mine. A waiter, in white cotton gloves, whom I at first took for Winch junior, received us at the door, and ushered us up-stairs to our respective dressing-rooms. Here were various other gentlemen, giving the finishing touch to their scented and glistening hair, and drawing on their new white kids. I imitated their movements, and tried my best to appear at ease and *au fait* to such occasions. When we descended to the parlor, Mr. Gamble came forward at once to greet us, and presented us with a respectful flourish to the obdurate Winch *père*, who looked imposing in his blue coat with gilt buttons, buff Marseilles vest, and high white cravat. Mrs. Winch, dark, like her daughter, but shrivelled, which the latter was not, stood beside her lord, in black satin, evidently as happy as she could well be. The reconciliation, in fact, was supposed to be mainly her work.

We, as the son-in-law's friends, received conspicuous attention. Mrs. Gamble welcomed us like old acquaintances, and glided hither and thither with a lazy grace, as she strove to stir up and blend us with the other social elements of which the party was composed. This was not difficult in the case of my companions, and I resolved, in my ignorance of New York habits, to imitate them in everything. Accordingly, when Mrs. Gamble asked me if I should not like to be introduced to a young lady "of a literary turn," in whom I might discover "a congenial spirit," I acquiesced with enthusiasm, and soon found myself seated beside Miss Levi, a remarkable girl, with very black hair and eyebrows, and a prominent nose. Her forehead was so low, that, at a distance, it looked like a white stripe over her eyebrows. She wore a dress which not merely showed her shoulders, but the upper undulations of her bosom, so that, whenever she bent forward, my gaze fell into a wonderful twilight region, which caused me to blush with the sense of having committed an impropriety.

"Mrs. Gamble tells me you are a poet, Mr. Godfrey," she said. (How had Mrs. Gamble learned that so soon?)

"Oh, I write a little," I modestly answered.

"How charming! I doat on poetry. Won't you repeat to me some of yours?"

I was rather taken aback at this proposition, but, taking it for granted that Miss Levi knew the ways of society better than myself, I repeated to her, in a low voice, and with some confusion, the last song I had written.

"It is beautiful!" she exclaimed, fixing her large, jet-black eyes upon me with a power I could scarcely endure to meet. "Beautiful! You must have been inspired — does she live in the city?"

"Who?" I asked, feeling that my face sufficiently betrayed me.

"How can you ask 'who?' Mr. Godfrey? Ah, you poets are a sad class of men. I'm afraid you are all inconstant; tell me, do you think you can be faithful to her?"

Some imp prompted me to reply, "I never had any doubt of it before this evening."

"Oh, Mr. Godfrey!" she exclaimed, "that is too bad! Now I know you are not in earnest." But she looked at me very much as if she would like me to insist that I was. I could not carry the farce any further, so endeavored to change the subject by asking, "Do you write, Miss Levi?"

"I ought not to tell you," she answered; "but I can *feel*."

Our talk was here interrupted, probably on the brink of sweet intellectual disclosures, by the sound of the piano. It was Swansford, whom Mrs. Gamble had persuaded to favor the company with one of his compositions. He gave, to my surprise, the very song I had just repeated to Miss Levi, with a tender and beautiful melody of his own. This generosity touched me, — for generosity it really was, when he might have sung his own words. He looked towards me and smiled, at the close, seeing my gratitude in my eyes.

Shortly afterwards I was released from Miss Levi, who took Swansford's place, and sang, "You 'll Remember Me," in a piercing voice. Various songs of the same class followed, and, even with my own uncultured taste, I could easily understand the look of distress on Swansford's face.

The double parlor was crowded, and it was not long before the songs gave way to the music of two violins and a harp, stationed under Mr. Winch's portrait, between the front windows. The carpets had been taken up, so that everybody expected dancing. Having a slight familiarity with quadrilles, from the "gatherings" in Upper Samaria, I secured Miss Dunlap, as the partner with whom I should be least embarrassed, and, after that, was kept well supplied through the efforts of the Gambles and young Winch. When the waltz came, I withdrew to a corner and watched the softly whirling pairs, conspicuous among whom were the hero and heroine of the evening. It was delightful to see the yielding grace with which she trusted herself to his arm, drifting like a swan on the eddies of a stream, while her hands lay clasped on his shoulder, and her large, dark eyes lifted themselves to his. Happy pair! If I were he, and she were Amanda!—but I ground the thought between my teeth, and stifled the impatience of my heart.

Towards midnight we marched down to a room in the basement, where a superb supper was arranged. Mrs. Very supposed that it must have cost fifty dollars, and she was capable of forming an opinion. There were oysters, salads, patés, jellies, brandy-peaches, and bon-bons, with tea, coffee, ices, and champagne. I now discovered that I had a natural taste for these luxuries, and was glad to see that Swansford partook of them with a relish equal to my own. The iced champagne, which I had never before tasted, seemed to me the nectar of the gods. Young Winch filled my glass as often as it was emptied, for a few short, jolly speeches were made and a great many toasts drunk. The ladies filtered away before we knew it, and we were first aroused from our delightful revelry by Mr. Mortimer, who came, hat in hand, to announce that the Misses Tatting and Dunlap were waiting for us.

On the way home I confided to the latter my interview with Miss Levi, and had it on my tongue's end to tell her about Amanda. I longed to pour out my heart to a sympathizing ear, and would probably have done it, had Hester Street been a little farther off.

On reaching the attic I went into Swansford's room for a little chat, before going to bed. He was highly excited. He looked up at the lithographs of Mendelssohn and Beethoven, shook his fist, and cried, "Oh, you grand old Trojans, did you ever have to endure what I have? I don't believe it! You had those around who knew what you were, and what your art is, but I,—see here, Godfrey! This is the insane, idiotic stuff that people go into ecstasies about."

He sat down to the piano, played a hideous, flashy accompaniment, and sang, with extravagant voice and gesture, one of the sentimental songs to which we had been treated.

I threw myself back on his bed, in convulsions of laughter.

"My words are poor enough," he continued, "but what do you say to these: —

"'When ho-hollow hearts shall wear a mask,
'T will break your own to see-he-hee,
In such a mo-homent, I but ask
That you 'll remember — that you 'll re-MEM-ber
— you 'll re—ME-HE-HEM—be-e-e-r me!'

— oh, and the young ladies turn up their eyes like ducks in a thunder-storm, at *that*, and have no ear for the splendid passion of 'Adelaïda'! It 's enough to make one despise the human race. I could grind out such stuff by the bushel; why not take my revenge on the fools in this way? Why not give them the absurdest satire, which they shall suck down as pure sentiment? I'll laugh at them, and they 'll pay me for it! Come, Godfrey, give me some nonsense which will pass for a fashionable song; I 'm in the humor for a bit of deviltry to-night."

"Agreed!" I cried, springing from the bed. I eagerly caught at the idea, for it seemed like a personal discharge of my petty spite against Miss Levi. I took a pencil and the back of a music-sheet, and, as sense was not material to the composition, in a short time produced the following: —

"Away, my soul! This withered hand
No more may sing of joy:
The roses redden o'er the land
Which autumn gales destroy;
But when my hopes shall shine as fair
As bowers beneath the hill,
I 'll bid the tempest hear my prayer,
And dream you love me still!

"The sky is dark: no stars intrude
To bind the brow of day.
Oh, why should love, so wildly wooed,
Refuse to turn away?
The lark is loud, the wind is high,
And Fate must have her will:
Ah, nought is left me but to die,
And dream you love me still!"

"The very thing!" exclaimed Swansford, wiping away tears of the laughter which had twice interrupted my reading. "I've got the melody; give me the candle, and we'll have the whole performance."

He sang it over and over with the purest, most rollicking relish introducing each time new and fantastic ornaments, until the force of burlesque could no farther go. My intense enjoyment of the fun kept up his inspiration, and the melody, with its preposterous accompaniment, was fairly written before our merry mood began to decline. The piece was entitled "A Fashionable Song," and we decided that it should be offered to a publisher the very next day.

It was late when I awoke, and in the practical reaction from the night's excitement I thought very little of the matter until the sound of Swansford's piano recalled it. He met me, smiling, as he said, "Our song is really not a bad thing of its kind, though the kind is low enough. But, of course, we need never be known as the authors."

He put on his hat, and went out, with the manuscript in his hand. I accompanied him as far as the Park, in order to make a call, to which I did not attach any particular hope, (I had been too often disappointed for that!) but in fulfilment of a promise. Among the new acquaintances I had made at the Winch ball, was a Mr. Lettsom, who was acting as a law reporter for various daily papers. In the course of a little conversation which I had with him, I mentioned my wish to obtain literary employment of some kind, and asked whether he knew of any vacancy. He informed me that reporting was the surest resource for a young man who was obliged to earn his living by his pen. Most of the prominent editors, he said, had begun life either as reporters or printers, and there could be no better school in which to make one's talent ready and available.

Something in Mr. Lettsom's plainness, both of face and manner, inspired me with confidence in his judgment, and I eagerly accepted his invitation to call upon him at the office of the *Daily Wonder*, where I hoped, at least, to hear something that would put me on the right track.

I found him in the fourth story of the building, at a little desk in the corner of a room filled with similar desks, at which other gentlemen were either writing or inspecting enormous files of newspapers. A large table in the centre of the room was covered with maps, dictionaries, and books of reference. There was not much conversation, except when a man with smutty hands, a paper cap on his head, and a newspaper tied around his waist, came in and said, "Hurry up with that foreign news copy! It 's time the Extra was out!" To me the scene was both strange and imposing. This was the Delphic cave whence was uttered the daily oracular Voice, which guided so many thousands of believing brains; these were the attendant priests, who sat in the very adytum of the temple and perhaps assisted in the construction of the sentences of power.

There was nothing oracular about Mr. Lettsom. With his thin face, sandy eyebrows, and quiet voice, he was as ordinary a man in appearance as one will meet in a day's travel. He seemed, and no doubt was, incapable of enthusiasm; but there was a mixture of frankness, kindness, and simple good-sense in him which atoned for the absence of any loftier faculty. I had no claim whatever upon his good offices; he scarcely knew more of me than my name, and had only asked me to step in to him at an hour when he should have a little leisure for talk. I was, therefore, quite overcome, when, after the first greetings, he said, —

"I have been making inquiries this morning, at the newspaper offices. It is a pity I did not meet you sooner, as the Anniversaries, when extra work is always needed, are nearly over; but there may be a chance for you here. It depends upon yourself, if Mr. Clarendon, the chief editor of the *Wonder*, is satisfied to try you. An insignificant post, and poorly paid, at first, — but so are all beginnings. So many young men come to the city with high expectations, that there would be no difficulty in getting any number of full-grown editors and critics, while the apprentices' places are rarely in demand. I tell you this beforehand. We will now call on Mr. Clarendon."

Before I could recover my breath, we were in the sacred presence, in a small adjoining room. Mr. Clarendon sat at a library table, which rested on a countless array of drawers. He was writing rapidly on long, narrow slips of paper, which he numbered and transferred from his right to his left hand as they were finished. He must have heard our entrance, but neither lifted his head nor noticed us in any way until Mr. Lettsom announced, —

"This is Mr. Godfrey, the young gentleman about whom I spoke to you this morning."

"Very well, Lettsom," — and the latter left the room. Mr. Clarendon bowed in an abstracted way, pointed with the top of his quill to a chair on the other side of the table, and resumed his writing.

He was a man of middle age, good presence, and with an expression of penetration, shrewdness, and decision in his distinctly moulded features. His head was massive and finely formed; the hair, once light-brown, was now almost wholly gray, and the eyes of that rich golden-bronze tint which is as beautiful as it is rare. Although his frame was large, I was struck by the smallness, whiteness, and symmetry of his hand.

I took the seat indicated, and waited for him to speak. He wrote half of one of his slips, and then, having apparently finished a paragraph, said, without looking up, —

"So, you want to try your hand at newspaper work?"

I assented, stating that I was willing to perform any kind of literary labor of which I might be capable.

"You have never done anything of the sort, I suppose. Have you ever written for publication?"

"Yes."

"What?"

The few poems and the accepted story seemed very insignificant now, — but they were all I had. I mentioned them.

"That is hardly a recommendation," he said, resuming his writing; "rather the reverse. We want a plain style, exact adherence to facts, and above all — quickness. You may have these qualities, nevertheless. Let us see."

He turned over a pile of newspapers at his right hand, selected, almost at random, the *Baltimore American*, and handed it to me, saying, "You will find the city-news on the third page. Look over it and tell me if you see anything of sufficient importance to copy."

"Nothing, unless it is this — 'Conflagration at Fell's Point,'" I answered, after rapidly running my eye up and down the columns.

"Now go to yonder table — you will find pen and paper there — and condense this half-column account into fifteen lines, giving all the material facts."

How lucky it is, I thought, as I prepared to obey, that I went through such a thorough course of amplification and condensation at the Honeybrook Academy! My mind instantly reverted to the old drill, and resumed something of its mechanical dexterity. In fifteen or twenty minutes I had performed the work, Mr. Clarendon, in the mean time, writing steadily and silently on his narrow slips.

"It is done, sir," I said, venturing to interrupt him.

"Bring it here."

I handed him both the original article and my abbreviated statement. He compared them, as it seemed to me, by a single glance of the eye. Such rapidity of mental action was little short of the miraculous.

"Fairly done, for a beginner," he then remarked. "I will try you, Mr. Godfrey. This will be the kind of work I shall first give you. You will make blunders and omissions, until you are better broken to the business. Six dollars a week is all you are worth now; will that satisfy you?"

Satisfy? It was deliverance! It was a branch of Pactolus, bursting at my feet, to bear me onward to all golden possibilities! I blundered forth both my assent and gratitude, which Mr. Clarendon, having completed his article, cut short by conducting me to the larger room, where he presented me to one of the gentlemen whom he addressed as Mr. Severn, saying, "Mr. Godfrey is to be set at condensing the miscellaneous. He will come here at ten o'clock to-morrow morning. Have an eye to him now and then."

Mr. Severn, who had a worn and haggard look, was evidently glad to learn that I was to relieve him of some of his duties. His reception was mildly cordial, and I was a little surprised that he betrayed no more curiosity to know who or what I was.

Overflowing with joy at my unexpected good fortune, I hastened back to Mrs. Very's to communicate the happy news to Swansford. But I was obliged to control my impatience until late in the afternoon. When at last I heard his step coming up the stairs, I threw open my door and beckoned him in. He, too, seemed no less excited than myself. Flinging his hat upon my bed, he cried out, "Godfrey!" at the same instant that I cried—

"Swansford! *such* news! hurrah!"

"Hurrah!" he echoed, but his face fell. "Why, who told you?"

"Who told me?" I asked, in surprise; "why, it happened to me!"

"*What* happened to you? Good God!" he exclaimed in sudden alarm, "you have not gone and sold the song to somebody else?"

In the tumult of my thoughts, I had forgotten all about the song. With a hearty laugh at the comical expression on Swansford's face, I pushed him into a chair and triumphantly told him my story.

"I congratulate you, Godfrey," he said, giving me his hand. "This is a lucky day for both of us. I thought I should astonish you, but there 's not much chance of that, now, and I 'm heartily glad of it."

"What do you mean?"

"Let me tell *my* story. When I left you at the Park Gate, I started to go down to Kettlewell's, but, by the time I had reached the Astor House, it occurred to me, that, as he deals in just such sentimental songs as we have burlesqued, I should have but a small chance of doing anything with him. Besides, I dislike the man, although he published my compositions when no one else would. So I turned about and went up street to Mackintosh, who 's at least a gentlemanly fellow. I produced the song, first told him what it was, saw that he thought the idea a good one, and then sang it as well as I could. There was another gentleman in the store, and they both laughed like the deuce when I wound up with the grand final cadenza. Mackintosh, I think, would have taken the song, but the other gentleman came up, clapped his hand on my shoulder, and said, 'I must have that. I 'll buy it, out and out. Joe shall sing it this very night!' I did n't know who he was, but Mackintosh then introduced him to me as Bridger, of Bridger's Minstrels. 'What 's your price, copyright and all?' he asked. Thinking it was a joke, I retorted with, 'A hundred dollars.' 'Fifty,' said he. 'No, a hundred,' I answered, keeping up the fun. 'Well — split the difference. Say the word, and here 's your money.' 'Seeing it 's you' — I began to say, but before I had finished there were seventy-five dollars in my hand, — here they are! — — and Bridger was writing a bill of sale, including the copyright. Mackintosh opened his eyes, but I pretended to take the matter coolly, though I hardly knew whether I was standing on my head or heels. But what a shame and humiliation! Seventy-five dollars for a burlesque to be sung by Ethiopian Minstrels!"

"There 's neither shame nor humiliation about it!" I protested. "It 's grand and glorious! Only think, Swansford, — ten weeks' board each for an hour's work!"

"*I* think of years of work, and not an hour of appreciative recognition," said he, relapsing into sudden gloom.

But my sunshine was too powerful for his shadow. I insisted on crowning this *dies mirabilis* with an Olympian banquet in the best oyster-cellar of the Bowery, and carried my point. We had broiled oysters, a little out of season, and a bottle of champagne, though Swansford would have preferred ale, as being so much cheaper. I was in a splendid mood, and again carried my point.

This ravishing dawn of prosperity melted my soul, and there, in the little stall, scarcely separated from roystering and swearing bullies on either side, I whispered to Swansford my love for Amanda and my dreams of the future which we should share.

He bent down his head and said nothing, but I saw a tear drop into his wine.

We rose and walked silently homewards, arm in arm.

CHAPTER XVII.

WHICH "CONDENSES THE MISCELLANEOUS" OF A YEAR.

The next day commenced for me a new life — a life of responsible, regulated labor, and certain, if moderate reward. It was not difficult to resume the harness, for my temporary freedom had not been sufficiently enjoyed to tempt me to prolong it. My life already possessed a serious direction, leading, I fondly believed, to that home of my own creation which my poor mother had foreseen upon her death-bed. This hope was stronger at that time than any literary aspirations. Indeed, I would have sacrificed the latter without much regret, provided another and more speedy path to wealth and distinction had presented itself. But my mind had received its bent from my cheaply won triumphs at the Honeybrook Academy, and I had too little experience of life to know how easily a young and plastic nature accommodates itself to different forms of training.

I took my appointed desk in the editorial room of the *Daily Wonder*, and commenced my allotted labor of "condensing the miscellaneous." I was so anxious to give satisfaction that no paper — even the most insignificant country sheet — passed through my hands without being carefully inspected. I sat at my desk from ten to twelve hours a day, selecting, condensing, and polishing my items, until Smeaton, the foreman of the composing-room, — the man with smutty hands and paper cap, — informed me, as he took my slips, "You do pile up the Miscellaneous in an awful way; half of that will be crowded out of to-night's make-up."

Not a fire, murder, railroad disaster, daring burglary, shocking accident, tragic occurrence, curious phenomenon or singular freak of nature, escaped my eyes; and I was beginning to congratulate myself on my expertness, when, on the third day, I received a most unexpected humiliation. I had overlooked the result of an election to fill a vacancy in the Fourth Congressional District of Tennessee, — a circumstance which my colleagues who "condensed the miscellaneous" for the *Marvel*, the *Monitor*, and the *Avenger*, had all duly commemorated, thus distancing the *Wonder* for that day. Mr. Clarendon's wrath was both strong and freely expressed. It would have been still more severe, Mr. Severn informed me, but for the lucky chance that the "city editor," in reporting a fire in Broome Street, had obtained both the amount of insurance and the names of the companies, which were not mentioned in the rival dailies, and thereby partly compensated my oversight. I found that the rivalry extended to the smallest details in the composition of a paper, and was felt as keenly by the subordinates of the establishment as by the principals. There was an eager comparison of the various journals every morning, and while the least advantage of the *Wonder* in point of news was the subject of general rejoicing, so the most insignificant shortcoming seemed to be felt by each as a personal grievance. I very soon caught the infection, and became as sensitive a partisan as the rest.

There was a marked change in Mr. Jenks's manner towards me when he discovered my new position. My short story with the unmistakable moral was accepted with some flattering remarks, to the effect that I was already improving in style, and he thought he could afford to pay me ten dollars instead of five. He called me back when I was leaving his office, adding in a careless way, "Of course you know Mr. Withering, the literary critic of the *Wonder*. I wish you would just call his attention to the June number of 'The Hesperian.' Here is an extra copy for him."

On Saturday afternoon I received the stipulated six dollars, which I felt had been well earned. This sum was sufficient to pay my board and all other necessary expenses, thus making me independent of literature and its scanty, uncertain returns. I was already so fortunate as to possess an occupation and a taste; the narrow bounds of my life were satisfactorily filled. I not only felt but saw that others recognized in me a new importance. Even Mr. Mortimer, identifying me with the *Wonder*, seemed to take it for granted that I was the depository of much secret intelligence, in matters of current gossip, politics, or finance. The demand for my opinion on these matters created the supply, and it was astonishing how soon my words, until now shy, hesitating, and painfully self-distrustful, became assured and oracular. Rand's opinion, as to the necessity of certain metals, either in face or pocket, seemed about to be justified.

When I returned home that evening, a new delight awaited me. Mrs. Very handed me a letter, addressed to "Mr. John Godfrey," in a coarse, awkward hand, which puzzled me a little until I noticed the post-mark, "Cardiff," in one corner. Then I rushed up to my room, locked the door, and tore open the envelope with trembling haste. A delicate enclosure, of silky pink paper, and redolent of patchouly, dropped out; but I resolutely inspected the rough husk before feasting my heart on the honeyed kernel. This was Dan's letter: —

"SUNDAY, May the 23d.

"Respected Friend, I recd. your favor in which you informed me that you was getting on so well and gave the other as you directed. Thought it best to wait for the other's answer, though there is no particular news. Sep Bratton goes to The Buck every day, and there 's high goings on between him and the squire. Your friend Mr. Rand was there again. People say the squire is speculating about Pottsville, and will cut up pretty fat some day, which is no business of mine, but thought you might like to hear. We are all well, and mother and Sue says remember me to him. I guess Ben and her is satisfied with one another, but you need not say I told you. There is a mistress at the school this summer, a right smart young woman, her name is Lavina Wilkins. And hoping these few lines will find you enjoying good health, I remain,

"Yours, respectfully,

"DANIEL YULE."

This letter was almost like the touch of Dan's broad, honest hand; it brought a breeze from the valley with it and a burst of sunshine, in which I beheld the pond, the shaded foot-path, and the lonely bank beside the old hemlock-tree. With a sigh of yearning tenderness I stretched forth my empty arms and murmured, "Dear Amanda!" Then I kissed the fragrant pink of the little note, and gloated over my own name, traced in fine Italian hand. The words looked so smooth, so demure, so gently calm — in short, so like herself! My heart thrilled with joy as I deciphered, on the fairy seal of sky-blue wax, scarcely larger than a three-cent piece, the words "*toujours fidèle.*" After this, I had no more power of abstinence. The coming joy must be tasted.

Her letter was very short in comparison with mine, — so short, indeed, that after three readings I knew it by heart, and could repeat it to myself as I walked down Chatham Street. I can still recall it, word by word.

"Dear John," (there were volumes of withheld confession for me in that one adjective): —

"How pleased I was to get your *beautiful* letter! Ma was not at home, so I was *alone* and could read it undisturbed, fancying you were *near* me. Do you really think of me *so much?* Do I *always* seem present to you? I can scarcely believe it yet, although you say it, and I *feel* in my *heart* that you are *true.* I am not afraid that when you get to be a *great* writer, you will forget me or any of us. Oh, it is a *bliss* to find *one* upon whom we can rely! You may imagine how much I have thought about you since you left. It was so sudden, and I was so *bewildered* by what you said, and I cannot remember what *I* said or did. But I do not forget any of *your* words. They cannot be unsaid, can they? Tell me truly, now, do you wish it could be so? — but no, I will not *ask* the question. We were at Carterstown last Sunday, and Mr. Perego preached from the text — Love is strong as death, Jealousy cruel as the grave. I wished you could *only* have heard it! How *some* people can be so jealous is past my comprehension: they can't have much *faith*, it seems to me.

"Oh, your letter was *so* beautiful! *so poetic!* I am quite ashamed to send you my *prose* in return. I have not your *gift* of expressing myself, and you must *imagine* all that I am not able to say. Do not ask too much of me. I am afraid you do not know all my *deficiencies*, and perhaps I had better stop now, lest I might disclose them to your gaze. Don't you think, with me, that *speech* is not necessary, where people understand each other's *feelings?* I could be silent for *years*, if *fate* required it, not but what there is a great *consolation* in the interchange of thoughts. Your description of your life in New York was *very* interesting, and I want to hear more of it; but now I must say good-bye, for fear of interruption. I *cannot* repeat, even with the pen, *your* words at the close of your letter, but you won't care about it *now*, will you? A. B.

"P. S. — Oh, do not write very often — not more than once in two or three months. It would be *dreadful* if Pa or Ma or Sep should find it out. They all think I am a child with no mind of my own. And I cannot look Dan Yule in the face: he *must* suspect something, and what if he should get drunk and tell! Not that he drinks, but we can't tell what *may* happen, and I am *so* frightened for fear our *poor, harmless letters* should fall into somebody's hands.

"N. B. — I have received the Hesperian through the Post-office. Sep brought it, but he did not know your hand. How lucky! Leonora's Dream is *lovely!*"

How easily I read, in those artless, timid sentences, her shy, pure, yet steadfastly faithful maiden heart! Even my own tumultuous utterances of passion lost their eloquence, beside the soft serenity of her voice. The tender playfulness with which she avoided repeating the fond epithets I had used, quite charmed me. Love had donned a witching, coquettish mask, well knowing that his own immortal eyes shone through it. I was completely happy, but an instinct told me not to intrude my joy on Swansford's mysterious sorrow: so, that night, I kept my room and wrote another poem.

My life now assumed a somewhat monotonous sameness. For months I strictly performed my appointed duties, increasing my circle of acquaintances but slightly, and acquiring no experiences which seem worthy of being recorded. My nature, apparently, was resting from the excitements of the previous year, and its rapid, partly enforced development was followed by a long period of repose. Little by little, however, I was gaining in knowledge of life, in self-reliance, and in power of discriminating between the true and the false, in men and things; but in all these particulars I suspect I was still behind most young men of my own age. Certainly I saw not yet the out-cropping of the grosser elements of human nature which a great city brings to light, yet I began to feel a dim conviction that there *was* something, that my own innocence and ignorance were exceptional, and that, whether in the way of observation or experience, I had much to learn.

About the beginning of winter, Mr. Clarendon, after informing me that he considered me tolerably well broken to the harness, and expressing his satisfaction with my punctual, steady habits of work, raised my salary to ten dollars a week. I was by this time able to do "the Miscellaneous" much more rapidly, and was frequently called upon, in addition, to write short items about the weather, the appearance of the city on particular occasions, or such other indefinite subjects as might be safely intrusted to a new hand. Thus I became more and more, in my own estimation, an integral part of the *Daily Wonder*, but fortunately did not feel the loss of the individuality which it absorbed.

The increase of my salary, added to an occasional windfall from "The Hesperian," enabled me now to set about gratifying a secret desire which I had long cherished. This was nothing less than to publish a volume. Swansford, who had great faith in my abilities, advised me to this step; but no persuasion was necessary to convince me of its expediency. As the author of a popular book, I believed that Squire Bratton would bow his haughty crest before me, and Uncle Amos approach me with a penitent confession of misdemeanor. Instead of running at the stirrup, as I had been doing, it was a bold leap into the saddle. Raised thus, a head and shoulders above the "heartless, unheeding crowd," I should spatter instead of being spattered. It was an enticing idea, and I had scarcely patience to wait for its fulfilment.

In another respect, however, Swansford was perverse, and his perverseness greatly annoyed me. Our "Fashionable Song" proved to be very popular. It was published as the composition of Bridger (of Bridger's Minstrels), and he, of course, received all the fame. It was even reported in the papers that his commission on the sale, he being owner of the copyright, amounted to more than a thousand dollars. I was furious when I read this to Swansford, but he only smiled, in his melancholy way, as he remarked, —

"He is welcome to the money, and his success with that stuff reconciles me to my share of the pay. He would give a hundred dollars for another, Mackintosh tells me."

"Don't do it!" I cried, eagerly. "A hundred dollars and half the gains of the copyright will be little enough. Think what we have lost on the first one!"

"You forget, Godfrey, how glad we were to get it. Why, we should have been satisfied with one tenth of the sum. But I wrote the thing in a freak of disgust, which I have outlived, thank God! Why should I allow such themes to enter my brain at all? The time is too short, the mission too solemn, for this profane trifling."

"But, Swansford," I cried, "you surely don't mean that you will not write another, if I furnish the words?"

"Yes," said he, gravely, and lowering his voice almost to a whisper; "I am writing a symphony. It will be my first effort at a work which might be worthy to offer to those two Masters yonder, if they were alive. The first movement is finished — wait — sit down — don't interrupt me!"

He took his seat at the piano, drew up his coat-sleeves, turned back his wristbands, and commenced playing. It was a sad, monotonous theme, based, for the most part, on low, rumbling chords, which reminded me, more than anything else, of distant thunder on the horizon of a summer night. A certain phrase, running into the higher notes, and thence descending by broad, lingering intervals, was several times repeated. The general effect of the composition was weird and mystic; I felt that I did not fully comprehend its meaning.

Swansford at last ceased and turned towards me with excited eyes. "There!" he cried; "I have carried it so far, but beyond that there is a confusion which I cannot yet unravel. This is only the presentiment of the struggle; its reality is to come. I feel what it should be, but when my mind tries to grasp it, I encounter cloud instead of form. Oh, if I were sure of reaching it at last, I would gladly give sweat, blood, and agony!"

He covered his face with his hands, and bent forward over the piano. I recognized and envied in him the presence of a consuming artistic passion. Involuntarily, I asked myself whether my love of literature possessed me with the same intensity, and was obliged to confess that it did not. I was a lover, not a worshipper. I was not strong enough to spurn an avenue of success, though it did not point to the highest goal. But I was at least capable of fitting reverence for Swansford's loftier and more delicately constituted nature, and made no further reference, then, to the offer he had received.

When I returned to the subject, a few days afterwards, I found him as stubborn as ever. My share of the money which we might earn so easily would have enabled me at once to publish my volume; and as I was conscious of no special degradation in the first instance, so I could not for the life of me feel that a repetition of the joke would be a flagrant offence against either his art or mine. My representations to this effect were useless. He was completely absorbed in his symphony, and filled with a rapt, devotional spirit, which, by contrast with my position, made me seem a tempter, assailing him with evil suggestions. I was silent, and Bridger did not get his second song.

During the winter my circle of experience was considerably enlarged. A small portion of the "complimentary" privileges of the *Wonder* fell to my share, and I made acquaintance with lectures, concerts, the drama, and the opera. Swansford sometimes accompanied me to the latter, and from him I learned the character and significance of works which had else impressed me with a vague, voluptuous, unintelligent delight. In my leisure hours I undertook the task of preparing my poems for publication. I had too great a liking for my own progeny to reject any of them, but, even then, there were not more than enough to form a thin volume of a hundred and twenty pages. The choice of a title puzzled me exceedingly. I hesitated for a long time between "The Wind-Harp" and "Æolian Harmonies," until Swansford informed me that both were equally suggestive of monotonous effect. Then I went to the opposite extreme of simplicity, and adopted "First Poems, by

John Godfrey," — which the publisher, who was to lend me his imprint (I paying all the expenses of printing and binding and receiving half the proceeds of the sales), rejected as fatal to success. It would never do, he said, to announce "*First* Poems"; nobody would buy them; I must presuppose that the public was familiar with my productions; many persons bought, simply to show that they kept up with the current literature, and the word "First" would tell them the whole story. Why not say "Leonora's Dream," (he saw that was the name of the leading poem,) "and Other Poems"? And so it was settled.

During all this time I had tried to gratify Amanda's wish with regard to the correspondence. It was hard, very hard, to endure three months' silence, but as she begged it for *her* sake, I tried to quiet my impatient heart and console myself with the knowledge of our mutual constancy. Her letters were short, but precious beyond computation. Her expressions were none the less sweet that they were constantly repeated; did not I, also, repeat over and over, without the possibility of exhausting their emphasis, my own protestations of unalterable love? I communicated my good fortune, with sure predictions of the bright future it heralded, but kept back, as a delicious surprise, the secret of my intended publication, and another plan which was to follow it. As it was now evident that the book could not be given to the world before May, and my twenty-first birthday occurred in June, I determined to steal a few days for a visit and present myself and my fame at the same time. I should come into possession of my legacy, and it would therefore be necessary to make a journey to Reading.

How my dreams expanded and blossomed in the breath of the opening spring! Love, Manhood, and Money, — though the last was less than it had once seemed to me, — how boundless was the first and how joyous the second!

CHAPTER XVIII.

IN WHICH I AGAIN BEHOLD AMANDA.

TOWARDS the end of May the important book appeared. I am sure that no immortal work was ever watched, through its different processes of incarnation, with such tender solicitude. I lingered over the first proofs, the revised proofs, and the printed and folded sheets, with a proud, luxurious interest, and the final consummation — the little volume, bound and lettered — was so precious that I could have kissed the leaves one by one. It seemed incredible that the "John Godfrey" on the title-page really meant myself! A book for me had hitherto possessed a sublime, mystical individuality of its own, and this, which had grown beneath my hand, by stages of manufacture as distinctly material as those which go to the formation of a shoe or a stove, was now to be classed among those silent, eloquent personalities! It might be placed side by side with "Paradise Lost" or "Childe Harold," on book-shelves; who could tell whither chance or fortune might not carry it, or what young and burning lips it might not help unseal?

A year previous, I should have been ready to expect the event announced by portents, such as precede the incarnation of a prophet, — murmurs in the air, — restless movements of the sea, — strange moods of expectancy in men. But all my boyish pyrotechnics of fancy had already dwindled down to a modest tallow-candle, and I had, now and then, my moments of severe doubt. My book, I now knew, was a venture, but whether strikingly and immediately successful, or the reverse, it would at least serve a purpose by bringing my name before the reading public, to say nothing of the dearer service which I confidently awaited from its publication.

Copies were sent to all the principal newspapers and periodicals of Boston, New York, and Philadelphia, and to all prominent authors, inscribed on the fly-leaf: "With the respects of John Godfrey." My position in the *Wonder* office gave me an opportunity of seeing whatever criticisms it might call forth, and from the day of publication I looked at the column of "Book Notices," before searching among the local news for condensable items. For nearly a week I saw nothing, and was nigh unto despair; then came a few scattering notices, then dozens of them all together. They were mostly brief, but very pleasant. I was accredited with "tender sentiment," "sweetness of versification," and "much promise." The result of these judgments not only satisfied, but elated me. A little poem, entitled "The Winter Wind," which I esteemed much less than the longer and more ambitious productions, was extensively copied. In the words of a western editor, it was "worthy of the pen of Amelia B. Welby." The faults of the volume were indicated in the same indefinite way as its merits; — they were "want of maturity," "occasional violation of metre," or "redundancy of images, attributable to youth." Thus, although very few copies of the book were demanded of the publisher, I considered it a flattering success.

All these notices I cut out and carefully preserved in a separate pocket of my portfolio. I have them still. The other day, as I took them out and read them over with an objective scrutiny in which no shadow of my former interest remained, I was struck with the vague, mechanical stamp by which they are all characterized. I sought in vain for a single line which showed the discrimination of an enlightened critic. The fact is, we had no criticism, worthy of the name, at that time. Our literature was tenderly petted, and its diffuse, superficial sentiment was perhaps even more admired than its first attempts at a profounder study of its own appropriate themes and a noble assertion of its autonomy. That brief interregnum in England, during which such writers as Moir, B. Simmons, T. K. Hervey, and Alaric A. Watts enjoyed a delusive popularity, had its counterpart on our side of the Atlantic. All our gentle, languishing echoes found spell-bound listeners, whom no one — with, perhaps, the single exception of Poe — had the will to disenchant. Hillhouse and Dawes, Grenville Mellen and Brainard still sat high on Parnassus, and Griswold astonished us by disinterring a whole Pantheon of forgotten worthies.

For my own part, I am grateful that it was so. I was warmed and cheered by generous words of welcome, of which I only felt the sincerity, not the critical nullity. My life was brightened and made hopeful at a time when — but I will not anticipate my story. The reader will learn, before I close, how far my maturer powers justified my early ambition, and he will acquit me of selfishness when I express the hope that all brambles may be put away from before the feet of others, as they were put away from mine. Whether or not I deserve the fame I then coveted, I am still grateful for the considerate kindness which did not venture to disturb a single illusion. What if those poems were but bubbles thrown up by the first warm fermentation of youth? For me they displayed, none the less, their fragments of rainbow color, and I do not see why I should not rejoice in them while they lasted. Why, also, should any one say to me, "These are air and froth, not the imperishable opals you imagine?" No; let rather me, and all such as brighten their lives with similar dreams, be deceived!

I had worked steadily and faithfully for a year, at my desk in the *Wonder* office, and Mr. Clarendon did not refuse my petition for a week's holiday. Severn agreed to perform my duties, in addition to his own, during my absence, with the understanding that I should return the service, later in the summer. To Swansford I confided so much of my intention as regarded the business with my uncle, reserving the rest until my return, for I was still uncertain how Squire Bratton would receive the knowledge of my attachment to Amanda. The dear fellow sympathized heartily with my improving prospects. He believed in the promise of my volume, because it was better than he could have done, and his predictions of my success in literature were even more enthusiastic than my own secret hopes. He was a faithful friend; would that my conscience allowed me to say the same of myself!

My last letter from Amanda had been received in March. It was brief and hurried, and at any other time would have failed to satisfy the cravings of my heart. But I was already deep in the ecstasy of my "first proofs," and looking forward to the double surprise I was hoarding up for her. "John," she wrote, "do not be angry at my short letter, today, for *indeed* I am dreadfully afraid Sep, or Dan, or somebody suspects *something*. Sep asked me the other day whether I had heard from you. I thought I should sink into the ground, but I had to look him in the face and *tell a fib*. I know it was n't right, and you would not like me to do it, but there were Pa and Ma in the room. I am well, only *so nervous*, you cannot think. Dan looks at me so queer, every time we meet. I am not sure that it is *right* for us to correspond in this *underhanded* way, but you know it was *your* proposition. I hope you won't take it hard that I should say so, but indeed I wish there was some other way in which we could *exchange our thoughts*. Mr. Perego and his wife are here to tea, and I have only five minutes to myself. We see a good deal of company now, and it takes up all my time, nearly. I sometimes wish I was my own mistress, but I suppose such thoughts are wrong. At any rate, I am *patient*, and you can be a little so, too,— can't you? A. B."

I did not much wonder that Amanda should be somewhat uneasy lest our correspondence — the manner of which, to her frank, truthful nature, involved a certain amount of deception — should be discovered. I felt a slight twinge of conscience on perceiving that I was responsible for her disquiet, and confessed that her faith in me, as measured by her patience, must exceed mine in her. My love, certainly, did not need the nourishment of letters; but silence was a pain, and I was much better constituted to enjoy than to endure. My answer was long and consolatory in its tone. I admitted my impatience, hinting, however, that I hoped the cause of it would soon terminate; that I fully appreciated her position, so much more delicate and difficult than mine, and would release her from it as soon as the improvement in my fortunes would allow. Meanwhile, I said, she should only write when she felt assured that she ran no risk in so doing. It was no great magnanimity in me to grant this, under the circumstances, yet I involuntarily let it appear that I was making a sacrifice for her sake. She could not help feeling, I reasoned, that the balance of patience was now restored between us.

At last the happy morning of my first holiday dawned. I was fully prepared for the journey, in order to take the ten o'clock train for Trenton. A small and elegant travelling valise, packed the night before, stood on the top of my honest old trunk, and its shining leather winked at me, with an expression of eagerness for its mission. Among the contents, I need not say, were several copies of "Leonora's Dream, and Other Poems," *one* of them bound in green morocco, with gilt edges. After I had arrayed myself in a new travelling-suit of light-brown, and carefully adjusted the bow of my cinnamon-colored cravat, I took a good look at my face in the little mirror, and commended what I saw. I can still remember, as if it were somebody else's face, the dark, earnest, innocent eyes, filled with such a joyous light; the low brow and thick, wavy locks of hair; the smooth cheeks, already pale from my confined life, and the thin, sensitive lips, shaded by a silky moustache, which *would* be red, no matter how my hair had darkened. My features were not regular, and I never thought of making any claim to be called handsome; but I was vain enough to imagine that there was something "interesting" in my face, and that I would not disappoint the expectations of my Amanda. My country awkwardness, at least, had disappeared, and the self-possessed air which had come in its stead enabled me to use, instead of obscure, my few physical advantages.

My ride to Trenton was shortened by the active, excited imagination, which ran in advance and prefigured, in a thousand ways, the coming meeting. When I arrived I found that I was too late for the afternoon stage, and, on account of the distance across the country to Cardiff, would be obliged to wait until morning. This was a sore interruption, but it came to end, and sunrise saw me once more looking on the green Pennsylvanian hills from the driver's box. I enjoyed the fresh summer glory of the country as never before; success was behind me and love beckoned me on. What wonder if the meadow-larks piped more sweetly than ever the nightingale in Cephissian thickets, or if the blue and green of sky and earth held each other in a lovelier harmony than that of which Herbert sang? As we drove onward, the two hills which rise to the eastward of Cardiff lifted their round, leafy tops, afar off, over the rim of the horizon. I thought them the gates of Paradise.

It was noon when the stage drew up beside the white porch of the well-known tavern, and the driver announced to the four inside passengers, "Fifteen minutes for dinner!" His statement was noisily verified by a big bell, which issued from the central door, followed by the arm and then the body of the stout landlord, who looked at me doubtfully as I entered, but did not seem to recognize me. I was rather glad of this, as it proved that I had changed considerably in my appearance, and, I hoped, for the better. I was too hungry to slight the announcement of dinner, especially as I had determined on walking over to Upper Samaria, as on that well-remembered autumn day, a year and a half before.

Taking the green morocco book from my valise, which I left in the landlord's charge, I set forth on my journey, in a tumult of delicious feelings. I know that I was frequently obliged to pause when my breath came short with the rapid beating of my heart. I anticipated and measured off the distance, and computed the time, saying to myself, "In an hour more — in fifty minutes — in three-quarters" —

When I reached the top of the second hill from Cardiff, and looked across the hollow to the next rise, where the road skirts Hannaford's Woods, I saw a neat open wagon coming up towards me. The team had a familiar air, and I stopped and inspected it with some curiosity. I scarcely knew whether to be pleased or alarmed when I recognized Squire Bratton and his wife. My first impulse, I fancy, was to leap over the fence and take a wide circuit across the fields to avoid them; but then I reflected that they were probably going to Cardiff, leaving the coast clear for my interview with Amanda. It would be my duty to see them when they returned, and my reception then could not be prejudiced by greeting them now. I therefore resumed my walk, but more slowly, down the hill.

As the wagon approached, I could see that Squire Bratton looked more than usually spruce and important. His hat was set well back upon his head, and the ends of his upright shirt-collar made two sharp white triangles upon the broad red plain of his cheeks. He snapped his whip-lash continually in the air, and the sound prevented me from hearing the remarks which, from the motion of his head and the movement of his mouth, he was evidently making to his wife. He did not seem to recognize me until we were but a few paces apart.

"Hallo! Why, here 's Godfrey!" he exclaimed, checking the horses.

I approached the wheel, and shook hands with both.

"Should hardly ha' known you, with that bit of squirrel's tail under your nose," said the Squire. "Coming over to see us all again? That 's right."

"Yes," I answered; "I am on my way to Reading, and did not like to pass as near as Cardiff, without calling upon my friends in Upper Samaria. I hope you are all well."

"First-rate, first-rate. I need n't ask *you*. You 've got into better business than school-teaching, I should reckon?"

I smiled in conscious triumph, as I replied, "Oh yes, much better in every way."

"Glad to hear it. Well — we must push on. See you again to-night. You 'll find our house open, and *somebody* there you 'll like to see: ha, ha!"

With a chuckle of satisfaction and a pistol-volley from his whip, Squire Bratton drove away, leaving me in a state of profound astonishment. What did he mean? Could it be that he had accidentally discovered, or that Amanda had confessed, the truth, and that he intended to give me a hint of his approbation? It seemed almost too complete a joy to be real, and yet I could give his words no other interpretation. As for Mrs. Bratton, she had laughed and nodded her head, as much as to say, "Go on — it 's all right!" The more incredible my fortune seemed, the more sure I felt that it must be true. An instant feeling of gratitude and affection for the old couple sprang up in my heart. I turned about, as if to thank them on the spot for my perfect happiness, but their team had gone over the hill. Then I hastened forward, up the long rise, with feet that scarcely felt the road.

Again the charming valley — how dear its every feature now! — lay spread before me. There was Yule's Mill, and the glassy pond, and the chimneys of Bratton's house, rising out of a boss of leaves; and down the stream, over the twinkling lines of the willows, I could just see the ragged top of the old hemlock, sacred to the first confession and surrender of love. I never saw a lovelier, happier, more peaceful scene: I never expect to see its like again.

Now my road led down between the sloping fields which caught the full warmth of the sun, and let their grain romp and roll in the sweet summer wind, until it bent to the level of the creek, around the knoll where I had sought for trailing arbutus, on that day whence my life as a man ought to be dated. I there determined to cross the stream above the pond, and make my way straight through the narrow field beyond, to Bratton's house. First Amanda, and the positive assurance of my bliss! I said.

Hot and panting with excitement and the rapidity of my motions, I gained the top of the knoll at last, but a stone's throw from the house. All was quiet around. The trees hid the windows, and even the front veranda, from the point where I stood, and I thought of the magic hedge around the palace of the Sleeping Beauty. The hundred years had passed, and I was the fortunate prince, come to waken my beloved with a kiss. I paused, and held back the joy at my lips, that I might the longer taste its perfect flavor. All at once I heard the voice of some one singing, — a voice moving along under the trees. It was she! — I saw the rose-tint of her dress through the gaps in the shrubbery. I saw her glide along towards an open arbor of lattice-work, overgrown with clematis, which stood on the top of the lawn, a little to the left of the house.

Now was my fortunate moment! I sprang over the fence, crept down behind the clumps of lilac and roses, and reached the arbor as she was singing the line, "*And I've seen an eye still brighter.*" (How well I remember it.) Her back was towards me: she was looking out, over the railing, down the road to the mill. How lovely her slender figure, clad in pink lawn, showed in the green frame! I could no longer contain myself, but cried out, in a voice which I vainly strove to soften to a whisper, —

"Amanda! Dear Amanda!"

She started, with a gasp, rather than a scream, of surprise. She turned and recognized me: a fiery blush ran over her face and neck, but instantly died away, leaving her very pale. Her eyes were fixed upon mine with an expression of alarm; her lips moved a little, but she seemed unable to speak.

"I did n't mean to frighten you so, Amanda," I said,—"but I am so glad, so happy!" And I rushed forward, threw my arms around her waist, and bent down to give her the kiss for which I had hungered so long.

But she screamed, covered her face with her hands, and twisted herself out of my embrace. "Leave me alone!" she said, in a low, hard voice, as she escaped to the other side of the table, and stood there, pale, and trembling a little.

"Don't be angry, darling!" I pleaded. "Is n't it true, then, that your father and mother know everything? I met them on the road, and they told me to come here at once — that you would be glad to see me. I thought they *must* know, you see, and that all our troubles were over, for I'm free at last,—I am my own master, and now I can speak to your father. It will all come out right, and we will be rewarded for our patience."

I gently approached her as I spoke these words. But she put out her hand to keep me away, and said, with her face turned from me, "You must not say such things to me, Mr. Godfrey."

Something in the tone of her voice seemed to chill my very blood. I was so startled and astonished that the first thought which came into my head forced for itself a passionate utterance.

"Amanda!" I cried, "tell me what all this means! What have you heard? Has anybody dared to slander me in my absence, and have you believed it?"

I had scarcely finished speaking before she sprang forth from the arbor, crying, "Charles! Charles!"

I had not heard the approaching step on the lawn, but close at hand arose a familiar masculine voice, "Why, what 's the matter, dear?" Looking out, I was petrified at beholding, three paces off, my Amanda (I still thought her mine) clinging to Charley Rand, who already had his arm about her waist. Nor did he relinquish his clasp when he lifted his head and saw me.

"Godfrey!" he exclaimed; "where did you drop from, all at once?"

He stretched out his hand, as if expecting me to come forward and take it. I stood motionless, striving to realize the fact of this double treachery. My tongue clove to my jaws, and I was unable to articulate a word.

"What has happened, Amanda?" he asked.

"Oh, Charles!" she murmured, tenderly, with her head on his shoulder, "Mr. Godfrey has *so* frightened me."

He laughed. "Never mind," he said; "you seem to have frightened him quite as badly."

Disengaging his arm, he now approached me. I involuntarily retreated a step, and my voice returned to me.

"Stand back, Rand!" I cried. "What are you doing here? What right have you to hold Miss Bratton in your arms?"

"Come, now, that 's a good joke!" said he, with an insolent air, — "Miss Bratton? Mrs. Rand, you mean! Mrs. Rand since two days. I thought, to be sure, you had come down on purpose to congratulate us."

I could not yet believe it. "Amanda!" I said, turning to her, and speaking with a voice which I hardly recognized as my own, "is it true? Are you married to that man?"

She stood up and looked me full in the face. There was not a quiver of her eyelids, nor a shade of deeper color on her pale, quiet face. "Certainly," she said.

"Good God!" I cried; "you could break your faith with me, without a word! This is your *truth!* This is your *patience!* You, whom I have so loved, for whose sake I have so labored! Rand, did *you* know that she and I were engaged — that she had given her heart to me — that she has been mine, in the sight of God, for more than a year past?"

I saw, while I was speaking, that his face was beginning to grow dark. Amanda must have noticed it also, and have instantly decided what course to take, for she confronted me without flinching, the settled calm of her face stiffening into a hard, cold, cruel mask, in which I saw her true nature expressed, — the mingled nature of the cat and the serpent, false, selfish, and venomous.

"It is a lie!" she exclaimed. "How dare you say such things? I never was engaged to you — I never told you that I loved you!"

"Amanda!" was all I could utter. But the helpless appeal of love, the bitter reproach, the hot indignation of an honest heart, which together found expression in that one word, were shattered against the icy visage of her treachery. She turned to Rand, with a tender, frightened air, saying, "Charles, make him go away: he is certainly crazy!"

"Come," said he, "we 've had quite enough of this, Godfrey! You were always a little vain, you know, and you must n't think that because a young lady behaves friendly, and admires your writings, and all that sort of thing, that she 's dead in love with you. I don't mind your prancing around in this way, so far as I 'm concerned, but I won't see my wife insulted."

I could have borne anything better than his flippant, patronizing tone; but, indeed, my back was not then strong enough to bear another feather's-weight of burden. It was not merely that the cherished bliss of my life was dashed to pieces in a moment: I was outraged, humiliated, wounded at all points. My conflicting feelings, all surging towards the same centre, possessed me wholly, body and brain, and I can no longer disentangle them, in memory. I was mad.

"Then see yourself insulted!" I shouted. My muscles acted of themselves, with wonderful rapidity. Rand received a blow in the face and tumbled over backwards upon the grass. His wife screamed and seemed to be making towards me, her quiet eyes lighted up horribly with a white, steely blaze. I remember turning away with a contemptuous laugh, stumbling down the lawn like a drunken man, with a dizzy humming in my ears, and finding my way, somehow, to a lonely nook under the willows, a short distance below the mill. There I sat down, and after sharp, convulsive pangs, as on that night at school when Penrose soothed me, the storm broke into tears. I covered my face with my hands and wept long and passionately. It was impossible to think, or to call to my help the least of the consolations which afterwards came. I could feel nothing but the deadly hurt of the wound.

All at once, as the violence of my passion was wearing itself out, I felt a hand gently pressing my shoulder. I need not have started, with a sudden, angry suspicion of further treachery: it was only Dan Yule. I took his hand, and tried to say something.

He sat down beside me, and patted my leg, with a kind familiarity. "Don't mind *me*," said he: "I guess I know what 's the matter, havin' had a suspicion of it from the first. I seen what was goin' on over t' the Squire's, and had a good mind to ha' writ to you about it, — but, thinks I, it a'n't none o' my business, and like as not she 's told him herself, and so I 'd better keep clear. But I did n't like it none the more. I 'd just got in a big saw-log this afternoon, when I seen you comin' down from the Squire's, and turnin' into the willers — seemed like as if you did n't exackly know where you was goin'. So I set Jim to shut off the water when the saw got to t' other end, and sneaked across to see what had become o' you."

Dan kept his eyes on the ground while he spoke, and mechanically went on patting my leg, as if both anxious to comfort me in some way and fearful lest his presence was embarrassing. I said something at last about my disappointment being so unexpected — something which he interpreted as an apology for my weakness.

"You need n't be ashamed on it," said he. "Lots o' fellows takes on that way, only a man does n't like to be seen. I s'pose people thinks it is n't jist manly, but there 's times when you can't help yourself. You don't mean that you had no idee she was married, till you come here and found it out?"

I thereupon told Dan the whole story, and in telling it, I saw the trick which Amanda had played with me and with her own conscience. It was true that she had never said, either when I declared my love, or afterwards in her letters, *in so many words*, that she loved me : but this discovery only made the actual lie more enormous. There was conscious, cold-blooded deception from the beginning: I was bound, but not she. I suppose she must have liked me, in her passive way; or I may have been the first fish that came into her net. Whatever her motive was, in allowing me to believe my love returned, her selfish calculation in the matter, from beginning to end, was now apparent. When I came to the closing scene of the wretched history, Dan became a little excited. Instead of patting my leg, he gave it a spanking slap, and swore, in a general way, without launching his words at anybody in particular. The blow I had administered to Rand put him in a good humor again.

"I dunno but I 'd ha' done it myself, in your place," he said. "Though it is n't likely that *he* was so much to blame, after all, if he did n't know nothin' about it before."

The thought had not occurred to me. I immediately recognized its justice, and began to feel ashamed of myself.

"Well, John," Dan continued, "I reckon, now, you 'll come over and stay with us to-night. Miss Lavina 's back again this summer, and she has your room; but Ike 's away, and you can put up for the night with me. Miss Lavina, I need n't mind tellin' *you*, is likely to stay with us. Sue 'll be married after harvest, and I 've kind o' prevailed on Lavina to take her place."

Dan looked so sheepish and happy that I understood him. I thanked him for all his past and present kindness, and congratulated him with fresh tears in my eyes, on the fortune which I never, never should know. I felt, nevertheless, that it was impossible to accept his invitation, — impossible for me, in my agitated state, to spend more time in Upper Samaria than would be required to get over the borders of the township. I told him this, and he seemed to understand it. He had lighted his pipe, and was leaning against one of the willows, comfortably smoking. As I arose from my seat on the log, some hard substance in my breast-pocket struck my arm.

"Dan," I said, "have you a match?"

"Yes. Have you learned to smoke, at last?"

I said nothing, but took the match he offered, and the green morocco, gilt-edged copy of "Leonora's Dream," on the fly-leaf of which I had written a sonnet, — O misery! — a sonnet full of the truest and the tenderest love, to the wife of Charley Rand! I doubled back the sumptuous covers, and turned the leaves from me, that I might not see one word of that mockery, which I, poor fool! had written with tears of joy dimming my eyes; then, striking fire with the match, I held it to the book.

"Gosh!" exclaimed Dan; "what 's that for?"

The flames soon devoured not only the manuscript but all the hundred and twenty pages of my immortal verse. Then I threw the glittering cover on the ground, and stamped on it with fiendish satisfaction. When it had been so bruised and disfigured that the title was illegible, I flung it down the bank into the stream.

I watched it as it drifted slowly along, past rotting snag and slimy grass, past oozy banks, and flats of rank skunk-cabbage, and felt that my own gilt-edged dreams were flung with it to as foul a fate. I had lost my love, and it left no consecration behind,—nothing but shame, and bitterness of heart, and contempt for what I had reverenced in myself as most holy!

CHAPTER XIX.

RELATING HOW I CAME INTO POSSESSION OF MY INHERITANCE.

An hour before sunset I found myself again on the ridge overlooking the valley. I was weak and tired, and as I leaned upon the fence after climbing the long ascent, I was conscious of the dismal change which had come upon the beautiful world of three hours before. I saw the same woods and hills, but the foliage had become hard and black, the fields dreary in their flat greenness, and the sky seemed to hold itself aloof in a cold divorce from the landscape to which it had so lately been softly wedded. Night, or storm, or winter, would have been less cheerless. An unutterable sense of loneliness filled my heart. I was still young enough to suppose that all emotions were eternal simply because they were emotions. I was sure that my love would never have faded or changed; now it was violently torn from me, leaving a pang in its place, to inherit its own enduring life. The world could give nothing to compensate me for this loss. Better would it be if I could die, and so escape the endless procession of dark, blighted, hopeless days. Then I saw, for the first time, and stood face to face with that Doubt which suspends us, trembling, over the abyss of nothingness. I asked that question which no human mind dare long entertain, — that question, the breath of which crumbles Good and Evil, Time, Faith, and Providence, making of life a terror and a despair. The outer crust of thought, upon which I had lived, gave way, and I looked shudderingly down into central deeps of darkness and of fire.

The struggle which my nature was undergoing will be better understood when its mixed character is considered. Either pure sorrow for a lost love, or vain yearning for a love which had been withheld, could have been comprehended by the heart, and therefore so grasped as to be best borne; but this — what was it? A tumult of love and hate, — for the habit of a year could not be unlearned in a moment, — disappointed hope, betrayed faith, devotion ignorantly given to heartless selfishness, a revelation of the baseness of human nature shed upon a boundless trust in its nobility! It assailed all my forms of faith at once, depriving me not only of love, but of the supports which might have helped me to bear its loss.

I knew that she, henceforth, would hate me. Even if some rudimentary hint of a conscience existed in her nature, and the remembrance of her deception were able to give it an occasional uneasiness, the blow I inflicted on her husband, before her eyes, more than cancelled the wrong. She would now justify herself to herself, as fully as to him. If the story were ever disclosed, both, of course, would be considered the aggrieved parties in the eyes of the world, and I the vain, adventurous miscreant.

I walked slowly and wearily back to Cardiff, keeping a good lookout for the vehicle of the elder Brattons, which I discerned far enough in advance to avoid successfully. The landlord by this time had found out who I was, and tortured me with stories about the marriage, which I had not tact enough to escape. It appeared, from what he said, that Squire Bratton, Mulford, and Rand's father, with some others, were concerned in a speculation for buying coal-lands, the profits whereupon were to be realized when a certain projected railroad had been built. Rand himself was believed to have a minor share in the enterprise; he was reckoned to be "a mighty smart business-man," and the Squire took to him from the start. He had frequently come down from Reading during the previous winter, but the match had not been talked about until a few weeks before it took place. They were going to Reading to live, the landlord said, and the old folks were quite set up about it.

I gave a melancholy groan of relief, when I at last found myself in bed, and surrounded by congenial darkness. I tried to compose my thoughts to my accustomed prayer, but the spectre I had invoked showed a blank where I had once seen the face of God. Men were nothing but accidental combinations of atoms, it said; Life was a temporary condition, and joy, sorrow, duty, love, were things of education, unreal and perishable; there was neither Virtue nor Vice but in imagination, — neither happiness nor misery, nor anything positive but physical sensation — and that only while it lasted. So far from shrinking from these suggestions, I took a fearful pleasure in following them to their common termination, on the brink of that gulf where all sentient existence melts into nothing, as smoke into air.

The next day I took the stage to Reading, performing the journey in the same hardened, apathetic mood. There was even, at times, a grim satisfaction in the thought that I was now free from every emotion which could attach me to my fellow-beings, — free from the duties of blood, the tender allegiance of love, the services of friendship. I saw nothing but selfishness in the world; I would be selfish too.

Reaching Reading in the evening, I took up my quarters at the "Mansion House." I was in no mood to claim my uncle's hospitality, although the grievance I had borne against him now seemed a very insignificant thing. I was neither afraid of him nor his efforts to procure me "a change of heart." Nearly two years had elapsed since that episode of my life, and I was beginning to see how much I had exaggerated its character. I had no dread of the approaching interview. Indeed, I so far relented towards Aunt Peggy as to take a copy of my volume for presentation to her.

When I went down Penn Street after breakfast, the next

morning, to the well-known corner, I saw that a change — which, nevertheless, did not surprise me — had occurred in the establishment. The old, weather-beaten sign had disappeared, and in its place was a new one, white ground and black letters, shaded with blue: "WOOLLEY AND HIMPEL'S GROCERY STORE." Bolty was not so stupid as his heavy face and sleepy eyes proclaimed. He had already made his nest, and would not be long in feathering it comfortably.

There he was, behind the counter, a little more brisk in his movements than formerly, and with every bit of his familiar loquacity. He was a trifle taller, and his white hair was brushed straight up from his forehead instead of being cut short. His thick, pale lips hung half-open, as usual, and his eyes expressed the same lazy innocence, but I fancied I could see the commencement of a cunning wrinkle at their corners. He wore a short jacket of grass-cloth, buttoned in front, which arrangement I admired, for I knew that the bosom of his shirt was not wont to be in a presentable condition.

As I appeared at the door, he recognized me at once. Catch him, indeed, forgetting any face he had ever known! I suspect he still retained a sort of phlegmatic liking for me, or at least was now satisfied that I could no longer interfere with his plans, for he slipped along the counter towards me with every appearance of cordiality, stretching out his fat hand as he cried, "Why, John Godfrey! Is that you now? And you 've come back to see us, after so long! I declare I did n't know what had become o' you; — but you 're lookin' well — *wery* well — better as ever I see you. — Yes, ma'am! The 'Peruvian Preventative,' did you say? You could n't take nothin' better; we sells cart-loads o' boxes — cart-loads, and the more people use 'em the more they wants 'em!"

He was off and waiting upon the customer, — a woman from the country, with very few front teeth and a sun-bonnet, — before I could say a word. I was so amused at this exhibition of his old habits, that, for the first time in two days, I felt the sensation of laughter creeping back to its accustomed nook. Presently the woman left, and, the store being now empty, Bolty returned to me.

"You was a little surprised, was n't you?" he asked, "to see my name over the door. It 's been up sence Easter, and we 're doin' wery well — wery well, indeed. 'T a'n't much of an int'rest I 've got, though, — only a quarter, but it 's a good beginnin'. The customers knows me, you see, and they stick to me. Mr. Woolley 's got a good deal of other business on his hands now."

"Yes," said I, "I have heard of it."

"Coal-lands? Yes; you 've heerd right. Not that I know much about it. He 's awful close, Mr. Woolley is, — keeps his own counsel, as he says, and Mulford and Rand's too, I guess. But what have *you* a-been carryin' on? You look mighty smart, so I guess it ha'n't been a bad spec."

I told Bolty as much in reference to my position in New York as I thought proper, and then asked for my uncle.

"He 's gone down to the canawl," said Bolty; "but he 'll be back as soon as the Banks is open."

"Then I 'll go in and see Aunt Peggy."

I entered the little back-parlor. The sofa and chairs were more shiny and slippery than ever, and a jagged abattis of horse-hair was beginning to project from the edges of the seats. There was no improvement in the atmosphere of the room since I had left; — nothing had been taken away, and nothing added except a mezzotint of the Rev. Mr. Mellowby, in a flat mahogany frame. My aunt was not there, but I heard noises in the kitchen, and went thither without further ceremony.

Aunt Peggy was bending over the stove, with a handkerchief around her head, an old calico apron over her dress, a pot-lid in one hand and a pewter spoon in the other.

"Well, Aunt Peggy," said I, "how do you do by this time?"

She was very much surprised, of course; but she transferred the spoon to the hand which held the pot-lid, and greeted me with a mixture of embarrassment and affection. A few tears certainly dropped from her eyes, but I knew how easily they came, and did not feel encouraged to make any great show of emotion.

"I 'm glad you 've come to see us, John," she said, in her most melancholy tone. "Walk into the settin'-room. I 'd like to hear that you don't bear malice against your relations, that meant to do for your good. It seemed hard, goin' away the way you did."

"Oh, Aunt Peggy, let bygones be bygones. I dare say you meant to do right, but it has turned out best as it is."

"I had mournin' enough," she said, "that things could n't have gone as me and your uncle wanted; but I s'pose we 've all got to have our trials and tribulations."

That was all we said about the matter. I was well dressed, and gave a most favorable account of my worldly prospects, and my aunt seemed considerably cheered and relieved. I suspect that her conscience had been tormented by the fear of her sister's son becoming a castaway, and that she had therefore been troubled with doubts in regard to the circumstances which drove me from her roof. My success removed that trouble, at least. Then I presented the book, in which I had turned down leaves to mark a few poems of a religious character, which I thought she might read with some satisfaction. Such things as "The Lament of Hero," I knew, would be quite unintelligible to her. She was greatly delighted with the present, promising to show it to Mr. Cutler, the new minister.

We were getting on very pleasantly together, when my uncle entered from the shop. As Bolty had apprised him of my arrival, his face expressed more curiosity than surprise. His greeting was cordial, but its cordiality did not strike me as being entirely natural. His hair had grown grayer, but there was no shade of difference in the varnished cheeks and the large tight mouth. Intercourse with his new associates had already given him a more worldly air. It was certain that neither his unworthiness nor his fortunate assurance of "grace" occupied his thoughts so much as formerly. Considering what had passed between us, I felt more at ease in his presence than I had anticipated.

"You look very well, John," said he. "I hope you have been at least successful in temporal things."

He could not deny himself this insinuation, but I was no longer sensitive on the point, and did not notice it. Of course, I represented my affairs to him in the most prosperous light, setting forth my promising chances for the future, while feeling in my heart their utter hollowness and vanity.

"Well, you 're settled at a business that seems to suit you," he said. "That 's a good thing. You 've gone your way and I 've gone mine, but there need not be any difficulty between us."

"No, Uncle Amos," I replied. "I have learned to take care of myself. The principal object of my visit is to relieve you from all further trouble on my account."

"In what way?" he asked.

"Why," I exclaimed, a little astonished, "don't you know that I am twenty-one?"

"Twenty-one! Oh — ah! Yes, I see. Are you sure of it? I did not think it was so soon."

Somehow, his words made an unpleasant impression upon me. I soon convinced him, by the mention of certain dates, that I knew my own age, and then added, "I am now entitled to my money, you know. If you put out last year's interest, there must have been more than eighteen hundred dollars due to me on the first of April."

"Yes," said he, "of course I put it out. But I really did n't suppose you would want the capital at once. I did n't — hm, well — make arrangements to have it ready at a moment's warning. You see, John, you should have notified me in the proper way beforehand. This, I may say, is not notifying me at all. Besides, why should you want the money now? What will you do with it? You surely would n't think of speculating in the stock-market; that 'd be throwing it to the four winds. If you put it in the savings-bank, you 'll only get five per cent. instead of six, as you get now. Why not let it be where it is? Use the interest if you want: I might advance you this year's, though it 's put out too, — but when you 've got your capital safe, keep it so."

"I wish to have my own money in my own hands," I answered, rather coldly. "I never supposed a notification would be necessary, as you knew I was entitled to receive the money as soon as I came of age. I consider myself capable of taking care of it, and even if I should lose it, that is altogether my own business."

"Oh, no doubt, no doubt," said my uncle. He rubbed his shiny cheek and stretched out his lower jaw, as if perplexed. "You are entitled to the money, that is all right enough, but — but it 's still *out*, and I don't see how I could get it, just now."

"At any rate, you can transfer the bond — or whatever it is — to me. That will be equivalent to the money, for the present."

Uncle Amos grew very red in the face, and was silent for a few minutes. His arm-chair seemed to be an uneasy seat. He looked at me once, but instantly turned his eyes away on encountering mine. At last he said, "I can't well do that, John, because it a'n't invested separately — it 's along with a good deal of my own. You see, it 's this way, — I 'll tell you all about it, and then I think you 'll be satisfied to leave things as they are. I 've gone into an operation with some other gentlemen, — we keep rather dark about it, and I don't want you to say anything, — and we 've bought up a big tract of land in Monroe County, among the mountains, where there 's sure to be coal. It a'n't worth much now, but when the railroad is opened, there 's no telling what we may n't sell out for. The road 's pretty sure to be put through in a year or two, and then the loss of interest in the mean time will be nothing in comparison to the profit we shall make by the operation. There are ten thousand acres in all, and I was put down for one thousand; but there were other expenses, surveyors, and we had to pay a geologist a big price to take a quiet look at the place; so I had n't enough of my own, without putting yours with it. I intend you shall go share and share with me in the profits. You may get six hundred, or six thousand per cent. instead of six. Don't you see how much better that will be for you?"

"No, I don't!" I cried. I was again thunderstruck, and the bitter tumult of my feelings began to rage anew. "I see only this, that you had no right to touch a cent of my money. It was put in your charge by my poor mother, to be returned to me when it should become due, not to be risked in some mad speculation of yours, about which I know nothing except that one infernal scoundrel at least is engaged in it! You to warn me against risking it in stocks, indeed! If you meant me to go share and share with you, why did you ask me to be satisfied with six per cent.?"

My uncle's eyes fell at these words. I saw my advantage, and felt a wicked delight in thus holding him at my mercy. His face looked clammy, and his chin dropped, giving a peculiarly cowed, helpless expression to his mouth. When he spoke, there was a tone in his voice which I had never before heard.

"I know, John," he said, "that you don't like me overly, and perhaps you won't believe what I say; but, indeed, I did mean to share the profits with you. I thought, only, if you 'd leave the money in my hands, I would n't say anything about the operation yet awhile. It 's done now, and can't be helped."

"Why not?" I asked. "You can borrow the money, on your house and store. Give me what belongs to me, and you may keep all the profits of your 'operation,' — if you ever get any!"

He looked around with an alarmed air, carefully closed the kitchen-door, and then, resuming his seat, bent forward and whispered, "I had to do that, as it was. I raised all I could — all the property would bear. It was 'most too much for me, and I could n't have turned the corner if I had n't sold out a quarter interest in the grocery to Bolty. I wish you could understand it as I do, — you 'd see that it 's a sure thing, perfectly sure."

It was enough for me that Bratton, Mulford, and the Rands were concerned in the business. That fact stamped it, in my mind, as a cheat and a swindle, and my uncle, it seemed, was no better than the others. I was fast hardening into an utter disbelief in human honesty. It was not so much the loss of the money which I felt, though even that had a sanctity about it as the double bequest of my dead father and mother, which I had hoped would bring me a blessing with its use. I had learned to earn my living, and knew that I should not suffer; but I was again the dupe of imposition, the innocent victim of outrage.

I was conscious of a strong bodily chill: the teeth chattered in my head. I rose from my seat, turned to him for the last time, and said, "Amos Woolley, you know that you have acted dishonestly, — that you have broken your trust, both to my mother and me. I thought once that you were trying sincerely to serve God in your own blind, bigoted way; but now I see that Mammon is your master. Get *you* a change of heart before you preach it to others. I will not prosecute and ruin you, by showing to the world your true character, though you seem to have cared little whether or not I was ruined by your act. If you should ever repent and become honest, you will restore me my inheritance; but, until you do it, I shall not call you 'uncle,' I shall not take your hand, I shall not enter your door!"

His chin dropped lower, and his eyes were fixed on me with a reproachful expression, as he listened to my sharp words. I put on my hat and turned towards the door. "John!" he cried, "you are wrong — you will one day be sorry for what you have said."

Aunt Peggy at that moment entered from the kitchen. "You 're not goin' away, John?" she said; "you 'll come back to dinner at twelve?"

"No, aunt," I answered; "I shall probably never come back again to see you. Good-bye!" And I picked up her hanging hand.

"What ails you? What has happened?"

"Ask your husband."

I went into the store, closing the door behind me. When I saw Bolty's face I felt sure that he had been eavesdropping. He did not seem surprised that I was going away, and I fancied there was something constrained and artificial in his parting, "Come back right soon, and see us again!" Perhaps I wronged him, but I was not in a mood to put the best construction upon anybody's acts or words.

I walked up Penn Street at a rapid rate, looking neither to the right nor left, and found myself, before I knew it, high up on the side of Penn's Mount, beyond and above the city. The walk had chased away the chill and stagnation of my blood. I was flushed and panting, and choosing a shady bank, I sat down and looked once more upon the broad, magnificent landscape. I was glad that my brain, at last, had become weary of thought — that I could behold the sparkle of the river and the vanishing blue of the mountains with no more touch of sentiment or feeling than the ox grazing beside me. I accepted my fortune with an apathy which, it seemed, nothing could ever break. If I could but live thus, I said, seeing men as so many black mites in the streets of yonder city, hearing only a confused hum of life, in which the individual voice of every passion is lost, and be content myself with the simple knowledge of my existence and the sensations which belong to it, I might still experience a certain amount of happiness.

CHAPTER XX.

IN WHICH I DINE WITH MR. CLARENDON AND MAKE THE ACQUAINTANCE OF MR. BRANDAGEE.

I WAS back again at my post before my stipulated leave of absence had expired. Mr. Clarendon was evidently surprised, but not disagreeably so, at my unexpected return, and, when I reported myself to him in his private office, asked me to take a seat, — a thing he had never done since my first interview. Beyond an occasional scolding, varied by a brief word of commendation, my intercourse with him had been very limited, but I had acquired a profound respect both for his character and his judgment.

After I was seated, he laid down his pen, pushed the long slips of paper to one side, and looked at me across the table.

"How old are you, Godfrey?" he asked, after a pause.

"Just twenty-one."

"So much the better. You have plenty of time yet to find out what you can do best. Or are you like most young men who can write a little, and suppose that you are capable of everything?"

"I never supposed that," I protested.

"I have looked through your book," he continued. [I had presented him with a copy soon after its publication.] "It is about like nine-tenths of the poetry that is published nowadays, — a good deal of genuine feeling and sentiment, but no art. Judging by the degree of literary cultivation in the public, — which I have had a fair opportunity of learning, — I should think it would be generally liked. But

I don't want you to be misled by this fact. You have a ready pen; your talents are quick and flexible, and, with proper schooling, you may become a useful and successful newspaper writer. But I don't think you will ever achieve distinction as a poet. Are you not very fond of reading Moore, Scott, and Mrs. Hemans?"

I assented, with a mixture of surprise and embarrassment. Mr. Clarendon's unfavorable opinion, however, affected me much less than it would have done a fortnight sooner.

"Let me advise you," he said, "to drop those authors for a while, and carefully read Wordsworth. I would not ask you to cease writing, for I know the request would be useless; and, except in the way of fostering a mistaken ambition, it can do you no harm. Your prose style will be none the worse from the greater compactness of thought and the richer vocabulary which poetry gives. Only," he added, with a smile, "pray keep the two in separate boxes. It is a great mistake to mix them as some writers do."

I assured Mr. Clarendon that I was by no means certain of my vocation; that the volume was an experiment, which seemed to me to be tolerably successful, but I did not suppose it finally settled the question. I was greatly obliged for his good opinion of my talents, and would read Wordsworth as he recommended. I was then about to withdraw from the room, but he detained me a moment longer.

"I am going to propose a change in your duties," he said. "You are now familiar with the composition of a newspaper, and can do better service, I think, in the City Department. It is not so mechanical as your former work, — requires quickness, correctness, and a sprightly style. You will be much out-of-doors, of course, and you may find it a little harassing at the start. But there will be an increase of salary, and you must expect to earn it."

I willingly accepted the proposal, for, to be candid, I was getting tired of the monotony of "condensing the miscellaneous." The increase of my salary to fifteen dollars a week was also welcome. My satisfaction in saving a portion of my earnings was gone, but a gloomier motive supplied its place. It was well to be independent of the selfish race of men, — to work out the proud and contemptuous liberty, which I proposed to myself as my sole future aim.

Mrs. Very welcomed me back with the *empressement* due to a member of her domestic circle. Mr. Mortimer shook hands with me as we went down to dinner, with an air which said, "I admit your equality;" and Mrs. Mortimer bent her neck some three quarters of an inch more than usual, as she allowed her tightly gloved hand to rest for a second in mine. Miss Dunlap being absent on a visit to her friends in the country, my seat fell next to Miss Tatting, who made loud and particular inquiries as to how I found my relatives, and was it a nice part of the country, and which way do you go to get there, and did the ladies come to New York to buy their trimmings, — all of which I could have well spared. Swansford, I could see, was truly happy to have me again as his vis-à-vis, and in spite of my determination to trust no human being, I could not help acknowledging that he really seemed to think himself my friend. When we had talked for an hour or two, in the attic, I was almost sure that he was, and that I was his. The numb, steady ache of my wounds was beginning to tire me; I longed to cry out, even though I were heard.

It was a still, sultry evening. We sat together at the window until the stars came out, and looked down on the felt partitions between the back-yards, and the mosquitoes began to rise from a neighboring rain-water cistern. Swansford had played to me his last composition, — something in the minor key, as usual, — and I felt the hardness and coldness of my mood give way.

"Come, old fellow," I said, "I am five dollars a week richer than I was. Let us go out and baptize the circumstance."

He was quite ready to join me. He had a pinched and hungry look; Mrs. Very's provender was not adapted to his delicate taste, and there were days when he scarcely ate enough to support life. We walked up the Bowery, arm in arm, crossed through Grand Street to Broadway, and finally descended into a glittering cellar under the Metropolitan Hotel. I had resolved to be as splendid as possible. It was not long before we were installed in a little room, as white and bright as paint and gas could make it, with dishes of soft-shell crabs and lettuce before us, and a bottle of champagne, in ice, on the floor.

I had a presentiment that I should tell Swansford everything, and I did. But it was not until the crabs and lettuce had disappeared, and an additional half-bottle found its way to the cooler. I had no fault to find with his sympathy. He echoed my bitterest denunciations of the treachery and selfishness of men, but would not quite admit the utter falsehood of women, nor, moreover, my claim to be considered the most wronged of human beings.

"What *can* be worse?" I cried, quite reckless whether or not my voice was heard in the neighboring stalls. "Can you tell me of any harder blow than that? I don't believe it!"

There were tears of outraged love in my eyes, and his seemed to be filling too. He shook his head mournfully, and said, "Yes, Godfrey, there is a worse fate than yours. Your contempt for her will soon heal your love: but think, now, if she were true, if she were all of womanly purity and sweetness that you ever dreamed her to be, if you *knew* that she could never love but yourself, — and then, if she were forced by her heartless family to marry another! Think what it would be to know her, day and night, given to *him*, — to still believe that her heart turned to you as yours to her, — to add endless pity and endless agony to the yearning of love!"

His hands were tightly clasped on the table before him,

and the tears were running down his thin cheeks as he spoke. I knew his story now, and my pity for his sufferings beguiled me into semi-forgetfulness of my own. I was unable to speak, but stretched out my hand and grasped his. Our palms met in a close, convulsive pressure, and we knew that we were thenceforth friends.

The next day I was both surprised and flattered on receiving an invitation to dine with Mr. Clarendon. Mr. Severn, who shared the honor, stated to me confidentially, "He would n't have done it, if he did n't look upon you as one of our stock workers." It was one of his *Wonder* dinners, as they were called, embracing only gentlemen connected in some way with the paper. He was in the habit of giving three or four every year, — a large anniversary dinner in the winter, and smaller ones at intervals of three months. Mr. Horrocks, the chief editor of the *Avenger*, gave similar entertainments to his subordinates, and there was a standing dispute between them and us of the *Wonder* as to which gentleman had the honor of originating the custom.

I dressed myself in my best to do fitting honor to the occasion, and punctually as the clock struck six rang the bell of Mr. Clarendon's door, on Washington Square. A mulatto gentleman, with a dress-coat rather finer than my own, ushered me into the drawing-room, which was empty. Mr. Clarendon, however, immediately made his appearance and received me with great heartiness of manner. He had entirely put off his official fixity of face and abruptness of speech, and I hardly knew him in his new character of the amiable, genial host.

"We shall have but few guests to-day," he said, "as my family leaves for Newport next week. Mrs. Clarendon and my niece will join us at dinner, and there will be another young lady, I believe. Mr. Brandagee and yourself are the only bachelors, and I must look to you to entertain them."

He smiled as he said this, and I felt that I ought to smile and say something polite in return; but the effort, I am afraid, must have resulted in a dismal grin. I was not in a condition to sit down and entertain a young lady with flippant and elegant nothings. However, there was already a rustling at the other end of the room, and three ladies advanced towards us. First, Mrs. Clarendon, a ripe, buxom blond of forty, in dark-blue silk, — altogether a cheery apparition. Then the niece, Miss Weldon, tall, slender, with a long face, high forehead, black eyes, and smooth, dark hair. She had the air of a daughter, which I presume she was, by adoption. Mr. Clarendon had but one child, a son, who was then at Harvard. Miss Weldon's friend, as I judged her to be, was a Miss Haworth (I think that was the name — I know it reminded me of Mary Chaworth), a quiet creature, with violet eyes, and light hair, rippled on the temples. Her face seemed singularly familiar to me, and yet I knew I had never seen her before. I mutely bowed to both the young ladies, and then turned to answer a remark of Mrs. Clarendon, inwardly rejoicing that she had saved me from them.

Mr. Severn presently entered, carrying his unhappy face even to the festive board. He had the air of being, as he perhaps was, permanently overworked, and was afflicted with the habit, which he exercised unconsciously, of frequently putting his hand on his side and heaving a deep sigh. Yet he was a shrewd, intelligent fellow, and, although usually a languid, hesitating talker, there were accidental moments when he flashed into respectable brilliancy. After the greetings were over, I was glad to see that he addressed himself to the niece, leaving Mrs. Clarendon to me.

It was a quarter past six, and Mr. Clarendon began to show signs of impatience. "Withering stays," said he to his wife; "as for Brandagee, I should not much wonder if he had forgotten all about it. He seems to have the run of a great many houses."

A violent ringing of the bell followed his words, and the two delinquents entered together. I already knew Mr. Withering, and felt grateful to him for his kindly notice of my volume, but he was not otherwise attractive to me. He was a man of thirty-six, with a prematurely dry, solemn air. He wore a full, dark-brown beard, and his thick hair was parted in the middle, so as to hide two curious knobs on his temples. I used to wonder what Miss Hitchcock would predict from those organs: I was sure there were no bumps of the kind on my own skull. Perhaps they represented the critical faculty, for Mr. Withering never wrote anything but notices of books. He read all the English reviews, and was quite a cyclopædia of certain kinds of information; but, somehow, a book, in passing through his alembic, seemed to exhale its finer aroma, to part with its succulent juices, and become more or less mummified. Names, at the sound of which I felt inclined to bow the knee, rattled from his tongue as dryly as salts and acids from a chemist's, and I never conversed with him without feeling that my imaginative barometer had fallen several degrees.

Mr. Brandagee was barely known to me by name. He was the author of several dashing musical articles, which had been published in the *Wonder*, during the opera season, and had created a temporary sensation. Since then he had assailed Mr. Bellows, the great tragedian, in several sketches characterized rather by wit and impertinence than profound dramatic criticism: but everybody read and enjoyed them none the less. He was said to be the scion of a rich and aristocratic family in New-Haven, had passed through college with high honors, and afterwards spent several years and a moderate fortune in rambling all over Europe and the East. He had now adopted journalism, it was reported, as an easy mode of making his tastes and his talents support him in such splendor as was still possible.

He made his salutations with a jolly self-possession — a

noisy, flashy glitter of sentences — which quite threw the rest of us into the shade. The ladies, I saw, were specially interested in making his acquaintance. When dinner was announced, he carried off Mrs. Clarendon, without waiting for the host's beckon or looking behind him. Mr. Withering followed with Miss Weldon, and then Mr. Clarendon offered his arm to Miss Haworth. Severn, pressing his side, and heaving profound sighs, brought up the rear with me. I hastened to take the unoccupied seat at Mrs. Clarendon's left hand, though it did not properly belong to me. The lady was too well-bred even to look her dissatisfaction, and Mr. Withering was thus interposed between me and the niece.

My share of the entertainment was easily performed. Mr. Brandagee, on the opposite side, monopolized the conversation from the start, and I had nothing to do but look and listen, in the intervals of the dinner. The man's face interested me profoundly. It was not handsome, it could hardly be called intellectual, it was very irregular: I could almost say that it was disagreeable, and yet, it was so mobile, it ran so rapidly through striking contrasts of expression, and was so informed with a restless, dazzling life, that I could not turn my eyes away from it. His forehead was sloping, narrowing rapidly from the temples down to the brows, his eyes dark-gray and deeply set, and his nose very long and straight, the nostrils cut back sharply on either side, like the barbs of an arrow. His upper lip was very short, and broken in from the line of his profile, as if he had been kicked there by a horse when a child. It was covered with a moustache no thicker than an eyebrow, — short, stubby hairs, that seemed to resist growth, and resembled, at a little distance, a coarse black powder. The under lip and chin, on the contrary, projected considerably, and the latter feature terminated in a goat-like tuft of hair. His cheeks were almost bare of beard. When he spoke slowly, his voice seemed to catch somewhere in the upper jaw and be diverted through his nose, but as he became lively and spirited in conversation, it grew clear and shrill. It was not an agreeable voice: the deep, mellow chest-notes were wanting.

The impression he made upon me was just the reverse of what I had felt on first meeting Penrose. The latter repelled me, in spite of the strong attraction of his beauty; but Mr. Brandagee repelled me in every feature, yet at the same time drew me towards him with a singular fascination. His language was bold, brilliant, full of startling paradoxes and unexpected grotesquenesses of fancy; withal, he was so agile and adroit of fence that it was almost impossible to pin him except by weapons similar to his own. It seemed to me that Mr. Clarendon at once admired and disliked him. The ladies, however, were evidently captivated by his brilliancy, and helped him to monopolize the attention of the table.

He had just completed a very witty and amusing description of Alexandre Dumas, and there was a lull in the talk, while a wonderful *mayonnaise* was brought upon the table, when Miss Weldon, bending around Mr. Withering, addressed him with, —

"Oh, Mr. Brandagee, did you ever hear Rubini?"

"I *did*," said he. "Not on the stage. I 'm hardly old enough for that, if you please. But when I was living in Turin, I called one evening on my old friend, Silvio Pellico, and found him dressed to go out. Now I knew that he lived like a hermit, — I had never seen him before in swallow-tails, — so I started back and said, '*cos' è?*' 'To Count Arrivamale's,' says he, 'and only for Rubini's sake.' 'Will Rubini be there?' I yelled; 'hold on a minute!' I took the first fiacre I could find, gave the fellow five *lire* extra, galloped home and jumped into my conventionalities, snatched up Silvio, and off we drove to Arrivamale's together. True enough, Rubini was there, old and well preserved, but he sang — and I heard him!"

"What did you think of his singing?" asked the delighted Miss Weldon.

"All *fioriture.* The voice was in rags and tatters, but the method was there. You know how Benedetti sings the *finale* of Lucia? — lifting up his fists and carrying the *sostenuto* the whole breadth of the stage; — well, Rubini would have kept it dancing up and down, and whirling round and round, like a juggler with four brass balls in the air. That was what he sang, and I shall never forget the *bell' alma innamora-ha-ha-hoo-hoo-hoo-hoo-ah-ha-ha-ta!*"

There was a general shout of laughter at this burlesque imitation of poor Rubini, which Mr. Brandagee gave in a cracked falsetto. There seemed to be no end to his accomplishments. After taking a fork-full of the *mayonnaise,* he turned to Mrs. Clarendon with an enthusiastic face, exclaiming, "Admirable! I congratulate you on your cook; or is Mr. Clarendon himself the author? It is a part of my *credo* that the composition of a salad requires a high order of intellect, as well as character, tact, and the instincts of a gentleman. Horace, Cervantes, and Shakspeare would have been good hands at it; St. Paul would have done it splendidly!"

In spite of what had gone before, I was startled and shocked at this, and I believe Mrs. Clarendon did not like the irreverence. But Mr. Brandagee rattled on without regarding her, — "It is n't modest in me to proclaim my own skill, but, then, nobody ever accused me of modesty. Modesty is an inconvenient article for gentlemen's use. I am prouder of my triumph at the *Trois Frères* than of anything else in my life. There were only three of us, — Paul de Kock and poor Alfred de Musset. When we came to the salad I saw their eyes sparkle; so much the better — I had planned a surprise. So I picked up the dish, turned it around, smelled it suspiciously, pulled it about a little with a fork, and then said to the *garçon,* '*otez ça!*' I wish you could have seen their faces; I am sure De Kock ground '*barbare!*' between his teeth. But I promised to give them a substitute, started them on their old, everlasting dispute about the battle of Zara, — one maintained that there had been such a battle, and the other that there had n't, — got the ingredients I wanted, and set to work. They were hard at it, throwing Barbarossa and Dandolo, and I don't know who else, across the table at each other's heads, when I put their plates before them and said, '*essayez!*' Each of them made a grimace, and took a little morsel with an air of suspicion. When they had fairly tasted it, they looked at each other for a full minute without saying a word. Then De Kock drew a long breath and cried out, '*incroyable!*' and De Musset answered, '*énorme!*' We shook hands all around, with tears in our eyes, and always *tutoyed* each other from that very night. Poor De Musset!"

After the ladies had withdrawn, cigars were brought on the table. Mr. Clarendon, I noticed, did not smoke, and I thought he seemed pleased that I followed his example. Mr. Severn and Mr. Withering puffed their cigars delicately and cautiously, and drew nearer to their chief, while Mr. Brandagee, blowing a great cloud, poured out a glass of claret and then pushed the decanter across to me.

"They are talking over *Wonder* matters," he said, taking Mrs. Clarendon's chair. "That is very fair Lafitte; try it. But I prefer Clos-Vougeot after dinner."

I took a glass of the wine rather than confess my ignorance of the proper thing, in the presence of such an authority.

"By the way," he asked, "are you the Mr. Godfrey who has just published a volume of poems? I read Withering's notice of it; I wish you would send me a copy."

I gratefully promised to comply.

"I think we all begin in that way. I published, in my senior year, 'Alcibiades at Syracuse;' — don't say you 've heard of it, because I know you have n't. I have not seen the thing for ten years, but I dare say it 's insufferable trash. Poetry does n't pay. Do you know there are not six poets in the world who could live on the profits of their verses ? "

" But it is not money alone," — I began, and then stopped, seeing the ends of his projecting under-lip curl around the ends of the short upper one, in a peculiar, mocking smile. I felt instantly how green and sentimental I must appear in his experienced eyes.

" I know all you were going to say," he remarked, noticing my silence. " I was tarred with the same brush, ages ago. It 's pretty well scrubbed out of me, but I recognize the smell. You believe in fame, in a sort of profane coming-down of the fiery tongues, don't you ? You 've been anointed, and shampooed, and brushed, and combed by some barber-Apollo, for an elegant ' mission,' have n't you ? And the unwashed and uncombed multitude will turn up their noses and scent you afar off, and say to each other, ' Let us stand aside that The Poet may pass ! ' "

I was too dazzled by the grotesque fancy of the image to feel much hurt by its irony. On the contrary, I was curious to know what a man, whose youth, he confessed, had known dreams similar to mine, now thought of Literature and of Life, after such a large experience of both. I therefore laughed, and said, " I don't expect any such recognition as that ; — but is it not better to have some faith in the work you undertake ? Could any one be a good poet who despised his mission, instead of believing in it ? "

" The greatest poet of this generation," he said, " is Heine, who is n't afraid to satirize himself, — who treats his poetic faculty very much as Swift treated Celia. The mission, and the anointing, and all that, are pleasant superstitions, I admit ; but one can't live in the world and hold on to them. The man who is n't afraid to look at the naked truth, under all this surface flummery, is the master. You believe, I suppose, that all men are naturally kind, and good, and honest, — that politicians are pure patriots, and clergymen are saints, and merchants never take advantage of each other's necessities, — that all married couples love each other, and all young lovers will be true till death" —

I could not bear this. My blood was up, and I interrupted him with a passionate earnestness which contrasted strangely with the cold-blooded, negligent cynicism of his manner.

"I am not quite such a fool as that," I said. "I believe that men, and women too, are naturally selfish and bad. I have no particular respect for them; and if I should desire fame, it would only be for the sake of making them respect me."

He looked at me more attentively than before, and I felt that his keen gray eyes were beginning to spy out my secret wound. I took another sip of the claret, in the hope of turning aside his scrutiny. This movement, also, he seemed to understand, but could not resist imitating it. He filled his glass, emptied it, and then turned to me with, —

"So, you would like to be respected by those for whom you have no respect. What satisfaction is there in that?"

"Not much, I know," I answered; "but if they honored me for saying what I feel to be true and good, I should think better of them."

"Ho, ho! *That*'s it, is it? Your logic is equal to the puzzle of Epimenides and the Cretans. You despise men; therefore they respect you; therefore you respect them. I should n't wonder if you had gone through the converse experience, to arrive at such a conclusion."

I was quite bewildered by his rapid, flashy sentences, and knew not how to reply. Besides, I saw how keenly he tracked my expressions back to their source in my life, and made a feeble effort to throw him off the scent.

"Then you don't think a literary reputation is worth having?" I said.

"By all means; it is positive capital, in a certain way.

It makes publishers indorse your promissory notes, opens the doors of theatres and opera-houses to you, supplies you with dinners without end, gives you the best rooms in hotels, — sometimes complimentary passes on steamboats and railways; in the words of the pious, smooths the asperities of this life, and does you no harm in the world beyond the grave. I should n't in the least object to those advantages. But if only the school-girls weep over my pages, and pencil the words 'sweet!' and 'beautiful!' on the margin, their tears and their remarks won't butter my bread. I 'd rather sit on velvet, like Reynolds the Great, propped up by forty-seven flash romances, than starve, like Burns, and have the pilgrims come to kneel on my bones. Fame 's a great humbug. 'Who hath it? — he that died o' Wednesday!'"

I was not prepared to disagree with him. His words gave direction to the reflux of my feelings from their warm, trusting outflow. I acknowledged the authority which his great knowledge of life conferred; and though his hard, mocking tone still affected me unpleasantly, I was desirous to hear more of views which might one day be my own.

"Then there is no use in having any ambition?" I remarked.

"*Cela dépend.* If a man feels the better for it, let him have it. Théophile Gautier used to say, there are but three divinities — Youth, Wealth, and Beauty. Substitute Health for Beauty, and I agree with him. I have no beauty; — I 'm as ugly as sin, but I don't find that it makes any difference, either with women or men. Give me health and wealth, and I 'll be as handsome as the Antinous. One must get old some day; but even then, what is given to youth can be bought for age. Hallo! the Lafitte is out. Stretch down your arm and get the other decanter. Severn won't miss it."

I did as he requested, and Mr. Clarendon, noticing the movement, got up and took a seat near me. "Brandagee," he said, "I hope you have not been putting any mischief into Godfrey's head."

"I have none to spare," he replied. "I am keeping it bottled up for my article on Mrs. Pudge in Ophelia. By-the-by, it 's nine o'clock. I must go down to Niblo's to see her once more in the mad scene. These are capital Figaros, Mr. Clarendon. I 'll take another, to give me a start on the article."

He took *six*, went into the drawing-room to take leave of the ladies, and departed.

"A brilliant fellow," said Mr. Clarendon, "but spoiled by over-praise when young, and indulgence abroad."

"He 's good company, though," said Severn.

As for myself, I found myself mentally repeating his words, on the way home. Youth, health, and wealth — was he not right? What else was there to be enjoyed, — at least for me?

CHAPTER XXI.

IN WHICH I ATTEND MRS. YORKTON'S RECEPTION.

A FEW days after the dinner, Mr. Brandagee, being in the *Wonder* office to read the proof of his article on Mrs. Pudge, came to my desk and entered into conversation. I had just completed my graphic description of the fall, death, and removal of an omnibus-horse on the slippery pavement of Broadway (an item afterwards copied in all the country papers), and had half an hour to spare, in the course of which time quite a pleasant familiarity was established between us. He had looked over my book, which he pronounced better than "Alcibiades at Syracuse," to the best of his recollection. As he was leaving, he said, —

"Do you go to Mrs. Yorkton's on Friday evening?"

"Mrs. Yorkton?"

"Yes — the poetess. Though she mostly writes under the signature of 'Adeliza Choate.'"

Was it possible? Adeliza Choate, — the rival of my boyish ambition, — the sister of my first poetic dreams! I had always imagined her as a lovely, dark-eyed girl, with willowy tresses and a lofty brow. And she was Mrs. Yorkton, — married, and giving receptions on Friday evenings! That fact seemed to bring her down to common earth, — to obscure the romantic nimbus in which my fancy had enveloped her form; yet I none the less experienced a violent desire to see her.

"Oh!" I exclaimed, "I have read her poems, but I do not know her personally. I should very much like to go."

"Nothing easier: I'll take you. Friday night, remember. She lives in Fourth Street, and you may as well call at the Smithsonian for me. Come early. I had a note from her this morning, and she wants me to be there by eight o'clock, to assist her in some deuce of a mysterious arrangement. She always gets up some sentimental claptrap or other — 'to start conversation in intellectual channels,' she says. You 'll find all the literary small fry on hand, — Smithers, Danforth, Clara Collady, and the like. You need n't dress particularly, — it 's quite Bohemian. Smithers always wears a scarlet cravat, and an old black velvet coat, with half the buttons off."

This information was rather attractive than otherwise. It denoted a proper scorn of conventionalities, which I had always looked upon as one of the attributes of genius. A side-door, at least, was now opened for me into the enchanted circle which I so longed to enter. The anticipation of the event diverted my mind from its gloomy apathy, and helped me along more swiftly through the weary days.

Fortunately, when the evening arrived, there was no moral, charitable, political, or religious meeting to report, — no pyrotechnic display or torch-light procession to describe, — and I could venture to be absent from the office until midnight, at which time I was obliged to revise the fires and accidents. Notwithstanding Mr. Brandagee's hint as to costume, I put on my evening dress, and sprinkled my handkerchief with jockey-club. Reaching the Smithsonian at half-past seven, I found my *chaperon* in his room on the third story, reading a volume of Balzac, with his feet on a chair and a mint-julep at his elbow.

"By Jove, I forgot!" he exclaimed, jumping up. "Damn Adeliza Choate and the whole tribe! I 'd ten thousand times rather go on with *La Peau de Chagrin.* But it won't do to have you get out of your bandbox for nothing, Godfrey. Whew! You have come from Araby the Blest, — will you let me 'pursue your triumph and partake your gale?' Adeliza will have a sonnet 'To J. G.' in the next 'Hesperian,' commencing, —

'On thine ambrosial locks my heart reclines.'"

But he changed his coat and brushed his black hair while talking, and we set out for the eastern part of Fourth Street. The Yorkton Mecca was a low and somewhat ancient brick house, with a green door and window-blinds. Heavy, badly smelling ailanthus-trees in front conveniently obscured the livery-stable and engine-house on the opposite side of the street, and as there happened to be no fires at the time, and no carriages in requisition, the place had a quiet, contemplative air. The bell was answered by a small mulatto-boy, whose white jacket and trousers were ornamented with broad red stripes down the arms and legs, giving him the air of a little yellow harlequin.

He grinned on seeing Mr. Brandagee, said, "She 's in the parlor," and threw open the door thereto.

Only one gas-burner was yet lighted, but, as the rooms were small, I could very well observe the light-blue figure which advanced to meet us. Heavens and earth! where was the lovely creature with dark eyes and willowy tresses? I saw, to my unutterable surprise, a woman of forty-five, tall, lean, with a multitude of puckers about her yellowish-gray eyes, and long thin lips. On her faded brown hair she wore a wreath of blue flowers. Her nose was aquiline, and her neck seemed to throw out strong roots in the direction of her shoulders. As I looked at the back of it, afterwards, I could not help thinking I saw a garland of forget-me-nots laid on the dry, mossy stump of a sapling.

"Faithful friend! Fidus Achates!" (which she pronounced *Akkatees*,) she exclaimed, holding out both hands to Brandagee. "You are just in time. Adonis," (this to the striped mulatto-boy,) "light the other burners!"

"You know you can always depend upon me, Adeliza," Brandagee replied, with a side-wink to me; "I consider myself as your *fidibus*. Let me present to you my friend, Mr. Godfrey, whose name is familiar to you, no doubt, as one of our dawning bards, — 'Leonora's Dream, and Other Poems.'"

"Is it possible? This is an unexpected acquisition to our circle of choice spirits. Mr. Godfrey! I am delighted to make your acquaintance. I have long known and admired your poetical self: we are fellow-Hesperians, you know."

Though I was so confounded by the reality of Adeliza's appearance, I could not help being flattered by the warmth of her reception. I glowed with gratified vanity, as I took her offered hand, and said I was very happy to meet Miss Choate, whose poems I had read with so much pleasure.

Brandagee burst into a laugh at my blunder, which I also perceived, the moment after it was uttered. Much embarrassed, I stammered some awkward words of apology.

Mrs. Yorkton, however, was rather pleased than offended.

"No apology is necessary, Mr. Godfrey," she said: "I am quite as accustomed to my poetic as to my prosaic name. I adopted the former when I first began to write, on account of the prejudice which The Herd manifests when a woman's hand dares to sweep the strings of the Delphic lyre. But the secret was soon discovered by those friends who knew my Inner Self, and they still like to address me by what they call my 'Parnassian name.'"

By this time the remaining burners had been lighted, and all the features of this bower of the Muses were revealed to view. The furniture was well-worn, and had apparently been picked up piece by piece, without regard to the general harmony. Over the front mantelpiece hung a portrait in crayons of the hostess, with a pen in her hand, and her eyes uplifted. On a small table between the windows stood a large plaster bust of Virgil, with a fresh wreath of periwinkle (plucked from the back-yard) upon its head. On the two centre-tables were laid volumes of poetry, and some annuals, bound in blue and scarlet cloth. The most remarkable feature of the room, however, was a series of four oblong black-boards, suspended like picture-frames on the walls, each one bordered with a garland of green leaves. Upon two of these there were sentences written with chalk; the other two were still empty.

"There, Mr. Brandagee!" she exclaimed, waving her thin arm with an air of triumph; "that is my idea for to-night. Don't you think it suggestive? Instead of pictures, a pregnant sentence on each of these dark tablets. It seems to symbolize Thought starting out in white light from the midnight of Ignorance. Words give mental pictures, you know, and I want to have these filled up by distinguished masters. Come, and I'll show you what I have done!"

She led the way to the farthest black-board, stationed herself before it, with Brandagee on one side and myself on the other, and resumed her explanation. "This *I* have written," she said, "not because I could not find any sentence adapted to the purpose, but because my friends seem to expect that I should always offer them some intellectual food. '*Congenial Spirits Move in Harmonious Orbits,*' — how do you like it? There must be a great deal of meaning compressed into a very few words, you know, — oracular, suggesting various things. Now, I want to have the same thought, or a kindred one, in other languages, on the other boards. The next, you see, is French, but I can't go any further without your help. What do you think of this?"

"'*Les beaux esprits se rencontrent,*'" read Brandagee. "Very appropriate, indeed! Not only abstractly true, but complimentary to your guests. And you want the same thing in other languages, — what languages?"

"One must be German, of course," said she. "Can't you remember something from Schiller, or Goeethy, or Rikter?"

"I have it! Give me the chalk. Your own Orphic utterance reproduced in the immortal words of Goethe! Did you know it?—the finest line in 'Faust';—what a singular coincidence of genius?"

Taking the chalk from the ready hand of the delighted Mrs. Yorkton, Brandagee wrote on the third black-board: "*Gleiches gesellt sich gern mit Gleichem!*" I understood the words, and was a little at a loss to account for his enthusiasm about them.

"Now for the last!" said he. "It must be Italian, Spanish, Swedish, or Dutch. I might take a line from Dante,—'*Lasciate ogni speranza,*' and so forth, but that would be too palpable to some of the *beaux esprits.* You want something more vague and mystical. Who is there,—Tegner, Calderon, Lope de Vega?—Calderon is best, and now I recall the very sentence for you. There it is, white on black: '*Cada oveja ha sin pareja.*'"

"It has a lovely sound," she murmured; "what is the meaning?"

"Something like this," he answered; "'No gentle creature is condemned to solitude,'"—but he afterwards whispered to me that the sentence actually read: "Every sheep has its fellow."

Mrs. Yorkton grasped his hands with gratitude, and twice made the circuit of the rooms to inspect, with radiant satisfaction, her suggestive mental pictures. Then, as Brandagee had flung himself into a chair, and was tossing over the leaves of the annuals, she invited me to take a seat beside her on the sofa.

"Tell me now, Mr. Godfrey," said she, "what is your usual process of composition? I don't mean the fine frenzy, because all poets must have *that,* of course; but *how* do you write, and when do you find the combination of influences most favorable? It is a subject which interests me greatly; my own temperament is so peculiar. Indeed, I have found no one upon whom the Inspiration seizes with such power. Does it visit you in the garish light of day, or only awake beneath the stars? Must you wear a loose dressing-gown, like Mr. Danforth, or is your Muse not impeded by the restraints of dress?"

I scarcely knew what answer to make to these questions. In fact, I began strongly to suspect that I was no poet. I had never supposed that any particular time or costume was required for the exercise of the faculty, — had never thought of instituting a series of observations upon myself, for the purpose of determining what conditions were most favorable.

"I am really unable to say," I answered. "I have always been in the habit of writing whenever I felt that I had a good subject, whether by day or night."

"How fortunate!" she exclaimed; "how I envy you! Your *physique* enables you to do it; but with *my* sensitive frame, it would be impossible. I feel the approach of Inspiration in every nerve; — my husband often tells me that he knows beforehand when I am going to write, my eyes shine so. Then I go up-stairs to my *study*, which is next to my bedroom. It always comes on about three o'clock in the afternoon, when the wind blows from the south. I change my dress, and put on a long white gown, which I wear at no other time, take off my stays, and let my hair down my back. Then I prance up and down the room as if I was possessed, and as the lines come to me I *dash* them on the black-board, one after another, and chant them in a loud voice. Sometimes I cover all four of the boards — both sides — before the Inspiration leaves me. The frail Body is overcome by the excitement of the Soul, and at night my husband often finds me lying on the floor in the middle of the room, panting — panting!"

She gave this information in so wild and excited a manner, flapping her hands up and down before her to illustrate the operation of prancing, hurling forth one arm, and making a convulsive, tremulous line in the air with her closed fingers when she came to dashing the words on the black-board, and panting so very literally at the close, that

I began to be alarmed lest the Inspiration was approaching. I looked at her head, and was reassured on finding that the forget-me-nots still crowned it, and that her hair was not coming down behind.

"I should think it must be very exhausting," I ventured to remark.

"Killing!" she exclaimed, with energy. "I am obliged to take restoratives and stimulants, after one of these visits. It would n't be safe for me to have a penknife in the room, — or a pair of scissors, — or a sharp paper-cutter, — while the frenzy is on me. I might injure myself before I knew it. But it would be a sweet, a fitting death. If it ever comes, Mr. Godfrey, you must write my thanatopsis!"

Here Brandagee, sitting at the table with his back to us, startled us by bursting into the most violent laughter. Mrs. Yorkton evidently did not find the interruption agreeable.

"What is the matter?" she asked, in a stiff voice.

"Oh," said he, "these things of Mrs. Mallard. I have just been turning over the 'Female Poets.' The editor has given her ten pages. I wonder what she paid him; there *must* have been an equivalent."

"Ten pages, indeed!" ejaculated Mrs. Yorkton, with bitterness, "and barely *three* for me! That is the way literature is encouraged. How anybody can find the traces of Inspiration in Mrs. Mallard's machinery — I won't call it poetry — I cannot comprehend. I am told, Mr. Brandagee, that she has become very spiteful, since my receptions have made a noise in the literary world."

"I don't doubt it. Detraction and Envy are the inevitable attendants of Genius. But the Eagle should not be annoyed at the hostile gyrations of the Vulture."

"What grand dashes of thought you strike out!" she cried, in an excess of delight and admiration. "That image would close a sonnet so finely. If it should return to my mind, hereafter, in some Inspired Moment, you will know whose hand planted the Seeds of Song."

"You don't know what a poet I am!" he said, in his mocking way. "If I dared to write. Dr. Brown-Sequard said to me one day, in Paris, when he was attending me for the rupture of a blood-vessel, caused by writing a poem on hearing a nightingale singing in Rue Nôtre Dame de Lorette, — said he, 'Brandagee, my boy, avoid these exaltations, if you don't want to bring up at Père la Chaise or Charenton. Your nature is over-balanced: you must drop the spiritual and cultivate the animal.' It was a hard sentence: but I wanted to live, and I was forced to obey."

He heaved a deep sigh, which was echoed, in all seriousness, by Mrs. Yorkton. I admired the amazing command of face and manner, which enabled him to perpetrate such barefaced irony, without exciting her suspicion. It was evident that she both believed and admired him.

The arrival of guests interrupted the conversation. Two gentlemen and a lady entered the room. I recognized Mr. Smithers at once, by the scarlet cravat and velvet coat; the others, as Mrs. Yorkton whispered before presenting me, were "appreciative sympathizers, not authors." The black-board answered their purpose by furnishing immediate subjects for talk, and I got on very well with the appreciative sympathizers. Presently Mr. Danforth arrived, escorting Clara Collady, and followed by Mr. Bluebit, a sculptor, and Mr. S. Mears, a painter. Brandagee persisted in calling the latter "Smears." I looked curiously at the gentleman who could only write in a loose dressing-gown, and found the peculiarity intelligible, supposing he usually went as tightly clad as at present. His coat was buttoned so that there were horizontal creases around the waist, and the seams were almost starting, and it seemed impossible for him to bend forward his head without having respiration suspended by his cravat. Whenever he nodded in conversation, his whole body, from the hips upward, shared the movement.

Clara Collady was a dumpy person of twenty-eight or

thirty, with a cheerful face and lively little black eyes. I sought an introduction to her, and soon found that we were mutually ignorant of each other's works. I was surprised to learn that her name was genuine and not "Parnassian." She was disposed to enjoy the society without criticizing its separate members, or suspecting any of them of the crime of overlooking her own literary importance.

"I like to come here," she said. "It rests and refreshes me, after a week in the school-room. Mrs. Yorkton is sometimes a little too anxious to show people off, which I think is unnecessary. They are always ready enough to do it without instigation. But it is very pleasant to say and do what you please, and I find that I generally learn something. I could n't aspire to the higher literary circles, you know."

Loud talking, near at hand, drew my attention. It was Smithers engaged in a discussion with S. Mears.

"Classical subjects are dead — obsolete — antediluvian!" cried the former. "Take the fireman, in his red flannel shirt, with the sleeves rolled up to his shoulders, — the clam-fisher, bare-legged on the sea-shore, — the wood-chopper, — the street-sweeper: where will you find anything more heroic?"

"Very good for *genre*," said S. Mears, "but you would n't call it High Art?"

"It 's the Highest, sir! Form and Action, in their grand primitive sublimity! That 's the mistake you painters make; you go on forever painting leather-faced Jeromes, and Magdalens with tallow bosoms, instead of turning to Life! Life 's the thing! A strong-backed 'long-shore-man, with his hairy and sunburnt arms, and the tobacco-juice in the corners of his mouth, is worth all your saints!"

"Very well," said S. Mears; "will you let me paint yourself, with vine-leaves in your hair, and only a bit of goat-skin around your loins? I 'll call it Silenus. You 'll have your 'Life,' and I 'll have my classic subject."

Mr. Smithers was evidently getting angry, and would have hotly retorted, but for the interposition of Mr. Bluebit, who took an arm of each and shook them good-humoredly, saying, "Congenial spirits move in harmonious orbits." Brandagee, also, had been attracted by the voices, and joined the group. The other three gentlemen, I noticed, treated him with a cautious deference, as if they had been pricked by his tongue and did not wish to repeat the sensation.

Other guests dropped in, by ones and twos, until the small apartments were well filled, and the various little centres of animated talk blended in an incessant and not very harmonious noise. Mrs. Yorkton seemed to consider me as an acquisition to her circle, — probably because it embraced more "appreciative sympathizers" than authors, — and insisted on presenting me to everybody, as "one of our dawning bards." The kindly cordiality with which I was received awoke my benumbed ambition, and cheated me into the belief that I had already achieved an enviable renown.

While I was talking to a very hirsute gentleman, — Mr. Ponder, who wrote short philosophical essays for "The Hesperian," — I heard a familiar female voice behind me. Turning around, I beheld the nose, the piercing Oriental eyes, and the narrow streak of a forehead of Miss Levi, whom I had not seen since Winch's reconciliation ball. She was dressed in a dark maroon-colored silk, and the word "Titianesque!" which I heard S. Mears address to his friend Bluebit, must have been spoken of her. Among so many new faces she impressed me like an old acquaintance, and I bowed familiarly as soon as I caught her eye. To my surprise, she returned the salutation with an uncertain air, in which there was but half-recognition.

"How have you been, since we met at Mr. Winch's?" I asked, taking a vacant seat beside her.

"Oh, very true! It was *there* we met: I remember

the song you sang. What a pity Mrs. Yorkton has no piano!"

I was too much disconcerted by the mistake to set her right; but Mrs. Yorkton, beholding us, bent down her forget-me-nots and whispered, "And you never told me, Miss Levi, that you knew Mr. Godfrey! Why did you not bring him into our circle before?"

Miss Levi cast a side-glance at me, recalled my personality, and answered, with perfect self-possession, "Oh, I think poets should find their way to each other by instinct. I can understand them, though I may not be of them. Besides, *he* is false and faithless. You know you are, Mr. Godfrey: you are like a bee, going from flower to flower."

"Which is worse, Miss Levi," I asked, — "the bee that visits many flowers, or the flower that entertains many bees?"

She spread her fan, covered the lower part of her face with it, and fixed me with her powerful eyes, while Mrs. Yorkton nodded her head and observed, "An admirable antithesis!"

"Now, Mr. Godfrey," Miss Levi resumed, removing her fan, "that is a spiteful remark, and you know it. You must repeat to me your last poem, before I can forgive you."

"Pray do!" cried Mrs. Yorkton, clasping her hands in entreaty. "Let *us* be the first to welcome it, before you cast it forth to the hollow echoes of the world. Mr. Danforth has promised to read to us the first act of his new tragedy, and your poem will be a lyrical prelude to the sterner recitation."

But I was steadfast in my refusal. I had written nothing since the publication of my volume, and how was I to utter to the ears of others the words of love which had become a mockery to my own heart? The controversy drew the eyes of others upon us, until Brandagee came to my rescue, by proclaiming his own lack of modesty, and demanding a test upon the spot.

"What shall it be?" he asked: "a recitation, a lyrical improvisation, or an extemporaneous dramatic soliloquy? There 's no difference between writing a thing for others to read, and speaking it for others to hear. Poetry is only a habit of the mind — a little practice makes it come as pat as prose. There was my friend, Von Struensee, the great composer, who took it into his head, when he was fifty years old, to write the librettos of his own operas. Never had attempted a line of poetry before; so he began by lifting the calf, and it was n't long before he could shoulder the ox. The first day he wrote two lines; the second, four; the third, eight; the fourth, sixteen; doubling every day until he could do eighteen hundred lines without stopping to take breath. Do you know that Sir Egerton Brydges wrote fourteen thousand sonnets, and I 've no doubt they were as good as Cardinal Bembo's, who took forty days to a single one. Give me an inspiring subject, — the present occasion, for instance, or an apostrophe to our talented hostess, — and I 'll turn out the lines faster than you can write them."

The proposal was hailed with acclamation, and the little interval which occurred in choosing a subject gave Brandagee time to collect his thoughts for the work.. He had skilfully suggested a theme, which, having been mentioned, could not well be overlooked, and, to Mrs. Yorkton's intense satisfaction, she became his inspiration. He rattled off with great rapidity a string of galloping lines, in which there was not much cohesion, but plenty of extravagant compliment and some wit. However, it passed as a marvellous performance, and was loudly applauded.

Other subjects were immediately suggested, considerably to Mr. Danforth's annoyance. This gentleman had been fidgeting about the room uneasily, with one hand in his pocket, occasionally drawing forth a roll of paper tied with red ribbon, and then thrusting it back again. Brandagee, perceiving the movement, said, —

"Do not run the Pierian fountain dry all at once, I beg of you. But, if Mr. Danforth will allow me, I will read the portion of his tragedy with which he intends to favor us. I flatter myself that I can do justice to his diction."

The proposal met with favor from all except the author. Thrusting the roll deeper into his pocket, and stiffening his head angrily, he protested that no one could or should read his own manuscript except himself. Besides, he had not positively promised that the company should hear it; the plot was not yet developed, and hence the situations would not be properly understood. It would be better, perhaps, if he waited until the completion of the second act.

"Wait until all five are finished!" said Mr. Smithers. "It is a bad plan to produce your torsos; I never knew of any good to come of it. Give me the complete figure, — bone, muscle, and drapery, and *then* I'll tell you what it is!"

Brandagee seconded Mr. Smithers's views so heartily that the postponement of the reading was soon accepted, as a matter of course, by the company. Mr. Danforth was consequently in a very ill humor for the rest of the evening. He would have gone home at once but that Clara Collady, whom he escorted, declared that she was very well pleased with the entertainment and was determined to remain.

Adonis now reappeared with a tray, and we were regaled with cups of weak tea, and cakes of peculiar texture. Under the influence of these stimulants, harmony was restored, and the orbits of the congenial spirits ceased to clash. The midnight reports of fires and accidents called me away soon afterwards, and I tore myself from Miss Levi's penetrating eyes, and Mrs. Yorkton's clutching hands, promising to return on successive Friday evenings. Brandagee left with me, satisfied, as he said, with having "choked off Danforth."

As I was leaving the room, I caught sight of a mild, diminutive gentleman, seated alone in the corner nearest the door. He was looking on and listening, with an air of modest enjoyment. None of the others seemed to notice him, and I suspected that he had been even forgotten by Adonis and the tea-tray. Catching my eye, he jumped up briskly, shook hands, and said, —

"Very much obliged to you for the call. Come again!"

It was Mr. Yorkton.

CHAPTER XXII.

IN WHICH I ENTER GENTEEL SOCIETY AND MEET MY RELATIVES.

WHEN the first bitterness of my humiliation and disappointment had subsided, and the conviction penetrated my mind that it might still be possible for me to take a moderate delight in life, I found that I had quite broken loose from my youthful moorings and was more or less adrift, both in faith and morals. I do not mean that I was guilty of actual violations of my early creed; my life was so far correct, through the negative virtue of habit; but I was in that baseless condition where a strong current — not much matter from what side it came — might have carried me far enough to settle the character of my future life. I have always considered it a special blessing that so much of my time was given to responsible and wearying labor in those days. I retained my position on the *Wonder*, because I had not sufficient energy to seek an easier situation, and no desire to try new associations. The variety of my work prevented steady thought, and I found less difficulty in escaping from the contemplation of my wrongs. Not yet, however, was I able to congratulate myself on the treachery which had released my heart from a mistaken bond.

I attended Mrs. Yorkton's receptions quite regularly for some weeks. As the steady summer heats came on, her bower was partly deserted, the artists and authors having gone into the rural districts and taken many of the "appreciative sympathizers" with them. Miss Levi departed, early in July, for "old Long Island's sea-girt shore" (as she remarked). I afterwards discovered that she meant Fire Island. It was at once a relief and a regret to me, when she left. I began to enjoy the sham skirmishes of sentiment in which we indulged, especially as there was no likelihood of either being damaged by the pastime; and, on the other hand, I was a little afraid of her bewildering glances, which seemed to increase in frequency and power of fascination every time we met.

Brandagee did not again attend. He left the city, soon after our acquaintance commenced, for a tour of the watering-places, and his sharp, saucy, brilliant letters from Newport and Saratoga took the place of his dramatic criticisms in the columns of the *Wonder*. I prevailed on Swansford to accompany me, on two occasions, and Mrs. Yorktown was very grateful. Music, she said, had not yet been represented in her society, and she was delighted to be able to present what she called "The Wedded Circle of the Arts," although certain that Mrs. Mallard would be furious when she should hear of it. The thinness of the attendance during the dog-days gave me an opportunity to cultivate Mr. Yorkton's acquaintance, and the modest little man soon began to manifest a strong attachment for me.

"Bless you, Mr. Godfrey!" he said, I don't know how many times, "I s'pose I'm of no consequence to you Genusses, but I *do* like to exchange a friendly word with a body. These is all distinguished people, and I'm proud to entertain 'em. It does credit to Her — I can see that. I'm told you can't find sich another Galaxy of Intellex, not in New-York. A man in *my* position has a right to be proud o' that."

Although he often referred to his position in the same humble manner, I never ascertained what it was. When I ventured to put forth a delicate reconnoissance, he looked at his wife, as if expecting a warning glance, and I then surmised that she had prohibited him from mentioning the subject.

I made but little progress in my literary career during this time. Not more than seventy-five copies of my book had been sold, and although the publisher did not seem to be at all surprised at this result, I confess I was. Nevertheless, when I read it again in my changed mood, sneering at myself for the under-current of love and tenderness which ran through it, — recalling the hopes with which I had written, and the visions of happiness it was to herald, — I found there was not left sufficient pride in my performance to justify me in feeling sensitive because it had failed. I contributed two or three stories to "The Hesperian," but early in the fall Mr. Jenks became bankrupt, and the magazine passed into other hands. My principal story was published the month this disaster occurred, and it has not been decided to this day, I believe, which party was responsible for the payment. All I understand of the matter is that the payment was never made.

My increased salary, nevertheless, suggested the propriety of living in a somewhat better style than Mrs. Very's domestic circle afforded. It was hard to part from my daily companionship with Swansford, but he generously admitted the necessity of the change in my case, and I faithfully promised that we should still see each other twice or thrice a week. It was more difficult to escape from Mrs. Very. "It 's an awful breaking up of the family," said she, "and I did n't think you 'd serve me so. I 've boarded you reasonable, though I say it. I may not be Fashionable," (giving a loud sniff at the word,) "but I 'm Respectable, and that 's more!"

At dinner, that day, she made the announcement of my departure in a pleasant voice and with a smiling face. But the constrained vexation broke out in her closing words, — "There 's some that stands by me faithful, and some that don't."

Mr. and Mrs. Mortimer expressed their regret in phrases which the Complete Letter-Writer could not have improved, while Miss Tatting, in whom Impulsiveness waged a continual war with Conventionality, came plumply forth with her real sentiments.

"I see how it is," said she; "you are getting up in the world, and Hester Street is too much out of the way. It 's natural in you, and I don't blame you a bit. I 've often said it would turn out so, — have n't I, Martha?"

This was to Miss Dunlap, who glanced at me with a stealthy look of reproach, as she murmured, "Yes, aunt."

I knew that I was a monster of ingratitude in Mrs. Very's eyes, a fortunate man in the Mortimers', and a proud one in those of Miss Tatting and her niece. My last dinner in Hester Street was therefore constrained and uncomfortable, and I made all haste to evacuate the familiar attic room. My new residence was the elegant boarding-house of Mrs. De Peyster, in Bleecker Street, west of Broadway. Here I paid six dollars a week for a fourth-story room back, furnished with decayed elegance, having a grate for winter, a mosquito-net for summer, and a small mahogany cabinet and bookcase for all seasons. The latter, in fact, was the lure which had fascinated me, on the day when Mrs. De Peyster, waiting in state in the parlor below, sent me up-stairs with the chambermaid to inspect the room.

When my effects had been transferred to these new quarters, and I had arranged my small stock of books on the shelves, placed my manuscript in the drawers of the cabinet, and seated myself with Wordsworth in an arm-chair at the open window, I seemed to be enveloped at once in an atmosphere of superior gentility. The backyards embraced in my view were not only more spacious than those under Swansford's window in Hester Street, but the board-partitions between them were painted, and a row of grape-arbors hid the lower stories of the opposite block. From one of the open windows below me arose the sound of a piano. It was not a favorable post for reading enthusiastic lines about celandines and daffodils, and I frankly admit that I found Wordsworth rather tame.

This was during the half hour before dinner. When the bell rang, I descended, not to the basement, but to the back-parlor, where Mrs. De Peyster introduced me to my neighbor at the foot of the table, Mr. Renwick, a clerk in an importing house down town. He was a younger, taller, and more elegant variety of the Mortimer type: correctness was his prominent characteristic. There was also a young married couple, a family consisting of father, mother, and two daughters, and four gentlemen of various ages, all bearing the same stamp of unimpeachable propriety. The dinner was a much more solemn affair than at Mrs. Very's. Thin morsels of fish succeeded the soup, and the conversation, commencing with the roast and vegetables, in a series of tentative skirmishes, only became fairly established towards the close of the meal.

Mr. Renwick, oblivious of my presence for the first ten minutes after the introduction, suddenly startled me by saying, —

"I see that Erie went up at the Second Board, to-day."

"Indeed?" I remarked, feeling that a slight expression of surprise would not be out of place; though what "Erie" was, and why it should go up at the Second Board, was a mystery to me.

"Yes. Five eighths," said he. Then, as if conscious that he had done his duty, he became silent again until the close of the dessert, when, warming up over a slice of watermelon, he observed, in a lower and more confidential tone, —

"I should n't wonder if the balance of Exchange were on our side before Christmas."

"What reasons have you for thinking so?" I asked at random.

"Crops. I always keep the run of *them*."

"They are very fine, I suppose," I ventured to say, with fear and trembling.

"You mean *here?* Yes. And I see that the prospects of Pork are flattering. Everything combines, you know."

I did n't know in the least, but of course I nodded and looked wise, and said I was glad to hear it. Of all talk I had ever heard, this seemed to me to be the most dreadfully soulless. I looked up the table and listened. The two girls were talking with the young wife about a wonderful poplin at Stewart's, — silver gray with green sprigs; the gentlemen were discussing the relative speed of Scalpel and Oriana, and the heavy mother was lamenting to the attentive Mrs. De Peyster that they had been obliged to leave Newport before the regatta came off, "on account of Mr. Yarrow's business, — the firm never can spare him for more than a month at a time."

How I longed for the transparent pretension of the table in Hester Street, constantly violating the rules of its own demonstrative gentility! For my easy chat with Swansford, for Miss Dunlap's faded sentiment, Miss Tatting's fearless impulsiveness, and even Mrs. Very's stiffly stereotyped phrases! There, the heavy primitive cooking was digested by the help of lively nothings of talk and the peristaltic stimulus of laughter: here, the respectably dressed viands, appearing in their conventional order of procession, were received with a stately formality which seemed to repel their attempts at assimilation. "Erie" and the "balance of exchange" mixed, somehow, with the vanilla-flavored *blanc mange*, and lay heavy on my stomach: the prospect of Mr. Renwick's neighborhood embarrassed and discouraged me, but I could not see that any advantage would be gained by changing my place at the table.

After dinner I hurried across to my old quarters, for the relief of Swansford's company. He laughed heartily at my description of the genteel society into which I was now introduced, and said, —

"Ah, Godfrey, you 'll find as I have done that Art spoils you for life. It is the old alternative of God or Mammon:

you can't serve two masters. Try it, if you like, but I see how it will end. I have made my choice, and will stick to it until I die: you think you have made yours, but you have not. You are getting further from Art every day,"

I resented this opinion rather warmly, because I felt a suspicion of its truth. I protested that nothing else but Literature was now left me to live for. It was true I had seemed to neglect it of late, but he, Swansford, knew the reason, and ought to be the last man to charge me with apostasy to my lofty intellectual aims. He half smiled, in his sweet, sad way, and gave me his hand.

"Forgive me, Godfrey," he said; "I did n't mean as much as you supposed. I was thinking of that single-hearted devotion to Art, of which few men are capable, and which, God knows, I should not wish you to possess, unless you were sure that you were destined to reach the highest place. Most authors and artists live in the border land, and make excursions from time to time over the frontier, but there are few indeed who build their dwellings on the side turned away from the world!"

"I understand you now, Swansford," I answered, "and you are right. I am not destined to be one of the highest; don't think that I ever imagined it. I am cast alone on the world. I have been cheated and outraged, as you know. I see Life before me, offering other — lower modes of enjoyment, I will not deny; but where else shall I turn for compensation? Suppose I should achieve fame as an author? I have a little already, and I feel that even the highest would not repay me for what I have lost. I shall not reject any other good the gods provide me. I 've tried purity and fidelity of heart, to no purpose. I don't say that I 'll try the opposite, now, but you could n't blame me if I did!"

"Come, Godfrey," said he, "I 've written a voluntary for the organist of St. Barnaby's. He paid me to-day, and

I have two dollars to spare. We 'll go out and have a little supper together."

Which we did, and in the course of which we put the World on its trial, heard all the arguments on either side, rendered (without leaving our seats) a verdict of "Guilty," and invoked the sentence which we were powerless to inflict. What should I have done without that safety-valve of Swansford's friendship?

By-and-by I grew more accustomed to my life in Bleecker Street. I found that Mr. Renwick could talk about Mrs. Pudge and the drama, as well as Erie and the Second Board; and that Mr. Blossom, the very same gentleman who had bet ten dollars on Scalpel at the Long Island races, was an enthusiastic admirer of Tennyson. He had a choice library of the English Poets in his room, and occasionally lent me volumes. I learned to read Wordsworth at my window, to the accompaniment of the fashionable redowa on the first-floor piano, and after many days there dawned upon my brain the conviction that there was another kind of poetry than Tom Moore's and Felicia Hemans's.

I grew tolerably skilful in the performance of my labor for the *Wonder*, having fallen into an unconscious imitation of Brandagee's smart, flashy style, which gave piquancy to my descriptions and reports. Mr. Clarendon was quite satisfied with my performance, though he let fall a word of warning. "This manner," he said, "is very well for your present department, but, if you want to advance, you must not let it corrupt you entirely."

Thus the summer and part of the autumn passed away, without bringing any occurrence worthy of being recorded. Towards the end of October, however, a sudden and most unexpected pleasure came to cheer me.

I had gone into the St. Nicholas Hotel on some errand connected with my newspaper labors, and was passing out again through the marble-paved lobby, when a gentleman suddenly arose from the row of loungers on the broad, carpet-covered stalls, and stepped before me. A glance of his dark, questioning eyes seemed to satisfy him; he seized my hand, and exclaimed, —

"John Godfrey, is this really you?"

Penrose! my cousin! I had not forgotten him, although our correspondence, after languishing for a few months, had died a natural death before I left Reading. For two years I had heard no word of him, and, since my bitter experience of the past summer, had reckoned it as one of the improbable possibilities of life that we should ever meet again. His boyish beauty had ripened into an equally noble manhood. He was taller and stronger limbed, without having lost any of his grace and symmetry. A soft, thick moustache hid the sharp, scornful curve of his upper lip, and threw a shade over the corners of his mouth, and the fitful, passionate spirit which once shot from his eyes had given place to a full, steady ray of power. As I looked at him, I felt proud that the same blood ran in our veins.

We sought out a vacant corner in the reading-room and sat down together. He looked once more into my eyes with an expression of honest affection, which warmed the embers of my school-boy feeling for him in an instant.

"We should not have lost sight of each other, John," he said. "It was more my fault than yours, I think; but I never forgot you. I could scarcely believe my eyes when we met, just now. Yours is a face that would change more than mine. There is not much of the boy left in it. Come, give me your history since you left Dr. Dymond's."

I complied, omitting the most important episode. Penrose heard the story with keen interest, interrupting me only with an ejaculation of "The old brute!" when I related my uncle's management of my inheritance.

"Now," said he, when I had finished, "you shall have my story. There is very little of it. I was twenty, you may remember, when I left the Doctor's school, and went into my uncle's office. I had no expectation of ever receiving any assistance from my father, and worked like a young fellow who has his fortune to make. I believe I showed some business capacity; at least my uncle thought so; and after I came of age my father found it prudent to make an outside show of reconciliation. Matilda insists that the Cook had a hand in it, but I prefer not to believe it. If she had, I rather think she was disappointed at the result; for, when my father died, a year ago, he only left her the legal third. The rest was divided between Matilda and myself. I 'm sure I expected to be cut off with a shilling, but it seems his sense of justice came back to him at the last. His fortune was much less than everybody supposed, — barely a hundred thousand — and I have my suspicions that the Cook laid away an extra share in her own name before his death. It makes no difference to me now; we are well rid of her. Matilda was married a month ago, and, though I can't say that I particularly admire the brother-in-law she has selected for me, I am satisfied that she is out of the hands of that woman."

"Are you living in New York, Alexander?" I asked.

"Not now; but I may fix my home here, very soon. I shall have another motive, old fellow, now that I know you are here. I have a chance of getting into a firm down town, if my little capital can be stretched to meet the sum demanded. I have luxurious tastes, — they are in the Hatzfeld blood, are they not? — and I could not be content to sit down at my age, with my two thousand a year. I suppose I shall marry some day, and then I must have ten thousand."

It did not surprise me to hear Penrose speak slightingly of a fortune which, to me, would have been a splendid competence. It belonged to his magnificent air, and any stranger could have seen that he would certainly acquire whatever his ambition might select as being necessary to his life. I never knew a man who, without genius, so impressed every one with a belief in his powers of commanding success.

As I stretched out my hand to say good-bye, he grasped me by the arm, and said, "You must see Matilda. She is in her private parlor, and I think Shanks, her husband, will be at home by this time."

I had no very strong desire to make the acquaintance of my other cousin, and I suppose Penrose must have read the fact in my face, for he remarked, as we were mounting the stairs, "Now I remember, there was something in one of Matilda's letters which was not very flattering to you. But I have told her of our friendship since, and I know that she will be really glad to see you. She has not a bad heart, when you once get down to it; though it seems to me, sometimes, to be as grown over with selfish habits and affectations as a ship's hull with barnacles."

When we entered the private parlor on the third floor, I perceived an elegant figure seated at the window.

"'Till," said Penrose, "come here and shake hands with our cousin, John Godfrey!"

"R-really?" she exclaimed, with as much surprise as was compatible with a high-bred air, and the next moment rustled superbly across the room.

"How do you do, cousin?" she said, giving me a jewelled hand. "*Are* you my cousin, Mr. Godfrey? Aleck explained it all to me once how you found out the relationship, somewhere in a wild glen, was n't it? It was quite romantic, I know, and I envied him at the time. You have the Hatzfeld eyes, certainly, like us. I 'm sure I 'm very glad to make your acquaintance."

I expressed my own gratification with as much show of sincerity as I could command. Matilda Shanks was a tall, fine-looking woman, though by no means so handsome as her brother. Her eyes and hair were dark, like his, but her face was longer, and some change in the setting of the features, almost too slight to be defined, substituted an expression of weakness for the strength of his. She must have been twenty-seven, but appeared to be two or three years older, — a result, probably, of the tutorship she had assumed on her step-mother's behalf.

"Well, 'Till," said Penrose, when we had seated ourselves in a triangular group, "do you find him presentable?"

Her eyes had already carefully gone over my person from head to foot. "*Très comme il faut*," she answered; "but I took your word for that, beforehand, Aleck."

"You must know, Godfrey, that Matilda is a perfect dragon in regard to dress, manners, and all the other requisites of social salvation. It 's a piece of good luck to pass muster with her, I assure you. I have not succeeded yet."

She was beginning to put in an affected disclaimer when Mr. Shanks entered the room. I saw his calibre at the first glance. The wide trousers, flapping around the thin legs; the light, loose coat, elegantly fitting at the shoulders and just touching its fronts on the narrow ground of a single button; the exquisite collar, the dainty gloves and patent-leather boots, and the gold-headed switch, all proclaimed the fashionable young gentleman, while the dull, lustreless stare of the eyes, the dark bands under them, and the listless, half-closed mouth, told as plainly of shallow brains and dissipated habits. He came dancing up to his wife, put one arm around her neck and kissed her.

She lifted up her hand and gave his imperial a little twitch, by way of returning the caress, and then said, "Edmund, my cousin, Mr. Godfrey."

"Ah!" exclaimed Edmund, hastily thrusting an eye-glass into his left eye and turning towards me. Retaining his hold of the switch with two fingers, he graciously presented me with the other two, as he drawled out, "Very happy, sir."

I was vexed at myself afterwards that I gave him my whole hand. I know of no form of vulgarity so offensive as this offering of a fractional salutation. None but a snob would ever be guilty of it.

A conversation about billiards and trotting-horses ensued, and I broke away in the midst of it, after promising to dine with the Shanks at an early day.

CHAPTER XXIII.

DESCRIBING MY INTERVIEW WITH MARY MALONEY.

One result of my out-door occupation was to make me familiar with all parts of the city. During the first year of my residence I had seen little else than Broadway, from the Battery to Union Square, Chatham Street, and the Bowery. I now discovered that there were many other regions, each possessing a distinct individuality and a separate city-life of its own. From noticing the external characteristics, I came gradually to study the peculiarities of the inhabitants, and thus obtained a knowledge which was not only of great advantage to me in a professional sense, but gave me an interest in men which counteracted, to some extent, the growing cynicism of my views. Often, when tired of reading and feeling no impulse to write, (the greatest portion of my literary energy being now expended on my regular duties,) I would pass an idle but not useless hour in wandering around the sepulchral seclusion of St. John's Park, with its obsolete gentility; or the solid plainness of East Broadway,—home of plodding and prosperous men of business; or the cosmopolitan rag-fair of Greenwich Street; or the seething lowest depth of the Five Points; the proud family aristocracy of Second, or the pretentious moneyed aristocracy of Fifth Avenue, — involuntarily contrasting and comparing these spheres of life, each of which retained its independent motion, while revolving in the same machine.

I will not trouble the reader with the speculations which these experiences suggested. They were sufficiently commonplace, I dare say, and have been uttered several millions of times, by young men of the same age; but I none the less thought them both original and profound, and considered myself a philosopher, in the loftiest sense of the word. I imagined that I comprehended the several natures of the rich and the poor, the learned and the ignorant, the righteous and the vicious, from such superficial observation, — not yet perceiving, through my own experience, the common flesh and spirit of all men.

One afternoon, as I was slowly returning towards my lodgings from a professional inspection of a new church in Sixth Avenue, I was struck by the figure of a woman, standing at the corner of Bleecker and Sullivan Streets. A woman of the laboring class, dressed in clean but faded calico, — leaning against the area-railing of the corner house, with a weak, helpless appeal expressing itself in her attitude. Her eyes were fixed upon me as I passed, with a steady, imploring gaze, which ran through me, like a palpable benumbing agency, laming my feet as they walked. Yet she said nothing, and could scarcely, I thought, be a beggar. I was well accustomed to the arts of the street-beggars, and usually steeled myself (though with an unconquerable sense of my own inhumanity) against their appeals. Now and then, however, I met with one whom I could not escape. There was a young fellow, for instance, with both his legs cut off at the thighs, who paddled his way around the Park by means of his hands. I had been told that he was in good circumstances, having received heavy damages from the Hudson River Railroad Company; but I could not stand the supplication of his eyes whenever we met, and was obliged either to turn my head away or lose two shillings. There was the same magnetism in this woman's eyes, and before I crossed the street, I felt myself impelled to turn and look at her again.

She came forward instantly as I did so, yet not so rapidly that I could not perceive the struggle of some powerful motive with her natural reluctancy. I stepped back to the sidewalk.

"Oh, sir!" said she, "perhaps you could help a poor woman."

I was suspicious of my own sympathy, and answered coldly, "I don't know. What is the matter with you?"

"It 's the rent," she said. "I can always airn my own livin' and *have* done it, and the rent too, all to this last quarter, when I 've been so ailin', and my boy gits no wages at all. If I don't pay it, I 'll be turned into the street to-morrow. I 'm no beggar: I niver thought to ha' beseeched anybody while my own two hands held out: but there it is, and here I am, and if it was n't for my boy I would n't care how soon the world 'd come to an end for me. The best things was pawned to pay the doctor, only my weddin'-ring I can't let go, for Hugh's sake. His blessed soul would n't be satisfied, if I was buried without *that* on my finger."

She was crying long before she finished speaking, turning the thin hoop of very pale gold with her other thumb and finger, and then clasping her hands hard together, as if with an instinctive fear that somebody might snatch it off. This action and her tears melted me entirely to pity.

"How much must you have?" I asked.

"It 's a whole quarter's rent — fifteen dollars. If that was paid, though I 'm a little wake yet, I could wurrk for the two of us. Could you help me to it any way?"

"Where do you live?"

"It 's jist by here — in Gooseberry Alley. And the Feenys will tell you it 's ivery word true I 've said. Andy, or his wife aither, was willin' enough to help me, but she has a baby not a week old, and they 've need of ivery penny."

She turned, with a quick, eager movement, and I followed, without any further question. Gooseberry Alley was but a few blocks distant. It was a close, dirty place, debouching on Sullivan Street, and barely wide enough for a single cart to be backed into. The houses were of brick, but had evidently been built all at once, and in such a cheap way that they seemed to be already tumbling down from a lack of cohesive material. A multitude of young children were playing with potato parings or stirring up the foul gutter in the centre of the alley with rotting cabbage-stalks. I remember thinking that Nature takes great pains to multiply the low types of our race, while she heedlessly lets the highest run out. A very disagreeable smell, which I cannot describe, but which may be found wherever the poor Irish congregate, filled the air. That alone was misery enough, to my thinking.

About half-way up the alley, the woman entered a house on the right-hand, saying, "It 's a poor place, sir, for the likes of you to come into, but you must see whether I spake the truth."

In the narrow passage the floor was so dirty and the walls so smutched and greasy that I shuddered and held the skirts of my coat close to my sides; but when we had mounted a steep flight of steps and entered the woman's own apartment, — a rear projection of the house, — there was a change for the better. The first room was a bedroom, bare and with the least possible furniture, but comfortably clean. Beyond this there was a smaller room, which seemed to be a combined kitchen and laundry, to judge from the few necessary implements. The woman dusted an unpainted wooden stool with her apron and gave it to me for a seat.

"My boy made it," said she; "the master let him do that much, but it 's little time he gits for such things."

She then entered into an explanation of her circumstances, from which I learned that her name was Mary Maloney; that she was a native of the North of Ireland, and had emigrated to America with her husband ten years before. They had had many ups and downs, even while the latter lived. I suspected, though she did not say it, that he was a reckless, improvident fellow, whose new independence had completed his ruin. After his death, she had supported herself mostly by washing, but succeeded in getting her boy, Hugh, admitted as an apprentice into a large upholstery establishment, and might have laid up a little in the Savings-Bank, if she had not been obliged to feed and lodge him for the first two years, only one of which was passed. Hugh was a good boy, she said, the picture of his father, and she thought he would be all the better for having a steady trade. After a while he would get wages, and be able to keep not only himself but her, too. Would I go into Feeny's — the front rooms on the same floor — and ask them to testify to her carackter?

I did not need any corroborative evidence of her story. The woman's honesty was apparent to me, in her simple, consistent words, in her homely, worn features and unshrinking eyes, and in the utter yet decent poverty of her dwelling. I determined to help her, — but there were scarcely five dollars in my pocket and fifteen were to be paid on the morrow. It was drawing near to Mrs. De Peyster's dinner-hour, and I recollected that on two or three occasions small collections for charitable purposes had been taken up at that lady's table. I therefore determined to state the case, and ask the assistance of the other boarders.

"I must go now," I said, "but will try to do something for you. Will you be here at seven o'clock this evening?"

"I niver go out o' th' evenin'," she answered, "and not often o' th' day. Hugh 'll be home at seven. If you could only lend me the money, sir, — I don't ask you to give it, — I 'd do some washin' for y'rself or y'r family, a little ivery wake, to pay ye back ag'in."

When we had reached a proper stage of the dinner, I mentioned the matter to Messrs. Renwick and Blossom, asking them whether they and the other gentlemen would be willing to contribute towards the sum required.

"You are satisfied that it is a case of real distress, and the money is actually needed?" asked the latter.

"I am quite sure of it."

"Then here are two dollars, to begin with. I think we can raise the whole amount." He took advantage of a lull in the conversation and repeated my statement to the company. After a few questions which I was able to answer, pocket-books were produced and note after note passed down the table to me. Upon counting them, I found the sum contributed to be nineteen dollars. I stated this fact, adding it was more than was required. Some one answered, "So much the better, — the woman will have four dollars to begin the next quarter with." The others acquiesced, and then resumed their former topics of conversation, satisfied that the matter was now settled. I was greatly delighted with this generous response to my appeal, and began to wonder whether the shallow, superficial interests with which my fellow-boarders seemed to be occupied, were not, after all, a mere matter of education. They had given, in a careless, indifferent way, it was true; but then, they had given and not withheld. I had no right to suppose that their sympathy for the poor widow was not as genuine as my own. I have learned, since then, that this noble trait of generosity belongs to the city of my adoption. With all their faults, its people are unstinted givers; and no appeal, supported by responsible authority, is ever made to them in vain.

When I returned to Gooseberry Alley in the evening, I found Mary Maloney waiting for me at the door, her face wild and pale in the dim street-light. When she saw me I suppose she read the coming relief in my face, for she began to tremble, retreating into the dirty, dark passage as she whispered, "Come up-stairs, will you, plase — my boy 's at home!"

An ironing-board was laid across two boxes in the kitchen, and Hugh, a short, stout lad of seventeen, was ironing a shirt upon it. His broad face, curly red hair, and thick neck were thoroughly Irish, but his features had already the Bowery expression, — swaggering, impudent, and good-humored. His bare arms, shining milk-white in the light of the single tallow-candle, showed the firmness and fulness of the growing muscle. The picture of his father — his mother had said. I did not doubt it; I saw already the signs of inherited appetites which only the strictest discipline could subdue. He stopped in his work, as we entered, looked at me, then at his mother, and something of her anxiety was reflected on his face. I even fancied that his color changed as he waited for one of us to speak.

In the interest with which I regarded him, I had almost forgotten my errand. There was a sudden burning smell, and an exclamation from Mrs. Maloney, —

"Hugh, my boy — look what y 're a-doin'! The shirt, — whativer shall I do if y 've burnt a hole in it?"

Hugh's hand, holding the iron, had rested, in his suspense, fortunately not upon the shirt, but the blanket under it, making a yellow, elliptical scorch. He flung down the iron before the little grate, and said, almost fiercely: —

"Why couldn't you tell me at once, mother!"

"I have the money, Mrs. Maloney," I answered for her, — "the fifteen dollars and a little more."

"I knowed you'd bring it!" she exclaimed; "what didn't I tell you, Hugh? I was afeared to be too shure, but somethin' told me I'd be helped. Bless God we'll see good times yit, though they've been so long a-comin'!"

The tears were running down her face, as she tried to say some words of thanks. Hugh's eyes were moist, too; he darted a single grateful glance at me, but said nothing, and presently, seating himself on the wooden stool, began to whistle "Garryowen." I delivered into Mrs. Maloney's hands the fifteen dollars, and then seven more (having added three, as my own contribution) for any additional necessities. I explained to her how the sum had been raised as a free and willing gift, not a loan to be repaid by painful savings from her scanty earnings. Then, beginning to look upon myself as a benefactor, I added some words of counsel which I might well have spared. With a more sensitive subject, I fancy they would have annulled any feeling of obligation towards me; but Mary Maloney was too sincerely grateful not to receive them humbly and respectfully. She begged to be allowed to take charge of my washing, which I agreed to give her on condition that I should pay the usual rates. Her intention, however, as I afterwards discovered, included the careful reparation of frayed linen, the replacement of buttons, and the darning of stockings; and in this way my virtue was its own reward.

I turned towards Hugh, in whom, also, I began to feel a protecting interest. After a little hesitancy, which mostly originated in his pride, he talked freely and quite intelligently about his trade. It was a large establishment, and they did work for a great many rich families. After another year, he would get five dollars a week, taking one season with another. He liked the place, although they gave him the roughest and heaviest jobs, he being stronger in the arms than any of the other boys. He could read and write a little, he said, — would like to have a chance to learn more, but there was ironing to do every night. He had to help his mother to keep her customers; it was n't a man's work, but he did n't mind that, at all, — it went a little ways towards paying for his keep.

Something in the isolated life and mutual dependence of this poor widow and son reminded me of my own boyish days. For the first time in many months I spoke of my mother, feeling sure that the humble understandings I addressed would yet appreciate all that I could relate. My heart was relieved and softened as I spoke of mother's self-denial, of her secret sufferings and her tragic death; and

Mary Maloney, though she only said "Dear, dear!" took, I was sure, every word into her heart. Hugh listened attentively, and the impudent, precocious expression of manhood vanished entirely from his face. When I had finished, and rose to leave, his mother said, —

"I must ha' felt that you was the son of a widow, this afternoon, when I set eyes on ye. Her blessed soul is satisfied with ye this night, and ye don't need my blessin', but you have it all the same. Hugh won't forgit ye, neither, will ye, Hugh?"

"I reckon not," Hugh answered, rather doggedly.

I had a better evidence of the fact, however, when Christmas came. He found his way to my room before I was dressed, and with an air half sheepish, half defiant, laid a package on the table, saying, —

"Mother says she sends you a Merry Christmas, and many of 'em. I 've brought an upholstery along for you. I made it myself."

I shook hands and thanked him, whereupon he said, "All right!" and retired. On opening the package, I found the "upholstery" to be a gigantic hemispherical pincushion of scarlet brocade, set in a gilt octagonal frame of equal massiveness. A number of new pins, rather crookedly forming the letters "J. G.," were already inserted in it. It was almost large enough for a footstool, and reminded me of Hugh's red head every time I looked at it but I devoutly gave it the place of honor on my toilet table.

It was the only Christmas gift I received that year.

CHAPTER XXIV.

A DINNER-PARTY AT DELMONICO'S.

I SAW very little of Penrose for some weeks after our first meeting. He was much occupied with his arrangements for entering the mercantile firm with the beginning of the coming year, and these arrangements obliged him to revisit Philadelphia in the mean time. Matilda — or, rather, Mr. Edmund Shanks — invited me to dine with them at the St. Nicholas, but pitched upon a day when my duties positively prevented my acceptance of the invitation. This was no cause of regret, for I was not drawn towards my cousin, and could not forgive the two fingers of her husband. For Penrose I retained much of the old attachment, but his nature was so different from mine that the innermost chamber of my heart remained closed at his approach. I doubted whether it ever would open.

One evening in December he called upon me in Bleecker Street. However I might reason against his haughtiness, his proud, disdainful air when he was absent, one smile from those superb lips, one gentler glance from those flashing eyes disarmed me. There was a delicate flattery, which I could not withstand, in the fact that this demigod (in a physical sense), with his air of conscious power, became human for me, — for me, alone, of all his acquaintances whom I knew, laid aside his mask. Nothing made me respect myself so much as the knowledge that he respected me.

"You have a very passable den, John," he remarked, darting a quick, keen glance around my room; "rather a contrast to our bed in Dr. Dymond's garret. How singularly things turn out, to be sure! Which of us would have suspected this that night when the Doctor made me share sheets with you? Yet, I had a notion then that you would be mixed up somehow with my life."

"You were very careful not to give me any hint of it," I answered, laughing.

"I was right. Even if you are sure that an impression is a prophetic instinct, not a mere whim, it is best to wait until it proves itself. Then you are safe, in either case. There is no such element of weakness as superfluous frankness. I don't mean that it would have done any harm, in our case, but when I deliberately give myself a rule I like to stick to it. Only one man in a hundred will suspect that you have an emotion when you don't express it. You are thus, without any trouble, master of the ninety-nine, and can meet the hundredth with your whole strength."

"Are you frank now?" I asked.

"John," said he, gravely, "don't, I beg of you, play at words with me. I will confess to you that I should become morally *blâsé* if I could not, once in a year or so, be utterly candid with somebody. I'm glad you give me the chance, and if I recommend my rule to you, don't turn it against me. You are not the innocent boy I knew in Honeybrook, —I can see that, plainly, —but you are an innocent man, compared with myself. I hope there will always be this difference between us."

"I can't promise that, Alexander," I said, "but I will promise that there shall be no other difference."

He took my hand, gave it a squeeze, and then, resuming his usual careless tone, said, "By the bye, I must not forget one part of my errand. Shanks is to give a little dinner at Delmonico's next Saturday, — ten or a dozen persons in all, — and he wants you to be one of the party. Now, don't look so blank; *I* want you to come. Matilda has been reading your book, and she has persuaded Shanks (who knows no more about poetry than he does about horses, though he buys both) that you are a great genius. You can bother him, and bring him to your feet in ten sentences, if you choose. The dinner will be something superb, — between ourselves, ten dollars *par couvert*, without the wine, — and I have private orders from Matilda not to accept your refusal, on any pretext."

I frankly told Penrose that I did not like Shanks, but would accept the invitation, if he insisted upon it, rather than appear ungracious. I stipulated, however, that we should have neighboring seats, if possible.

When the time arrived, I took an omnibus down Broadway, in no very festive humor. I anticipated a somewhat more solemn and stiff repetition of Mrs. De Peyster's board and its flat, flippant conversation. The servant conducted me to a private parlor on the second floor, where I found the host and most of the guests assembled. Matilda welcomed me very cordially as "Cousin Godfrey," and Shanks this time gave me his whole hand with an air of deference which I did not believe to be real. Knowing Matilda's critical exactness, I had taken special pains to comply with the utmost requirements of custom, in the matter of dress and manners, and if my demeanor was a little more stiff than usual, I am sure that was no disparagement in the eyes of the others. My apprenticeship at Mrs. De Peyster's table had done me good service; I could see by Penrose's eyes that I acquitted myself creditably.

The remaining guests arrived about the same time. We were presented to each other with becoming formality, and I made a mechanical effort to retain the names I heard, for that evening, at least. They were only important to me for the occasion, for I neither expected nor cared to see any of them again. I noticed that there were three ladies besides Matilda, but merely glanced at them indifferently until the name "Miss Haworth" arrested my attention. Then I recollected the violet eyes, the low white brow, and the rippling light-brown hair. Seeing a quick recognition in her face, I bowed and said, "I have already had the pleasure, I believe."

At these words, a gentleman standing near her, to whom I had not yet been introduced, turned and looked at me rather sharply. She must have noticed the movement, for she said to me, with (I thought) a slight embarrassment in her tone, "My brother, Mr. Floyd."

Mr. Floyd bowed stiffly, without offering me his hand. I was amazed to find that he could be the brother of Miss Haworth, — so different, not only in name but in feature. I looked at them both as I exchanged the usual commonplaces of an incipient acquaintance, and was more and more convinced that there could be no relationship between them. His face struck me as mean, cunning, and sensual; hers frank, pure, and noble. It was a different type of face from that of any woman I remembered, yet the strong impression of having once seen it before returned to my mind. I was surprised at myself for having paid so little attention to her when we first met in Mr. Clarendon's house.

Though her voice had that calm, even sweetness which I have always considered to be the most attractive quality in woman, it was not in the least like Amanda Bratton's. Hers would have sounded thin and hard after its full, melting, tremulous music. It belonged as naturally to the beauty of her lips as tint and pearly enamel to a sea-shell. Her quiet, unobtrusive air was allied to a self-possession almost beyond her years, — for she could not have been more than twenty. Though richly and fashionably dressed, she had chosen soft, neutral colors, without a glitter or sparkle, except from the sapphires in her ears and at her throat. I was not yet competent to feel a very enthusiastic admiration, but I was conscious that the sight of her filled me with a pleasant sense of comfort and repose.

"Isabel," said Mrs. Shanks, tapping Miss Haworth's shoulder with her fan, "*on a servi*. Will you take Mr. Godfrey's arm?"

I bowed and crooked my elbow, and we followed the other ladies into the adjoining room. The touch of the gloved hand affected me singularly; I know not what soft, happy warmth diffused itself through my frame from that slight point of contact. The magnetism of physical nearness never before affected me so delicately yet so powerfully.

Matilda seated the guests according to her own will, and with her usual tact. Her brother's future partners were her own supporters, while Shanks was flanked by their wives. Miss Haworth was assigned to the central seat on one side of the oval table, between Penrose and myself, with Mr. Floyd and two other young fashionables facing us. The table was resplendent with cut-glass and silver, and fragrant with gorgeous piles of tropical flowers and fruit, the room dazzling with the white lustre of gas, and the accomplished French servants glided to and fro with stealthy elegance. The devil of Luxury within me chuckled and clapped his hands with delight. If Life would furnish me with more such dinners, I thought, I might find it tolerably sunny.

The dinner was a masterpiece of art. Both the natural harmonies and the conventional stipulations were respected. We had oysters and Chablis, turtle-soup succeeded by glasses of iced punch, fish and sherry, and Rüdesheimer, Clicquot, Burgundy, Lafitte, and *liqueurs* in their proper succession, accompanying the wondrous alternation of courses. Hitherto, I had been rather omniverous in my tastes, — only preferring good things to bad, — but now I perceived that even the material profession of cooking had its artistic ideal.

The conversation, as was meet, ran mostly upon the dishes which were placed before us. Mr. Shanks developed an immense amount of knowledge in this direction, affirming that he had given special directions for a single clove of garlic to be laid for five minutes on a plate with certain *cotelettes en papillotes*, under a glass cover; that the canvas-back ducks should be merely *carried through* a hot kitchen, which was cooking enough for them; and that the *riz de veau* would have been ruined if he had not procured, with great difficulty, a particular kind of pea which only grew in the neighborhood of Arras. The Lafitte, he said, was "the '34, — from the lower part of the hill; Delmonico won't acknowledge that he has it, unless you happen to know, and even then it 's a great favor to get a few bottles."

"Many persons can't tell the '34 from the '46," said one of the partners, setting the rim of his glass under his nostrils and sniffing repeatedly; "but you notice the difference in the *bouquet*."

It really seemed to me that this voluptuous discussion of the viands as they appeared, — this preliminary tasting, this lingering enjoyment of the rare and peculiar qualities, this prelusive aroma of the vine, tempering yet fixing its flavor, — constituted an æsthetic accompaniment which balanced the physical task of the meal and called upon the brain to assist the stomach. I drank but sparingly of the wines, however, being warned by the growing flush on the faces of the three young gentlemen opposite, and restrained by the sweet, sober freshness of Miss Haworth's cheek, at my side.

As the conversation grew riotous in tone, and laughter and repartee (mostly of a stupid character, but answering the purpose as well as the genuine article) ruled the table, my gentle neighbor seemed to encourage my attempts to withdraw from the noisy circle of talk and establish a quiet *tête à tête* between our two selves. Penrose was occupied with one of his partners and Matilda with the other; Mr. Floyd was relating the last piece of scandal, with the corrections and additions of his neighbors, and each and all so absorbed in their several subjects that we were left in comparative privacy.

"Have you long known my cousin, Mrs. Shanks?" I asked.

"Only familiarly since last summer, when we were at Long Branch together. We had met before, in society, once or twice, but one never makes acquaintances in that way."

"Do you think we can ever say that we are truly acquainted with any one?" said I.

"Why not?" she asked, after a look in which I read a little surprise at the question.

I felt that my words had been thrown to the surface from a hidden movement of dislike to the society present, which lurked at the bottom of my mind. They shot away so suddenly and widely from my first question that some explanation was necessary; yet I could not give the true one. She waited for my answer, and I was compelled to a partial candor.

"I believe," I said, "that the word 'acquainted' put the question into my head. I have been obliged to reverse my first impressions so often that it seems better not to trust them. And I have really wondered whether men can truly know each other."

"Perhaps nearly as well as they can know themselves," said she. "When I see some little vanity, which is plain to every one except its possessor, I fancy that the same thing may very easily be true of myself."

"You, Miss Haworth!" I exclaimed.

"I as well as another. You do not suppose that I consider myself to be without faults."

"No, of course not," I answered, so plumply and earnestly that she smiled, looking very much amused. But the fact is, I had made a personal application of her first remark, and answered for myself rather than for her. Perceiving this, I could not help smiling in turn.

"I confess," I said, "that I have mine, but I try to conceal them from others."

"And you would be very angry if they were detected?"

"Yes, I think I would."

"Yet all your friends may know them, nevertheless," said she, "and keep silent towards you as you towards them. Do you think universal candor would be any better? For my part, I fancy it would soon set us all together by the ears."

"Just what I told you, John," said Penrose, striking in from the other side. "Candor is weakness."

"I begin to think so, too," I remarked gloomily. "Deceit seems to be the rule of the world; I find it wherever I turn. If the outside of the sepulchre shows the conventional whitewash, it makes no difference how many skeletons are inside."

I took up a little glass toy which stood before me, filled, apparently, with green oil. It slid down my throat like a fiery, perfumed snake.

"Penrose!" cried Mr. Floyd, "is that the Chartreuse before you?"

"No," said the former, turning the bottle, "it 's Curaçoa."

"Ah, that reminds me," — cried Mr. Shanks, commencing a fresh story, which I did not care to hear. The old feeling of sadness and depression began to steal over me, and the loud gayety of the table became more hollow and distasteful than ever.

"Mr. Godfrey," said Miss Haworth, a little timidly.

I looked up. Her clear violet eyes were fixed upon me with a disturbed expression, and there may have been, for a second, a warmer tinge on her cheek, as she addressed me, —

"I am afraid you misunderstood me. I think a candid nature is the highest and best. I only meant that there is no use in constantly reminding our friends, or they us, of little human weaknesses. We may be candid, certainly, without ceasing to be charitable."

"Yes, we *may* be," I said, "but who *is?* Where is there a nature which may be relied upon, first and forever? I once thought the world was full of such, but I am cured of my folly."

The trouble in her eyes deepened. "I am sorry to hear you say so," she said, in a low voice, and began mechanically pulling to pieces a bunch of grapes.

My bitter mood died in an instant. I felt that my words were not only false in themselves, but false as the utterance of my belief. There were, there must be, truth and honor in men and women; I was true, and was there no other virtue in the world than mine? I could have bitten my tongue for vexation. To retract my expressions on the spot, — and I now perceived how positively they had been made, — would prove me to be a whimsical fool, and Miss Haworth must continue to believe me the negatist I seemed. In vain I tried to console myself with the thought that it made no difference. A deeper instinct told me that it *did*, — that the opinion of a pure-hearted girl was not a thing to be lightly esteemed. I had flattered myself on the social tact I had acquired, but my first serious conversation told me what a bungler I still was, in allowing the egotism of a private disappointment to betray itself and misrepresent my nature to another.

While these thoughts flashed through my mind, Penrose had commenced a conversation with Miss Haworth. Glancing around the table, I encountered Matilda's dark eyes. "Cousin Godfrey!" she called to me, "how do you vote? — shall we stay or go? Edmund always sits with his head in a cloud, at home, and very often Aleck with him; so I think if we open the door and let down the windows, the atmosphere will be endurable, — only you gentlemen generally prefer to banish us. I don't believe it's any good that you say or do when you get rid of us."

"Stay," said I. "There will be no cloud from my lips. Why should you not keep your seats, and let the gentlemen withdraw, if there must be a division?"

"Gallantly spoken, cousin. But I see that Edmund has the consent of his neighbors, and is puffing to make up for lost time. I congratulate you on your wives, gentlemen: I thought I was the only veteran present. Isabel! they are not driving you away, I hope?"

"Oh, no!" said Miss Haworth, who had risen from her seat; "but father is home from the Club by this time, and he always likes to have a little music before going to bed. Tracy, will you please see if the carriage is waiting?"

Mr. Floyd put his head out of the window and called, "James!" "Here, sir!" came up from the street, and Miss Haworth, giving a hand to Matilda and her husband, and leaving a pleasant "Good-night!" for the rest of us, collectively, glided from the room. Mr. Shanks escorted her to her carriage.

This little interruption was employed by the company as an opportunity to change their places at the table. A sign from Matilda called me to an empty chair beside her.

"I 'm so glad you 're a poet, Cousin Godfrey," she said, — "the first in our family; and I assure you we have need of the distinction to balance the *mésalliance,* — you know all about it from Aleck, though you 're not near enough related to be hurt by it as we were. I think we shall come to New York to live: Edmund prefers it, and one gets tired of Philadelphia in the long run. We have plenty of style there, to be sure; but our set is very much the same from year to year. Here, it may be a little too free, too — *qu' est ce que c' est?* easy of entrance, — but there 's a deal more life and variety. Don't you think so? but, of course, you gentlemen are never so particular. Society would fall into ruin, if it was n't for *us.*"

"It 's very well you save society, for you ruin individuals," I remarked.

"Hear that, Aleck!" she exclaimed; "I did n't think it was in him. You have certainly been giving him lessons in your own infidelity. He will spoil you, Cousin Godfrey,"

Penrose looked at me and laughed. "I 'm glad you are a match for 'Till, John," he said. "If I 've taught you, the pupil surpasses the teacher."

Much more of this badinage followed. My apprenticeship to words and phrases gave me an advantage in the use of it, and I was reckless enough to care little what I said, so that my words had some point and brilliancy. Penrose was more than a match for me, but he considerately held back and allowed me to triumph over the others. It was as he predicted; I brought Mr. Edmund Shanks to my feet in ten sentences. He called me "Cousin Godfrey," and said, repeatedly, in a somewhat thick voice, "If you only smoked, you would be a trump."

"He 'll come to that after a while; he can't have all the virtues at once," remarked Mr. Floyd. I liked neither the tone nor the look of the man: a sneer seemed to lurk under his light, laughing air. He was one of the two or three who had lighted their cigars, and substituted brandy and ice for the soft, fragrant wines of Bordeaux. A sharp retort rose to my tongue, but I held it back from an instinct which told me that he would welcome an antagonism *I* had authorized.

It was near midnight when the guests separated, and as we descended in a body to the street, we found the three coachmen asleep on their boxes.

"Are you not going to get in, Aleck?" said Matilda, as Penrose slammed the door.

"No; I am going to walk with Godfrey. Good-night!"

Mr. Floyd joined us, smoking his cigar, humming opera-tunes and commenting freely upon the company, as we walked up Broadway. When we reached the corner of Howard Street, he muttered something about an engagement, and turned off to the left.

Penrose laughed as he gave utterance to certain surmises, in what seemed to me a very cold-blooded manner. He took my arm as he added: "I don't know that Floyd is any worse than most of the young New Yorkers; but he 's rather a bore to me, and I 'm glad to get rid of him. I see so much of the class that I grow tired of it, — yet I suppose I belong to it myself."

"Not in character, Alexander!" I protested: "you have talent, and pride, and principle!"

"None too much of either, unless it be pride," he said. "Take care you don't overrate me. I can be intensely selfish, and you may discover the fact, some day. Whatever I demand with all the force of my nature I must have, and will trample down anything and anybody that comes between. You have only seen the mother's blood in me, John. There is a good deal of my father's, and it is bad."

I saw the dark knitting of his brows in the lamplight, and strove to turn aside the gloomy introversion of his mood. "How is it," I asked, "that this Floyd is a brother of Miss Haworth?"

"Step-brother, by marriage," he answered. "He is in reality no relation. Old Floyd was a widower with one son when he married the widow Haworth, — some ten years ago, I believe: Matilda knows all about it, — and the boy and girl called themselves brother and sister. The old man has a stylish house on Gramercy Park, but he 's an inveterate stock-jobber, and has failed twice in the last five years. I suspect she keeps up the establishment."

"How?"

"She 's an heiress. Two thirds of her father's property were settled on her, — some hundreds of thousands, I 've been told. No wonder Floyd would like to marry her."

"He? Is it possible?" I exclaimed.

"That 's the gossip; and it *is* possible. He is no relation, as I have said, but I fancy she has a mind of her own. She seems to be a nice, sensible girl. What do you think? You saw much more of her than I did."

"Sensible, — yes," said I, slowly, for I had in fact not

decided what I thought of her, — "so far as I could judge; and almost beautiful. But her face puzzles me: I seem to have seen it already, yet —— "

Penrose interrupted me. "I know what you mean. I saw it, also, and was bothered for two minutes. The engraving of St. Agnes, from somebody's picture, in Goupil's window. It is very like her. Here is the St. Nicholas; won't you come in? Then good-night, old fellow, and a clear head to you in the morning!"

Yes; that was it! I remembered the picture, and as I walked homeward alone, along the echoing pavement, I murmured to myself, —

"The shadows of the convent-towers
Slant down the snowy sward,
Still creeping with the creeping hours
That lead me to my Lord."

I don't know what strange, poetic whim possessed me, that I should have made the purchase of the engraving my first business on Monday morning.

CHAPTER XXV.

CONTAINING, AMONG OTHER THINGS, MY VISIT TO THE ICHNEUMON.

After the first of January, Penrose became a member of the firm of Dunn, Deering & Co., whose tall iron warehouse on Chambers Street is known to everybody. Having very properly determined to master the details of the business at the start, he was so constantly occupied that I saw little of him for two or three months thereafter. Mr. and Mrs. Shanks lingered still a few weeks before returning to Philadelphia, but their time was mostly devoted to up-town balls, which I had no wish to attend, although Matilda offered herself as godmother of my social baptism. My days and the greater part of my nights were appropriated, and by no means unpleasantly, to my business duties. Little by little, I found my style increasing in point and fluency, and the subjects assigned to my pen began to present themselves in a compact, coherent form. I was proud enough not to accept an increase of salary without endeavoring to render adequate service, and thus the exertions I made rewarded themselves.

In my case, Schiller's "Occupation, which never wearies — which slowly creates, and destroys nothing," was a helping and protecting principle, — how helpful, indeed, I was yet to learn. I had been wounded too deeply to wear a painless scar; the old smart came back, from time to time, to torment me, — but my life was much more cheerful than I could have anticipated. My affections still lacked an object, constantly putting forth tendrilled shoots to wither in the air, but my intellectual ambition began to revive, though in a soberer form. I had still force enough to control the luxurious cravings of my physical nature, — the thirst for all the enjoyments of sense, which increased with my maturing blood. When I coveted wealth, I was aware that it was not alone for the sake of leisure for study and opportunities of culture; it was for the wine as well as the bread of Life. I saw that velvet made a pleasanter seat than wood; that pheasants tasted better than pork; that a box at the opera was preferable to leaning out of a garret-window and listening to *Casta diva* played on a hand-organ, — in short, that indulgence of every kind was more agreeable than abstinence.

I know that many good people will draw down their brows and shake their heads when they read this confession. But I beg them to remember that I am not preaching, nor even moralizing; I am simply stating the facts of my life. Nay, the fact, I am sure, of most lives; for, although I do not claim to be better, I steadfastly protest against being considered worse, than the average of men. Therefore, you good people, whose lips overflow with professions of duty towards your fellow-beings, and the beauty of self-denial, and the sin of indulgence, look, I pray you, into your own hearts, whether there be no root of the old weed remaining, — whether some natural appetite do not, now and then, still send up a green shoot which it costs you some trouble to cut off, — before weighing my youth in your balance. It is no part of my plan to make of myself an immaculate hero of romance. I fear, alas! that I am not a hero in any sense. I have touched neither the deeps nor the heights: I have only looked down into the one and up towards the other, in lesser vibrations on either side of that noteless middle line which most men travel from birth to death.

My affection for Swansford kept alive in my heart a faint but vital faith in the existence of genuine emotions. I saw him once a week, for we had agreed to spend our Sunday afternoons together, alternately, in each other's rooms. He still disposed of an occasional song, as I of a story, but his great work was not completed, — had not been touched for months, he informed me. He was subject to fits of profound dejection, which, I suspected, proceeded from a physical cause. He was decidedly paler and thinner than when I first made his acquaintance. The drudgery of his lessons frequently rendered him impatient and irritable, and he was anxious to procure a situation as organist, which would yield enough to support him in his humble way. I wanted to bring him together with Penrose, in the hope that the latter might be able to assist him, but feared to propose a meeting to two such diverse characters, and, up to this time, accident had not favored my plan.

The Friday evening receptions of Mrs. Yorkton — I beg pardon, Adeliza Choate — continued to be given, but I did not often attend them. I had been fortunate enough to obtain entrance to the literary *soirées* of another lady whom I will not name, but whose tact, true refinement of character, and admirable culture drew around her all that was best in letters and in the arts. In her *salons* I saw the possessors of honored and illustrious names; I heard books and pictures discussed with the calm discrimination of intelligent criticism; the petty vanities and jealousies I had hitherto encountered might still exist, but they had no voice; and I soon perceived the difference between those who aspire and those who achieve. Art, I saw, has its own peculiar microcosm, — its born nobles, its plodding, conscientious, respectable middle-class, and its clamorous, fighting rabble. To whatever class I might belong, I could not shut my eyes to the existing degrees, and much of my respect for the coarse assertion of Smithers, the petulant conceit of Danforth, and the extravagant inspiration of the once adored Adeliza evaporated in the contrast.

To Brandagee all these circles seemed to be open; yet I could not help noticing that he preferred those where his superior experience made him at once an authority and a fear. The rollicking devil in him was impatient of restraint, and he had too much tact to let it loose at inopportune times and places. I sometimes met him in those delightful rooms which no author or artist who lived in New York at that time can have forgotten, and was not surprised to see that, even in his subdued character, he still inspired a covetable interest. He now came to the *Wonder* office but seldom. He could never be relied upon to have his articles ready at the appointed time, and there had been some quarrel between him and Mr. Clarendon, in consequence of which he transferred his services to the *Avenger*. I had become such a zealous disciple of the former paper that I looked upon this transfer as almost involving a sacrifice of principle. Mr. Clarendon, however, seemed to care little about it, for he did not scruple still to send to Brandagee for an article on some special subject.

He had at one time a scheme for publishing a small fashionable daily, to be devoted to the opera and the drama, artistic and literary criticism, the turf, dress, and other kindred subjects; the type and paper to be of the utmost elegance, and the contents to rival in epigrammatic brilliancy, boldness, and impertinence the best productions of the Parisian *feuilletonistes*. Had the wealth of many of the New York families been any index of their culture, the scheme might have succeeded, but it was too hazardous to entrap any publisher of sufficient means. He then determined to repeat the attempt in a less ambitious form, — a weekly paper instead of a daily, — which would involve little preliminary expense, and might be easily dropped if it failed to meet expectations. It was to be called "*The City Oracle*," and to bear the familiar quotation from Shakspeare as its device. I had heard Brandagee discuss the plan with Mr. Withering (who decidedly objected to it, very much preferring a Quarterly Review), and had promised, incidentally, to contribute a sketch for the first number, if it should ever make its appearance.

Towards the close of winter, — I think it was in February, — I met Brandagee one evening, as he was issuing from the Smithsonian, cigar in mouth, as usual.

"Ha!" he exclaimed; "I was this moment thinking of you. You have nothing to do at this hour, — come around with me to the Ichneumon. We are going to talk over *The Oracle*. Babcock has as good as promised to undertake the publication."

"Indeed?" said I. "When will you begin?"

"The first number ought to appear within ten or twelve days. That will leave me three weeks of the opera season, — long enough to make a sensation, and have the paper talked about. Notoriety is the life of a new undertaking of this kind. I can count on six pens already, including yours and my own. In fact, I could do the whole work alone on a pinch; though I don't profess to be equal to Souville. You never heard of Thersite Souville, I dare say: he wrote the whole of *Gargantua*, — just such a paper as I intend to make my *Oracle*, — editorials, criticisms, gossip and *feuilleton;* and everybody supposed that the best intellect in Paris was employed upon it, regardless of expense. He was up to any style, but he always changed his beverage with his pen. For the manner of Sue, he drank hot punch; for Dumas, cider *mousseux;* Gautier or De Musset, absinthe; Paul de Kock, Strasburg beer, — and so on. It was a great speculation for his publisher, who cleared a hundred and fifty thousand francs a year, one third of which was Souville's share. If he had not been so vain as to blab the secret, he might have kept it up to this day. Come on; you'll find all my coadjutors at the Ichneumon."

"Where is the Ichneumon," I asked, "and what is it?"

"Not know it! You *are* a green Bohemian. Close at hand, in Crosby Street. The name is my suggestion, and I'm rather proud of it. When the landlord — Miles, who used to be bar-tender at the 'Court of Appeals' — took his new place, he was puzzled to get a title, as all the classic epithets, Shades, Pewter Mugs, Banks, Houses of Commons, Nightingales, Badgers, and Dolphins, were appropriated by others. I offered to give him a stunning name, in consideration of occasional free drinks. I first hit on the *Ornithorhynchus paradoxus*, which was capital; but Miles was fool enough to think that nobody could ever pronounce or remember it. Then I gave him the Ichneumon, with which he was satisfied, — he, as well as all Crosby Street, calls it 'Ike Newman.' I 've persuaded him to give us a backroom, and keep a bed up-stairs for any fellow who is boozy or belated. We shall make a classic place of it, and if the *Oracle* once fairly open its mouth, the crocodiles must look out for their eggs!"

We reached the house, almost before he had done speaking. It was an old-fashioned brick dwelling, the lower story of which had been altered to suit the requirements of the times. An octagonal lantern, on the front glass of which an animal "very like a weasel" was painted, hung over the door, and through the large adjoining window there was a spectral vision of a bar somewhere in the shadowy depths of the house.

The landlord was leaning over the counter, talking to a group of flashy gents, as we entered. He had the unmistakable succulent flesh and formless mouth of an Englishman, but with his hair closely cropped behind, and the back of his neck shaved in a straight line around from ear to ear, like a Bowery boy.

"Miles," said Brandagee, "another of us, — Mr. Godfrey."

"Y'r most obedient — 'ope to see you often," said Miles, rising to an erect posture and giving me his hand.

"Anybody in the Cave, Miles?"

"There 's three gents, Mr. Brandagee, — Smithers, for one, the painter chap, and the heavy gent."

"Come on, then, Godfrey," said Brandagee, laughing. "It 's Ponder and Smears. I 'll bet a thousand ducats Ponder wants to help us out, but, between you and me, his didactics would be a millstone around our necks. I 'll manage him. This is the way to the Cave — of Trophonius, you understand."

He entered a narrow passage on the right of the bar, pushed open with his foot a door at the further end, and we found ourselves in a room of tolerable size, with a dense blue atmosphere which threatened to eclipse the two sickly gas-lights. Smithers had untied his scarlet cravat, and, with head thrown back over the top of his arm-chair, suffered his huge meerschaum pipe, lazily held between his teeth, to dangle against his hairy throat. Mr. S. Mears was drawing his portrait in a condition of classic nudity, on the margin of a newspaper, with the end of a burnt match. Mr. Ponder, on the other side of the table, was talking, and evidently in as heavy a style as he wrote. Both the latter were smoking. All three started up briskly in their seats at our entrance.

"Ouf!" puffed Brandagee, with an expiration of delight. "Well done! This reminds me of the *salon des nuages*, as Frédéric Soulié called it, in the rear of the Cafe Doré. We used to hire two or three of the servants to smoke in it for an hour before our arrival. It was a special close communion of our own, and there was competition to get admitted, though few could stand the test. Cherubini had to leave in a quarter of an hour, and as for Delacroix, I never saw a sicker man. Let us improve this atmosphere before the others come. Here, Godfrey, is a *claro;* don 't be afraid, — you must commence some day."

I lighted the cigar, and made a feint of smoking it. But I never could acquire any liking for the habit, and my associates, after finding that I always spoiled an entire cigar in the process of burning half an inch, finally ceased to waste any more upon me.

"Well, Godfrey," said Brandagee, turning to me, "since you are to be one of us, we 'll take your initiation fee."

"What shall it be?" I asked.

"Oh, we won't be hard upon you. Beer through the evening, with a modest bowl of punch as a stirrup-cup."

He rang a bell as he spoke, and we were all presently supplied with corpulent mugs. There were two other arrivals, — one a reporter of the *Avenger*, the other a young gentleman who had a clerkship in the Custom-House and wrote for the magazines. I found myself more at home in this company than at Mrs. Yorkton's. Though there was rather a repellant absence of sentiment, there was, at least, nothing of the mock article. Nobody attempted to play a part, knowing the absurdity of wearing a mask behind the curtain, and suspecting how soon it would be torn off, if attempted. Thus the conversation, if occasionally coarse, if unnecessarily profane, if scoffing and depreciative of much that I knew to be good and noble, was always lively, racy, and entertaining. I surmised that my associates were not the best of men; but then, on the other hand, they were not bores.

The plan of the *Oracle* was first discussed. Each one, I perceived, was quite willing to dictate the best possible programme; but Brandagee steadily kept before them the fact that he was the originator of the idea, and would resent dictation, while he was willing to receive suggestions. Besides, Babcock, the publisher, had not yet fully committed himself, and it all might end in smoke. His own specialty of musical and dramatic criticism was an understood matter; Mears was to undertake the art notices ("he paints badly, and therefore he is tolerably sure to write well," Brandagee whispered to me); the *Avenger* reporter was selected to prepare the city gossip, while to the clerk and myself was allotted the writing of short, lively stories or sketches of character for the first page. There now only remained Smithers and Ponder to be disposed of. The former of these informed us that he was willing to contribute passages from his "Edda of the Present," an heroic, muscular poem, in irregular metre; and the latter thought that an essay on "The Influence of Literature upon National Character" would be an indispensable feature of the new journal.

"Not in the first number," replied Brandagee; "*that* must be all foam and sparkle. I don't contemplate many heavy articles at any time. It might do for Vienna. When my old friend Grillparzer founded his light *Sonntagsblatt*, — something like the *Oracle* in form, — he began with articles on Hegel's Philosophy, the Cretan-Doric dialect, the religion of the Ostiaks and a biography of Paracelsus. Locality makes all the difference in the world. We are nearer the latitude of Paris than any other capital, and there, if anything new has a didactic smell, the public won't touch it."

"But the national feeling" — commenced Mr. Ponder.

"Very well for the rural districts; I don't find much of it here. We are cosmopolitan, which is better. If I were beginning in Boston I would give you eight columns — four for the Pilgrim Fathers, and four for a description of the Common, as viewed from Bunker Hill Monument; or if it were Philadelphia, you should write a solid article, setting forth the commercial decline of New York, — but here we care for nothing which does not bring a sensation with it. We are not provincial, not national, not jealous of our neighbors; we live, enjoy, and pay roundly in order to be diverted. The *Oracle* must be smart, pert, hinting what may not properly be said outright, never behind with the current scandal, and brilliantly, not stupidly, impudent. With these qualities it can't fail to be a success. It will be a tongue which hundreds of people would pay well to keep from wagging."

"The devil!" exclaimed Mears; "do you mean to make a black-mail concern of it?"

"Don't be so quick on the trigger, young man! I merely referred to the power which we should hold. A thing may be bid for, but you are not obliged to sell it. In the way of advertising, however, there would be great and certain profits; we might enter into competition with Napoleon B. Quigg, or Gouraud's medicated epic. There are scores of retail dry-goods merchants who would give fifty dollars a piece to have their establishments mentioned in a novel or a play. I have a grand scheme for raising the wind, but I won't disclose it to you just now."

Our mugs were replenished, and Brandagee, who seemed to be in the mood for a harangue, went on again.

"There 's plenty of money in the world," he said, "if it were only in the right hands. Of all forms of Superstition which exist, that concerning money is the most absurd. It is looked upon as something sacred, — something above intellect, humanity, or religion. Yet it is an empty form — a means of transfer, being nothing in itself — like the red flame, which is no substance, only representing the change of one substance into another. You never really possess it until you spend it. What is it to knowledge, to the results of experience, or the insight of genius? But you come to me for advice or information which cannot be bought in the market, — the value of which gold cannot represent; I give it and you go your way. Then I borrow a hundred dollars from your useless surplus; you oblige me to sign a note payable in so many days, and consider me dishonored if I fail to meet it! Why should I not take of your matter as freely as you of my spirit? Why should this meanest of substances be elevated to such mysterious reverence? They only who turn it to the enrichment of their lives — who use it as a gardener does manure, for the sake of the flowers — have the abstract right to possess it. Jenkins has a million, but never buys a book or a picture, does n't know the taste of Burgundy, and can't tell 'Yankee Doodle' from '*Il mio tesoro*' — does that money belong to him? No, indeed, — it is mine, ours, everybody's who understands how to set it in motion and bring the joy and the beauty of life bubbling up to the surface!"

"Bravo!" cried the others, evidently more than half inclined to be of the same way of thinking. I did not suppose that Brandagee was entirely in earnest, but I was fascinated by the novelty of his views, and unable, at the time, to detect wherein they were unsound.

"Do you know, fellows," he continued, "that our lives are far more in accordance with the pervading spirit of Christianity than those of the men who devote themselves to earning and hoarding? We are expressly commanded to take no thought for the morrow. There is nowhere in the Bible a commendation of economy, of practical talent, even of industry in a secular sense. It was so understood in the early ages of Christianity, and the devotees who adopted lazy contemplation as a profession never starved to death. Perhaps they lived better than the contemporary men of business. I don't mean that their ways would suit us, but then they lived out their own idea, and that 's all we can do. Work, and the worry that comes with it, are relics of paganism. The stupid masses always were, and will be, pagans, and it was meant that they should labor in order to give leisure to what little intelligence there is in the world. If they are stiff-necked and rebellious, I hold that there is no particular harm in using our superior cunning to obtain what justly belongs to us. Suppose they make an outcry? Of course they look at the subject from their, which is the lower, the pagan point of view. Pagans, you are aware, have no rights which elected Christians are bound to respect."

Brandagee had trenched, before he was aware of it, on the favorite hobby of Smithers. The latter began to puff furiously at his meerschaum, now and then snorting the smoke from his nostrils in long blue lines.

"It 's a bit of adroit sophistry!" he exclaimed. "These pagans, as you call them, with their strong bones, their knotted muscles, their thick cerebellums and their cast-iron stomachs, are the very men who understand how to use life.

They could soon crush out your scanty breed of forced and over-refined Epicureans, if they cared to do it: you should be glad that they suffer you to exist. What you call work is only the sportive overplus of their colossal energy. If they did not keep alive the blood of the race, which you are trying all the while to exhaust, there would soon be, not only an end of Art and Literature, but an end of Man on this planet!"

"Smithers," said Brandagee, coolly, "if you would take a little more of the blood that circulates in your big body and send it in the direction of your brains, you would see that you have not come within a mile of meeting my assertion. I take *you* as my living verification. You like work no better than the rest of us, and you mix with your stevedores and sailors and 'longshoremen only to exploit them in your 'Edda.' I have often seen you, sitting on a pier-head with your pipe in your mouth, but I don't believe that 'the sportive overplus of your colossal energy' ever incited you to handle a single bale or barrel. I don't object to your hobby: it's a good one to ride, so far as the public is concerned, but we, here in the Cave, understand each other, I take it."

Smithers began to grow red about the gills, and would have resented the insinuation, but for the opportune arrival of Miles, bearing a curiously-shaped vessel of some steaming liquid and fresh glasses. The interest which these objects excited absorbed the subject of debate. Mears threw himself into a statuesque attitude and exclaimed in a Delphic voice, "The offering is accepted;" while Brandagee chanted, —

"Fill the cup and fill the can,
Have a rouse before the morn,"

and all shoved their glasses together under the nose of the ladle.

"Here, Godfrey," said Brandagee, striking his glass against mine, "welcome and acceptance from the mystic brotherhood! Here you have your money, as I was explaining: it has taken form at last, instead of lying, as a dry idea, in the pocket. I hold that we have the right to seize on shadows wherever we find them, for the sake of converting them into substance. Hence, if a man thinks I am taking away his shadow, in the Peter Schlemihl sense, let him apply the law of *similia similibus*, and parting with another shadow shall give him peace of mind. This you, Smears, would call levying black-mail. But you artists always take the gross, material view of things,—it belongs to you. The senses of Color and Form are not intellectual qualities. Never mind, I mean no disparagement. The value of mind is that it teaches us how to make the right use of matter; so we all come back to the same starting-point."

The conversation now became general and noisy, and I will not undertake to report it further. In fact, I have but an indistinct recollection of what followed, except that some time after midnight we parted affectionately at the corner of Spring Street and Broadway. The next morning I arose heavy in head, but light in purse,—so much lighter that I suspect the punch-bowl was filled more than once in the course of the evening.

Various impediments prevented *The Oracle* from appearing before the close of the opera season, and the plan was therefore suspended until the next fall. But the Cave of Trophonius still existed, under the guardianship of the Ichneumon, and I often seized an hour to enjoy forgetfulness of the present, in the lawless recklessness of the utterance to which it was dedicated.

CHAPTER XXVI.

IN WHICH I TALK WITH TWO GIRLS AT A VERY SOCIABLE PARTY.

I HAVE said that I still felt but little inclination to mingle in society, although I might easily have found opportunities. I fancy, however, that this reluctance was more imaginary than real: it belonged to the soberer *rôle* which I had chosen in the great drama. I could not quite justify my participation in the gayeties of the season to that spirit of stern indifference which I ought, logically, to have preserved. My nature, however, was not so profound as I supposed, and when once I was led to forget myself in the presence of others, I speedily developed a lively capacity for enjoyment. More than once I went slowly and moodily to a scene, whence I returned with buoyant, dancing spirits. Whenever I thought of Amanda Bratton, a feeling of congratulation at my escape tempered the bitterness of the memory, and I began to believe again (hardly admitting to myself that I did so) in the purity of woman and the honor of man.

The remembered expression of Miss Haworth's eyes troubled me, and I longed for an opportunity of presenting myself to her in a more correct light. It was some time before such an opportunity occurred. I passed her once on Broadway, on a sunny afternoon, and sometimes saw her through the window of a carriage, but nearly three months elapsed before I was able to speak to her again. Mr. Deering, with whom I had made a slight acquaintance during the dinner at Delmonico's, invited me to call "very sociably" at his house in Fourteenth Street, on a certain evening. I accepted, mainly because I expected to find Penrose there, and, as my duties required me to leave early, made my appearance precisely at the appointed hour. In this respect I was misled by the words "very sociably," for no other guests had yet arrived, and the rooms were decorated as if for a ball. I experienced a foolish sensation for a moment, as I stood alone in the strong light of gas and the glitter of gilding, but Mrs. Deering did not leave me long in waiting. With her entered, to my surprise, Miss Haworth.

Mrs. Deering was a frail-looking woman, with large dark eyes, and pale, melancholy, interesting face. She received me with perfect grace, and a kindly, winning air, which seemed — I knew not why — to ask for sympathy. At any rate, I gave it, and still I knew not why. In greeting Miss Haworth I offered her my hand, forgetting that my slight acquaintance hardly warranted me in assuming the signs of familiarity; but she took it with a natural, simple courtesy, in which there was no trace of mere conventional politeness. We seated ourselves at the bottom of the apartment, and I had ample time to overcome the first formal stages of conversation before the next arrival. The hostess and Miss Haworth were evidently familiar, if not intimate friends; they called each other "Fanny" and "Isabel," and frequently referred to mutual experiences and mutual impressions. I saw that both were amiable, cultivated, refined women. The point of difference seemed to be in character — in a certain gentle, reliant, hesitating quality in Mrs. Deering, and its latent opposite in Miss Haworth — for I did not think the latter old enough for marked development. Nevertheless, through all her maidenly sweetness and simplicity, I felt the existence of a firm, heroic spirit. Her pure, liquid voice could under no circumstances become shrill or hard, but its music might express a changeless resolution. Some sense within me, underlying the surface of my talk, continually contrasted her with Amanda Bratton. The consciousness of it annoyed me, but I could not escape from the perverse spirit.

Finally, Mrs. Deering rose and advanced to receive the coming guests, and we were left alone. My thoughts went back to our conversation at the dinner, and I longed for the tact to bring it up naturally. I introduced Matilda Shanks, — a subject soon exhausted; then Penrose, and here a happy thought came to my aid. I had become not only unembarrassed, but frank, and, almost before I knew it, had described the manner in which we had discovered our relationship.

"I had hardly liked him before that," I said. "I had thought him haughty, cold, and almost incapable of affection — but this was only the outside. He was truly happy to find that we were kin, although I was at that time a raw country-boy, far below him in everything. Since then, we have learned to know each other tolerably well. He is so handsome that I am very glad I can honestly esteem him."

I saw a light like a smile in Miss Haworth's eyes, but it did not reach her lips. "He *is* strikingly handsome," she said, "but it is not a face that one can read easily."

"I think I like it all the better for that," I answered. "It keeps up one's interest; there are so many surprises, as you discover new traits."

"If they were always agreeable surprises."

"I have found them so, in his case."

"You are fortunate, then," said she. Her tone was calm and passionless, and I detected no reason for my suspicion that she did not like Penrose. It almost seemed as if we had changed characters, — as if now the faith were on my side and the distrust on hers. I presently shook off this impression as absurd, and attempted to introduce my explanation before the new guests should interrupt us.

"I think my cousin frequently does injustice to himself," I said. "He is fond of proclaiming a hard, unsympathetic view of life, which does not correspond with his practice. I was at one time in danger of imitating him, because everything did not go according to my wishes. I can't quite recall the words I used in my talk with you at the dinner," (this was false — I knew them every one,) " but I am sure they did not express my true sentiments. I had rather be thought inconsistent than cynical."

" So would I!" she exclaimed, with a merry laugh. " Consistency is a jewel, you know, but the color of it don't happen to suit my complexion. I am heterodox enough to dislike the word; to me it signifies something excessively stiff, prim, and tiresome."

I was relieved, but a little surprised, at such an unexpected latitude of opinion in Miss Haworth.

" It dates from my school-days in Troy," she continued, by way of explanation. " Our teacher in Moral Philosophy had a habit of saying, — ' Be consistent, girls!' on every possible occasion. We all decided that if she was an example of it, consistency was a disagreeable quality, and I am afraid that we tried to get rid of what little we had, instead of cultivating it. I like a character upon which one can depend, but we may honestly change our views."

" Then," said I, " there are also such differences in our moods of feeling. We change like the scenery of land or sea, through green, gray, blue and gold, according to the sun and the clouds. You are right; the same tints forever would be very tiresome; but we should not half possess our opinions, if we were always conscious that we might soon change them for others."

" I wish Mrs. Deering had heard you say that. We were looking at a new dress of hers just before you came. There was a mixture of colors in it, which, I knew, had only caught her eye by its novelty, and the effect would soon wear off. But when I said so, she put her hand on my mouth, and pleaded, — ' Please don't say a word against it; let me like it as long as I can.' I laughed and called her a child, as she is in her frankness and gentleness."

"She is a very lovely woman," I said, "but there is something about her which seems to call for help or sympathy. I do not understand it."

"Is it so palpable?" asked Miss Haworth, in a low voice, as if speaking to herself. The approach of other guests interrupted our conversation, and I had no chance of resuming it during the evening, although we frequently crossed each other's paths, and exchanged a few words. The "very sociable" entertainment was something more than a reception and something less than a ball. Most of the guests came in full dress, and I was very glad that I had profited by a hint which Brandagee had once let fall. "In New York," said he, "it is always safer to over-dress than to under-dress. The former is looked upon as a compliment to the hosts, and no excuse is ever accepted for the latter." The young ladies were all *decolletées*, and their bright heads rose out of wonderful folds and cloudy convolutions of white mist, which followed with soft rustling noises the gliding swing of their forms. I was leaning on the narrow end of the grand piano, listlessly watching them as they moved through the figures of a quadrille, when Mrs. Deering suddenly addressed me with, —

"Don't you dance, Mr. Godfrey?"

"Sometimes," I answered; "but I think I enjoy seeing dancing even more. Somebody says, if one would stop his ears and shut out the music, one would find the movements of the dancers simply ridiculous. I can imagine that this might be true of the gentlemen, — but, certainly, not of the ladies."

"Are we so much more graceful?" she asked.

"No," said I, with plump sincerity; "it is rather the advantage of dress, — the difference between drapery, which falls into flowing and undulating lines, and a close shell, like that of a tortoise. Besides the shell is black, which robs it of light and shade. Suppose the gentlemen wore Roman togas, — white, with a border of purple, or blue and silver, or crimson and gold, — don't you think the effect would be immensely improved?"

"I must confess the idea never entered my head. You must give me time to think about it, before I can answer. It is something new to hear a gentleman speak for the beauty of his sex; *we* are generally allowed the monopoly of that."

I felt embarrassed, and there was an unpleasant sense of heat in my face, which increased as I encountered Miss Haworth's laughing, expectant eyes. She was standing near, and must have heard the whole conversation.

"If I thought myself handsome," I said, at last, "I should never lay myself open to such a charge; but it gives me pleasure to see beauty, Mrs. Deering, whether in woman or man, and I do not understand why custom requires that one sex should help it with all possible accessories and the other disguise it."

"Oh, you men don't really need it," began Mrs. Deering. "You have courage and energy and genius." — Here she stopped, turned pale, and after a little pause, added with a gayety not altogether natural; "Shall I find you a partner for the next quadrille?"

I assented, thinking of Miss Haworth, but Mr. Deering came up at that moment and secured her. Mrs. Deering laid her hand on my arm, and we began to thread the disentangling groups as the music ceased. The elegant young gentlemen were already dodging to and fro, and taking their places in anticipation of the next dance: the blooming, girlish faces were snatched away as we approached them, and Mrs. Deering, with a little laugh at our ill-fortune, said, "I must pick out the best of the wall-flowers, after all, — ah! here is one chance yet!"

A moment after, I found myself face to face with — Miss Levi!

"Mr. Godfrey wishes for the pleasure," — Mrs. Deering began to say, by way of presentation and request.

"Now, Mr. Godfrey!" exclaimed Miss Levi, jumping up and giving me a smart rap with her sandal-wood fan, — "you know you don't deserve it! You would never have seen me without Mrs. Deering's help, — and if I accept you, it 's for her sake only. He 's as false and heartless as he can be, Mrs. Deering!"

If my thought had been expressed in words, I am afraid there would have been a profane verb before Miss Levi's name. I was exasperated by the unexpected encounter, and less than ever disposed to hear her flippant, affected chatter, to which I had responded so often that I was powerless to check it now. As we took our places on the floor, and she spread the scarlet leaves of her fan over the lower part of her face, her jet-black eyes and hair shining at me above them, I thought of the poppy-flower, and the dark, devilish spirit of the drug which feeds it. I tried to shake off the baleful, narcotic influence which streamed from her, and which seemed to increase in proportion as I resisted it. By a singular chance, Mr. Deering and Miss Haworth were our *vis-à-vis*. I had scarcely noticed this, when the preliminary chords of the quadrille were struck, and the first figure commenced.

"Confess to me, now, Mr. Godfrey," said Miss Levi, when our turn came to rest, "that you are as false in literature as you are in love. You have not been at Mrs. Yorkton's for ever so long."

"I am false to neither," I answered, desperately, "for I believe in neither."

"Oh, I shall become afraid of you." I knew her eyes were upon my face, but I steadily looked away. "You are getting to be misanthropic, — Byronic. Of course there is a cause for it. It is *she* who is false; pardon my heartless jesting; I shall never do so again. But you never thought it serious, did you? I always believed in your truth as I do in your genius."

The last sentences were uttered in a low, gentle, confidential tone, and the fingers that lay upon my arm closed tenderly around it. I could not help myself: I turned my head and received the subdued, sympathetic light of the large eyes.

"You are mistaken, Miss Levi," I said; "there is no '*she*' in the case, and there will not be."

"Never?" It was only a whisper, but I despair of representing its peculiar intonation. It set my pulses trembling with a mixture of sensations, in which fear was predominant. I dimly felt that I must somehow disguise my true nature from this woman's view, or become her slave. I must prevaricate, lie, — anything to make her believe me other than my actual self.

The commencement of the second figure relieved me from the necessity of answering her question. When we had walked through it, and I was standing beside her, she turned to me and said, —

"Well?"

"Well?" I echoed.

"You have not answered my question."

I summoned all the powers of dissimulation I possessed, looked her full in the face with an expression of innocence and surprise, and answered, "What question?"

Her dark brows drew together for an instant, and a rapid glance hurled itself against my face, as if determined to probe me. I bore it with preternatural composure, and, finding she did not speak, repeated, "What question?"

She turned away, unaware that something very like a scowl expressed itself on her profile, and muttered, —

"It is of no consequence, since you have forgotten it."

My success emboldened me to go a step further, and not merely defend myself, but experiment a little in offensive tactics.

"Oh, about being false to literature?" I said. "You probably thought I was pledged to it. That is not so; what I have done has been merely a diversion. Having attempted, of course it would not be pleasant to fail; but there is no great satisfaction in success. With your knowledge of authors, Miss Levi, you must be aware that they cannot be called either a happy or a fortunate class of men!"

Again she scrutinized my face, — this time over her fan. I was wonderfully calm and earnest: there is no hypocrisy equal to that of a man naturally frank.

"I am afraid it is true," she answered, at last. "But there are some exceptions, and, with *your* genius, you might be one of them, Mr. Godfrey."

"If my 'genius,' as you are pleased to call it," I said, "can give me a house like this, and large deposits in the banks, I shall be very much obliged to it. I should much rather have splendor than renown: would n't you?"

Looking across the floor I met Miss Haworth's eyes, and although she turned them away at once, I caught a glimpse of the quiet, serious observance with which they had rested upon me. I rejoiced that she could not have heard my words. The game I had been playing suddenly became distasteful. Miss Levi's answer showed that she had fallen into the snare; that her enthusiasm for literature and literary men was a shallow affectation, which I might easily have developed further, but I took advantage of the movements of the dance to change the subject. When the quadrille was finished, I conducted her to a seat, bowed, and left her almost too precipitately for courtesy.

In the mean time Penrose had arrived. I had not seen him for some weeks, and we were having a pleasant talk in a corner of the room when Mrs. Deering, in her arbitrary character of hostess, interrupted us, by claiming him for presentation to some of her friends.

"The partnership is social as well as commercial, is it?" said he. "Then I must go, John."

An imp of mischief prompted me to say to Mrs. Deering, "Introduce him to Miss Levi. Dance with her, if you can, Alexander; I want to hear your impression of her beauty."

"Oh, ho!" he exclaimed, "is she the elected one? By all means. I shall try to find her bewitching, for your sake."

"Alexander!" I cried. But the twain were already moving away, Mrs. Deering looking back to me with a gay, significant smile. I was provoked at myself, and at Penrose. I had honestly wished, for my own satisfaction, to subject Miss Levi to the test of his greater knowledge of the world, his sharp, merciless dissection of character. Perhaps I thought he could analyze the uncanny, mysterious power which she possessed. But the interpretation he had put upon my words spoiled the plan. And Mrs. Deering, I feared, had accepted that interpretation only too readily. Could she really believe that I was attracted towards Miss Levi? If so, and she mentioned the discovery to Miss Haworth, what must the latter think of me? She, too, had noticed the intimate character of our conversation during the dance; yet she could not, must not be allowed to misunderstand me so shockingly. I worried myself, I have no doubt, a great deal more than was necessary. My surmises involved no compliment to the good sense of the two ladies, and the excitement they occasioned in my mind was inconsistent with the character I had determined to assume.

I looked around for Miss Haworth before leaving the parlor. She was seated at the piano, playing one of Strauss's airy waltzes, while the plain, weary-looking governess, who had been performing for the two previous hours, was taking a rest and an ice on the sofa. Among the couples which revolved past me were Penrose and Miss Levi, and there was a bright expression of mischief in the former's eye as it met mine.

I went down town to my midnight duties in the office of the *Wonder*, very much dissatisfied with myself. It seemed that I had stupidly blundered during the whole evening, and had made my position worse than it was before in the eyes of the only woman whom I was anxious to please. The latter fact was now apparent to my consciousness, and when I asked myself "Why?" there was no difficulty in finding reasons. She was handsome; she resembled St. Agnes; I believed her to be a pure, true, noble-hearted girl.

Then I asked myself again, "Anything more?"

And as I stepped over the booming vaults, in which the great iron presses of the *Wonder* revolved at the rate of twenty thousand copies per hour, and mounted to the stifling room where the reports on yellow transfer-paper awaited me, I shook my head and made answer unto myself, "No; nothing more!"

CHAPTER XXVII.

WHICH SHOWS THAT THERE WAS SOMETHING MORE.

My ill-humor extended over several days, and even showed itself in my professional duties. I don't suppose that the blustering March weather of New York was ever so savagely and bitterly described as in some of my articles at that time. I wrote a hideously ironical sonnet to Spring, which some country editor maliciously copied, side by side with Bryant's poem on "March," bidding his readers contrast the serene, cheerful philosophy expressed in the lines, —

> "But in thy sternest frown abides
> A look of kindly promise yet — "

with "the spleenful growling of Mr. J. Godfrey," contemptuously adding, "whoever he may be."

This latter castigation, however, came back to me at a time when I could laugh over it, and acknowledge that it was deserved. It was not long before the fact recurred to my mind that Custom required me to call upon Mrs. Deering, and, admitting that Custom sometimes makes very sensible and convenient arrangements, I consoled myself with the prospect of soon knowing how far Penrose had implicated me.

Mrs. Deering received me with the same winning, melancholy grace, which, from the first, had inspired me with a respectful interest. We conversed for some time, and, as she made no allusion to Miss Levi, I was obliged to introduce the subject, "butt-end foremost."

"I saw that you presented Penrose to Miss Levi," I said.

"Of course you did n't believe his jesting, when I asked you to do so?"

"Oh, no," she answered, with a smile; "I am accustomed to that sort of badinage among gentlemen. There was some joking about it afterwards between Mr. Penrose and Miss Haworth."

"Good heavens!" I exclaimed, quite startled out of my propriety; "Miss Haworth, I hope, does not suppose it to be true?"

Mrs. Deering's eyes rested on my face a moment, with a sweet, gentle interest. "I do not think she does," she presently remarked: "it was Mr. Floyd, her step-brother, who seemed to be most interested. He asked Mr. Penrose to introduce him also to Miss Levi."

"It is too bad!" I cried, in great vexation: "what shall I do to contradict this ridiculous story?"

"Pray give yourself no uneasiness, Mr. Godfrey. I will contradict it for you, should I hear anything of it, but I really imagine that it has already been forgotten."

I gave her grateful thanks and took my leave, somewhat comforted, if not quieted in spirit.

A few days afterwards I received a little note from her inviting me to tea. I wrote a line of acceptance at once, and gladly, surmising that she had something to tell me, — feeling quite sure, at least, that I should hear of Miss Haworth. But I did not venture to anticipate the happiness which awaited me. Miss Haworth, whether by accident or through Mrs. Deering's design, was present. There were also two or three other guests, who, as they have no concern with the story of my life, need not be particularized. Before we were summoned to the tea-table, Mrs. Deering found an opportunity to whisper to me, —

"Make yourself quite easy, Mr. Godfrey. It was all taken as a jest."

I knew that she referred to Miss Haworth, and felt that any reference to the subject, on my part, would be unnecessary. I was at once reconciled to the vexation which had procured me another interview with her, and in the genial, unconstrained atmosphere of the small company, became my own frank, light-hearted self, as Nature designed me to be. Our acquaintance ripened apace: we conversed, during the evening, on books and music, and men and their ways, developing, not always accordant views, but an increasing freedom in the utterance of them. I was still too ignorant of the change that was going on in my feelings to be timid or embarrassed in her presence, and my eyes constantly sought hers, partly because I was absorbed in the beauty of their dark-violet hue, and partly because they never shunned my gaze, but met it with the innocent directness of a nature that had nothing to conceal. Naturalists say that an object steadily looked at in a strong light, produces an impression upon the retina which remains and reproduces the image for hours afterwards. I am sure this is true; for those eyes, that rippled golden hair, that full, sweet mouth and round, half-dimpled chin, haunted my vision from that time forth. When I close my eyes, I can still see them.

My enjoyment of the evening would have been perfect but for the appearance of Mr. Tracy Floyd, who dropped in at a late hour to escort his step-sister home. We were sitting together, a little apart from the rest of the company, when he entered, and I could see that his face assumed no very friendly expression as he noticed the fact. After greeting the hostess and the other guests, he turned towards us.

"Bell, I have come for you," he said. "Ah, Mr. Godfrey, how do you do? Are you to be congratulated?"

"No!" I exclaimed, with a quick sense of anger, the expression of which I could not entirely suppress.

"Very complimentary to you, Bell! Rather a decided expression of distaste for your society."

"That was not what you meant," I said, looking him steadily in the eye.

He avoided my gaze, laughed, and said he was sorry I did n't seem to understand a joke. There was a heightened color in Miss Haworth's face, as she replied to a previous remark of mine, but in no other way did she notice what had passed between her step-brother and myself. Presently she rose to accompany him, giving me her hand frankly and kindly as she said good-night. I took leave of Mrs. Deering very soon after her departure.

I postponed all reflection — all examination of the confused, shining sensations which filled my heart — until my work was done, and I could stretch myself in the freedom and freshness of my bed. There was too much agitation in my blood for sleep. At first I left the gas-burner alight, that I might see, from my pillow, the picture of St. Agnes — but presently arose and turned out the flame. The color, the life, and spirit of the face in my memory made the engraving tame. I admitted to myself the joy of Isabel Haworth's presence, with a thrill of ecstasy, which betrayed to me at once towards what shore this new current was setting. At first, it is true, there was an intrusive consciousness, not precisely of inconstancy, but of something very like it — of shallow-heartedness, in so soon recovering from a hurt which I had considered mortal; but it was speedily lost in the knowledge, which now came to me, of the growth of my nature since the days of that boyish delusion. I suddenly became aware of the difference between sentiment and passion. My first attachment was shy, timid, dreamy, — shrinking away from the positive aspects of life. It flattered my vanity, because I looked upon it as an evidence of manhood, but it had not directly braced a single fibre of my heart. This, on the contrary, filled me, through and through, with a sharp tingle of power: it dared to contemplate every form of its realization; were its blessing but assured, I should proudly proclaim it to the world. Its existence once recognized, I took it swiftly into every chamber of my being: my kindled imagination ran far in advance of the primitive stage of my experience, and before I fell asleep I had almost persuaded myself that the fortune of my life was secured.

I have said but little of Miss Haworth, because, up to this time, I had seen so little of her. My love was half instinct, — the suspicion of a noble and steadfast character which was yet unproved. She did not seem to be considered, in society, a marked beauty; she rather evaded than courted observation, — but I felt that she was one of those women whom one would like to meet more frequently in what is called "fashionable" society, — of faultless social culture, yet as true and unspoiled as the simplest country maiden. It was no shame to love her without the hope of return. Indeed, I admitted to my own heart that I had no right to any such hope. What could she find in me? — she, to whom the world was open, who doubtless knew so many men more gifted in every way than myself! Nevertheless, I should not tamely relinquish my claim. I might have to wait for a long time, — to overcome obstacles which would task my whole strength,— but she was too glorious a prize to sit down and sigh for while another carried her off.

All this occurred in the first thrill of my discovery. I could not always feel so courageous; the usual fluctuations of passion came to cheer or depress me. I could only depend on seeing her, through accidental opportunities, and my employment prevented me from seeking to increase them. Often, indeed, I hurried through my afternoon duties in order to prolong my walk up Broadway, in the hope of meeting her, but this fortune happened to me but twice. One evening, however, at Wallack's, a little incident occurred which kept me in a glow for weeks afterwards. Mr. Severn had given me two of the complimentary tickets sent to the *Wonder* office, and I took Swansford with me, delighted with the chance of sharing my recreation with him. We selected seats in the parquet, not too near the brass instruments; his ear suffered enough, as it was, from the little slips and false notes which were inaudible to me. Looking around the boxes at the end of the first act, my heart gave a bound on seeing Miss Haworth, in company with an unknown lady and gentleman. She wore a pale lilac dress, with white flowers in her hair, and looked unusually lovely. They were conversing cheerfully together, and I could study the perfect self-possession of her attitude, the grace of her slightest movements, without being observed.

Having made this discovery, I had thenceforth but half an eye for the play. My seat, fortunately, was nearly on a line with the box in which she sat, and I could steal a glance by very slightly turning my head. Towards the close of the second act, an interesting situation on the stage absorbed the attention of the audience, and feeling myself secure, I gazed, and lost myself in gazing. The intensity of my look seemed to draw her palpably to meet it. She slowly turned her head, and her eyes fell full upon mine. I felt a sweet, wonderful heart-shock, as if our souls had touched and recognized each other. What my eyes said to her I could not guess, — nor what hers said to me. My lids fell, and I sat a moment without breathing. When I looked up, her face was turned again towards the stage, but a soft flush, "which was not so before," lingered along her cheek and throat.

I might have visited the box during the *entr'acte*, but my thoughts had not yet subsided into a sufficiently practical channel. The play closed with the third act, and at its close the party left. Once more our glances met, and I had sufficient courage to bow my recognition, which she returned. I had no mind, however, to wait through the farce, and hurried off Swansford, who was evidently surprised at my impatient, excited manner, following so close on a fit of (for me) very unusual taciturnity. I answered his comments on the play in such a manner that he exclaimed, as we reached the street, —

"What is the matter with you, Godfrey? You don't seem to have your senses about you to-night."

I laughed. "I am either the blindest of bats, the stupidest of owls," I said, "or my senses are miraculously sharpened. I have seen either all, or nothing, — but no, it must, it *shall* be all!"

I caught hold of Swansford's arm and hurried him along with me. As we passed a corner lamp-post, he looked at my face in the light with a puzzled, suspicious expression, which moved me to renewed mirth. He was as far as possible from guessing what was the matter with me.

"Here is Bleecker Street," said I. "Come up to my room, old fellow, and you shall judge whether I am a fool or not."

He complied mechanically, and we were presently seated in opposite arm-chairs, before the smouldering grate. I gave him a glass of Sherry, — a bottle of which I kept on purpose for his visits, — and when I saw that he looked refreshed and comfortable, began my story in an abrupt, indirect way.

"Swansford," I asked, "can a man love twice?"

"I do not know," he answered sadly, after a pause,— "*I* could not." But he lifted his face towards me with a quick, lively interest, which anticipated my confession.

I began at the beginning, and gave him every detail of my acquaintance with Miss Haworth, — the dinner at Delmonico's, the glimpses in the street, the "very sociable" party at Mr. Deering's, the invitation to tea, and finally the meeting of our eyes that very evening. There was no shyness in my heart, although I knew that the future might never give form to its desires.

"That is all," I concluded, "and I do not know what you may think of it. Whether or not I am fickle, easily impressed, or deceived in my own nature, in all other respects, I know that I love this girl with every power of my soul and every pulse of my body!"

I had spoken with my eyes fixed on the crimson gulfs among the falling coals, and without pausing long enough for interruption. There was so little to tell that I must give it all together. Swansford did not immediately answer, and I looked towards him. He was leaning forward, with his elbows on the arms of the chair and his face buried in his hands. His hair seemed damp, and drops of perspiration were starting on his pale forehead. A mad fear darted through my mind, and I cried out, —

"Swansford! Do you know Miss Haworth?"

"No," he replied, in a faint, hollow voice, "I never heard her name before."

His fingers gradually crooked themselves until the tendons of his wrists stood out like cords. Then, straightening his back firmly in the chair, he seized the knobs on the ends of the arms and appeared to be bracing himself to speak.

"I have — no business — with love," he began, slowly; "you should not come to me for judgment, Godfrey. I know nothing about any other heart than my own; it would be better if I knew less of that. You are younger than me; there is thicker blood in your veins. Some, I suppose, are meant to be happy, and God grant that you may be one of them! I am not surprised, only" —

He smiled feebly and stretched out his hand, which I pressed in both mine with a feeling of infinite pity.

"Give me another glass of Sherry," he said, presently. "I am weaker than I used to be. I think one genuine, positive success would make me a strong man; but it 's weary waiting so long, and the prospect no brighter from one year's end to another. Is it not inexplicable that I, who was willing to sacrifice to Art the dearest part of my destiny as a Man, should be robbed of both, as my reward? If I had my life to begin over again, I would try selfish assertion and demand, instead of patient self-abnegation, — but it is now too late to change."

These expressions drew from me a confession of the same stages of protest through which I had passed, — or, rather, was still passing, — for the rebellious thoughts only slumbered in my heart. We exchanged confidences, and I saw that while Swansford admitted to himself the force of the selfish plea, he still considered it with reference to his art. If some master of psychology had said to him, "Sin, and the result will be a symphony!" I believe he would have deliberately sinned. If Mendelssohn had murdered the basso, for his slovenly singing in "Elijah," he would none the less have revered Mendelssohn as a saint. I did not know enough of music to judge of Swansford's genius; but I suspected, from his want of success, that his mind was rather sympathetic than creative. If so, his was the saddest of fates. I would not have added to its darkness by uttering the least of doubts: rather I would have sacrificed my own hopes of literary fame to have given hope to him.

The days grew long and sunny, the trees budded in the city squares, and the snowy magnolias blossomed in the little front-gardens up town. Another summer was not far off, and my mind naturally reverted to the catastrophes of the past, even while enjoying the brightness of the present season. No word from Pennsylvania had reached me in the mean time, and I rather reproached myself, now, for having dropped all correspondence with Reading or Upper Samaria. The firm of Woolley and Himpel, I had no doubt, still flourished, — with the aid of my money; Rand and *his* Amanda (I could not help wondering whether they were happy) probably lived in the same city; Dan Yule was married to the schoolmistress; and Verbena Cuff, I hoped, had found a beau who was not afraid of courting. How I laughed, not only at that, but at many other episodes of my life in Upper Samaria! Then I took down "Leonora's Dream, and Other Poems," for the first time in nearly a year. This was the climax of my disgust. My first sensation was one of simple horror at its crudities; my second one of gratitude that I had grown sufficiently to perceive them.

I was now ambitious of culture rather than fame. I saw that, without the former, I could never rise above a subordinate place in literature, — possibly no higher than the sphere represented by Mrs. Yorkton and her circle; with it, I might truly not attain a shining success, but I should be guarded against failure, because I should know my talents and not misapply them. The thirst for acquiring overlaid, for a time, the desire for producing. After Wordsworth I read Pope, and then went back to Chaucer, intending to come down regularly through the royal succession of English authors; but the character of my necessary labors prevented me from adopting any fixed plan of study, and, as usual, I deserved more credit for good intentions than for actual performance.

Only once more, in the course of the spring, did I secure a brief interview with Miss Haworth. During the Annual Exhibition of the Academy of Design, I met her there, one afternoon, in company with Mrs. Deering. It was a gusty day, and the rooms were not crowded. We looked at several of the principal pictures together, and I should have prolonged the sweet occupation through the remaining hours of daylight, had not the ladies been obliged to leave.

"Do you go anywhere this summer?" Mrs. Deering asked.

"No further than Coney Island," I said, with a smile at the supposition implied by her remark; "a trip of that length, and an absence of six hours, is all the holiday I can afford."

"Then we shall not see you again until next fall. Mr. Deering has taken a cottage for us on the Sound, and Miss Haworth, I believe, is going to the Rocky Mountains, or somewhere near them. Where is it, Isabel?"

"Only to Minnesota and Lake Superior. I shall accompany a friend who goes for her health, and we shall probably spend the whole summer in that region."

"How I wish I could go!" I exclaimed, impetuously. Then, recollecting myself, I added, "But you will tell me all about Minne-ha-ha and the Pictured Rocks, will you not? May I call upon you after your return?"

"I shall always be glad to see you, Mr. Godfrey."

I held her hand and looked in her eyes. It was only for a moment, yet I found myself growing warm and giddy with the insane desire of drawing her to my breast and whispering, "I love you! I love you!"

When they left the exhibition-room, I followed, and leaning over the railing, watched them descending the stairs. At the bottom of the first flight Miss Haworth dropped her parasol, turned before I could anticipate the movement, and saw me. I caught a repeated, hesitating gesture of farewell, and she was gone.

Then began for me the monotonous life of summer in the city, — long days of blazing sunshine and fiery radiations from pavements and brick walls, — nights when the air seemed to wither in its dead sultriness, until thunder came up the coast and boomed over the roofs, — when theatres are shut, and fashionable clergymen are in Europe, and oysters are out of season, and pen and brain work like an ox prodded with the goad. Nevertheless, it was a tolerably happy summer to me. In spite of my natural impatience, I felt that my acquaintance with Miss Haworth had progressed as rapidly as was consistent with the prospect of its fortunate development. If it was destined that she should return my love, the first premonitions of its existence must have already reached her heart. She was too clear-sighted to overlook the signs I had given.

There was one circumstance, however, which often disturbed me. She was an heiress, — worth hundreds of thousands, Penrose had said, — and I a poor young man, earning, by steady labor, little more than was necessary for my support. While I admitted, in my heart of hearts, the insignificance of this consideration to the pure eyes of love,

I could not escape the conventional view of the case. My position was a mercenary one, and no amount of sincerity or fidelity could wash me clear of suspicion. Besides, it reversed what seemed to me the truest and tenderest relation between man and woman. If I won her heart, I should be dependent on her wealth, not she upon my industry and energy. For her sake, I could not wish that wealth less: she was probably accustomed to the habits and tastes it made possible; but it deprived me of the least chance of proving how honest and unselfish was my devotion. All appearances were against me, and if she did not trust me sufficiently to believe my simple word, I was lost. This was a trouble which I could not lighten by imparting it to any one, — not even Swansford. I carried it about secretly with me, taking it out now and then to perplex myself with the search of a solution which might satisfy all parties, — her, myself, and the world.

The summer passed away, and the cool September nights brought relief to the city. One by one the languid inhabitants of brown-stone fronts came back with strength from the hills, or a fresh, salty tang from the sea-shore. The theatres were opened, oysters reappeared without cholera, and the business-streets below the Park were crowded with Western and Southern merchants. The day drew nigh when I should again see my beloved, and my heart throbbed with a firmer and more hopeful pulsation.

CHAPTER XXVIII.

WHICH GIVES AN ACCOUNT OF A FIRE AND WHAT FOLLOWED IT.

During the summer of which I am writing, there was an unusual demand for short, sketchy articles, moral in tendency, but without the dulness of moral essays. They were weak concoctions of flashy, superficial philosophy, generally starting from the text of some trivial incident, and made piquant with a delicate flavor of slang. The school exists to this day, and may be found, in the hectic of its commencing decline, in the columns of certain magazines and literary newspapers. In the days of its youth, it possessed an air of originality which deceived ninety-nine out of every hundred readers, and thus became immensely popular. The demand, increased by the emulation of rival publishers, and accompanied by fabulous remuneration (if the advertisements were true), soon created a corresponding supply, and the number of Montaignes and Montaignesses who arose among us will be a marvel to the literary historian of the next century.

My practice in what the foreman of the *Wonder* composing-room called "fancy city articles," enabled me to profit at once by this new whirl in the literary current. My sketches, entitled "The Omnibus Horse," "Any Thing on This Board for Four Cents," and "Don't Jump!" (the latter suggested by the Jersey City Ferry,) had already been extensively copied, and when Mr. G. Jenks, — rising presently to his feet after the failure of "The Hesperian," as publisher of *The Ship of the Line*, an illustrated weekly, in which the same head did duty as Gen. Cass, Pius IX., and the inventor of the Air-Tight Stove, — when Mr. Jenks, I say, occupied another back-office, and badgered new aspirants for publicity with, "What 's the handle to your Brown? — or Jones?" — he summoned me to his presence and graciously offered me five dollars for a weekly sketch of the popular kind, not to exceed half a column in length.

"Not *too* moral," he added, by way of caution, "though they must *lean* that way. If you can make 'em a little racy, — you understand, — but not so that it can be taken hold of, they 'll go all the better. There 's that book, 'Pepper Pot,' for instance, sold a hundred and fifty thousand copies in six months, — puffed in all the religious papers, — would have been a fortune to me."

I naturally rebelled against this sort of dictation, but having encountered it wherever I turned, I supposed that it was a universal habit of publishers, and must of necessity be endured. The articles required could be easily enough produced, and the fee, small as it was, might accumulate to a respectable little sum if laid aside, week by week, with whatever else I could spare. I therefore accepted the offer, and was laughed at by Brandagee for not having asked twenty dollars.

"If you want to be valued," said he, "you must be your own appraiser. Taking what 's offered is admitting that you 're only worth so much. There was Fleurot, — I knew him when he had but one shirt, and washed it with his own hands every night, but he would n't take a centime less than five thousand francs for the picture on his easel, and got it, sir! — got it, after waiting eighteen months. Then he doubled his price and played the same game. *Now*, if you want anything from his brush, you must order it six years in advance."

There was a large kernel of truth in Brandagee's words, as I afterwards had occasion to discover. He had been absent during the summer, as the *Avenger's* correspondent at the watering-places, claiming his rights as "dead-head" on railways and in hotels, and now returned more audacious and imperious than ever. During his absence, the Cave of Trophonius had been, for the most part, deserted. Miles confessed that he had been obliged to accommodate "other parties" with the use of its oracular walls, but he promised that "you literary gents shall 'ave it agin, 'avin' a sort o' fust claim."

These things, however, belong to the unimportant incidents of my life. An event occurred — as I find by a reference to the files of the *Daily Wonder* for the year 185– — on the night of the 27th of September, which was of vital consequence to my subsequent fortunes.

One of the assistant reporters was sick, and in case anything of interest should transpire, it was expected that I should perform his duty. I had been unusually busy through the day, and at eleven o'clock at night had just corrected and sent into the composing-room my last "copy" for the morning's paper, when the bell on the City Hall began to boom the announcement of a fire. I forced open my heavy eyelids, gave up, with a sigh, the near prospect of sleep and rest, seized my pencil and note-book, and hurried off in the direction indicated by the strokes.

It was a damp, misty night, I remember, and as I reached the elevation of Broadway at Leonard Street, I could distinguish a dull glimmer over the tops of the tall houses on the western side. I could hear the sharp, quick rattle of a fire-engine dashing up Church Street, while others, coming from the eastern part of the city, shot through the Canal Street crossing. The fire was somewhere in the Tenth Ward, it seemed, — a trifling affair, not worth keeping me from my bed, I thought, but for the certainty of the *Avenger's* reporter being on hand, eager to distance the *Wonder* in the morning, and then proclaim the fact, next day, as a triumph of "newspaper enterprise."

A few minutes more brought me to the scene. It was in

Green Street, near Broome. The flames were already bursting out of the windows of a tall brick house; three or four streams from as many engines were sparkling and hissing in the red light, having as yet made no headway against the conflagration; and a line of policemen, on either side, kept back the increasing mass of spectators. There were shouts of command, cries, exclamations; alarm and excitement in the opposite and adjoining houses, and a wet, sooty, dirty chaos of people, furniture, beams, and bricks, pouring out from below, or hurled down from above the fiery confusion. I was accustomed to such scenes and thought only of following my professional instinct, — ascertaining the name of the owner of the property, its value, and the amount of insurance upon it.

A word to a captain of police, and the exhibition of my pencil and note-book, procured me admission into the space cleared for the engines and hose-carriages in front of the fire. Here I was alternately sprinkled by upward spirts from pin-holes in the snaky hose, and scorched by downward whiffs of air, but I had the entire scene under my eye and could pick up my information from the tenants of the burning house, as soon as they had done saving their mattresses and looking-glasses, — the objects first rescued on such occasions.

The second house on the left, just opposite my perch on the top of a shabby chest of drawers, was brilliantly lighted. The shutters being thrown back and the windows opened, I looked directly into a sumptuous double parlor, which appeared to be the scene of an interrupted entertainment. The lid of the piano was lifted, and a table in the centre was covered with glasses and bottles. At each window were grouped three or four girls, with bare white shoulders and arms, talking and laughing loudly with such firemen as took a moment's breathing-spell on the sidewalk under them. Glasses, I could see, were occasionally passed down to the latter.

"It 's a chance if Old Western is n't smoked out of her hole," remarked one policeman to another.

"Faith, she might be spared from this neighborhood," the latter answered, laughing. "They are carrying the hose up to her roof, now!"

I looked up and saw the helmet and red shirt of a fireman behind the eaves. The street-door was entered without ceremony, and I presently noticed a commotion among the careless inmates. A policeman made his appearance in the parlor; the bottles were swiftly removed, and, at a signal from a middle-aged woman, with a hawk's beak of a nose, the girls disappeared.

All at once, a part of the roof of the burning building fell in. A cloud of fiery dust arose, raining into the street as it rolled across the inky sky. The heat became intense: the men who worked the nearest engine were continually drenched with water to prevent their clothes taking fire. My position became untenable, without more risk than a reporter is justified in running for the sake of an item of twelve lines, and I hastily retreated across the street. By this time many other engines had arrived, and larger space was required for their operations. I was literally driven to the wall by the press of wheels and water-jets and the reckless earnestness of the firemen.

Perceiving a narrow, arched passage between the two houses, — an old-fashioned kitchen-entrance, — I took refuge in it. The conflagration lighted up the further end, and showed me that a hose had been already laid there and carried to the rear. I therefore determined to follow it and ascertain what could be seen from the other side. By the help of some stakes and the remains of a grape-arbor, I climbed to the top of the board-fence which inclosed the back-yard. The wind blew from the west, and thus, although I found myself quite near to the fire, I was not much incommoded by the heat. The brave fellows on the roof of the nearest house moved about in dark relief against the flickering, surging background of dun and scarlet light. I shuddered as I saw them walking on the brink and peering down into the fatal gulf. A strong reflected lustre was thrown upon the surrounding houses from the low-hanging mist, and revealed every object with wonderful distinctness.

There was a rear wing to the house designated by the policeman as belonging to "Old Western," and I had taken my stand near one corner of it, at the junction of the fences with those of two back-yards belonging to the opposite houses in Wooster Street. I had not been stationed thus two minutes, before an agitated, entreating voice came down to me, —

"Oh, sir, good sir, — please help me to get away!"

I looked up. A window in the end of the rear wing was open, and out of it leaned a girl, partly dressed, and with her hair hanging about her ears, but with a shawl closely drawn over her shoulders and breast. She was not more than seventeen or eighteen. The expression of her face was wild, frightened, eager, and I imagined that she was so confused by fear as to have forgotten the ready means of escape by the street-door.

"Please help me, quick — quick!" she repeated.

"The house is not on fire yet," I said; "you can go out through the front without danger."

"Oh, not that way, — not that way!" she exclaimed. "It 's not the fire, — it 's the *house* I 'm afraid of. Oh, save me, sir, save me!"

I had read, in the *Police Gazette* and other classical papers which sometimes fell into my hands, of innocent girls decoyed into dens of infamy, very much as I had read of human sacrifices in Dahomey, without supposing that any such case would be brought directly home to my own experience. This seemed to me to be an instance of the kind, — the girl, at least, desired to escape from the house, and I could not doubt, one moment, the obligation upon me to give her assistance.

"I will save you if I can," I said, "but it is impossible for you to come down from that window. Can I get into the house?"

"There is no time," she panted, — "you do not know the way, — she might come back. I will go down into the yard, and you can help me over the fence. Wait, — I'm coming!"

With these words she disappeared from the window. I shared her haste and anxiety, without comprehending it, and set about devising a plan to get her over the inclosure. The floor of the yard was paved, and, I judged, about ten feet below me: I might barely reach her hand by stooping down, but it would be very difficult to lift her to the top without a stay for my own exertions. All at once I caught an idea from the dilapidated arbor. It was an easy matter to loosen one of the top-pieces, with its transverse lattice-bars, and let it down in the corner. This furnished at the same time a stay for me, and an assistance to her feet. I had barely placed it in the proper position before a lower door opened, and she hurried breathlessly up the pavement.

"Quick!" she whispered; "they are all over the house, — they may see us any minute!"

I directed her how to climb. The lowest strip of lattice broke away; the second held, and it enabled her to reach my hand. In two more seconds she stood, tottering, on the narrow ledge beside me.

"Now," I said, "we must get down on the other side."

"Here, — here!" she exclaimed, pointing into the garden of one of the Wooster-Street houses, — "we must get out that way. Not in front, — she would see me!"

She was so terribly in earnest that I never thought of disputing her will. I carefully drew up the rough ladder, let it down on the other side, and helped her to descend. Then I followed.

There was not a moment to spare. I had scarcely touched the earth, before a strong, stern woman's voice cried, "Jane! Jane!" from the room above us. The girl shuddered and seized me by the arm. I bade her, with a gesture, crouch in the corner, where she would be safely hidden from view, and stole along the fence until I caught sight of the window. Once the hawk's beak passed in profile before it, and the same voice said, "Damn the girl! where is she?"

A strong light shone into the room through a window on the north side. There was a slamming of doors, a dragging noise accompanied by shouts, and then a male voice, which seemed very familiar to my ear, said, as if in reply to "Old Western's" profane exclamation, —

"What's the matter, old woman? Lost one of 'em?"

In a moment, the hose being apparently adjusted, a stout, square figure in a red shirt came to the window. I could plainly see that the hair, also, was red, the face broad, the neck thick, — in short, that it was my young friend, Hugh Maloney.

"She can't ha' jumped out here," he said. "You need n't be worrited, — you 'll find her down in front among your other gals."

A minute or two of further waiting convinced me that there was no danger of the means of escape being detected. The occupants of the Wooster-Street houses were all awake and astir, and I must procure an exit for us through the one to which the garden belonged. I spoke a word of encouragement to the girl, picked up the light bundle of clothes she had brought with her, and boldly approached the rear of the house. This movement, of course, was observed by the spectators at the bedroom windows, and, after a little parley, a man came down with a candle and admitted us into the back-kitchen. When he had carefully refastened the bolts, darting a suspicious glance at myself and my companion, he conducted us through to the front door. A woman's face, framed in a nightcap, looked down at us around the staircase-landing, and, just before the door slammed behind us, I heard her call out, "Don't let any more of those creatures pass!"

I fancy the girl must have heard it too, for she turned to me with a fresh appeal, — "I 'm not safe yet, — take me away, — away out of danger!"

I gave her my arm, to which she clung as if it were a fluke of Hope's own anchor, and said, as we walked up the streets, —

"Where do you wish to go? Have you no friends or acquaintances in the city?"

"Oh, none!" she cried. "I don't know anybody but — but one I ought n't to have ever known! I 'm from the country; I did n't go into that house of my own will, and I could n't get out after I found what it was. I know what you must think of me, sir, but I 'll tell you everything, and maybe, then, you 'll believe that I 'm not quite so wicked as I seem. Take me anywhere, — I don't care if it 's a shanty, so I can hide and be safe. Don't think that I meant your own house; you 've helped me, and I 'd die rather than put disgrace on you. The Lord help me! — I may be doing that now."

She covered her face with her hands and began to cry. I felt that she spoke the simple truth, and my pity and sympathy were all the more keen, because I had never before encountered this form of a ruined life. I was resolved to help her, cost what it might. As for disgrace, the very fear she expressed showed her ignorance of the world. In a great city, unfortunately, young men may brave more than one aspect of disgrace with perfect impunity.

"Would you not like to go back to your friends in the country?" I asked, after a moment's reflection.

"I could n't," she moaned. "I think it would kill me to meet any of them now. It was a sin to leave them the way I did. If I could get shelter in some out-of-the-way street where there 'd be no danger of *her* finding me, — no matter how poor and mean it was, — I 'd work night and day to earn an honest living. I 'm handy with the needle, — it 's the trade I was learning when" —

A plan had presented itself to my mind while she was speaking. I think that vision of Hugh's head at the window suggested it. I would go with her to Mary Maloney and beg the latter to give her shelter for a day or two, until employment could be found. In Gooseberry Alley she would be secure against discovery, and I believed that Mary Maloney, even if she knew the girl's history, would be willing to help her at my request. Nevertheless, I reflected, it was better, perhaps, not to put the widow to this test. It would be enough to say that the girl was a stranger who had come to the city, had been disappointed in obtaining employment, and now found herself alone, friendless, and without means. Then I remembered, also, that my own stock of linen needed to be replenished, and I could therefore supply her with occupation for the first week or two.

I stated this plan in a few words, and it was gladly accepted. The girl overwhelmed me with her professions of gratitude, of her desire to work faithfully and prove herself deserving of help. She knew she could never recover her good name, she said, but it should not be made worse. I, who had saved her, must have evidence that I had not done it in vain.

As we turned down Houston in the direction of Sullivan Street, we met a party of four aristocratic youths, in the first stage of elegant dissipation. The girl clung to my arm so convulsively and seemed so alarmed that I crossed with her to the opposite sidewalk. They stopped and apparently scrutinized us closely. I walked forward, however, without turning my head until we reached the corner of Sullivan Street. When I looked back, they had disappeared, — there was only a single person, standing in the shadow of the trees.

Gooseberry Alley was quiet, and the coolness of the

night had partly suppressed its noisome odors. I stopped under the lamp at the corner, and, while I said, " This is the place I spoke of, — are you willing to try it ? " — examined the girl's face for the first time.

She was rather short of stature, but of slight and graceful build. Her face was pale, but the bloom of her lips showed that her cheeks could no doubt match them with a pretty tint of pink. Her eyes — either of dark gray or hazel — were troubled, but something of their girlish expression of innocent ignorance remained. A simple, honest loving heart, I was sure, still beat beneath the mask of sadness and shame. It never occurred to me that I was too young to be her protector, — that the relation between us would not only be very suspicious in the sight of the world, but was in itself both delicate and difficult. Neither did it occur to me that I might have dispensed with the confession she had promised to make, sparing her its pain, and allowing her to work out her redemption silently, with the little help I was able to give. On the contrary, I imagined that this confession was necessary, — that it was my duty to hear, as hers to give it.

" I have not time to hear your story to-night," I said. " I will see you again soon. But you have not yet told me your name."

" Jane Berry," she whispered.

" And mine is John Godfrey."

I knocked at the door of the tenement-house, and after some delay, and the preliminary projection of Feeny's sleepy head from the second-story window, was admitted by Mary Maloney herself. She had sprung out of bed and rushed down-stairs in a toilette improvised for the occasion, — a ragged patch-work quilt held tightly to her spare body and trailing on the floor behind her, — under the impression that something must have happened to Hugh. In order to allay her fears, I came within an ace of betraying that I had seen the latter. I told her the fictitious story

(Heaven pardon me for it!) which I had composed, and asked her assistance. The fragment of burning tallow in her hand revealed enough of Jane Berry's pretty face and tearful, imploring eyes, to touch the Irishwoman's heart.

"Indade, and it 's little I can do," she said, "but you 're welcome to that little, Miss, even without Mr. Godfrey's askin'. And to think that you met him in the street, too, jist as I did! It 's a mercy it was *him*, instid o' the other young fellows that goes ragin' around o' nights."

I could imagine the pang which these words caused to the poor girl's heart, and therefore, saying that I had still work to do, and they must both go to rest at once, hurried away from the house.

My notes were incomplete, and I was obliged to return to the scene of the fire, where I found smoke and ruin instead of flames. Two or three engines were playing into the smouldering hollows, sending up clouds of steam from the hot bricks and burning timbers, and the torches of the firemen showed the piles of damaged furniture in the plashy street. Two houses had been destroyed, and the walls of one having fallen, there was a gap like a broken tooth in the even line of the block.

I soon learned that there had been an accident. The front wall, crashing down unexpectedly, had fallen upon a fireman who was in the act of removing a ladder. They had carried him to the nearest druggist's on Broadway, and it was feared that his hurt was fatal. The men talked about it calmly, as of an ordinary occurrence, but performed their duties with a slow, mechanical air, which told of weariness and sadness.

Of course, I was obliged to visit the druggist's, and obtain the name and condition of the unfortunate man. The business of a reporter precludes indulgence in sentiment, prohibits delicacy of feeling. If the victim of a tragedy is able to give his name, age, and place of residence, he may then die in peace. The family, drowned in tears and despair, must nevertheless furnish the particulars of the murder or suicide. Public curiosity, represented by the agent of the newspaper, claims its privilege, and will not abate one item of the harrowing details.

The policeman, guarding the door from the rush of an excited crowd, admitted me behind the blue and crimson globes. The injured man, bedded on such cushions as the shop afforded, lay upon the floor, surrounded by a group of his fellow-firemen. His shirt had been cut off, and his white, massive breast lay bare under the lamp. There was no external sign of injury, but a professional eye could see knobs and protrusions of flesh which did not correspond to the natural overlapping of the muscles. A surgeon, kneeling beside his head, held one arm, with his finger on the pulse, and wiped away with a sponge the bloody foam which bubbled from his lips.

Presently the man opened his eyes, — large, clear, solemn eyes, full of mysterious, incomprehensible speech. His lips moved feebly, and although no sound came from them, I saw, and I think all the others saw, that the word he would have uttered was, " Good-bye ! "

" He has but a minute more, poor fellow ! " whispered the surgeon.

Then, as by a single impulse, each one of the rough group of firemen took off his helmet, knelt upon the floor, and reverently bowed his head in silence around the dying man. I knelt beside them, awed and thrilled to the depths of my soul by the scene. The fading lips partly curved in an ineffable smile of peace; the eyes did not close again, but the life slowly died out of them ; a few convulsive movements of the body, and the shattered breast became stone. Then a hand gently pressed down the lids, and the kneeling men arose. There was not a sob, nor a sound, but every face was wet with tears unconsciously shed. They lifted the body of their comrade and bore him tenderly away.

It was nearly three o'clock in the morning before my task was finished, and I could go home to bed with a good conscience. I had passed the crisis of fatigue, and was preternaturally awake in every sense. The two incidents of the night powerfully affected me; dissimilar as they were, either seemed to spring from something originally noble and undefiled in the nature of Man. The homage of those firemen to the sanctity of Death made them my brothers; the ruder and more repellant aspects of their lives drifted away like smoke before this revelation of tenderness. To Jane Berry, however, my relation assumed the pride and importance of a protector, — possibly of a saving agent. The remembrance of what I had done in her case filled me with perfect, serene happiness. I will not say that vanity, — that selfishness (though Heaven knows how!) had no part in my satisfaction; many profound teachers and exceedingly proper persons will tell us so; — nor do I much care. I knew that I had done a good deed, and it was right I should deem that the approving smile of Our Father hallowed my sleep that night.

CHAPTER XXIX.

IN WHICH PENROSE FLINGS DOWN THE GLOVE AND I PICK IT UP.

Mary Maloney called upon me the next morning, as I had requested her to do. The girl, she said, had shared her own bed, and had risen apparently refreshed and cheerful. Hugh, who came home after midnight, had been inclined to oppose the acceptance of the new tenant, until she explained to him the "rights of it," whereupon he had acquiesced. She thought there would not be much difficulty in procuring work, as the busy season for tailors and sempstresses was coming on; and, meantime, she herself would attend to buying the linen and other materials for my new shirts.

Having furnished the money for this purpose, and added a small sum for the girl's support until she was able to earn something, I considered that nothing more could be done until my knowledge of her story gave me other means of assisting her. I was naturally curious to learn more about her, but my occupation during the days immediately succeeding the fire prevented my promised visit, and very soon other events occurred to delay it still further.

Mrs. Deering returned from her summer residence on the Sound during the first week of October, and I was not long in discovering the fact and calling upon her. She had corresponded with Miss Haworth during the summer, and gave, without my asking, an outline of the latter's journey, adding that she was now on her way home. If I had not already betrayed myself to Miss Deering's detective eye, I must certainly have done it then. I felt and expressed altogether too much happiness for a young gentleman to manifest in regard to the return of a young lady, without some special cause. I was perfectly willing that she should suspect my secret, so long as its disclosure was reserved for the one who had the first right to hear it.

From that day my walks at leisure times extended beyond Fourteenth Street. I watched the house in Gramercy Park, until observed (detected, I fancied) by Mr. Tracy Floyd, who tossed me an insolent half-recognition as he passed. In a week, however, there was evidence of Miss Haworth's arrival. I did not see her, but there was no mistaking the character of the trunks which were unloaded from an express-wagon at the door.

I allowed two days to elapse before calling. It was a compromise between prudence and impatience. The event was of too much importance to hazard an unsatisfactory issue. Not that I intended declaring my love, or consciously permitting it to be expressed in my words and actions; but I felt that in thus meeting, after an absence of some months, there would be something either to flatter my hope or discourage it wholly.

I dressed myself and took my way across Union Square and up Fourth Avenue, with considerable trepidation of mind. I was aware that my visit was sanctioned by the liberal conventionalism of the city, and, moreover, I had her permission to make it, — yet the consciousness of the secret I carried troubled me. My heart throbbed restlessly as when, three or four years before, I had carried my poem of the "Unknown Bard" to the newspaper office. But I never thought of turning back this time.

I was so fortunate as to find Miss Haworth at home and Mr. Floyd out. The latter, I suspect, had not credited me with boldness enough for the deed, and had therefore taken no precautions against guarding the beauty and the fortune which he was determined to possess.

I looked around the sumptuous parlor while awaiting Miss Haworth's appearance, and recognized in the pictures, the bronzes, the elegant disposition of furniture and ornaments, the evidence of her taste. It was wealth, not coarse, glaring, and obtrusive, but chastened and ennobled by culture. Thank God! I whispered to myself, money is her slave, not her deity.

The silken rustling on the stairs sent a thousand tremors along my nerves, but I steadily faced the door by which she would enter, and advanced to meet her as soon as I saw the gray gleam of her dress. How bright and beautiful she was! — not flashing and dazzling as one accustomed to conquest, but with a soft, subdued lustre, folding in happy warmth the heart that reverently approached her. Her face had caught a bloom and her eye an added clearness from the breezes of the Northwest; I dared not take to myself the least ray of her cheerful brightness. But I did say — for I could not help it — that I was very glad to see her again, and that I had often thought of her during the long summer.

"You must have found it long, indeed," she said, "not being allowed to escape from the city. I am afraid I have hardly deserved my magnificent holiday, except by enjoying it. You, who could have described the shores of Lake Superior and the cliffs and cataracts of the Upper Mississippi, ought to have had the privilege of seeing them rather than myself."

"No, no!" I exclaimed. "The capacity to enjoy gives you the very highest right. And I am sure that you can also describe. Do you remember your promise, when I had the pleasure of meeting you in the Exhibition Rooms? You were to tell me about all you should see."

"Was it a promise? Then I must try to deserve my privilege in that way. But here is something better than description, which I have brought back with me."

She took a portfolio from the table and drew out a number

of photographic views. The inspection of these required explanations on her part, and she was unconsciously led to add her pictures to those of the sun. I saw how truly she had appreciated and how clearly remembered the scenes of her journey; our conversation became frank, familiar, and in the highest degree delightful to me. A happy half-hour passed away, and I had entirely forgotten the proprieties, to the observance of which I had mentally bound myself, when the servant announced, —

"Mr. Penrose!"

I started, and, from an impulse impossible to resist, looked at Miss Haworth. I fancied that an expression of surprise and annoyance passed over her face, — but it was so faint that I could not be certain. My conversation with her concerning him, at Deering's "very sociable" party, recurred to my mind, and I awaited his entrance with a curious interest. There was nothing in the manner of her reception, however, to enlighten me. She was quietly self-possessed, and as cordial as their previous social intercourse required.

On the other hand, Penrose, I thought, was not quite at ease. I had not seen him before, since his return from Saratoga, and was prepared for the quick glance of surprise with which he regarded me. The steady, penetrating expression of his eyes, as we shook hands, drew a little color into my face; he was so skilful in reading me that I feared my secret was no longer safe. For this very reason I determined to remain, and assume a more formal air, in the hope of deceiving him. Besides, I was desirous to study, if possible, the degree and character of his acquaintance with Miss Haworth.

"Ah! these are souvenirs of your trip, I suppose," he said, glancing at the photographs as he rolled a heavy velvet chair towards the table and took his seat. "I only heard of your arrival this evening, from Mrs. Deering, and hoped that I would be the first to compliment you on your daring; but Mr. Godfrey, I see, has deprived me of that pleasure."

To my surprise, a light flush ran over Miss Haworth's face, and she hesitated a moment, as if uncertain what reply to make. It was but for a moment; she picked up some of the photographs and said, —

"Have you ever seen these views of Lake Pepin?"

"No," he answered, running over them like a pack of cards; "superb! magnificent! By Jove, I shall have to make the trip myself. But I would rather see a photograph of Lake George. What a pity we can't fix heroic deeds as well as landscapes!"

"Mr. Penrose," Miss Haworth remarked, with an air of quiet dignity, "I would rather, if you please, not hear any further allusion to that."

"Pardon me, Miss Haworth," he said, bowing gravely; "I ought to have known that you are as modest as you are courageous. I will be silent, of course, but you cannot forbid me the respect and admiration I shall always feel."

What did they mean? Something of which I was ignorant had evidently taken place, and her disinclination to hear it discussed prevented me from asking a question. My interest in the conversation increased, although the pause which ensued after Penrose's last words hinted to me that the subject must be changed. I was trying to think of a fresh topic, when he resumed, with his usual easy adroitness, —

"I don't suppose I ever did a really good deed in my life, Miss Haworth, — that is, with deliberate intention. One does such things accidentally, sometimes."

"Don't believe him!" said I. "He likes to be thought worse than he really is."

"If that is true, I should call it a perverted vanity," Miss Haworth remarked.

"You are quite right," Penrose replied to her, "but it is not true. I have no mind to be considered worse than I am, but to be considered better implies hypocrisy on my part. I might compromise for my lack of active goodness, as most people do, by liberal contributions to missions and tract-societies, and rejoice in a saintly reputation. But where would be the use? It would only be playing a more tiresome *rôle* in the great comedy. Because I am not the virtuous hero, I need not necessarily be the insidious villain of the plot. The walking gentleman suits me better. I know all the other characters, but they are my 'kyind friends,'— I treat them with equal politeness, avoid their fuss and excitement, and reach the *dénouement* without tearing my hair or deranging my dress."

He spoke in a gay, rattling tone, as if not expecting that his assertions would be believed. Miss Haworth smiled at the part he assumed, but said nothing.

"What will you do when the play is over?" I asked.

"Come, Godfrey, don't bring me to bay. Everything on this planet repeats itself once in twenty-eight thousand years. In the mean time, I may go on a starring tour (pardon the pun, Miss Haworth, it is n't my habit) through the other parts of the universe. Why should one be brought up with a serious round turn at every corner? It should be the object of one's life to escape the seriousness of Life."

"Death is the most serious aspect of Life," I said, "and it is not well that we should turn our faces away from it."

I could not talk lightly on subjects of such earnest import. Death and ruin had too recently touched my own experience. I began to tell the story of the crushed fireman, and Penrose, though at first he looked bored, finally succumbed to the impression of the death-scene. I found myself strangely moved as I recounted the particulars, and it required some effort to preserve the steadiness of my voice. When I closed there were tears in Miss Haworth's lovely eyes. Penrose drew a long breath and exclaimed,—

"That was a grand exit."

Then his face darkened, and he became silent and moody.

I heard the street-door open, and suspecting that it was Mr. Tracy Floyd, whom I had no desire to meet, rose to take leave. Penrose followed my example, saying, as he lightly touched Miss Haworth's hand, —

"Do not misunderstand me if I have failed to respect your delicacy of feeling. I assure you I meant to express no empty, formal compliment."

"The case has been greatly magnified, I have no doubt," she answered. "I simply obeyed a natural impulse, which, I am sure, any other person would have felt, and it is not agreeable to me to have a reputation for heroism on such cheap terms."

I presume my face expressed my wonder at these words, for she smiled with eyes still dewy from the tears I had called forth — a warm, liquid, speaking smile, which I answered with a tender pressure of her hand. The next moment, frightened at my own boldness, and tingling with rosy thrills of passion, I turned to meet Mr. Floyd at the door.

Penrose greeted him with a cool, off-hand air of superiority, and I answered his amazed stare with the smallest and stiffest fragment of a bow. We were in the street before he had time to recover.

We turned into and walked down Fourth Avenue side by side. I made some remarks about the night and the weather, to which Penrose did not reply. His head was bent, and he appeared to be busy with his own thoughts. Presently, however, he took hold of my arm with a fierce grasp, and exclaimed, —

"John, did *you* mention it to her? And did she allow you to speak of it?"

"What do you mean?" I asked. "What was it? You and she were speaking in riddles. I know nothing more than that she did something which you admire, but which she does not wish to have mentioned."

"And you really don't know? That girl is a trump, John

Godfrey. She saved a man's life at the risk of her own, a fortnight ago."

"Is it possible?" I exclaimed. "Where? How?"

"At Lake George. They were there on their return from the Northwest. The season was nearly over, you know, and there were not many persons at the hotel, but I had the story from Welford, our next-door neighbor in Chambers Street, who was one of them. It seems that she had gone off alone, strolling along the shore, and as the day was clear and hot, had taken a seat somewhere under a tree, near the water, beside a little point of rock. One of the Irish waiters went into the lake for a bath, and whether he got beyond his depth and could n't swim, or whether the coldness of the water gave him the cramp, I don't know, but the fact is he went down. Up he came again, splashing and strangling; she heard the noise, sprang upon the rock, and saw the fellow as he went down the second time. Another girl would have stood and screeched, but she walked straight into the lake — think of it, by Jove! — until the water reached her chin. She could see his body on the bottom, and perhaps he, too, saw her white dress near him, for he stretched out his arm towards her. She shut her eyes, plunged under and just caught him by the tip of a finger. Good God, if she had lost her balance! His hand closed on hers with a death-grip. She drew him into shallower water, then, by main force, — big and heavy as he was, — upon the sand, threw his clothes over his body, and stuck her parasol into the ground to keep the sun off his head. There was a scene at the hotel when she walked in, drowned and dripping from head to foot, and called the landlord to the rescue. The man was saved, and I hear there was no end to his gratitude. The other young ladies, Welford says, thought it very romantic and predicted a marriage, until they found it was an Irish waiter, when they turned up their noses and said, 'How could she do such a thing?'"

Penrose closed his story with a profane exclamation which I will not repeat. The noble, heroic girl! I was filled with pride and admiration — it was honor but to love her, it would be bliss unspeakable to win her!

"It was gloriously done!" I cried. "There is nobody like her." I quite forgot that I was betraying myself.

"John," said Penrose, "come into the square. You and I must have an explanation. You love Isabel Haworth, and so do I!"

"Good God, Alexander! Are you serious?"

"Serious?" he echoed, with a savage intensity which silenced me. We entered the eastern gate of the oval enclosure, which, at that hour, was almost deserted. Two or three footsteps only crushed the broad gravel-paths. The leaves were falling, at intervals, from the trees, and the water gurgled out of the pipes in the middle of the basin. I followed him to the central circle, where he stopped, turned, and faced me. His eyes shone upon me with a strong, lambent gleam, out of the shadows of the night. I was chilled and bewildered by the unexpected disclosure of our rivalry, and nerved myself to meet his coming words, the purport of which I began to forebode.

"John Godfrey," he said at last, in a low voice, which, by its forced steadiness, expressed the very agitation it should have concealed, — "John Godfrey, there is no use in trying to disguise the truth from each other. You would soon discover that I love Isabel Haworth, and I prefer telling you now. You and I have been friends, but if you are as much in earnest as I take you to be, we are from this time forth rivals, — perhaps enemies."

He paused. I tried to reflect whether this hostile relation — for so his words presented it — was indeed inevitable.

"Towards another man," he continued, "I should not be so frank. But I am ready to show you my hand, because I have determined to win the game in spite of you. I have told you that I am intensely selfish, and what my nature demands that it must have. You are in my way, and unless you prove yourself the stronger, I shall crush you down. I don't know what claims you make to the possession of this girl, — but it is not necessary to measure claims. I admit none except my own. When Matilda recommended her to me as an eligible match, I kept away from her, having no mind for matches *de convenance*, — least of all, of Matilda's making; but little by little I learned to know her. I saw, not her fortune, but a rare and noble woman, — such a woman as I have been waiting for, — welcome to me as Morning to Night. She is my Eos, — my Aurora."

The stern defiance of his voice melted away, and he pronounced the last words with a tender, tremulous music, which showed to me how powerfully his heart was moved by the thought of her. But was she not all this to me — and more? Not alone my future fortune, but compensation for a disappointed past? Yes: I felt it, as never before, and grew desperate with the knowledge, that, whatever the issue might be, at least one of us was destined to be unhappy forever.

"You say nothing," he said, at last. "I repeat to you I shall win her. Will you relinquish the field? or will you follow a vain hope, and make us enemies? I have given you fair warning, and want your decision."

"You shall have it at once, Alexander," I replied. "I will be equally frank. Like you, I admit no claims except my own. This is a matter in which your fortune, your superior advantages of person and social culture give you no additional right. It takes more than your own will to achieve success: you seem to leave *her* out of the account. So long as she has not spoken against me, I also may hope. I will *not* relinquish the field. You say I love her, and you ask me to act as if my love were a farce! Rivals we must be: it cannot be helped; but I will try not to become your enemy."

He laughed. "I warn you," he said, "not to depend on your ideal of human generosity and magnanimity. If you are fortunate, — I simply accept your own supposition, for the moment, — you would not feel hostility towards me. Oh, no! the fortunate can easily be generous. But don't imagine that I should play Pythias to your Damon in that case, or that you will be any more inclined to do it for me when the case is reversed. No; let us face the truth. One of us will never forgive the other."

"It may be as you say," I answered, sadly. "Would to God it had not happened so!"

"Cousin John," cried Penrose, suddenly, seizing me by the hand, "I know the world better than you do. I know that love, nine times out of ten, can be kindled and made to burn by the breath of the stronger nature that craves it. I am cool-headed, and know how to play my powers, — yes, my passions, if need be. You say I leave *her* out of the account, but it is only because I believe her affections to be free. The question is, which of us shall first catch and hold them? I shall succeed, because I most need to be successful. Think what a cold, isolated existence is mine, — how few human beings I can even approach, — and of those few what a miracle that one forces me to love her! See, then, how all the brightness of my life hangs on this chance. Give up the rivalry, John; it is not life or death with you; you have friends; you will have fame; yours is a nature to form new ties easily; you will find sunshine somewhere else without trying to rob me of mine!"

My feelings were profoundly touched by his appeal, and possibly some romantic idea of generosity may have weakened my resolution for a moment. My heart, however, reasserted its right, reminding me that love cancels all duties except its own. Possibly — and the thought stung me with a sharp sense of joy — I was speaking for her life as well as mine. But, whether or not, I dared not yield merely because his trumpet sounded a boast of triumph; I must stand and meet the onset.

"Alexander," I said, "ask me anything but this. When Isabel Haworth tells me with her own lips that she cannot love me, I will stand back and pray God to turn her heart to you. But, loving her as I do, that love, uncertain as is its fortune, binds me to sacred allegiance. While it lasts, I dare not and will not acknowledge any other law. If it meets its counterpart in her, I will not fear the powers you may bring to move her, — she is mine, though all the world were in league with you. I shall employ no arts; I shall take no unfair advantage; but if God has meant her for me, I shall accept the blessing when He chooses to place it in my hands."

Penrose stood silent, with folded arms. It was some time before he spoke, and when he did so, it was with a voice singularly changed and subdued. "I might have known it would end so," he said; "there is another strength which is as stubborn as mine. I have more reason to fear you than I supposed. It is to be a fight, then; better, perhaps, with you than with another. Hereafter we shall meet with lances in rest and visors down. Give me your hand, John, — it may be we shall never shake hands again."

Out of the night flashed a picture of the wild dell in Honeybrook, and the dark-eyed boy, first stretching out a cousin's hand to me from his seat on the mossy log. Was the picture also in his mind that our hands clung to each other so closely and so long? I could have sobbed for very grief and tenderness, if my heart had not been held by a passion too powerful for tears.

We walked side by side down Broadway. Neither spoke a word until we parted with a quiet "Good-night!" at the corner of Bleecker Street. There was but one contingency which might bring us together again as we were of old, — disappointment to both.

CHAPTER XXX.

WHICH BRINGS A THUNDERBOLT.

During my interview with Penrose, I was supported by the strength of an excitement which stimulated all my powers of mind and heart. The reaction followed, and showed me how desperate were my chances. He was in every respect — save the single quality of fidelity — my superior; and unless she should discover that hidden virtue in me, and accept it as outweighing culture, brilliancy, and manly energy, there was every probability that she would prefer my cousin, if called upon to choose between us. The first impression which he produced upon her did not seem to be favorable, but I drew little comfort therefrom. His face was "not easily read," she had said, which only indicated that she had not yet read it. Certain obvious characteristics may clash, even while the two natures are drawing nearer and nearer in the mystic, eternal harmony of love. On the other hand, I had flattered my hopes from the discovery of points of sympathy, little tokens of mutual attraction; but how deep did those signs reach? Had I any right to assume that they expressed more on her side than that æsthetic satisfaction which earnest minds derive from contact? Possessing literary tastes, she might feel some interest in me as a young author. It was all dark and doubtful, and I shrank from making the only venture which would bring certainty.

I had congratulated myself on the force of character, which, I fancied, had fully developed itself out of the circumstances of my life. No doubt I had made a great stride forwards, — no doubt I was rapidly becoming independent and self-reliant, — but the transformation was far from being complete. This new uncertainty set me adrift. My will seemed as yet but the foundation of a pier, not sufficiently raised above the shifting tides of my feelings to support the firm arch of fortune. I envied Penrose the possession of his more imperious, determined quality. Moreover, the gulf into which I had looked was not yet sealed; there were hollow echoes under my thoughts, — incredulous whispers mocked the voice of my hope, — and at times a dark, inexorable Necessity usurped the government of Life.

Through all these fluctuations, my love remained warm and unwavering. I clung to it, and order gradually returned out of the apparent chaos. It contained the promise of Faith, of reconciliation with the perverted order of the world.

I now recalled, with a sense of shame, my neglect of Jane Berry since the night of her rescue, and made it a point to visit Gooseberry Alley next morning, before going down town. I found her in Mary Maloney's kitchen, assisting the latter in starching her linen. Her hair was smoothly and neatly arranged, the bright color had come back to her face, and she was, in truth, a very pretty, attractive girl. A joyous light sparkled in her eyes when she first looked up, on my entrance, but her lids then fell and a deep blush mantled her cheeks.

"And it's a long time ye take, before you show y'rself, Mr. Godfrey," exclaimed Mary Maloney. "Here's Miss Jenny was beginnin' to think she'd niver see ye agin."

"You might have told her better, Mary," I said. "I have been remiss, I know, Miss Berry, but I wanted to discover some chance of employment for you before calling. I am sorry to say that I have found nothing yet."

"You are very kind, sir," she answered, "and I don't wish to trouble you more than can be helped. Mary has been making inquiries, and she expects to get some work for me very soon."

"Yes," said Mary; "she 's frettin' herself, for fear that she 's a burden on me; but, indade, she ates no more than a bird, and it is n't me that 's hard put to it to live, since Hugh airns his six dollars a wake. He pays the rint, ivery bit of it, and keeps hisself in clothes, and I don't begrudge the lad a shillin' or so o' spendin'-money, as well as his aiquals. I have my health, God be praised, and indade the company she 's to me seems to give me a power o' sperrit. But there 's them that don't like to be beholden to others, and I can't say as I blame 'em."

"Oh, it is n't that, Mary," here Jane Berry interposed; "I 'm sure you have n't allowed me to feel that I was a burden, but I am really able to earn my own living, and something more, I hope. It 's what I want to do, and I can't feel exactly satisfied until I 'm in the way of it."

I felt ashamed of my neglect, and resolved to atone for it as soon as might be. I assured Jane Berry that I should take immediate steps to secure her steady employment. But I could not say to her all that I desired; Mary Maloney was in the way. I therefore adopted the transparent expedient of taking leave, going part way down the stairs, and then returning suddenly to the door, as if some message had been forgotten.

She came hurriedly, at my call. I remained standing on the upper step, obliging her to cross the landing, the breadth of which and the intervening room removed us almost beyond earshot of the Irishwoman.

"I wanted to ask you," I said, in a low voice, and somewhat embarrassed how to begin, "whether she knows anything."

"I don't know," she answered. "It seems to me that everybody must mistrust me;—but I 've been afraid to tell her."

"Say nothing, then, for the present. But you wanted to

give me your history, and it must be told somewhere else than here. Could you go up into Washington Square, some evening, and meet me? You can say you need a walk and fresh air, or you can make an errand of some kind."

She appeared to hesitate, and I added, "The sooner I know more about you, the better I may be able to assist you."

"I will come, then," she faltered, "but please let it be some dark evening, when I would run no risk of meeting *her*, — that woman. You 've saved me once, and you would n't want me to run into danger again, sir?"

"God forbid! Choose your own time."

In the course of a few days, with the aid of Mary Maloney, I procured an engagement for plain needle-work, not very well paid, it was true, but still a beginning which would serve to allay her scruples and give her encouragement to continue the work of self-redemption. The establishment was in the upper part of the Bowery, and the proprietors required her to work on the spot, in company with a score of other needle-women, — an arrangement which she was nervously loath to accept, but there was no help for it.

On the following Saturday night I met Miss Haworth, quite unexpectedly, at a literary *soirée*. I was listening to a conversation between a noted author and an artist whose allegorical pictures were much admired in certain quarters. The latter asserted that a man must himself first feel whatever he seeks to express, — must believe before he can represent; in other words, that the painter must be a devout Christian before he can paint a Holy Family, or the poet a Catholic before he can write a good hymn to the Virgin. The author adduced Shakspeare as an evidence of the objective power of genius, which can project itself into the very heart of a great range of characters and recreate them for its purposes. I was greatly interested in the discussion, and naturally inclined to the artist's views. Not recognizing my own limited powers, my immaturity of mind and habit of measuring other men by my individual standard, I was glad to find a fact, true of myself, asserted as a general law. I expressed, very warmly, my belief that hypocrisy — as I called it — was impossible in Art; only that which a man really was, could he successfully express in words, on canvas, or in marble.

Suddenly I turned my head with the vague impression that somebody was listening to me, and encountered Miss Haworth's eyes. She was one of a lively group who were commenting on a proof-engraving of one of Kaulbach's cartoons, just imported from Europe, and appeared to have only turned aside her head for a moment. She acknowledged my bow, but her eyes fell, and when I sought her, as soon as I could escape from the discussion, her usual ease and grace of manner seemed to have been disturbed. The soft, sweet eyes rather shunned than sought mine while she spoke, and her words were so mechanical as to denote abstraction of mind. I feared, almost, that Penrose had hinted at my passion, but the next moment acquitted him of this breach of faith, and began to wonder whether she did not suspect it. If so, I felt that I had strong reason to hope. The serenity of her nature was evidently troubled, yet she did not avoid or repel me. On the contrary, I knew that her glances followed me. Without daring to watch her, I walked in the light and warmth of her eyes, in an intoxication of the heart which continually whispered to itself, "Your time has come, — you shall be blessed at last!"

Now I might venture to declare my love; for, even if its growth in me should encounter only its first timid development in her, I should still be sure of the end. But it required more resolution than I had supposed to take the important step. Perhaps Penrose had anticipated me, and — though unsuccessful, or rather, *because* of it — had untuned her heart for a time. Should I not wait for an intimacy which might foreshadow its object? Then the image of Amanda Bratton perversely returned to annoy me.

Some devilish attribute of memory held up, face to face, and forced me to see again my boyish raptures, my stolen embraces, and the mockery of my final interview. It was profanation to Isabel Haworth to couple her image with that other, but the latter had left its impress on my life, and its cold, hard features glimmered through the warm tints of the new picture.

I remember that I walked the streets much at this time, and I think it was in one of those aimless walks that I met Jane Berry returning from her day's labor. Her face was covered by a thick veil, and I did not recognize her, but she stopped and said, hesitatingly, "Mr. Godfrey?"

"Oh, it is you, Jane; are you going home?"

"Yes, but I am ready to keep my promise, if you wish it, sir. It's on my mind and troubles me, and I may as well begin first as last."

"Very well," said I; "here is Fourth Street. We shall find the square empty at this hour, and it's your nearest way home."

It was a cloudy evening and the dusk was rapidly deepening into night. The gas already flared in the Broadway shops, and the lamplighters were going their rounds from one street-corner to another. There were few persons in Fourth Street, and as I walked down it, beside Jane Berry, I was conscious that my interest in her had somewhat faded. Her rescue (if it might be called so) was a thing of the past, and the romantic victim had become a commonplace sempstress, — to be looked after, of course, and restored to her family as soon as practicable; but I felt that I should be relieved of an embarrassing responsibility when this duty had been discharged.

Thus occupied with my thoughts, we reached the southern gate of the square, and I stopped. The girl looked at me as if expecting me to speak. She wanted courage to commence, and I therefore asked, —

"Are you willing to tell me where your home is?"

"In Hackettstown, sir," she answered. "Though we used to live in Belvidere. My father and brother are raftsmen. I came to Hackettstown to learn the trade from an aunt of mine — my father's sister — who lives there, and does a good business. In the summer she works a good deal for the quality at Schooley's Mountain, and that 's how I became acquainted with — with *him*. Oh, pray, sir, don't ask me to tell you his name!"

"No, Jane," I said, "I don't care to hear it. It is enough to know what he is."

"He was staying at the hotel, too," she continued. "Some times I went up in the stage, on errands for my aunt, and walked back down the mountain. He used to meet me and keep me company. I was n't taken with him at first, he spoke so bold and would stare me out of countenance. Then he changed, and seemed to be so humble, and talked in a low voice, and put me above all the quality at the hotel, and said he loved me truly and would make a lady of me. I began to like his talk, then: I was foolish, and believed whatever he said. Nobody before ever praised me so, — not even — oh, sir! *that* was the worst thing I did! There was another that loved me, I am sure of it, and — and I am afraid now that I love *him!* What will become of me?"

She burst into a fit of passionate weeping. I saw by the lamp that her face was pale and her limbs trembling, and feared that her agitation might overcome her. I put one arm around her waist to support her, bent down and tried to cheer her with soothing words. Fortunately there was no one near, — only a carriage dashed along, and the coachman pulled up, as if about to stop at the opposite corner. I involuntarily drew her away from under the lamp, and into the shade of the trees beyond.

"Tell me no more," I said, "if it pains you to do so."

"I 've told you the worst now. I don't understand it at all. I can see the difference between the two, in thinking over what's happened, but then I was charmed, as I have heard say that a bird is charmed by a rattlesnake. The other one would n't praise me, — I thought him readier to scold, but oh! he meant it for my good. It was pleasant to be told that I was handsome, — that I had good manners, and that I should be a rich man's wife, and ride in my own carriage and live in ease all my life. Then, sir, there was to be a farm bought for father, — it was only to say yes, and everything should be just as I wanted, as fine as a fairy tale. And I believed it all! Only the going away so secretly troubled me, but he said we would be back in two or three days, and then what a surprise! The two other girls would be ready to tear my eyes out, for spite at my great fortune; — oh, and I dare n't look them in the face now. So we went away in the train, and I thought it was *his* house he took me to" —

She stopped here, unable to say more. It was needless: I could guess the rest. I saw the vanity and shallowness of the girl's nature, but a fearful retribution had followed her false step, and it was not for me to condemn her in her shame. But I stretched forth my arm and crooked my fingers, thirsting to close them around the throat of the villain who had deceived her.

"You do not wish to return, then?" I asked. "Would not your aunt receive you?"

"I have been thinking it all over. If I could say that I have been at work, and have a little money to show for it, and maybe a recommendation from the people I work for, you see, sir, it would n't look quite so bad. Only I might have to lie. That would be dreadful; but I think it would be more dreadful for me to tell the truth. Do you think, sir, that God would forgive me for the lie?"

Her simple question brought confusion upon my ethics. I was really unable to answer it. On the one hand, the unforgiving verdict of the world, — a life hopelessly disgraced by the confession of the truth; on the other, a positive sin, offering the means of atoning for sin and repairing a ruined life!

After a long pause I said, "God must answer that question for you. Go to Him and wait patiently until His will shall be manifest. But perhaps you are right in not wishing to return at once. I hoped you might have enabled me to assist you, but it seems best, now, that you should depend on yourself, unless — you spoke of another" —

"Don't mention him!" she cried. "I must try not to think of him any more. He 's as proud as the richest, and would trample me into the dust at his feet."

I saw that any further allusion to this subject would be inflicting useless pain, and proposed that she should return to her lodgings. On the way I encouraged her with promises of procuring better employment. I already began to plan what might be done, if Isabel Haworth should give herself to me, — I would interest her in Jane Berry's fate, and that once accomplished, all the rest would be easy. It was a case, moreover, for a woman's delicate hand to conduct, rather than a young man like myself.

I was fearful lest Mary Maloney might notice the traces of the girl's agitation, and therefore exerted myself to turn the conversation into a cheerful channel. On reaching Gooseberry Alley I went with her into the tenement-house, partly to divert the Irishwoman's attention. Feeny, smoking his pipe at the front-window, looked down and grinned, as we waited on the steps for the opening of the door.

Up-stairs, in the little back-kitchen, the table was spread for supper, and Hugh, with his shirt-sleeves rolled up as usual, was attending to the frying of some bacon. The lid of the tea-kettle danced an irregular jig to a tune whistled by the steam, and the aspect of the room was as cheery as its atmosphere was appetizing. Mary Maloney dusted the stool and handed it to me, saying, —

"Sure, now, and would you take a cup o' tay wi' the likes of us?"

I assented very willingly, and drank the cheap tea, out of a grotesque cup of "rale chaney, brought from th' old country," with a relish. Hugh, since his promotion to wages and his enrolment as a fireman, had acquired quite a manly air, but he struck me as being more taciturn than ever. The red curls were clipped close to his hard, round head, and his freckled chin was beginning to look stubby. When he spoke his voice betrayed the most comical mixture of the Irish brogue and the Bowery drawl. I caught him several times looking at me with a singular, questioning expression which puzzled me. The idea came into my head, without any discoverable reason, that he disliked me. Nevertheless, when his mother commanded him to light me to the street, he obeyed with alacrity, going in advance, and shading the dip with his big hand, to throw the most of its rays on the rickety steps.

I had not seen Mrs. Deering since my first visit after her return to the city. She was "indisposed," and her husband, whom I encountered in Broadway, informed me that Fashion prohibited her from appearing in society for three or four months. It was therefore useless to count on the chances of meeting Miss Haworth at her residence, and there was no certain way left to me but to repeat my call in Gramercy Park. I had now determined on the final venture, and only sought a lucky occasion. Twice or thrice I scouted around the house before finding appearances propitious; once there was a carriage in waiting, and another time I distinctly recognized the shadow of Mr. Floyd crossing the window-blinds. It was rather singular, I thought, that I did not happen to meet Penrose.

At last, it seemed that I had hit upon the right moment. The house was still, and the servant informed me that Miss Haworth was at home. I gave my name and entered the parlor to await her coming. I was in a state of fever; my cheeks burned, my throat was parched, and my heart throbbed so as almost to take away my breath. I strove to collect my thoughts and arrange my approaches to the important question, but the endeavor was quite useless; not only Amanda, but Penrose, Floyd, and Miss Levi, sent their wraiths to perplex me. The cold gray eyes of one woman, the powerful Oriental orbs of the other, were upon me, while each of the male rivals stretched out a hand to pull me back. What was I — an unknown country youth, hardly more than an adventurer as yet — to overleap, with easy triumph, all the influences banded against me?

There was the sound of a coming footstep. Swallowing down, by a mighty effort, a part of my agitation, I leaned on the back of a fauteuil, and looked at the reflected door in a large mirror between the windows. It opened swiftly, but the figure mirrored the next moment was not that of Miss Haworth. It was a servant-girl who was quick enough to deliver her errand.

"Miss Haworth says she 's not able to see you this evening, sir," she said; "and here 's a note she 's sent down."

I took it, — a folded slip of paper, without any address, but sealed at one corner.

"It is for me?" I asked.

"Yes — sir!" the girl replied, very emphatically.

I opened it; there were only two lines, —

"Miss Haworth informs Mr. Godfrey that her acquaintance with him has ceased."

The words were so unexpected — so astounding — that I could not at once comprehend their meaning. I felt marvellously calm, but I must have turned very pale, for I noticed that the girl watched me with a frightened air. My first impression was that the note was a forgery.

"Who gave you this?" I asked.

"*She* did, sir. I waited while she wrote it."

"Is Mr. Tracy Floyd in the house?"

"No, sir; he dined out to-day, and has n't come back yet."

There was nothing more to be said. I crushed the

slip of paper in my fingers, mechanically thrust it into my vest-pocket, and walked out of the house. I walked on and on, paying no heed to my feet, — neither thinking nor feeling, hardly aware of who I was. My nature was in the benumbed, semi-unconscious state which follows a stroke of lightning. There was even a vague, feeble effort at introversion, during which I whispered to myself, audibly, — "It don't seem to make much difference."

A lumber-yard arrested my progress. I looked around, and found myself in a dark, quiet region of the city, unknown to me. Over the piles of boards, I could see the masts of sloops. I had followed Twentieth Street, it appeared, across to the North River. I now turned down Eleventh Avenue, and walked until I came to a pier. The dark water which I heard, surging in from pile to pile, with a whishing thud at each, called me with an irresistible voice. I was not conscious of any impulse to plunge in and fathom the wearisome mystery of life; but if I had accidentally walked off the pier in the darkness, I would scarcely have taken the trouble to cry for help.

The pier-watchman confronted me with a rough, — "What do you want here?"

"Nothing," I said.

"Who are you?"

"Nobody."

"Then take yourself off, Mr. Nobody, or I'll make a Somebody of you."

I obeyed him.

CHAPTER XXXI.

IN WHICH I BEGIN TO GO DOWNWARDS.

It struck nine o'clock when I reached my lodgings. I was half-way up the first flight of steps when I suddenly asked myself the question, "What am I going to do?" My duties called me to the newspaper-office, but I felt that I was fit neither for labor, sleep, nor solitude. My only conscious desire was oblivion of the Present, — escape from myself. After a moment's reflection I turned, descended the stairs, went out of the house, and made my way straight to Crosby Street.

Miles welcomed me with, "Glad to see you, sir, — most of the gents is in," — and, as he spoke, the *Avenger's* reporter issued from the Cave.

"You 're just in time, Godfrey," said the latter; "they 're in the humor for making a night of it. I wish I could stay, but the Election plays the deuce with one's pleasures. No less than three meetings to-night: I must down to the office, and out again."

"Then," I observed, "you can do me a favor. I must write a line to Severn. Will you drop it in the business office, to be sent up to him?"

I got a scrap of paper from Miles, scribbled a few hasty words saying that I was ill and unable to attend to my work, inclosed it in a brown envelope and gave it to the reporter. Having thus shirked my duties, I entered the Cave.

The usual company was assembled, with the exception of Brandagee, who, however, had promised to be present.

The plan of the *City Oracle* had been revived, I was informed, and this time there would be no mistake. There were two additions to the company, both of them smart, comic writers, whose *debût* in the Sunday papers had been immensely successful, while "the millstone," as Brandagee was accustomed to call Mr. Ponder, had been fortunately removed. He had found a congenial place, as the writer of moral essays for a religious weekly, and came no more to the Ichneumon.

"I met him yesterday at the corner of the Bible House," said Smithers, "and I believe the fellow would have cut my acquaintance if he had dared. He was so pompously proper and pious that I said, 'Have you a tract to spare?' and turned down the collar of his overcoat, to see if he wore a white cravat. But what can you expect from the lymphatic temperament? There 's no muscle about him, only adipose substance, and his neck is as thin as the back of a rail."

Smithers untied his scarlet cravat and loosened his shirt-collar, as if to show that *his* neck was the reverse of thin, — and, indeed, it bore no slight resemblance to a plethoric column of the Indian cave-temples, surmounted by its poppy-head capital. He would have accepted this comparison as a compliment. He knew just enough of the Indian mythology to suppose that some of its features were rude, primitive forms of his own philosophy of life; he also adored the symbol of Siva, but under a less exalted significance.

All the initiation-fees of our clique or club had been contributed long since, and each individual was now forced to pay for his own refreshment; yet this necessity seemed to be no embarrassment. There might be no funds on hand for a new coat or pair of boots, but there was always enough for beer. I ordered a Toby of old ale, and drank it down, at one breath, from the cock of the hat. Mears immediately drew a caricature of me, holding a barrel aloft by the chines, with the bung-hole over my open mouth. Miles was an infallible judge of ales, and the keen, ripe fluid brought life and warmth back to my stagnant blood. I was too reckless to stop short of any extravagance, whether of potation or of speech.

"Godfrey, is it to be an epic or a tragedy?" cried Mears. "You've got a thirsty idea in your head, — a big plant, I should say, to require so much irrigation." Then he roared out a stanza of the old bacchanal of Walter de Mapes, which he had learned to sing at Düsseldorf.

"Tales versus facio, quale vinum bibo;
Neque possum scribere, nisi sumto cibo;
Nihil valet penitus quod jejunus scribo;
Nasonem post calices carmine præibo."

"That sounds more like a *jubilate* for a birth than a mass for the dead," said Brandagee, entering the room. "Has any of you just been delivered?"

"It's the inauguration hymn for the *Oracle*," I retorted, "and you are just in time to give the opening address."

"Here it is, — Babcock has come to terms. This time we shall begin *with* the Opera, and I fancy we'll make a sensation. The Impresario is all right; I've just had a bottle with him at Curet's. Now to lubricate my tongue, — what can I take after Béaume?"

"Whiskey," suggested Smithers.

"Yes, if I could order one of your famous 'long-shoremen's stomachs with it. But my taste is delicate to-night, — I want claret. Who'll lend me money at the risk of never being repaid?"

None of the others were eager to embrace the risk, which noticing, I handed Brandagee a five-dollar note across the table. The money had no value to me now, and I wanted the help of his reckless fancy and his audacious tongue.

"Godfrey, you deserve to make heavier profits," said he. "I'll put you in the way of it for the sake of a loan now and then. Meanwhile you shall have the half of what this brings, and I'll continue to owe you the whole of it. In that way we shall both gain by the operation."

Amid much laughter the order was given, and we were fairly launched on the fun of the evening. Miles, who was always in a good humor when there was a certainty of our spending a respectable sum, contributed a handful of cigars, and the air of the room soon put on its blue mysterious density, severe upon the eyes, but stimulating to the imagination.

"About the *Oracle*," said Brandagee, throwing his heels upon another chair and settling himself comfortably for talk, — "we must seriously begin to work for it. I think it would be best to open the first number with a burlesque platform, in the style of the political papers, — making our principles so broad that they would just amount to none at all. I had it in mind to copy the plan of *Le Flaneur*, which came out while I was in Paris. There was nothing about it to indicate a new paper: the leader began, 'In our article of yesterday we said' so and so; and the novel in the *feuilleton* was in its ninth chapter. It mystified everybody, as you may imagine. But I guess the joke would be too fine for the American mind to relish. What passes for wit among us, is simply a colossal absurdity; our burlesques are the most exaggerated the world ever saw. We must throw tubs to the whale and sops to Cerberus. After all, I rely most on the incidental sources of profit to keep up the paper."

"As how?" asked one of the company.

"Well, if there is audacity and arrogance enough among us, we'll soon get a reputation for critical knowledge. Once let the *Oracle* become *the* oracle of opinion in artistic, dramatic, and fashionable matters, and you see what our recommendation will be worth. Why, two or three theatres alone would club together to keep up a paper which sent the public to their ticket-offices, if there were any danger of it going down. This is the simple philosophy of the matter: *we* know what is good or bad, — the public don't. The public, let me tell you, always takes its opinion on such matters at second-hand, and is often put to much inconvenience by the absence of an infallible standard. Now, suppose we supply this standard; we then hold the fate of every book, picture, play, opera, — to say nothing of hotels, restaurants, tailors' and milliners' establishments, and the like, — in our own hands. We have a positive power, and the exercise of power is just what commands the highest price. All we want is talent enough to maintain our position. I think we have that, and the next thing is to work together. Somebody must take the lead and direct the operations of the concern, and the others must submit to his direction, or we 're ruined before we begin."

That somebody, we all understood, must be Brandagee himself. The prospect of entire submission to his dictation was not altogether pleasant to any of us, but he presented it as an ultimatum which must needs be accepted. I was not in a frame of mind to notice any other fact than that I should be well paid for a few sharp, bitter, racy articles, — such as I felt myself in a proper mood to write. As to Brandagee's hints of the channels through which the incidental profits were to be derived, they did not trouble me now. If people paid, they were supposed to receive an equivalent, — at least, *they* would think so, and they were the parties most concerned.

"Not a bad plan," said Smithers, referring to this branch of the business. "It 's a sort of literary filibustering which will develop mental courage and muscle, — qualities which this age sorely needs. We shall be like the wandering knights of the Middle Ages, going out to conquer domains and principalities, or like the Highland chieftains, swooping down on the plodding Lowlanders, and taking their surplus cattle. In fact, we could n't have a better motto than Rob Roy's."

"There 's Fiorentino, for instance," said Brandagee. "What he has done, we may do,—all the more easily here, where there are no intelligent rivals in the field. He 's a tolerably clever writer, but his chief power is in *management.* He knows everybody, and has the run of all the influential papers, so that whether his word is the strongest or not, it goes further than any one else's. I suppose the same thing might be tried here, if the chief dailies were not such damnable cats and dogs, but if we can lump the influence now scattered among them, and hold it as our own property, don't you see how the system will be simplified?"

The others all professed they saw it very clearly. In fact, as they began to understand "the system," they grew more willing to leave to Brandagee the task of carrying it into effect. Mears no longer hinted at "black mail," but rejoiced in the opportunity offered to him of demolishing Seacole, the allegorical painter. The opinions of the latter on the connection between Faith and Art, which I was wicked enough to betray, gave Mears the material for an exquisitely ironical description of his rival, letting his beard and nails grow and rolling himself in the ash-heap, to prepare his soul for the conception of a figure of St. Jerome.

There was another feeling which instigated me to join in this dishonorable scheme. My literary ambition, I have already said, was disturbed; its fresh, eager appetite was blunted, with increasing knowledge of myself, and from the other fluctuations of my fortunes,—but I was also disappointed, though I would not confess the fact to myself. After the kind, almost tender reception of my volume, I seemed to make no progress. I was welcomed at my entrance into the literary guild, and then—ignored. The curiosity attending the presentation of a new individuality in letters is soon satisfied, and many are the unfortunate authors who have accepted this curiosity as fame. But serious achievement is necessary to retain an interest which is liable to be overlaid by the next comer. The public seems to say, "This man *may* be a genius, — we have given him welcome and encouragement; now let him prove his right!"

The rule is natural, and I am satisfied that it is just. The firstlings of any author generally have an artless, unpretending beauty of their own, which is none the less interesting because it is not permanent. Poets are like apple-trees; there is a season of bloom and a season of fruit, — but between the two we often find a long period when the blossoms have fallen and the fruit is not yet ripe, — a silent, noteless, almost unlovely season of growth and transition. The world, at such times, passes heedlessly by the tree.

Though I professed to be indifferent to the neglect of my name, I was in reality embittered. I might value a literary reputation less than formerly, but it was not pleasant to feel that I was losing my chance for it. I saw that other young authors, comparison with whom — impartially made, although I did it — was not unfavorable to myself, kept their hold on the public attention, while others, in whom I found neither taste nor culture, were rising into notice. It would be well, I thought, to let the public see how egregiously it was mistaken in some of these cases; I would show that slang and clap-trap very often make the staple of a wide-spread reputation.

This petulant, captious disposition was encouraged by the tone adopted by my associates of the Cave of Trophonius. I was astonished and a little shocked at first, but I soon became accustomed to the cool, assured manner in which contemporary fames were pulled to pieces, and the judgment of posterity pronounced in anticipation. This sort of assurance is soon acquired, and in a short time I became as great an expert as the rest. Having already unlearned so much of my early faith and reverence, — making them responsible, indeed, for my misfortunes, — I rather exaggerated the opposite qualities, through fear of not sufficiently possessing them. It was a pitiful weakness, but, alas! we can only see correctly our former, not our present selves.

When I arose, late the next day, after a revel carried beyond midnight, I was in no better mood for resuming my regular labors. Duty, in any shape, had become "flat, stale, and unprofitable," and I felt strongly inclined to compensate for the lack of that luxurious indulgence which my nature craved, by lower forms of license. The blow of the previous evening had stunned rather than wounded me, and I felt that I should never again be sensitive to the good or ill report of men.

As for Miss Haworth, two explanations of her act presented themselves to my mind. Either Penrose or Floyd had misrepresented my character to her, or her position as an heiress had made her suspicious, and she attributed a mercenary object to my attentions. The latter surmise seemed the more plausible, as the circle in which she moved probably offered her few examples of pure, unselfish unions. The higher her ideal of love, the more cautious she would be to keep from her its baser semblance, and my principal cause of grievance was, that, in her haste and suspicion, she had misjudged my heart. I could not seek a justification; it was too delicate a subject to be discussed, except between confessed lovers. She might have dismissed me in less cruel a fashion, I thought, but it made little difference in the end. She was lost to me, without giving me a reason for ceasing to love her.

The more I reflected on this subject, the more sure I was of having guessed the true explanation. She had rejected me, not because I was poor, but because she was rich, — I, that would have thought it bliss to work for her, to wear out my life in making hers smooth and pleasant to her feet! I said, with a bitter ejaculation, that gold is the god of the world, — that no heart can beat with a natural emotion, no power of mind expand with a free growth, no life rejoice in the performance of its appointed work, without first rendering sacrifice to this Moloch! And yet, what Brandagee had said was true; it was no substance, it had not even the dignity of a material force: it was simply an appearance, — nothing when held and only turning into possession when thrown away.

I accepted, with stolid indifference, the prospect of a lonely life. Never again would I allow myself to love a woman, when the love of this one should have gradually perished (as I fancied it would), for want of sustenance. No home, no household joys, should ever be mine. The sainted spirit of my poor mother would never be called upon to bless the grandchildren whom she would fain have lived to kiss: I should go back to her alone, as on Saturday nights from my school at Honeybrook, — if, indeed, there was anything beyond the ashes of the grave. This life, that opened so sunnily, that promised so fairly, — what had it become? and why, therefore, should our dreams of rest and peace hereafter be more securely based? What sort of a preparation was there in the endurance of disappointment and injustice, to a nature whose natural food is joy?

So I reasoned — or, rather, thought I reasoned — with myself. There was no one to hold me up until my feet were strong enough to tread the safe and difficult track alone. Swansford was my only intimate friend, but, as I had not confided to him the growth of my passion, so now I withheld the confession of its untimely end. Besides, he seemed to be growing more sad and morbid. His views of life, if less cynical, were equally dark, and he often unconsciously encouraged me in my reckless determination to enjoy "the luck of the moment," whatever it might be. My position in Literature was similar to his in Musical Art; both had aspired and failed to achieve. The drudgery by which he supplied his personal wants was very irksome, but he would not replace it, as he might have done, by labors which he considered disgraceful to his art. Herein there was a difference between us, — a difference which at first had

26

made me respect him, but which I now turned to ridicule. If he were fool enough to sacrifice his few possibilities of enjoyment to an unprofitable idea, I would not imitate him.

After a few days of idle and gloomy brooding, followed by nights at the Ichneumon, I was driven back to the *Wonder* office, by the emptiness of my purse. I resumed my duties, performing them in a spiritless, mechanical fashion, with omissions which drew upon me Mr. Clarendon's censure. *The Oracle* was to appear in a fortnight or so, and I comforted myself with the pecuniary prospect which it held out to me, resolving, if it were successful, to cut loose from the daily treadmill round of the *Wonder*. My short articles for Jenks's *Ship of the Line* became smart and savage, as they reflected the change of my temper, and Jenks began to send back the proofs to me with a query on the margin, — "Is n't this a little too strong?" Following Brandagee's advice, I had demanded twenty dollars instead of the original five, but, as I lacked his brass, compromised for ten. This, however, was a small matter: I counted on receiving fifty dollars a week, at least, from the *Oracle*.

The days went by, fogs and chill, lowering skies succeeded to the soft autumnal days, and finally the opera season opened and the important paper appeared. There was an office in a third story in Nassau Street, a sign in illuminated Gothic letters, advertisements in the daily papers, negotiations with news-dealers, and all the other evidences of an establishment, intended not for a day but for — several years, at least. We celebrated the issue of the first number by a supper at Curet's, at which Mr. Babcock was present. It was unanimously agreed that nothing so spicy and brilliant had ever been published in New York. It transpired, in the course of the entertainment, that Babcock and Brandagee had equal shares in the proprietorship, and I was, consequently, a little disappointed when the latter handed me only fifteen dollars for one of my most dashing and spiteful sketches, three columns in length.

"We must have the power first," he said, "and then we 'll have the pay. Babcock is tight, and I don't want to make him nervous at the start. It will take about three or four weeks to get the reins in my hands."

He gave me a significant wink, and I was reassured. There was the great fact of the paper being actually in existence. Creation, of course, implied vitality, and the mere start, to my mind, involved permanence and success. An easy, careless life was before me for the immediate future, at least, and I did not care to look farther.

I knew, from Mr. Severn's hints, as well as from Mr. Clarendon's ominous looks, that I was getting into disgrace with both of them. Accordingly, I was not surprised one Saturday morning, on being summoned to the sanctum of the latter, — a call which I obeyed with a dogged indifference to the result.

"I am sorry to notice your remissness, Mr. Godfrey," said the chief, with a grave air, "and I have only postponed speaking of it, because I hoped you would have seen and corrected it yourself. The paper is injured, sir, by your neglect."

"I work as I am paid," I answered. "If you can find a better man, on the same terms, I am willing to give him my place."

"It is not that alone, Mr. Godfrey. You promised to become an available writer, and your remuneration would have been increased. I am afraid the company you keep or the habits you have formed are responsible for your failure to advance as fast as I anticipated. For your own sake, I shall be glad if you can assure me that this is not the case."

"I was not aware," I said, "that I was to look to some one else to choose my company and prescribe my habits."

"I suspect," he continued, without noticing this defiant remark, "that Brandagee has too much influence over you. I see your name in his new paper, — a clever rocket, but it will soon burn itself out. I advise you to have nothing more to do with it."

"No," said I, "I prefer giving up my place here."

"Very well, but I am sorry for it. Mr. Severn!" he called, rising and going to the door, "see Phelps this afternoon, and tell him to be on hand to-morrow evening!"

Severn looked at me, for the first time in his life, with a malignant expression. I laughed in his face, took a few private papers from the drawers of the desk I had used for two years and a half, thrust them into my pocket, and walked out of the office.

On the steps I met Mr. Lettsom, with his hands full of law-reports on transfer-paper. I had always liked the plain, plodding, kind-hearted fellow, and would fain present him in these pages as he deserved, but that, after his first service, he mingled no more in the events of my life.

"Good-bye, Lettsom," I said, giving him my hand; "you brought me here, and now I am taking myself off."

He looked bewildered and pained when I told him what had occurred. "Don't do it, — don't think of doing it!" he cried.

"It is already done."

I ran down the steps past him, and gained the street. My days of drudgery were over, but I could not enjoy the sense of freedom. There was a pang in breaking off this association which I could not keep down, — it was like pushing away from the last little cape which connected me with the firm land, and trusting myself to the unstable sea.

CHAPTER XXXII.

CONCERNING MARY MALONEY'S TROUBLE, AND WHAT I DID TO REMOVE IT.

One of the first results of the vagabond life into which I was rapidly drifting was a dislike for the steady, ordered, respectable circles of society. I looked, with a contempt which, I now suspect, must have been half envy, on the smooth, prosperous regularity of their ways, and only felt myself at ease among my clever, lawless associates, or among those who were poor and rude enough to set aside conventionalities. Thus it happened that I visited Mary Maloney much more frequently at this time than formerly. Jane Berry had been promoted, and was allowed to work at home, and I found a great pleasure in the society of two women who knew nothing of me — and would probably believe nothing — but good. They were both ignorant, and they looked up to me for counsel, and listened to my words with a manifest reverence, which, to a man of my years, was a most delicate flattery.

Sometimes I went in the early evening, with a few ounces of tea, or some other slight gift, as my excuse, but oftenest in the afternoons, when Hugh was sure to be absent. The silence of this growing bully, and the glances which he shot at me out of his bold eyes, were not encouragements to conversation in his presence. I fancied him to be one of those natures, at once coarse and proud, who bear an obligation almost as restively as if it were an injury.

After a while, however, I detected a change in Mary

Maloney's manner towards me. She no longer met me with the same hale, free welcome when I came: her tongue, wont to run only too fast, halted and stumbled; I could see, although she strove to hide it, that my presence was a constraint, yet could not guess why it should be so. This was annoying, not only on account of the old familiarity between us, but because I had a hearty liking for Jane Berry, who was almost the only person living in whose fate I was earnestly interested.

The latter, since the night when she had confided to me her history, no longer met me with a shy, blushing face, but showed a frank, fearless pleasure in my society. My visits seemed to cheer and encourage her, and with the growing sense of security, her hopeful spirit returned. She would soon be ready, I believed, to think of going back to the little New Jersey village.

It was near Christmas, — I remember trying to fix upon some appropriate, inexpensive gift for the only two female friends left to me, as I walked by the gayly decorated shops in Broadway, — when I turned, one afternoon, into Gooseberry Alley. I met Mary Maloney at the door of the tenement-house, with her bonnet on, and a basket of laundered linen in her hand.

"What! — going away, Mary?" I said. "I was about to pay you a visit."

She put down her basket on the floor of the passage, and looked at me with a troubled expression. "Miss Jenny 's at home," she said at last, with an air of hesitation, "but I s'pose, sir, you would n't want to see her, and me not there?"

"Why not?" I answered, laughing. "She 's not afraid of me, nor you either, Mary. Have I grown to be dangerous all at once?"

"Sure, and it is n't that, Mr. Godfrey. Would you mind comin' a bit down the strate wi' me? I 'd like to spake with you for a minute, jist."

"Oh, certainly," I said, turning and walking in advance between the gutter and the wall, until I reached the broader sidewalk of Sullivan Street. Here she joined me with her basket, and, when we were beyond hearing of any stragglers in the Alley, halted.

"I 'm a widow, Mr. Godfrey," she said, "and, askin' y'r pardon, sir, nigh old enough to be the mother o' you. There 's been somethin' I 've been a-wantin' to say to you, but it is n't a thing that 's aisy said; — howsiver, I 've spoke to the praste about it, and he says as you 're a proper young man and my intentions is right, it 's no sin, naither shame, but rather a bounden juty, sir, — and I hope you 'll take it so. It may n't seem right for me to go fornenst you, bein' so beholden to your goodness, and I wud n't if there was any way to help it."

Here she paused, as if expecting a reply. I had no idea, however, of the communication so solemnly preluded, and would have laughed outright but for the grave expression of her face. "I understand that, Mary," I said; "now tell me the rest."

"It 's about Miss Jenny, sir. The neighbors knowed of her comin', and who brought her, all along o' Feeny's bein' roused up in the night, and their tongues was n't idle, you may think. Girls wantin' sewin' a'n't to be picked up in the strates o' midnights, and though I knowed it was all right because you said so, it was n't quare, considerin', that folks should talk. You may think it 'd make little difference, anyhow, among us poor bodies; but we have our carrackters as well as our betters. Well — when they saw how handy and stiddy she was at her needle, they seemed to give me the rights of it; but now it 's all t' other way, along o' you comin' so fraiquently, sir, — and I 'm sure you 're welcome, ivery time, — and as for me, I 'm an honest woman, and nobody can say a word fornenst me, barrin' they lie,— but things is said, sir, as is n't agrayable to hear and hardly dacent to repate. Maybe you can guess 'em."

"What!" I exclaimed, "do they charge Jane Berry with being a mistress of mine? I suppose that is what you mean. You know, Mary, that it is a lie."

"I know, sir," she answered, "but my word goes for nothin' aginst appairances. Feenys takes my part, and says if it 's so, it 's unbeknowns to me, — which would be true if the t' other thing was, — but, in course, that don't stop their tongues. You see, sir, I can't bring it over my heart to tell her, — she 's a dacent, kindly, lovin' little body as iver was; but she 'll find it out to her sorra."

"Well," said I, "rather than that you and she should be annoyed and slandered in this way, I must give up my visits. Is there anything else I can do to satisfy those fools?"

"There was somethin' else I had on my mind, and there 's no use o' makin' two bites at a cherry," said she, with a curious misapplication of the proverb. But her face grew red and her voice dropped to a whisper. I began to fear — absurd as the thought was — that she also had been implicated in those amiable reports.

"It 's harder to tell," she said at last, wiping her face with her apron, "but maybe you 'll know what I mane, without my sayin' too much. I 'm thinkin' o' Hugh. I 've seen, plainly enough, that somethin 's the matter wi' the lad, iver since she come into the house. If he 's an honest likin' to her, it is n't to be thought that she 'll take up wi' the likes o' him, — though there a'n't a stouter and wholesomer boy o' his age in New York, — and if he *has n't*, it 's worse. He can't keep the eyes of him off her, and the temper of him 's jist ruint intirely. Maybe I 'm doin' wrong, bearin' witness aginst my own boy, but if you could hear him swear sometimes, sir, and grind his teeth in his slape, as I do, layin' awake and thinkin' what 's to be done!"

The widow's words threw a quick, strong light on Hugh's behavior. She was keener-sighted than I, and she had placed the whole situation clearly before me. Evidently, she relied upon me to relieve both her and Jane Berry from its certain distress, its possible danger, — and she must not be disappointed.

"Mary," I said, after a moment's reflection, "I am so surprised by all this that I must take time to think it over. You were quite right to tell me, and I give you my word that I will not stop until the matter is set right."

"Thank ye, sir!" she gratefully exclaimed. "I knowed you had the knowlidge and the willin' heart."

Then she went on down Sullivan Street, while I turned in the opposite direction, intending to go into Washington Square and turn the subject over in my mind, as I had promised. I was profoundly vexed, — not that *I* cared for the suspicions of that Irish pack, but on Jane Berry's account. Of course she must leave Gooseberry Alley without delay, and my principal task was to find a pretext for removing her.

What was the thought that suddenly caused me to stop, and then hurried me back the way I came? As this is to be an impartial history, it must be told; but I can best tell it by relating what followed. Every detail of the scene remains fresh and vivid in my memory.

I reëntered Gooseberry Alley, and in another moment knocked at the door of Mary Maloney's lodgings. It was opened, as I expected, by Jane Berry, and I carefully closed it behind me as I entered, lest any of the Feenys might be eavesdropping. Jane had taken her work to the window of the little kitchen, where there was more light of an afternoon, and briskly resumed her needle after admitting me. I noticed how fine and glossy her hair was where the light touched it.

"Mary 's not at home," she said, as I took a seat.

"I know it, Jane, and that is the reason why I have come to see you. I met her in the street."

I was embarrassed how to proceed further. She looked up with a wondering expectancy, and forced me to go on.

"I have heard something," I said, "which I am afraid will be very disagreeable news to you. I would not come to trouble you with it, if I did not think it was necessary."

She became so pale and frightened all at once that I saw what she suspected, and hastened to allay her fears.

"I know what you are thinking of, Jane; but it is not that. The woman has not found you out, — nay, I am sure she has ceased looking for you by this time. It is something which you could not have imagined, — something which affects myself as well as you. My visits, it seems, have been noticed by the poor, ignorant fools who live in these houses, and they can only explain them in their own coarse way. I see you don't understand me yet; I must say, then, that neither of us is considered as virtuous as the people think we should be."

"Oh, Mr. Godfrey!" she cried, "and I 've brought this on you! I 'm sure it must have been Mary who told you; she has n't seemed to me like the same woman for a week past, but I thought she might have troubles of her own. I felt that something was n't right, but I never thought of *that!* She don't believe it, surely?"

"She does not," I said; "but this wicked gossip spares her none the more for that. She is a good, kind-hearted woman, and must not be allowed to suffer on account of it."

"No, no, — I 'd rather tell her everything; but, then, it would n't help, after all. I ought n't to stay here since the story is believed; what can I do, if I leave?"

"Make the story true," I said.

Yes, those were my very words. What wonder if she did not understand them, — if her look of innocent bewilderment caused my wanton eyes to drop, and a sting of remorseful shame to strike through my heart? They were said, however, and could not be recalled, and I saw that her mind, in another moment, would comprehend their meaning. So I crushed down the rising protest of my better self, and repeated, —

"Make the story true. If we try to be good, we get no credit for it, and it is no worse to *be* what they say we are than to have them believe so."

She still looked at me incredulously, though the color was deepening on her cheek and creeping down over her slender throat. "Mr. Godfrey," she said at last, in a low, fluttering voice, "you are not saying what you really think?"

"It is true!" I exclaimed. "Look at the thing yourself; your life is ruined, and so is mine. Everything goes wrong with me, — doing right has brought me nothing but misfortune. You are more to be pitied than blamed, yet the villain who ruined you is a respectable member of society, no doubt, while *you* are condemned as long as you live. You see how unjust is the judgment of the world, — at any rate, *I* do, and I have ceased to care for it. If we unite our lives, we may be some comfort to each other. I can make enough money to keep you from want, and that is probably all you would ever have, if your friends were to take you back again. You may be sure, also, that I would be both kind and faithful."

The poor girl changed color repeatedly while I was uttering these cruel words. I thought she was deliberating whether to accept my proposition; but her heart, shallow as were its emotions, was still too deep for my vision to fathom. She was too agitated to speak; her lips moved to inaudible words, and her eyes looked an unintelligible question. I stooped down and took her hand; it was trembling, and she drew it gently out of my grasp. But the words were again repeated, and this time I heard them, —

"Do you love me?"

I felt, by a sudden flash of instinct, all that the question implied. In that moment, I became the arbiter of her fate. There was an instant's powerful struggle between the Truth and the Lie; but, thank God, I was not yet wholly debased.

"No," I said, "I will not deceive you, Jane. I do not love you. Love! I have had enough of loving. Yes, —

you may know the whole truth; I love as you do, — one who is lost to me, and through no fault of mine. What is left to me, — to either of us?"

She had covered her face with her hands, and was weeping passionately. I knew for whom her tears were shed, and how unavailingly, — but her grief was less than mine, by as much as the difference in the depth of our natures. I felt no movement of pity for her, because I had ceased to feel it for myself.

I waited until her sobs ceased, and then took her hand again. "Come, Jane," I said, "it does no good to remember him. I, too, will try to forget her who has cast me off, and perhaps you and I may come to love each other after a while. But we need n't make any pretence in the beginning, because we both know better."

Again she released her hand, but this time with a quick, impulsive motion. She rose from her seat and retreated a step from me. Her face was very pale, and her eyes wide with a new and unexpected expression. "Don't say anything more, Mr. Godfrey!" she cried; "I am afraid of you! Oh, is all the good you 've done for me to go for nothing? I 'll never believe this was in your mind when you picked me up, and set me on my feet, and put me in the right way again. I 've been praying God every night to bless you; you seemed to me almost like one of His angels, and it 's dreadful to see the Bad Spirit looking out of your eyes, and putting words into your mouth. I don't complain because what you 've said to me hurts me; I 've no right to expect anything else, — but it 's because *you* 've said it. Oh, Mr. Godfrey, don't say that it 's *my* fault, — that helping me has put such things into your head; please, don't say that! It would be the worst punishment of all!"

The intensity of her face, the piercing earnestness of her voice and words, struck me dumb. It came to my ear like the cry of a soul in agony, and I saw that I had here indeed blasphemously tampered with a soul's immortal interests. The selfish logic by which I had endeavored to persuade her fell into dust before the simple protest of her heart. I was too unskilled in the tactics of vice to renew the attack, even had I been unprincipled enough to desire it. But, in truth, I stood humiliated before her, sensible only of the fact that she would never more respect me. I had been an Angel to her artless fancy; henceforth I should be a Devil.

She waited for an answer to her last question, and what little comfort there might be in my reply she should have.

"Jane," I said, "you are not accountable for what I have been saying. You are far better than I am. I was honest in trying to help you, — *this* was not in my mind, — but I won't answer for myself any longer. You are right to be afraid of me: I will go!"

I turned as I said these words, and left the room. As I flung the door behind me, I saw her standing by the window, with her eyes following me. I fancied, also, that I heard her once more utter my name, but, even if it were true, I was in no mood to prolong the interview. As I opened the outer door hastily, I caught a glimpse of Mrs. Feeny dodging into the room on the other side of the passage.

On my way down Sullivan Street I remembered that I had done nothing towards relieving Mary Maloney of her trouble. But I soon dismissed the subject from my mind, resolved to let the two women settle it between themselves. Once in my room, I wrote a venomous sketch for the next number of the *Oracle*, and passed my evening, as usual, at the Ichneumon.

Two days afterwards the bells reminded me that it was Christmas morn; I had forgotten the day. I threw open my window, and listened to the musical clang, which came to my ears, crisp and sweet, through the frosty air. Having now more time at my disposal I had resumed my German studies, and the lines of Faust returned to my mind, —

> "Then seemed the breath of Heavenly Love to play
> Upon my brow, in Sabbath silence holy;
> And filled with mystic presage, tolling slowly,
> The church-bell boomed, and joy it was to pray."

Alas! I had unlearned the habit, and the beautiful day of Christian jubilee awoke but a dull reverberation in my heart. A Merry Christmas! Who would speak the words to me, not as a hollow form, but as a heart-felt wish?

There was a knock at my door. Mary Maloney entered and gave me the festive salutation. It came as a response to my thought, and touched my heart with a grateful softness. She carried a thin package in her hand, and said, as she laid it on the table, —

"I 've brought a Christmas for you to-day, Mr. Godfrey. It 's Miss Jenny's doin', and I don't mind tellin' you now, since she's left, that she sat up the biggest part of a night to get it ready. You see, sir, when I brought home your weskit, o' Wednesday, to fix the button, I said it would n't bear much more wearin', and you ought, by rights, to git y'rself a new one. With that she up and said she 'd like to make one herself, as a Christmas for you, and might she kape it and take the pattern. So she bought the stuff and hoped you 'd like it, and indade it 's a nate piece o' wurrk, as you may see."

I cast scarcely a glance at the waistcoat, so eager was I to hear what had become of Jane Berry. But Mary either could not, or would not, give me any satisfactory news.

"When I come home, t' other evenin'," she said, "I saw she 'd been cryin', and I mistrusted you 'd been havin' a talk with her, so I would n't add to her trouble by any words o' my own. And that was the night she finished the weskit. So next mornin' she went out airly and I did n't see her till nigh noon, when she had her things ready to laive. Says she, 'Mary, I 'm goin' away, but I sha' n't forgit you;' and says I, 'Naither will I forgit you, and I wish you hearty good luck, and where are you goin', for I expect to see you between whiles;' — but, says she, 'It 's best you don't come,' and 'I 'll always know where to find you,' and so she went off. Sure my heart ached wi' the thought of her, and it 's ached since, along o' Hugh. He won't believe I dunno where she is, and glowers at me like a wild baste, and stays away o' nights, till I 'm fearful, when there 's the laist noise in the house, it may be his blessed body brought home on a board."

I noticed, now, the haggard, anxious expression of the Irishwoman's face, and tried to encourage her with the assurance that Hugh was but a boy, and would soon forget his disappointment. But she clasped her hands and sighed, and there was a memory of Hugh's father in her fixed eyes.

After she had left the room, I picked up and inspected the present. It was of plain, sober-colored material, but very neatly and carefully made. I turned out the pockets and examined the lining, hoping to find some note or token conveying a parting message. There was nothing, and after a few inquiries, made to satisfy my remaining fragment of a conscience, I gave up the search for Jane Berry.

During the holiday week another incident occurred, — trifling in itself, but it excited a temporary interest in my mind. I had possession of one of the *Oracle's* passes to the Opera, and, at the close of the performance was slowly surging out through the lobby, with the departing crowd, when a familiar female voice, just in front of me, said, —

"But you men are such flatterers, — all of you."

"Present company excepted," replied another familiar voice, with a coarse, silly laugh.

If the thick coils of black hair, dropping pomegranate blossoms, had not revealed to me the lady, the flirt of a scarlet fan over her olive shoulder made the recognition sure. It was Miss Levi, of course, leaning on the arm of — could I believe my eyes? — Mr. Tracy Floyd. I kept as close to the pair as possible, without running the risk of being recognized, and cocked my ear to entrap more of their conversation. Eavesdropping in a crowd, I believe, is not dishonorable.

"It is a pleasure to hear music, under the guidance of such an exquisite taste as *yours*," remarked Miss Levi.

"Ah, you think I know something about it, then?" said her companion. "Deuced glad to hear it; Bell always used to snub me, — but a fellow may know as much as other people, without trying to show off all the time."

"Certainly; that is my idea of what a gentleman should be, — but how few such we meet!" Her voice was low and insinuating, and the pomegranate blossoms bent towards his shoulder. I knew, as well as if I had stood before them, that all the power of her eyes was thrown upon his face. I could see the bit of his neck behind his whisker grow red with pleasure, as he straightened his head and stroked his moustache.

There was a puff of cold air from the outer door, and she drew up the hood of her cloak. Somehow, it would catch in the wilderness of hair and flowers, and his assistance was required to adjust it to her head. Then they scuttled into the street, in a high state of mutual good-humor.

Is it possible, I asked myself, that he has been caught in the trap he laid for me? If so, I can afford to forgive him.

CHAPTER XXXIII.

WHICH SHOWS WHAT I BECAME.

THE reader may suppose that the part of my history most difficult to relate has already been written. If so, he is mistaken. It is easier to speak of an evil impulse which has been frustrated, than of a more venial fault which has actually been committed. Nay, I will go further, and state a fact which seems both inconsistent and unjust, — that the degree of our repentance for our sins is not measured by the extent to which they violate our own accepted standard of morals. An act which springs from some suggestion of cowardly meanness by which we may be surprised, often troubles us far more than an act due to bold, rampant, selfish appetite, though the consequences of the latter may be, beyond comparison, more unfortunate to ourselves and to others. There is in most men an abstract idea of manhood, — whether natural or conventional I will not here discuss, — which has its separate conscience, generally, but not always, working side by side with the religious principle. There are fortunate beings in whom the circumstances of life have never separated these distinct elements, — and such, alas! will not understand me. Perhaps the record I now set down against myself will make the matter more intelligible.

My circle of associates having become gradually narrowed down to Brandagee and his Oracular corps, with a few other *habitués* of the Ichneumon, who were not connected with the paper, — Swansford being almost the only old friend whom I cared to meet, — my life naturally took on, more and more, a reckless, vagabondizing character. The want of a basis of Faith, Patience, and Resolution, expressed itself in the commonest details of daily life. Mrs. De Peyster's respectable dinner company bored me to death; even the dishes wore the commonplace aspect of wholesome, insipid propriety. My stomach, like my brain, craved variety, piquancy, and excitement; health was a secondary consideration. I ceased to make any computation of my earnings and to guage my expenses accordingly. One day I would invite Brandagee or Smithers to some restaurant with a foreign *carte* and a list of cheap wines, and the next, perhaps, content myself with a lunch of black bread, Limburg cheese, and lager-beer. So long as I had company, the hours passed away rapidly, and with a careless, rollicking sense of enjoyment, but I shrank from being left face to face with the emptiness of my life.

With regard to my support, I was sufficiently assured. The ten weekly dollars of G. Jenks were punctually forthcoming, since the taste for scrappy, make-believe philosophy had not yet abated, and I also took to writing bilious, semi-mysterious stories, after the manner of Hoffman. The prospects of the *Oracle* were variable for the first few weeks: it attracted enough attention to keep up our hopes, and paid poorly enough to disappoint them. But, in one way or another, my income averaged twenty-five dollars a week, all of which went as fast as it came. When there was a temporary falling-off, Miles was ready enough to give me credit, — an accommodation which I found so convenient and used so frequently that there soon came a day when the very slender hoard I had spared was exhausted, and my bill for a fortnight's board in Bleecker Street still unpaid.

The evening on which I made this discovery, there happened to be an unusually large and jovial party in the Cave. I was in little humor for festivity: the recollection of Mrs. De Peyster's keen, suspicious glance, as she passed me on the stairs that afternoon, made me feel very uncomfortable, and I resolved to deny myself some indulgences which had grown to be almost indispensable, rather than encounter it a second time. Hitherto I had played something of an ostentatious part among my comrades, — had been congratulated on the evidences of my success, — and it was hard to confess that the part was now played out, and the sham velvet and tinsel spangles laid aside. I slunk into a corner and tried to appear occupied with a newspaper; but it was not long before Brandagee scented my depression.

"Hallo, Godfrey, what's the matter?" he cried, slapping me on the shoulder. "Ha! do I read the signs aright? Thou hast met the Dweller of the Threshold!"

I did not care to bandy burlesque expressions with him, and was too listless to defend myself from his probing eye; so I took him aside and told him my difficulty.

"Pshaw!" said he, "you are too innocent for this world. If I had the money I'd lend it to you at once, since you're so eager to feed the vultures; but I had the devil's own luck at *vingt-et-un* last night. Go to Jenks or Babcock, and get an advance; it's what every fellow is forced to do sometimes. Meanwhile, Miles will chalk your back for all you want to-night. Come, don't spoil the fun: that idea we developed last week was worth a hundred dollars, Babcock says. Two or three more such, and the *Oracle* is a made paper."

The "idea" of which he spoke was neither more nor less than a minute description of the costumes of various ladies at a grand private ball in Fifth Avenue, to which Brandagee had procured an invitation. It was written with a great apparent familiarity with the subject, and a reference to the dresses of the ladies of the Parisian noblesse, in a style breathing at once flattery and admonition. "You have done very well, this time," it seemed to say, "but take care,—I know all about it, and am on the look out for mistakes." Its publication was followed by greatly increased orders for *The Oracle* from up-town bookstores and newspaper stands. The musical criticisms, though much more cleverly done, failed to make anything like an equal sensation.

I succumbed to Brandagee's mingled raillery and persuasion, and entered my name on Miles's books. The circle joyfully opened to receive me, and in five minutes—so powerful is the magnetism of such company—no one was gayer and more reckless than I. We fell into discussing new devices for attracting attention to the paper,—some serious, some ironical, but all more or less shrewd and humorous. In fact, I have often thought, since those days, that a keen, wide-awake, practical man might have found, almost any evening, the germ of a successful enterprise among the random suggestions and speculations which we threw together.

"One thing is wanting yet," said Smithers, "and I'm a little surprised that it has n't occurred to you, Brandagee."

"Speak, Behemoth!" exclaimed the latter.

"Abuse. Not in a general way,—but personal. Take some well-known individual,—merchant, author, artist, politician,—it makes no difference,—and prick him deep enough to make him cry out. His enemies will all want to read the attack, in order to enjoy it, and his friends, out of a sympathetic curiosity. Men are made fools through the morbid sensitiveness which follows culture; their epidermis is as thin as the lining of an egg-shell. Take the strong, working-classes with their tanned, leathery hide"——

"Stop, there!" Brandagee interrupted. "I've got your suggestion, and we can dispense with your 'longshoremen. I *have* thought of the matter, but Babcock is fidgety. One's pen must be split to a hair, in order to sting and tickle just up to the edge of a personal assault or a libel suit, and not go over the line. I 'd like to see you try it, Smithers, with a nib as broad as your foot. I rather think you 'd have a chance of finding out the thickness of your epidermis."

Nevertheless, it was the general opinion that the proposition was worth considering. Several individuals even were suggested as appropriate subjects, but on Brandagee hinting that the suggester should first try his hand, the enthusiasm cooled very suddenly. Finally, it was decided to hold the plan in reserve.

"But," said Brandagee, "we must fix on some expedient. Heavens and earth! is all our inventive talent exhausted? We might find a new poet, of wonderful promise, or a pert female correspondent, with an alliterative horticultural name, such as Helen Honeysuckle or Belinda Boneset, but I don't know which of you could keep up the part successfully, and my hands are full. Then we must have a department of "Answers to Correspondents," at least two columns long; replies to imaginary queries on every subject under the Zodiac, — love, medicine, history, eclipses, cookery, Marie Stuart, and Billy Patterson. You fellows might do that while you are loafing here. There is nothing in the world easier to do, as for instance: 'Rosalie, — If the young gentleman, after picking up your pocket-handkerchief, put it into his own pocket instead of returning it to you, we should interpret the act as a sign of attachment. Should you desire a further test, ask him for it, and if he blushes, he is yours.' "

This suggestion met with great applause. We all went to work, and in the course of an hour concocted a number of answers. The reporter of the *Avenger*, who was accustomed to manufacture correspondence from various parts of the world, was called upon to write letters from Boston and Philadelphia, describing the sensation which the *Oracle* had produced in those cities; and by midnight, at which hour the atmosphere of the Cave was usually opaque, and the tongues of some of its occupants incoherent, we were all assured of the speedy triumph of our scheme.

I woke late next morning to an uncomfortable sense of my empty pockets. The excitement of the previous evening was followed by a corresponding depression, and I had no courage to face Mrs. De Peyster. I did not go down to breakfast, but waited until I felt sure that she would be occupied by the supervision of her household, and then quietly slipped out of the house.

There was no alternative but to adopt Brandagee's hint and solicit an advance from either Mr. Babcock or Mr. Jenks. The former gentleman being the more cultivated of the two, although I had had but little personal intercourse with him, he received my first visit. I proffered my request with a disgusting presentiment that it would be refused, — and the event proved that I was correct. It would be a violation of his business-habits, he said: still, if I were in immediate want of the sum, he might make an exception, if Mr. Brandagee had not just obtained an advance of fifty dollars! Since the paper could not yet be considered firmly established, he did not feel himself justified in anticipating the outlay to any further extent.

I now wended my way to the office of Mr. Jenks, and, knowing the man, put on a bolder face. It was not pleasant to ask a favor of him, but I could offer him security in the shape of articles; it would be simply anticipating the sums which would afterwards be due. After a good deal of hesitation, he consented, and I thus regained my good standing with Mrs. De Peyster, by cutting off a part of my future income. In the mean time, however, I had laid the basis of a new account with Miles, and thus commenced a see-saw of debt which kept me in continual agitation. When I was up on one side, I was down on the other, and each payment simply shifted my position. The disagreeable novelty of the experience soon wore off, and the shifts and manœuvres which at first were so repulsive became endurable from habit. When, after days of incessant worry, money came into my hands, I could not deny myself some coveted indulgence as a compensation. The former justified the latter, and the latter brought the former again into play.

I became, after a time, subject to extreme fluctuations of feeling. In moments of excitement, I experienced an exaltation of spirits, in which my difficulties and disappointments ceased to exist. I was elevated above the judgment of my fellow-men; I had courage to kick aside the trammels which inclosed them, and to taste a freedom which they were incompetent to enjoy. This condition was a substitute for happiness, which I mistook for the genuine article; I clung to it desperately when I felt the light fading and the colors growing dull, and the gray, blank fog dropping down from the sky. Then succeeded the state of aimless apathy, when my days seemed weighted with a weariness beyond my strength to bear. I could not fill the void space in my heart, once glowing with the security of Faith and the brightness of Love. I spread my coveted sense of Freedom over the gulf, but it would not be hidden; I dropped into it every indulged delight of appetite, only to hear a hollower clang. My principal satisfaction — or what seemed such — was in the belief that other men differed from myself only in hypocrisy, — outwardly appearing to obey laws they scoffed, and carefully concealing their secret trespasses.

But little more than two months had elapsed before I was forced into the conviction that my prospects were becoming precarious. The sales of the *Oracle* began to fall off; the paper was diminished in size, in order to reduce expenses, while professing (editorially) to be swimming along on a flood-tide of success, and the remuneration for my articles not only diminished in proportion, but was reluctantly paid. The final resource of personal abuse had been tried, and Brandagee must have been mistaken in the fine quality of his pen, for the immediate result was a libel suit, which so frightened Mr. Babcock that he insisted on avoiding it by retraction and apology. I had enough of experience to know that this was the death-knell of the enterprise, and was not deceived (neither was Brandagee, I think) by the galvanic imitation of life which remained.

About the same time my see-saw became so delicately poised that I lost my balance. My debt to Mrs. De Peyster had again accumulated; her eyes were not only coldly suspicious, but her tongue dropped hints which made me both angry and ashamed. I determined to leave her house as soon as it was possible to settle the account; but it was not possible, and, utterly unable to endure my situation, I put a single shirt and my toilet articles into my pocket, and leaving the rest of my effects behind, walked away. There was a miserable attic, miserably furnished, in Crosby Street, not far from the Ichneumon, to be had for five dollars a month, paid in advance. This was cheap enough, provided I could raise the five dollars. I remembered my loan of that amount to Brandagee, and asked him to return it.

"My dear fellow," said he, "I thought you understood that I never pay a loan. It would be ridiculous to contradict my principles in that way."

"Then," said I, "lend me the same amount."

"Ah, you put the matter in a more sensible form. I'll lend you five, or five hundred, as soon as I get it; but behold!"

He turned his pockets inside out.

I plainly told him what I had done, and that I was now without a penny to buy a meal or pay for a lodging.

"That's rather a bore," said he, coolly, "the first time you try it — but one gets used to it, like anything else. It's a seasoning that will do you no harm, Godfrey; I've been ground in that mill a dozen times, I presume. It would amuse you to hear of some of the dodges I 've been up to. Did I ever tell you about that time in Rome?"

I would not stop to hear his story, but left in a high state of exasperation. There remained one friend, who would help me if he could, though he straitened himself thereby. I had not seen him for some weeks, and felt, I am glad to say, a good deal of shame at seeking him now only to make use of him. I hurried across to Hester Street, and was about to ring the bell at Mrs. Very's door when it opened and he came out. I was shocked to see how his eyes had sunk and how hollow and transparent his cheeks had grown; but something of the old brightness returned when he saw me, and his voice had the old tone as he said, —

"I was afraid you had forgotten me, Godfrey."

"I have only been busy, Swansford, but I mean to make up for my neglect. You 'll think I take a strange way of doing it to-day, when I tell you that I come for help."

"And you so much stronger than I?"

"Not half so strong, Swansford. Here, in this pocket over the heart, and in all the others, animation is suspended. Can you lend me ten dollars for a day or two?"

I had known of his more than once sending that amount to his mother or sister, and supposed that he might have it on hand. The delay of a day or two, until I should repay him, would make little difference.

"I can," said he, after a moment's reflection, "but it will take about all I have. However, I can get along for two days — or three — without it. I hope you have not been unfortunate, Godfrey?"

Swansford had thought me wrong in giving up my situation in the *Wonder* office, and all my assurances of plentiful earnings afterwards had not reconciled him to the step. My present application seemed to justify his doubt, and this thought, I fancied, prompted his question. Not yet, however, could I confess to him — since I stubbornly refused to confess to myself — the mistake I had made.

"Oh, no," I said, assuming a gay, careless air. "I have been lending, too, and find myself unexpectedly short. In a day or two I shall be all right again."

Dear old fellow — how relieved he looked! I tried to persuade myself, for his sake, that I had spoken the truth; and, indeed, a little effort placed my condition in a much less gloomy light. My expenses, I reasoned, would now be reduced to the minimum; half the sum would give me lodging for a month, and the remaining half would supply me with food for a fortnight, in which time I could earn, not only enough to repay the loan but to relieve me from the necessity of making another. It would be necessary, however, to give up my dissipated way of life, and this I virtuously resolved to do — for a few weeks.

Swansford was on his way to give a music-lesson in Rutgers Street, but first went back to his room to get the money. I accompanied him, and could not help noticing how exhausted he appeared after mounting the last flight of steps. He dropped into a chair, panting; then, seeing my anxious look, said in a feeble voice, —

"It 's nothing, Godfrey. I 've been working a little too hard this winter. The symphony, you know, — it 's nearly finished, and I can't rest, now, until I 've written the last bar. I wish I had time to play it to you."

"You shall let me have the whole of it, Swansford. And I 'll bring Brandagee, who must write an article about it. He is always on the lookout for something new, and nobody better understands how to make a sensation. You 'll be a famous man before you 're six months older!"

A quick, bright spark flashed from his eyes, but instantly faded, leaving a faint, sad smile behind it. He sighed and murmured to himself, "I don't know." Then he gave me the money. I felt my hand trembling as I took it, but this might have been the faintness of hunger. I had eaten nothing for twenty-four hours.

On reaching the Bowery, I went into the first cellar and

strengthened myself with a beafsteak and a bottle of ale. Then I secured the attic for a month, purchased writing materials and sat down with the firm resolution to complete a sensational story before allowing myself a moment's pause, except for sleep. It was a dark, raw day of early March; there was no fire in the shabby room, and the dull daylight became almost dusk after passing through the unwashed panes. I had no table, but the rickety wash-stand would answer the purpose, and there was a single wooden chair. The meat and drink had warmed me, and thus, with my over-coat on my back, and the ragged bed-quilt, breaking out in spots of cotton eruption, over my knees, I commenced the work with a tolerable stock of courage. My subject was of the ghastly order, and admitted of an extravagant treatment, for which I was in the most congenial mood. Page after page of manuscript was written and cast aside, until the pen dropped from my benumbed fingers, and the chill from my icy feet crept up my legs and sent shudders through my body.

It was now dusk outside, and would soon be darkness within. The sense of my forlorn, wretched condition returned upon me, and the image of the Cave, with its comfortable warmth and its supply of mental and physical stimulus, came to tempt me away. But no, for Swansford's sake I would renounce even this indulgence. I would go out and walk the streets, to thaw my frozen blood, and arrange, in my brain, the remainder of my task.

How long I walked I cannot tell. I have an impression of having three times heard the wind sweeping through the leafless trees on the Battery, and as often through the trees in Union Square; but my mind was so concentrated upon the wild, morbid details of my story that they held it fast when I had grown weary of the subject, and would gladly have escaped it. Then I went to bed, to start and toss all night in that excited condition which resembles delirium rather than sleep, and leaves exhaustion instead of refreshment behind it.

By noon the next day the task was completed, and I left it in the hands of the editor of a popular magazine in which a few of my sketches had already appeared. I should have to wait a day or two for his decision; my brain, fagged by the strain upon it, refused to suggest a new theme, and yet my time was a blank which must be somehow filled. The flame of my good resolution burned lower and lower, — gave a final convulsive flicker as I passed the door of the Ichneumon, — went out, and I turned back and entered. Did I think of Swansford as the door closed behind me? Alas! I fear not. I only felt the warm atmosphere envelop me like a protecting mantle; I only heard, in the jovial voices which welcomed my coming, release from the loneliness I could no longer endure.

The season of late, bitter cold which followed seemed, like a Nemesis, to drive me back upon my vagabond life, and every other circumstance combined to fasten me in its meshes. By the time the editor had decided to accept my story, the sum I received for it was balanced by Miles's bill. He knew as well when there was money in my pocket as if he had counted it, and a refusal to pay would have shut me out from my only place of refuge. Jenks would no longer advance upon my articles, but began to hint that they now ceased to meet the popular taste. He thought of engaging one of the comic writers, whose misspelled epistles were in great demand, at a hundred dollars a week; it would pay better than ten for mine, — there was too much "cut and slash" in the latter. I saw what was coming.

Brandagee — against whose avowed selfishness, backed as it was by his powers of raillery, my indignation could not maintain itself — furnished me, now and then, with a morsel of occupation. But what an occupation it was for one who, three years before, had determined to write his name among the laurelled bards! I was to furnish poetic advertisements for the manufacturer of a new dentifrice! Once the imagined brother of Irving, Bryant, and Longfellow, I now found myself the rival of Napoleon B. Quigg and Julia Carey Reinhardt! I had reached, indeed, the lowest pit of literature, — but, no! there is a crypt under this, whose workers are unknown and whose works hide themselves in "sealed envelopes." Let that be a comfort to me!

I could not think of the manner in which I had sneaked away from Mrs. De Peyster, and deceived Swansford, without a pang of self-contempt. It has cost me no little effort to record my own humiliation, but I dare not mutilate the story of my fortunes. If the pure, unselfish aspirations of my early youth had been allowed to realize themselves in one smooth, unchecked flow of prosperity, I should have no story to relate. In an artistic sense I am my own hero, — but, —

> "What I seem to myself, do you ask of me?
> No hero, I confess."

CHAPTER XXXIV.

IN WHICH I HEAR FOOTSTEPS.

If the manner of life I have just described had come upon me naturally, through some radical deficiency of principle, I should have carelessly and easily adapted myself to it. I have known men who were always cheerful under similar embarrassments, and who enjoyed as well as admired the adroitness of their expedients of relief. Such are the true Zingari of a high civilization, who pitch the tent, light the camp-fire, and plunder the hen-roost, in the midst of great cities. They are born with the brown blood in their veins, and are drawn together by its lawless instinct.

I, however, had been pushed out of that sphere of order in which my nature properly belonged, partly by the shock of cruel disappointments and partly by the revolt of appetites common to every young man whose blood is warm and whose imagination is lively. When the keen edge of the former and the rampant exultation of the latter began to be dulled, there was no satisfaction left to me, except in forgetfulness of my former self. I heard, from time to time, the whispers of duty and the groans of conscience, and felt that if the two antagonistic powers within me were allowed to come together in a fresh struggle, the result would be — Despair. With my present knowledge I see that such a struggle was inevitable, — that a crisis was embraced in the very nature of my disease, — but then I only craved peace, and eagerly swallowed every moral narcotic which promised to bring it.

There were already symptoms of Spring, when my month

in the attic drew to an end. Days of perfect sunshine and delicious air fell upon the city, mellowing its roaring noises, softening into lilac and violet the red vistas of its streets, touching its marbles with golden gleams, and coaxing the quick emerald of the grass to its scattered squares. Most unhappy were such days to me, for the tender prophecies of the season forced my thoughts to the future, and into that blank I could not look without dismay.

By this time my condition was indeed wretched. My single suit of clothes grew shabby from constant wear, and my two shirts, even with the aid of paper-collars, failed to meet the requirements of decency. I had previously been scrupulously neat in my dress, but now I was more than slovenly, and I saw the reflection of this change in the manners of my associates. My degradation expressed itself in my garments, and covered me from head to foot, touching the surface of my nature in every point as they touched my skin.

For another month's rent of my lodging I depended on the six dollars which I was to receive for three poems inspired by the new dentrifice. The arrangement with the proprietor of this article had been made by Brandagee, who stated that he had a contract for furnishing the literature. He took to himself some credit for allowing me a portion of the work. I was anxious to meet him before evening, as Miles had a bill of some two dollars against me, and the most important debt must be first paid; but I visited all of Brandagee's usual haunts in vain. Tired at last, and quite desperate, I betook myself to the Cave and awaited his coming.

Any combination of circumstances which one specially fears, is almost sure to occur. My account at the Ichneumon was settled, as I had anticipated, and there was not enough left for the advance on my lodgings. Brandagee was in an ill-humor, and paid no attention to my excited representations of my condition.

"I tell you what, Godfrey!" he exclaimed; "it's ridiculous to make a fuss about such trifles when one of the best-planned schemes ever set a-foot is frustrated. Do you know that the *Oracle* is laid out, stark and stiff? The next number will be the last, and I've a mind to leave one side blank, as a decent shroud to spread over its corpse. Babcock swears he's sunk three thousand dollars, as if a paper must n't always sink five in the beginning to gain twenty-five in the end! If he had kept it up one year, as I insisted upon his doing, it would have proved a fortune for him and all of us."

I was not surprised at this announcement, nor was I particularly grieved, since the emoluments promised to me at the start had never been forthcoming. After a few potations, Brandagee recovered his spirits, and made merry over the demise of his great scheme. He proposed substituting the title of "Catacombs" for the Cave of Trophonius, and declared his intention of having a funeral inscription placed over the chimney-piece.

"Du Moulin," he said, — "you know him, — the author of '*La Fille Egarée*,' — always buried his unsuccessful works in the family cemetery. I spent a week with him once, at his chateau near Orleans, and he took me to see the place. There they were in a row, mixed together, — the children of the brain and the children of the body. First Elise, a little daughter; then 'Henriette,' a novel, with 'still-born,' on the tombstone; then his son Adolphe, and then the tragedy of 'Memnon,' the failure of which he ascribed to the jealousy of a rival author, so he had inscribed on the stone, '*assassiné!*' But only one impersonation of my plan dies with the *Oracle*, — there must be another avatar! There is no reason under heaven why I should not be as successful here as Fiorentino in Paris. I shall have to adopt his tactics, — work through the papers already established instead of setting up a new one. I am tolerably sure of the *Monitor* and the *Avenger*, and I might have the *Wonder* also, if you had not been such a fool as to give up your place on it, Godfrey."

"It was your representations that led me to do it!" I angrily retorted.

"Come, come, don't charge me with your own greenness! If a fellow takes my assertions for his guide, he'll have a devilish zigzag to run. I suspect you've been trying to strike a diagonal between morality and enjoyment, and have spoiled yourself for either. But it may be possible to get back your place: I always thought Old Clarendon had a sort of patronizing liking for you."

I knew what Brandagee's object was, — for what use he designed me, and feared the consummate dexterity of his tongue. There was something utterly repulsive to me in the idea of going back and humiliating myself before Mr. Clarendon, in order to insinuate articles intended to extort black-mail, — for Brandagee's "great" scheme meant nothing else, — into the columns of his paper. Yet, after what had happened, I no longer felt sure of myself.

For the first time in my life, I deliberately resolved to escape at once from my self-loathing and from this new temptation, by the intoxication of wine. In all my previous indulgence, — even when surrounded by a reckless and joyously-excited company, — I had never lost the control of brain or body. Some protecting instinct either held me back from excess, or neutralized its effects. I knew the stages of exhilaration, of confidence, of tenderness, and of boastful vanity, — but further than those vestibules, I had never entered the House of Circe.

I ordered a bottle of Sauterne — my favorite wine — and began to drink. I fancy Brandagee guessed the secret of this movement, and believed that it would deliver me the more easily into his hands. But I cannot be sure; my recollection of the commencement of the evening is made indistinct by the event with which it closed. There were, at first, two other persons present, — Mears and one of the comic writers, — and I do not know precisely at what hour they left, but I know that Brandagee waited until then to commence his attack.

I finished one bottle and was half-way down the second before I felt any positive effect from the beverage. Then, although my feet and hands glowed, and the humming of the quickened blood in my veins was audible in my ears, my mind seemed to brood, undisturbed and stern, above the tumult. The delicate flavor of the wine faded on my palate; a numbness, resembling a partial paralysis, crept over my body, — but in my brain the atmosphere grew more quiet, sober, and gloomy. The mysterious telegraph which carries the commands of the will to the obedient muscles seemed to be out of order, — I had lost, not the power, but the knowledge of using it. I sat like the Enchanted Prince, half marble, and my remaining senses grew keener from their compression. My mental vision turned inwards and was fixed upon myself with wonderful sharpness and power. Brandagee commenced his promises and persuasions, deceived by my silence, and not dreaming how little I heeded them. I heard his voice, thrust far away by the intentness of my thoughts, and nodded or assented mechanically from time to time. To talk — much less discuss the matter with him — was impossible.

I was in a condition resembling catalepsy rather than intoxication. While perfectly aware of external sounds and sights, I was apparently dead to them in that luminous revelation of my own nature which I was forced to read. I saw myself as some serene-eyed angel might have seen, with every white virtue balanced by its shadowed vice, every deviation from the straight, manly line of life laid bare in a blaze of light, I recognized what a part vanity had played in my fortunes, — with what cowardice I had shrunk from unwelcome truths, instead of endeavoring to assimilate their tonic bitterness, — and, above all, how contemptible had been the results of indulgence compared with the joyous release I had anticipated. It was a passionless, objective survey, which overlooked even the fluctuations of my feelings, and curiously probed the very wounds it gave.

I saw, further, that I had been miserably weak in allowing three circumstances — important as was their bearing on my happiness — to derange the ordered course of my life, and plunge me into ruin. For a youth whose only gifts were a loving heart, a sanguine temperament, and an easy, fluent power of expression, I had not been unsuccessful. I rather wondered now, perceiving my early ignorance, that so few obstacles had been thrown in my way. I supposed that I had performed marvels of energy, but here I had failed in the first test of my strength as a man. If Isabel Haworth had unjustly repulsed me, I had since then justified her act a hundred times. Fool and coward, — aspiring to be author, lover, man; yet flinging aside, at the start, that patience without which either title is impossible!

I saw clearly, I say, what I had become — but my clairvoyance went no further. There was the void space whence I had torn my belief in human honesty and affection, and close beside it that more awful chamber, once bright with undoubting reliance on The Father and His Wisdom, but now filled with a twilight which did not dare to become darkness. How was I to restore these shattered faiths, and, through them, my shattered life? This was the question which still mocked me. It seemed that I was condemned to behold myself forever in a mirror the painful brightness of which blinded me to everything else.

I had placed my elbows on the table and rested my face on my hands while undergoing this experience. It was late in the night. I had ceased to hear Brandagee's voice, or even to think of it, when, little by little, its tones, in conversation with some one else, forced themselves upon my ear.

"I tell you it 's trying to shirk your agreement," he said, "when I 've done my part. I 've almost made your fortune already."

"Not as I knows on, you ha 'n't!" replied another voice, which I recognized as belonging to Miles. "It 'ardly pays me. Leastways the profits on the gents you brings 'ere don't begin to pay for your drinks any longer. It won't do, Mr. Brandagee."

"Why, this one here has put six dollars into your pocket to-night."

"Can't 'e 'ear you?" whispered Miles.

"No: he 's drunk as a loon. Godfrey!"

He called in a low tone, then louder, — "Godfrey!" I do not believe I could have answered, if I had tried. My jaws were locked.

"They 'd spend more if you 'd pay 'em more," Miles continued. "I 'eard y'r bargain about the tooth-powder that day Dr. What's-'is-name was 'ere — five dollars apiece, it was, and you gives *'im* there two, and puts three in your *hown* pocket. Them three 'd be spent 'ere, if you hacted fairly. Besides, it was n't understood that you were to come and drink free, *hevery* day. I would n't ha' made that sort of a bargain; I knows 'ow much you can 'old."

Brandagee laughed and said, — "Well, well, I shall not come so often in future. Perhaps not at all. There 's a good fellow going to open in Spring Street, and he thinks of calling his place the *Ornithorhyncus paradoxus*, — the name you would n't have, Miles. If he does, it 's likely we shall go there."

Miles hemmed and coughed; he evidently disliked this suggestion. "There goes the door," he said, — "somebody for the bar. Come out and we 'll 'ave a brandy together before you go."

The disclosure of Brandagee's meanness which I had just heard scarcely excited a ripple of surprise or indignation on the fixed, glassy surface of my consciousness.

Wearied with the contemplation of my own failure, all my faculties united themselves in a desperate craving for help, until this condition supplanted the former and grew to the same intensity.

Presently Brandagee rose and went into the bar-room, and I was left alone. In the silence my feeling became a prayer. I struggled to find the trace of some path which might lead me out of the evil labyrinth, — but I could not think or reason: it was blind, agonizing groping in the dark.

Suddenly, I knew not how or where, a single point of light shot out of the gloom. It revealed nothing, but I trembled lest I was deceived by my own sensations, and was beginning to hope in vain. Far away, — somewhere in remote space, it seemed, — I heard the faint sound of a footstep. I could count its regular fall, like the beating of a slow, strong pulse; I waited breathlessly, striving to hold back the dull, rapid throb of my heart, lest I should lose the sound. But the sense of light grew, spreading out in soft radiations from the starry point, and, as it grew, the sound of the footsteps seemed to draw nearer. A strange excitement possessed me. I lifted my head from my hands, placed a hollow palm behind my ear, and threw my whole soul into that single sense. Still I heard the sound, — distant, but clearly audible in its faintly ringing beat, and clung to it as if its cessation were the beginning of deeper disgrace, and its approach that of a regenerated life!

It could not have been two minutes — but an age of suspense was compressed into the brief period — while I thus sat and listened. A voice within me cried out, "It is for me! Do not let it pass, — rise and go to meet it!" My marble enchantment was broken; I sprang to my feet, seized my hat, and hastened out of the Cave. Miles and Brandagee, with each a steaming glass in hand, were lounging against the bar. The latter called to me as I passed, but I paid no heed to him. Both of them laughed as the street-door closed behind me.

It was a cool, windless, starry night. The bells were striking midnight, and I set my teeth and clenched my fists with impatience for the vibration of the last stroke to cease that I might listen again for the footstep. One such sound, indeed, I heard between the strokes, — a man coming down the opposite side of the street, but it was not the step I awaited: it was too light and quick. When he had gone by and only the confused sounds of the night, far or near, stirred the air, I caught again the familiar footfall. It appeared to be approaching Crosby Street from Broadway, through the next cross-street below. I was sure it was the same: there was no mistaking the strong, slow, even march, slightly ringing on the flagged sidewalk. What would it bring to me?

Nearer and nearer, — but I could not advance to meet it. I waited, with fast-beating heart, under the lamp, and counted every step until I felt that the next one would bring the man into view. It came, — he was there! He made two steps forward, as if intending to keep the cross-street, — paused, and presently turned up the sidewalk towards me. My eyes devoured his figure, but there was nothing about it which I recognized. A strong, broad-shouldered man, moderately tall, with his head bent forward as if in meditation, and his pace as regular as the tick of a watch. Once he lifted his head and looked towards me, and I saw the outline of a bushy whisker on each side of his face.

In three seconds more he would pass me. I stood motionless, in the middle of the sidewalk, awaiting his coming. One step, — two, — three, and he was upon me. He cast a quick glance towards me, swerved a little from his straight course, and strode past. "Fool! fool!" I cried to myself, bitterly. As I did so, the footstep paused. I turned and saw him also turn and step rapidly back towards me. His head was lifted and he looked keenly and curiously into my face.

"Why, John — John Godfrey, is it you?"

He had me by both hands before the words were out of his mouth. One clear view of that broad, homely, manly face in the lamplight, and I cried, in a voice full of joy and tears, —

"Bob Simmons! Dear old friend, God has sent you to save me!"

Bob Simmons, my boyish comrade, whom I had almost forgotten! In the Providence which led him to me at that hour and in that crisis of my fortunes, my fears of a blind Chance, or a baleful, pursuing Fate, were struck down forever. Light came back to the dusky chamber of my heart, and substance to the void space. I prefer not to think that my restoration to health was already assured by the previous struggle through which my mind had passed, — that from the clearer comprehension of myself, I should have worked up again by some other path. It is pleasant to remember that the hand of a brother-man lent its strength to mine, and to believe that it was the chosen instrument of my redemption from evil ways.

My excited, almost hysterical condition was incomprehensible to Bob. I saw the gladness in his eyes change to wonder and tender sympathy. The next instant, I thought, he must see the debasement which was written all over me.

"Bob," I said, "don't leave me, now that I have found you again!" There was a noise of footsteps in the barroom of the Ichneumon: Brandagee was coming. Still holding the hand of my friend, I hurried him up the street.

"Where do you live, John?" he asked.

"Nowhere! I am a vagabond. Oh, Bob, you carried me once in your arms when I fell out of the apple-tree; give me your hand, at least, now, when I need your help so much more than then!"

Bob said nothing, but his hard fingers crushed mine in

a long grasp. Then he took my arm, and resuming his steady stride, bore me with him through Prince Street into the Bowery, and a long distance down Stanton Street. Finally he stopped before a house, — one of a cheaply-built, uniform block, — opened the door with a night-key, and drew me after him. After some dark groping up staircases, I found myself in a rear room. He found a match, lighted a candle, and I saw a small, modest apartment, befitting, in its simple appointments, the habits of a laboring man, but really luxurious in contrast to the shabby attic in which I had been housed.

"There!" he exclaimed, "these is my quarters, sich as they are. None too big, but you 're welcome to your share of 'em. It 's a long time, John, since you and me slept together at th' old farm. Both of us is changed, but I 'd ha' knowed you anywheres."

"It *is* a long time, Bob. I wish I could go back to it again. Do you recollect what you said to me when we were boys, just thinking of making our start in the world? It was my head against your hands; look, now, to what my head has brought me!"

Partly from shame and self-pity, partly also from the delayed effect of the wine I had drunk, I burst into tears. Poor Bob was inexpressibly grieved. He drew me to the little bed, sat down beside me, put his arm around me, and tried to comfort me in the way which first occurred to his simple nature, by diminishing the force of the contrast.

"Never mind, John," he said. "My hands ha'n't done nothin' yit worth mentionin'. I a'n't boss, only foreman, — a sort o' head-journeyman, you know. There 's the stuff in you for a dozen men like me."

I laid my head upon his shoulder with the grateful sense of reliance and protecting strength which, I imagine, must be the bliss of a woman's heart when she first feels herself clasped by the arms of the man she loves. Presently I grew calm again, and commenced the confession of my life, which, from beginning to end, I was determined that Bob should hear. But I had not made much progress in it, before I felt that I was growing deathly faint and sick, and my words turned to moans of distress.

Bob poured some water on a towel and bathed my head, then helped me to undress and laid me in his bed. I remember only that, some time afterwards, he lay down beside me; that, thinking me asleep, he tenderly placed his hand on my brow and smoothed back my ruffled hair; that a feeling of gratitude struck, like a soft, sweet pang, through the sensation of my physical wretchedness, — and then a gray blank succeeded.

When I awoke, it was daylight. I turned on my pillow, saw that Bob had gone and that the rolling curtain had been drawn down before the window. My head was pierced with a splitting pain; my eyelids fell of their own accord, and I sank again into a restless sleep.

It must have been afternoon when a light footstep aroused me. There was a plain, pleasant-faced woman in the room, who came forward to the bedside, at the movement I made.

"Where 's Bob?" I asked.

"He went off early to his work, sir. But you 're to keep still and rest; he 'll be back betimes, this evenin.' And I 've a cup o' tea ready for you, and a bit o' toast."

She brought them, placed them on a stand by the bedside, and left the room. I was still weak and feverish, but the refreshment did me good, and my sleep, after that, was lighter and more healthful. It was a new, delicious sensation, to feel that there was somebody in the world who cared for me.

It was nearly dark when Bob came softly into the room. I stretched out my hand towards him, and the honest fellow was visibly embarrassed by the look of gratitude and love I fixed on his face.

"You 're comin' round, finely!" he cried, in a cheery voice. "I would n't ha' left you, at all, John, but for the work dependin' on me; it 's that big buildin' down in Cortlandt Street, right-hand side. But to-morrow 's Sunday, as good luck will have it, and so we can spend the whole day together."

Bob brought me some more tea, and would have gone out for oysters, "patridges," and various other delicacies which he suggested, if I had allowed him. His presence, however, was what I most craved. After the morbid intellectual atmosphere I had breathed for the last few months, there was something as fresh and bracing as mountain breezes in the simple, rude commingling of purely moral and physical elements in his nature. The course of his life was set, from his very birth, and rolled straight forward, untroubled by painful self-questioning. If a temptation assailed him, he might possibly yield to it for a moment, but the next he would recover his balance. An influence of order flowed from him into me, and my views of life began to arrange themselves in accordance with it.

He was boarding, he informed me, with a married fellow-workman, whose wife it was that I had seen. He had been in New York since the previous autumn; it was the best place for his trade and he intended remaining. The day before one of the journeymen had been married; there was a family party at the bride's home, in Jersey City; he had been invited, and was on his way back when he met me in Crosby Street.

"Did you think of me?" I asked. "Had you a presentiment that you would meet an old friend?"

"Not a bit of it. I was thinkin' of — well, no matter. I no more expected to come across you, John, than — than Adam. But I 'm real glad it turned out so."

CHAPTER XXXV.

IN WHICH I HEED GOOD ADVICE, MAKE A DISCOVERY, AND RETURN TO MRS. VERY.

The Sunday which followed was the happiest day I had known for many months. I awoke with a clear head and a strong sense of hunger in my stomach, and after making myself as presentable as my worn and dusty garments would allow, went down with Bob to breakfast with the workman and his wife. The good people received me civilly, and asked no embarrassing questions. Bob, I surmised, had explained to them my appearance in his own way. So, when the meal was over, he remarked, —

"I guess I sha'n't go to church to-day. You won't want to go out, John, and I 'll keep you company."

I should gladly have accompanied him, humbled and penitent, to give thanks for the change in my fortunes, uncertain though it still was, but for the fear that my appearance, so little like that of a decent worshipper, would draw attention to me. For Bob's sake I stayed at home, and he for mine.

The time was well-spent, nevertheless. Confession is a luxury, when one is assured beforehand of the sympathy of the priest, and his final absolution. In the little back bedroom, Bob sitting with his pipe at the open window, I told him my story, from the day I had last seen him on the scaffold in Honeybrook, to the meeting of two nights before. I could not explain to him the bearing of my intellectual aims on the events of my life: he would not have understood it. But the episodes of my love touched our common nature and would sufficiently account, in his view, for my late recklessness. I therefore confined myself to those and to such other facts as I supposed he would easily grasp, since he must judge me, mainly, by external circumstances.

When I had finished, I turned towards him and said, — "And now, Bob, what do you think of me?"

"Jest what I always did. There 's nothin' you 've done that one of us hard-fisted fellows might n't do every day, and think no more about it, — onless it 's cuttin' stick without settlin' for your board, and borrowin' from a needy friend when you have n't the means o' payin' him. But *you* did n't know that when you borrowed, — I 'll take my oath on it. Your feelin's always was o' the fine, delicate kind, — mine 's sort o' coarse-grained alongside of 'em, — and it seems to me you 've worried yourself down lower than you 'd had any need to ha' gone. When a man thinks he 's done for, and it 's all day with him, he 'll step *into* the fire when he might just as easy step *out* of it. I s'pose, though, there 's more expected of a man, the more brains he has, and the higher he stands before the world. I might swear in moderation, for instance, and no great harm, while a minister would *be* damned if he was to *say* 'damned' anywheres but in his pulpit."

"But you see, Bob, how I have degraded myself!"

"Yes, I don't wonder you feel so. Puttin' myself in your place, I can understand it, and 't would n't be the right thing, s'posin' the case was mine. The fact is, John, we 've each one of us got to take our share of the hard knocks. There 's a sayin' among us that a man 's got to have a brickbat fall on his head once't in his life. Well — when you know it 's the rule, you may as well grin and bear it, like any other man. I know it comes hard, once't in a while — Lord God, *some things* is hard!"

Bob pronounced these last words with an energy that startled me. His pipe snapped in his fingers, and falling on the floor, was broken into a dozen pieces. "Blast the pipe!" he exclaimed, kicking them into a corner. Then he arose, filled a fresh pipe, lighted it, and quietly resumed his seat.

"What would you do now," I asked, "if you were in my place?"

"Forgit what can't be helped, and take a fresh start. Let them fellows alone you 've been with. That Brandagee must be as sharp as a razor; I can see you 're no match for him. You seem to ha' been doin' well enough, until you let him lead you; why not go back to the rest of it, leavin' him out o' the bargain? That editor now, — Clarendon, — I 'd go straight to him, and if I had to eat a mouthful or so o' humble pie, why, it 's of my own bakin'!"

I reflected a few minutes and found that Bob was right. Of all men whom I knew, and who were likely to aid me, I had the greatest respect for Mr. Clarendon, and could approach him with the least humiliation. I decided to make the attempt, and told Bob so.

"That 's right," said he. "And I tell you what, — it 's the rule o' life that you don't git good-luck in one way without payin' for it in another. I 've found that out, to my cost. And the Bible is right, that the straight road and the narrow one is the best, though it 's hard to the feet. The narrower the road, the less a man staggers in it. You seem, oftentimes, to be doin' your duty for nothin', — worse than that, gettin' knocks for doin' it, — but it 's my belief that you 'll find out the meanin', if you wait long enough. There 's that girl down in Upper Samaria, — you must ha' been awfully cut up about her, and no wonder, but did n't it turn out best, after all?"

Bob's simple philosophy was amply adequate to my needs. Without understanding my more complex experience of life, he offered me a sufficient basis to stand upon. Perhaps the thought passed through my mind that it was easy for his coarse, unimpressionable nature to keep the straight path, and to butt aside, with one sturdy blow, the open front of passions which approached me by a thousand stealthy avenues. I doubted whether keen disappointment — positive suffering — empowered him to speak with equal authority; but these surmises, even if true, could not weaken the actual truth of his words. His natural, unconscious courage shamed out of sight the lofty energy upon which I had prided myself.

I was surprised, also, at the practical instinct which enabled him to comprehend circumstances so different from his own, and to judge of men from what I revealed of their connection with my history. It occurred to me that the faculty of imagination, unless in its extreme potency, is a hindrance rather than an aid to the study of human nature. I felt assured that Bob would have correctly read the characters of every one of my associates in one fourth of the time which I had required.

It was arranged that I should make my call upon Mr. Clarendon the very next day. Bob offered me one of his shirts, and would have added his best coat, if there had been any possibility of adapting its large outline to my slender shoulders. He insisted that, whether or not my application were successful, I should share his room until I had made a little headway. I agreed, because I saw that a refusal would have pained him.

I own that my sensations were not agreeable as I rang the bell at Mr. Clarendon's door. It was necessary to hold down my pride with a strong hand, — a species of self-control to which I had not latterly been accustomed. When I found myself, a few minutes afterward, face to face with the editor in his library, the quiet courtesy of his greeting reassured me. It was not so difficult to make the plunge, as I did, in the words, somewhat bitterly uttered, —

"Another edition of the prodigal son, Mr. Clarendon."

He smiled with a frank humor, in which there was no trace of derision. "And you have come to me for the fatted calf, I suppose?" he said.

"Oh, a very lean one will satisfy me. Or a chicken, if there is no calf on hand."

"You must have been feeding on husks with a vengeance, in that case, Mr. Godfrey. If I ask for your story, believe me it is not from intrusive curiosity."

I was sure of that, and very willingly confessed to him all that it was necessary for him to know. In fact, he seemed to know it in advance, and his face expressed neither surprise nor condemnation. His eyes seemed rather to ask whether I was strong enough to keep aloof from those excitements, and I gratefully responded to the considerate, fatherly interest which prompted his questions.

The result of our interview was that I was reinstated in my employment, — in a somewhat lower position than formerly, it is true, and with a slightly diminished salary; but it was more than I had any reason to expect. Mr. Clarendon made his kindness complete by offering me a loan for my immediate necessities, which I declined in a burst of self-denying resolution. I was sorry for it, upon reflecting, after I had left the house, that Swansford might be suffering through my neglect, and my acceptance of the offer would have enabled me to relieve him.

This reflection was so painful that I determined to draw upon Bob's generosity for the money, and, until his return, employed myself in commencing a magazine story, of a much more cheerful and healthy tone than my recent productions. Bob was later than usual, and his footstep, as he ascended the stairs, was so slow and heavy that I hardly recognized it. He came bending into the room with a weight on his shoulders, which proved to be — the trunk I had left behind me at Mrs. De Peyster's!

"I thought you might want it, John, so I jest come up by way o' Bleecker Street, and fetched it along," said he.

"But how did she happen to let you take it? Oh, I see, Bob, you have paid my debt!"

"Yes; it's better you'd owe it to me than to her. I know you'll pay me back ag'in, and she don't."

Bob's view of the matter was so simple and natural that I did not embarrass him with my thanks. But I could not now ask for a further loan, and poor Swansford must wait a few days longer.

While Bob was smoking his evening pipe, I told him of the fortunate result of my visit to Mr. Clarendon.

"I knowed it," was his quiet comment. "Now we 'll take a fresh start, John, — your head aginst my hands. One heat don't win, you know; it 's the best two out o' three."

"Then, Bob!" I exclaimed, in a sudden effusion of passion, — "I 've lost where I most wanted to win. What are head and hands together beside the heart! Bob, did you ever love a woman?"

"I 'm a man," he answered, in a stern voice. After a few long whiffs, he drew his shirt-sleeve across his brow. I am not sure but it touched his eyes.

"John," he began again, "there 's somethin' queer about this matter o' love. I 've thought, sometimes, that the Devil is busy to keep the right men and women apart, and bring the wrong ones together. It goes with the rest of us as it 's gone with you. When I told you that you must grin and bear, t 'other night, I was n't preachin' what I don't practise myself. There was a little girl I knowed, last summer, over in Jersey, that I 'd ha' given my right hand for. I thought, at one time, she liked me, but jest when my hopes was best, she went off between two days" ——

"What?!" I exclaimed.

"Took herself away, without sayin' good-bye to anybody. Ha'n't been heard of from that day to this. Her aunt had a notion that she must ha' gone to New York, and I first come here, as much as for anything else, hopin' I might git on the track of her. I tell you, John, many 's the night I 've walked the streets, lookin' into the girls' faces, in mortal fear o' seein' hers among 'em. It may n't be so bad as that, you know, but a fellow can't help thinkin' the worst."

I was thunderstruck by the singular fancy which forced itself into my mind. If it were true, should I mention it? — should I relieve the torture of doubt only by the worse torture of reality? I looked at Bob's calm, sad, rugged face, and saw there the marks of a strength which I might trust; but it was with a hesitating, trembling voice that I said, —

"Did she live in Hackettstown, Bob?"

He started, turned on me a pair of intense, shining eyes, which flashed the answer to my question. The hungry inquiry of his face forced the name from my lips, —

"Jane Berry."

"Where is she, John? *What* is she?"

The questions were uttered under his breath, yet they had the power of a cry. I saw the task I had brought upon myself, and braced my heart for a pain almost as hard to inflict as to endure. His eyes, fixed upon me, read the struggle, and interpreted its cause. He groaned, and laid his head upon the window-sill, but only for a moment. I could guess the pang that rent his warm, brave, faithful heart, and the tears he held back from his own eyes came into mine.

Then, as rapidly as possible, — for I saw his eagerness and impatience, — I told him how and where I had first met Jane Berry, repeated to him her confession to me, and explained the mystery of her disappearance. I did not even conceal that passage where I had shamefully put off the character of helper and essayed that of tempter, because there might be a sad consolation in this evidence that her virtue, though wrecked, had not gone down forever. Though lost to him, she was not wholly lost to herself.

When I had finished, he drew a long breath and exclaimed, in a low voice, "Thank God, I know all now! Poor foolish girl, she 's paid dear enough for her folly.

What ought to be done is past my knowledge, savin' this one thing, that she must be found, — *must be*, I say, and you 'll help me, John?"

"I will, Bob, — here 's my hand on it. We 'll go to Mary Maloney at once."

In half an hour we were in Gooseberry Alley. It was little the Irishwoman could tell, but that little was encouraging. She had seen Jane Berry but once since her departure, and that, fortunately, within the past month. Jane had come to her house, "quite brisk and chirrupin'," she said; had inquired for me, and seemed very much disappointed that Mary was ignorant of my whereabouts; said she had been successful in getting work, that she was doing very well, and would never forget how she had been helped; but did not give her address, nor say when she would return. Mary confessed that she had not pressed her to repeat her visit soon; "you know the raison, Mr. Godfrey," she remarked.

The next day, I went with Bob to the Bowery establishment where I had first procured work for the unfortunate girl; but neither there, nor at other places of the kind, could we gain any information. Bob, however, at my request, wrote to her aunt in New Jersey, stating that he had discovered that Jane was supporting herself by her trade, and that he hoped soon to find her. I judged this step might prepare the way for her return; it was the only manner in which we could help her now. I did not despair of our finding her hiding-place, sooner or later. In fact, I accepted the task as an imperative duty, for *I* had driven her away. Bob, also, was patient and hopeful; he performed his daily labor steadily, and never uttered a word of complaint. But he sighed wearily, and muttered in his sleep, so long as I shared his bed.

Thanks to his forethought, I put on the feelings with the garments of respectability. My return to the *Wonder* office was hailed with delight by the honest Lettsom, and even with mild pleasure by the melancholy Severn. My mechanical tasks even became agreeable by contrast with exhaustive straining after effect, or the production of those advertising verses, which I never wrote without a sense of degradation. I was familiar with the routine of my duties, and gave from the start — as I had resolved to give — satisfaction. Mr. Clarendon, it appeared, had only intended to test my sincerity in his new offer of terms; for, at the close of the week, I found myself established on the old footing.

No sooner was the money in my pocket than I hastened to Mrs. Very's, palpitating with impatience to make atonement to Swansford. The servant-girl who answered the door informed me, not only that he was in, but that he never went out now. He had been very sick; the doctor would n't let him play on the piano, and it made him worse; so now he was at it from morning till night.

I heard the faint sounds of the instrument coming down from the attic, as soon as I had entered the door. The knowledge of him, sick, lonely, and probably in want of money, sent a sharp pain to my heart. As I mounted the last flight of steps, I distinguished his voice, apparently trying passages of a strange, sad melody, repeating them with slight variations, and accompanying them with sustaining chords which struck my ear like the strokes of a muffled bell.

He was so absorbed that he did not notice my entrance. When I called out his name, he turned his head and looked at me with a feeble, melancholy smile, without ceasing his performance. I laid the money on one end of the piano, and described my conduct in harsh terms, and begged his forgiveness; but still he played on, smiling and nodding from time to time, as if to assure me that he heard and forgave, while the absorbed, mysterious gleam deepened in his sunken eyes. I began to doubt whether he was aware of my presence, when the muffled bells tolling under his fingers seemed to recede into the distance, sinking into the mist of golden hills, farther and fainter, until they died in the silence of the falling sky. Then he turned to me and spoke, —

"Godfrey, was n't it Keats who said, 'I feel the daisies already growing over me'? You heard those bells; they were tolling for me, or, rather, for that in me which laments the closing of a useless life, a thwarted destiny. What is there left to me now but to write my own dirge? And who is there to charge me with presumption if I flatter my dreary departure from life by assigning to myself the fame of which I dreamed? Fame is but the echo of achievement, and I have sung into the empty space which sends no echo back. Listen! I celebrate myself — I give the 'meed of one melodious tear' to my own grave! No artist ever passed away in such utter poverty as that, I think."

He commenced again, and after an introduction, in the fitful breaks and dissonances of which I heard the brief expression of his life, fell into a sad, simple melody. There were several stanzas, but I only remember the following: —

"His golden harp is silent now,
And dust is on his laurelled brow:
His songs are hushed, his music fled,
And amaranth crowns his starry head:
Toll! toll! the minstrel 's dead!" *

Twice he sang the dirge, as if there were a mad, desperate enjoyment in the idea; then, as the final chords flickered and trembled off into the echoless space, his hands slipped from the keys, and, with a long sigh, his head dropped on his breast. I caught him in my arms, and my

* In searching among my papers for some relic of poor Swansford, I came upon a crumpled leaf, upon one side of which is written, —

"3 shirts 18
5 handkerchiefs 10
3 pr. socks 9
—
37 cts."

heart stood still with the fear that his excitement had made the song prophetic, and he was actually dead. I laid him on the bed, loosened his collar, and bathed his brow, and after a few minutes he opened his eyes.

"Godfrey," he said, "it 's kind of you to come. You see there is n't much left of me. You and I expected something else in the old days, but — any change carries a hope with it."

Regret or reproach on my part availed nothing. What was still possible, I resolved to do. When Swansford had somewhat recovered his strength, I left him and sought Mrs. Very. That estimable and highly genteel woman shed tears as she recounted the particulars of his illness, and hailed as a godsend my proposal to return to my old quarters — now fortunately vacant — in her house. I then hastened to Stanton Street, packed my trunk, and awaited Bob's return. He had not a word to say against my plan, and, moreover, offered his own help if it should be necessary.

Thus I found myself back again at the starting-point of three years before; but, ah me! — the sentimental, eager, inexperienced youth of that period seemed to be no relation of mine.

while in pencil, on the opposite side, is the stanza I have quoted, with the exception of the refrain, —

CHAPTER XXXVI.

WHICH BRINGS THE SYMPHONY TO AN END, BUT LEAVES ME WITH A HOPE.

Mr. Clarendon need not have feared that I might relapse into evil habits; every hour I could spare from my duties was devoted to the service of my dying friend. Since I had neglected and thoughtlessly injured him, I now resolved that no moment of his brief life should reproach me after its close. He was too feeble to deny me this satisfaction; and I saw, with a mournful pleasure, that no other hand was so welcome as mine, no other voice could so quickly bring the light back into his fading eyes. Bob insisted on relieving me, now and then, of my nightly watches, and I was surprised, not only at the gentleness and tenderness of his ministrations, but at Swansford's grateful acceptance of them. It almost seemed as if the latter had sent his Art in advance, into the coming life, and was content with human kindness and sympathy for the few days of this which remained.

The seeds of his disease were no doubt born with him, and their roots had become so intertwined with those of his life that only a professional eye could distinguish between the two. The impression left by my first visit was that he could not live twenty-four hours, but weeks had come and gone, and his condition fluctuated between the prospect of speedy death and the delusive hope of final recovery. There were times, even, when himself was deceived and would talk cheerily of the future. Neither of us knew how contradictory were these appearances, and that they should have prepared us for the opposite results.

One evening in the beginning of May, when Swansford's weakness and depression had reached a point whence it seemed impossible for him to rally, he beckoned me to his bedside. His voice was so faint that the words died away in whispers, but his face was troubled, and I saw from the expression of his eyes that he had a communication to make. I therefore administered a stimulating potion, and begged him to remain quiet until he felt its effects. Presently he was able to point to the upper drawer of his bureau, and ask me to bring him a package I should find in the right-hand corner. It was a heavy roll of paper, carefully tied and sealed. I laid it beside him on the bed, and he felt and fondled it with his white, wasted fingers.

"Here it is, Godfrey," he whispered, at last. "My symphony! I meant to have held it in my arms, in my coffin, and let it go to dust with the heart and the brain which created it; but now it seems that my life is *there*, not here, in my body. I might be killing something, you see, that had a right to live. God knows: but there is another reason. It belongs to *her*, Godfrey. Every note is part of a history which she alone can understand. Let her read it. I honor her too much to speak or write to her while I live, but there is no infidelity in her listening to the voice of the dead. Keep it until you have buried me: then give it into her hands."

"You have my sacred word, Swansford," I said; "but you must tell me who she is — where I shall find her."

"It is written there, I think. But you know her."

I feared his mind was wandering. Taking the package I held it to the light, and, after some search, discovered, feebly written in pencil, the words: "Mrs. Fanny Deering, from C. S." Of all the surprises of my life, this seemed the greatest.

"Swansford!" I cried, — "is it really she?"

"Yes, Godfrey; don't ask me anything more!"

He closed his eyes, as if to enforce silence. After a

while he seemed to sleep, and I leaned back in the rocking-chair which Mrs. Very had kindly provided for the watchers, busying my brain with speculations. I felt, more deeply than ever, the tragic close of Swansford's disappointed existence. She whom he had loved — whom he still loved with the despairing strength of a broken heart — who, I was sure, might silence, but could not forget the early memories which linked her to him — was here, within an hour's call of the garret where he lay dying. He was already within the sanctifying shadow of the grave, and the word, the look of tender recognition which she might anticipate beyond, could, in all honor and purity, be granted to him now. I would go to her — would beg her to see him once more — to give one permitted consecration of joy to his sad remnant of life. I knew that he did not dream of such an interview, — probably did not desire it, — and therefore it was best to keep my design secret.

In the morning Swansford had rallied a little, but it was evident that his life barely hung by a thread. I trembled with anxiety during the day, as I performed those mechanical tasks which were now more than ever necessary, for his sake, and hastened rapidly back at evening, to find him still alive, and in Bob's faithful charge. Then I set out, at once, for Mr. Deering's residence, in Fourteenth Street.

As I approached the house, my step slackened and I fell to meditating, not only on my errand, which I felt to be a matter of some delicacy, but on Mrs. Deering's apparent intimacy with Isabel Haworth. It will be remembered that I had not seen the former since the night of my mysterious repulse. I should no doubt have gone to her, as soon as Custom permitted, but for my ruinous and reckless course of life: she might possess the key to the treatment I had received, or, if not, could procure it. There was the hope of final knowledge in the present renewal of my acquaintance, and thus my own happiness suggested it, no less than my friend's.

I was but a few paces from the house when the door opened and a gentleman came out. I recognized Penrose at the first glance, and I saw that he also recognized me, before he reached the bottom of the steps. His appearance in the house of Isabel Haworth's friend started a thousand fierce suspicions in my breast. He had won, — he was the fortunate suitor — possibly the calumniator to whom I owed my disgrace! I stopped and would have turned, but he was already upon me.

" Cousin John," he said, and there was a tone in his voice which forced me to stand still and listen, though I could not take his offered hand, " where have you been? I tried to find you, at the old place, but your landlady almost turned me out of doors for asking. I thought you had anticipated me in clearing the field. Come, don't glower at me in that way, man! we can shake hands again."

He took mine by force.

" What do you mean?" I asked.

" That we are both floored. Floyd told me you had received your walking-papers long ago, and so I pushed on — to get mine. You were right, John; I *did* leave her out of the account, in my calculations. But I never saw all that I had lost until the moment of losing it. There, that 's enough; we need n't mention her any more. I 'll write to Matilda to-morrow to find a brace of elegantly finished machines, with the hinges of their tongues, knees, and ankles well oiled, — warranted to talk, dance, sit in a carriage, lounge at the opera, and do all other things which patent ladies may of right do. You shall have one, and I 'll take the other."

He laughed — a low, bitter laugh of disappointment.

" Alexander," I said, " I did not know of this before. I held back my hand because I feared that you were my fortunate rival. Now I give it to you, with my heart, if you will take it after I have said one more word. I have not ceased, and will not cease to love Isabel Haworth.

Something has come between us which I cannot yet understand, but, with God's help, I will remove it, and it may be — I scarcely hope, Alexander, but it *may* be — that her heart shall answer to mine. Now, will you take my hand?"

He looked at me, a moment, in silence. Then I felt my hand locked in a firm grasp, which drew me nearer, until our faces almost touched. His eyes read mine, and his lip trembled as he spoke, —

"God bless you, John! I was right to fear you, but it is too late to fear you now, and needless to hate you. I can't wish you success, — that would be more than human. But since she is lost to me there is less pain in the knowledge that you should win her than another. If it comes I shall not see it. I am going away, and it will be some comfort to think of you still as my friend."

"Going away?" I repeated; "you will leave New York — give up your business?"

"No; my excuse is also my necessity. Dunn and Deering have had an agency in San Francisco for two years past, and it is now to be made a branch, under my charge. The matter was talked of before, and I should probably have been there already, but for — well, for her. We understand each other now, and nothing more need be said. Try to think kindly of me, John, though you may not like the selfish and arbitrary streak I have inherited from my father; let the natures of our mothers, only, speak to each other in us!"

I had kept his hand in mine while he spoke. Little by little I was growing to understand his powerful, manly nature, mixed of such conflicting elements, and, in that comprehension, to feel how powerless were his coveted advantages of beauty, energy, and fortune, in the struggle for happiness. Again I turned to my own past history with shame. The three men nearest to me — Penrose, Swansford, and Bob Simmons — were equally unfortunate, yet each courageously met his destiny, while I alone had acted the part of a coward and a fool. I saw how shallow had been my judgment, how unjust my suspicions, and the old, boyish affection for my cousin came back to my heart.

"Alexander," I said, "I will remember you as a brother. If I ever thought unkindly of you, it was because I did not know you truly. God bless and keep you!"

He was gone, and I stood at the door. Our meeting had given me strength and courage, and I sought at once an interview with Mrs. Deering.

She entered the room with a colder and statelier air than I had before noticed in her. I felt, however, only the solemn importance of my errand, and the necessity of communicating it without delay. I therefore disregarded her somewhat formal gesture, inviting me to be seated, stepped nearer to her, and said, —

"Mrs. Deering, you will pardon me if I commit an indiscretion in what I have to say. It concerns a very dear friend of mine who was once a friend of yours, — Charles Swansford!"

She started slightly, and seemed about to speak, but I went on.

"He is lying on his death-bed, Mrs. Deering. He may have but a day — nay, perhaps only an hour — to live. He placed in my charge a musical work of his own composition, to be delivered to you after his death; but I have come now, unknown to him, to tell you that I believe no greater blessing could be granted to his last moments than the sight of your face and the sound of your voice. I need not say anything more than this. If your heart inclines you to fulfil my wish, — *mine*, remember, not *his*, — I am ready to conduct you. If not, he will never know that I have spoken it."

Her cold dignity was gone; pale and trembling, she leaned upon the back of a chair. Her voice was faint and broken. "You know what he is — was — to me?" she said.

"I knew it last night for the first time, and then only because he thought he was dying. I come to you at the command of my own conscience, and the rest must be left to yours."

"I will go!" she exclaimed; "it cannot be wrong now. God, who sees my soul, knows that I mean no wrong!"

"No, Mrs. Deering; since you have so decided, let me say to you that my poor friend's life of suffering and despair would have been ignobly borne for your sake, had you refused this last, pious act of consolation."

She grasped my hand in hers, crying, through her starting tears, — "Thank you, Mr. Godfrey! You have acted as a true friend to him and me. Let us go at once!"

Her carriage was ordered, and in a quarter of an hour we were on the way to Hester Street. She leaned back in the corner, silent, with clasped hands, during the ride, and when we reached the door was so overcome by her agitation that I was almost obliged to lift her from the carriage. I conducted her first to my own room, and then entered Swansford's, to prepare him for the interview.

He had been sleeping, and awoke refreshed; his voice was weak, but clear, and his depressed, unhappy mood seemed to be passing away. I sat down beside him on the bed, and took his hand in mine.

"Swansford," I said, "if you could have one wish fulfilled now, what would it be? If, of all persons you have ever known, *one* might come to visit you, whom would you name?"

A bright, wistful gleam flitted over his face a moment and then died out. "No one," he sighed.

"But there *is* some one, Swansford, — one who waits your permission to come to you. Will you admit her?"

"*Her?*"

His voice was like a cry, and such a wild, eager, wondering expression flashed into his features that I beckoned to Bob and we stole out of the room. Then I opened the door for Mrs. Deering, and closed it softly behind her, leaving them alone.

Do you ask what sacred phrases of tenderness, what confession of feelings long withheld, what reciprocal repentance and forgiveness, were crowded into that interview? I would not reveal them if I knew. There are some experiences of human hearts, in which God claims the exclusive right of possession, and I will not profanely venture into their sanctities.

Bob and I sat together in my room, talking in low tones, until more than an hour had passed. Then we heard the door of Swansford's room move, and I stepped forward to support Mrs. Deering's tottering steps. I placed her in a chair, and hastened to ascertain Swansford's condition before accompanying her to her home. His wasted face reposed upon the pillow in utter, blissful exhaustion; his eyes were closed, but tears had stolen from under the lids and sparkled on his white cheeks.

"Swansford," I said, kneeling beside him, "do you forgive me for what I have done?"

He smiled with ineffable sweetness, gently drew my head nearer, and kissed me.

When I left Mrs. Deering at her door, she said to me, —

"I must ask your forgiveness, Mr. Godfrey: I fear I have done you injustice in my thoughts. If it is so, and the fancies I have had are not idle, I will try to save you from" —

She paused. Her words were incomprehensible, but when I would have begged an explanation, she read the question in my face before it was uttered, and hastily exclaimed, as she gave me her hand, — "No, no; not to-night. Leave me now, if you please; but I shall expect to see you every day while — he lives."

As I walked homewards, pondering on the event of the evening, it was easy to perceive a connection between the formal air with which Mrs. Deering had received me and her parting words. I surmised that she had heard something to my disadvantage, either from Miss Haworth, or from the same source as the latter, and thus the clue I sought seemed about to be placed in my hand. I should no longer be the victim of a mysterious, intangible hostility, but, knowing its form, could arm myself to overcome it. Hope stole back into my heart, and set the suppressed pulses of love to beating.

From the close of that interview Swansford's condition seemed to be entirely changed. The last drop of bitterness was washed out of his nature; he was calm, resigned, and happy. He allowed me to send a message to his mother and sisters, which he had previously refused, and lingered long enough to see them at his bedside. He had insisted on being laid in an unmarked grave, among the city's poor, but now he consented that his body should be taken to his Connecticut home and placed beside its kindred. The last few days of his life were wholly peaceful and serene.

"He 's an angel a'ready," Bob said, and so we all felt. The decay of his strength became so regular towards the close that the physician was able to predict the hour when it would cease. We, who knew it, were gathered together, around the unconscious sufferer, who had asked to be raised and supported, in almost a sitting posture. His eyes wandered from one face to another, with a look too far removed from earth to express degrees of affection. All at once his lips moved, and he began to sing: —

> "His songs are hushed, his music fled,
> And amaranth crowns —— "

There his voice stopped, and his heart stopped with it.

I went to Connecticut with his family, and saw the last rites performed in the green little church-yard among the hills. Then I left his cheated hopes, his thwarted ambition, his shattered life to moulder there, believing that Divine Mercy had prepared a compensation for him in the eternal spheres.

Mrs. Deering's explanation, delayed by my constant attendance during the last days, and the solemn duties which followed, came at last; but it was not so satisfactory as I had hoped. All that I could clearly ascertain was that Miss Haworth had heard something — *knew*, indeed, the latter had declared to Mrs. Deering — to my prejudice, and had prohibited all mention of my name. Mrs. Deering naturally trusted to her friend's judgment, and my absence from a house where I had been so cordially received, confirmed her in the belief that her own vague suspicions must have a basis in reality. It was not necessary, she said, to mention them; she had heard nothing, knew nothing, except that Miss Haworth considered me unworthy of her acquaintance. She was now convinced that there was a mistake somewhere, and it should be her duty to assist in clearing up the mystery.

Mrs. Deering also informed me of another circumstance which had occurred some weeks before. Miss Haworth had left her step-father's house very suddenly, and gone alone to Boston, where she had relatives. It was rumored — but on what grounds nobody knew — that when she returned, it would not be to Gramercy Park. There must have been some disturbance, for she, Mrs. Deering, her most intimate friend, would otherwise have heard from her. She was on the point of writing, to inquire into the truth of the rumor, when my visit, and the excitement and preoccupation of her mind with Swansford's fate, had driven the subject from her thoughts. Now, however, she would lose no time. If the story were true, she would offer Miss Haworth a temporary home in her own house.

During these conversations, it was natural that my extreme anxiety to ascertain the nature of my presumed offence, and to be replaced, if possible, in Miss Haworth's good opinion, should betray its true cause. I knew that Mrs. Deering read my heart correctly, and added her hopes to mine, although the subject was not openly mentioned between us. She was never weary of recounting the noble womanly virtues of her friend, nor was I ever weary of listening. The two women had been educated in the same school, and were familiar with the circumstances of each other's lives. I thus made good progress in the knowledge of my beloved, even though she was absent and estranged.

While Mrs. Deering was waiting for an answer from Boston, Penrose sailed for California. The evening before his departure we spent together. Upon one subject there was a tacit understanding of silence, but on all others we were free and candid as brothers. With him went a portion of my life which I resolved must be renewed in the future, but when or how was as indefinite as the further course of my own fortunes.

CHAPTER XXXVII.

WHICH BRINGS MY FORTUNE AT LAST.

THROUGH all the period of agitation which I have just described I adhered faithfully to my work, and in spite of the demands upon my purse for poor Swansford's necessisities (and they were gladly answered), I slowly recovered my lost position of independence. Bob's generous loan was returned, I was free of other debt, and possessed once more an assured and sufficient income. Those months of vagabondage seemed like a dark, uneasy dream, in the steady light of resolution which now filled my life; it was as if a sultry haze in which the forms of Good and Evil were blended, and the paths of order and of license become an inextricable labyrinth, had been blown away, leaving the landscape clearer than ever before. I will not say that all temptations died, or no longer possessed a formidable power; but I was able to recognize them under whatever mask they approached, and patient to wait for the day when each conditional sin of the senses should resolve itself into a permitted bounty.

On one subject alone I was not patient, and my disappointment was extreme when Mrs. Deering informed me that she had received a letter from Boston stating only that the rumor was true, — Miss Haworth would not return to her step-father's house in Gramercy Park. She would accept her friend's invitation when she came back to New York, — probably in a fortnight, or thereabouts. There was a hint, it was true, of further confidences, when they should meet. I begged Mrs. Deering to write again, and ask, at least, an explanation of the mystery in which I was concerned. It was her right, I insisted, since she now permitted me to call myself her friend.

Four days afterwards, on returning to my lodgings late at night, after the completion of my editorial labors, I found a small note upon my table. It was addressed in a woman's hand, which struck my eye as familiar, although it was not Mrs. Deering's, and I had long since ceased to receive notes from any other lady, — even from Adeliza Choate. I opened it carelessly and read : —

"I have judged you unjustly, and treated you rudely, Mr. Godfrey. If I have not forfeited the right to make reparation, or you have not lost the desire to receive it, will you call upon me to-morrow evening, at Mrs. Deering's, and oblige

ISABEL HAWORTH."

I am not certain what I did during the next ten minutes after reading this note ; but I have a dim recollection of sinking on my knees at the bedside, and bowing my head on the coverlet, as my mother had taught me to do when a little boy. The work for which I had been trying to arm myself was already done. It mattered not now who was the enemy, nor what the weapon he had used against me ; she confessed her injustice, — confessed it fully, directly, and honorably, as became her nature. The only prayer to which I could bend my mind, before yielding to sleep that night, was, "God, give me Isabel Haworth!"

The next morning I wrote the single line, —

"I will come.

JOHN GODFREY," —

and carried it to Fourteenth Street myself, unwilling to trust the fate of the message to other hands. That day was the longest of my life. It was hard to force my mind into its habitual harness, and go over the details of a new sugar-refinery which was to be described for the morrow's paper, when my imagination was busy with the rippled hair and the soft violet eyes I had so long missed.

Let me overlook the memory of that gnawing impatience and hasten forward to the evening. At the earliest moment permitted by the habits of society, I presented myself at Mrs. Deering's door, and sent my name to Miss Haworth. I had not long to wait; she came into the room taller, it seemed to me, and more imposing in her presence, — but it was only the queenly air of right and justice which enveloped her. The sweet, frank face was pale, but firm, and the eyes did not droop or waver an instant, as they met my gaze. I forgot everything but the joy of seeing her again, of being restored to her society, and went forward to meet her, as if nothing had occurred since our last parting.

But she stopped and held me, by some subtle influence, from giving her the hand I was about to extend. "Wait, if you please, Mr. Godfrey," she said. "Before I can allow you to meet me as a friend, — even if you are generous enough to forgive, unexplained, the indignity with which I have treated you, — you must hear how far I have suffered myself to be misled by representations and appearances to do cruel wrong to your character as a man."

She stood so firm and resolute before me, bending her womanly pride to the confession of injustice with a will so noble that my heart bowed down at her feet and did her homage. It was enough; I would spare her the rest of her voluntary reparation.

"Miss Haworth," I said, "let it end here. You have already admitted that you judged me wrongly, and I ask no more. I do not seek to know what were your reasons for denying me the privilege of your — acquaintance; it is enough to know that they are now removed."

"It is not enough!" she exclaimed. "I claim to be accountable for every act of my life. You have a right to demand an explanation; you *would* demand it from a gentleman, and I am not willing to shelter myself under that considerate sentiment towards our sex which would spare me a momentary humiliation, by depriving me of the opportunity of satisfying my sense of justice. Be candid, Mr. Godfrey, and confess that the unexplained wrong would rest uneasily in your memory."

Her sense of truth struck deeper than my instinct of the moment. I felt that she was right; it was better that everything should be told now, and the Past made clear, for the sake of the Future.

"It is true," I said. "I am ready to hear all that you consider necessary to be told."

She paused a moment, but not from hesitation. She was only considering how to begin. When she spoke, her voice was calm and steady, and I felt that the purpose which prompted her was but the natural suggestion of her heart.

"I believe that one's instincts are generally true, and therefore I presume you already suspect that my step-brother, Mr. Tracy Floyd, is no friend of yours?"

I bowed in assent.

"Although I had no reason to attach much weight to Mr. Floyd's opinions, I will admit that other circumstances had shaken my faith, for a time, in the sincerity and honesty of men; that I was — perhaps morbidly — suspicious, and hence his insinuations in regard to yourself, though not believed, disposed me to accept other causes for belief. They assumed to be based on certain circumstances which he had discovered, and, therefore, when another circumstance, seeming to confirm them most positively, came under my own observation, I *did* believe. It was a shallow, hasty, false judgment, — how false, I only discovered a few weeks ago. I am ashamed of myself, for the truth bids me honor you for the very act which I interpreted to your shame."

Her words were brave and noble, but I did not yet understand their application. I felt my cheeks glow and my heart throb with happiness at hearing my own praise from her lips. She paused again, but I would not interrupt her confession.

"You may remember," she continued, "having called upon me, shortly after my return from the Northwest. Mr. Penrose was there at the same time, and you left the house together. My step-brother came into the room as you were taking leave. He was already in the habit of making depreciative remarks when your name happened to be mentioned; but on that evening he seemed particularly exasperated at your visit. It is not necessary for me to repeat all that he said, — the substance of it was that your habits of life rendered you unfit for the society of ladies, — that he, being, by the relation between our parents, permitted to look upon himself as my protector, warned me that any appearance of friendship towards you, on my part, would occasion me embarrassment, if not injury. I could not reconcile his assertion with the impression of your character which I had derived from my previous acquaintance with you; but, as I said before, Mr. Godfrey, I had had unpleasant experiences of human selfishness and hypocrisy, — my situation, indeed, seemed to expose me to such experiences, — and I became doubtful of my own judgment. Then came a singular chance, — in which, without my will, I played the spy upon your actions, and saw, as I supposed, the truth of all Mr. Floyd had declared."

My eyes were fixed upon her face, following her words with breathless interest. Not yet could I imagine the act or acts to which she referred. I saw, however, that the coming avowal required an effort of courage, and felt, dimly, that the honor and purity of her woman's nature were called upon to meet it.

"You have saved a woman," she said, "and it should not be hard for me to render simple justice to a man. I passed Washington Square one evening, Mr. Godfrey, when you were there to hear the story of an unfortunate girl. I saw you endeavoring to help and console her, — supporting her with your arm, — but I could hear neither your words nor hers. I trusted only to the evidence of my eyes, and they confirmed all that I had heard against you."

"What!" I exclaimed, "how was it possible?"

"I was in my carriage, bound on an errand which took me to the corner opposite the lamp under which you stood. As the coachman pulled up his horses, you moved away under the trees, as if fearful of being observed. The duplicity of your nature (as I took it to be) seemed to me all the darker and more repulsive from your apparent frankness and honesty; I was tired of similar discoveries, and I resolved, from that moment that I would know you no longer. It is my habit to act upon impulse, and I seized the first opportunity which occurred, — with what injustice, what rudeness I did not suspect until I learned the truth. I have tried to be as swift to atone as I was to injure, but you were not to be found; I knew not where a word from me might reach you until I received Mrs. Deering's last letter."

"Miss Haworth!" I cried, "say no more! you have acted nobly, — generously. I never accused you in my heart, — never." The next word would have betrayed my passion. I held it back from my lips with a mighty effort, but took her hand, bent my head over it and kissed it. When I looked up her eyes drooped, and the clear lines of her face were overspread with a wonderful softness and sweetness.

"Tell me only," I said, "how you learned anything more; who gave you an account of my interview with" —

I paused involuntarily. Her eyes were lifted steadily to mine, and she completed the unfinished sentence, —

"Jane Berry. From whom could I learn her story but from herself? She has told me all. It was she who went in my behalf to search for you."

It was my turn to drop my eyes. Had Jane Berry indeed told her *all?* No, it could not be; for in that case Miss Haworth might not have been so anxious to make reparation. She now overvalued as much as she had before undervalued my nature. What I seemed, in her pure, just eyes, I guessed with pain, as I remembered what I had been. But the mystery was not yet entirely clear; I thrust back the memory of my shame, and questioned her again, —

" How did you meet Jane Berry ? "

To my surprise, Miss Haworth seemed embarrassed what answer to give. She was silent a moment, and a light, rosy flush came into her face. Then she said, —

" Is it not enough, Mr. Godfrey, that I have met her ? — that I am trying to help her, as my duty bids me ? "

In what followed, I obeyed an irresistible impulse. Whence it came, I cannot tell; I was hurried along by a leap of the heart, so rapid that there was no time left to ask whither it was precipitating me. But the love nourished so long and sweetly, assailed by rivalry, suddenly hurled back, half held in check by the efforts of an immature will, and outraged by evil courses, now reasserted its mastery over me, filled and penetrated my being with its light and warmth, shone from my eyes, and trembled on my tongue. I was powerless to stay its expression. All thought of the disparity of our condition, of the contrast between her womanly purity and nobility and my unworthiness as a man, vanished from my mind. I only felt that we stood face to face, heart before heart, and from the overbrimming fulness of mine, I cried, —

" I know what you think, Miss Haworth, — how kindly you judge me. I know, still better, how little claim I have to be honored in your thoughts, and yet I dare, — how shall I say it ? — dare to place myself where only your equal in truth and in goodness ought to stand! I should give you time to know me better before telling you, as I must, that

I love you, — love you! Not first now, but long before I seemed to have lost you, and ever since, in spite of its hopelessness. I cannot thank you without betraying what is in my heart. I did not think to say this to-night; I came, too happy in the knowledge that you called me back, to dream of asking more, but your presence brings to my lips the words that may banish me forever. I ask nothing; love cannot be begged. I have no reason to hope; yet, Isabel Haworth, I love you, and believe that you will pardon if you cannot bless!"

A silence followed my words. I stood with bent head, as if awaiting a blow, while the gas-light fluttered and hummed in the chandelier above us. Presently a soft voice — my heart stood still, listening to its perfect music — stole upon the hush of the room.

"I knew it already."

"Then," — but I did not finish the sentence. Our eyes met, and tremulous stars of twilight glimmered through the violet of hers. Our hands met, and of themselves drew us together; drunken and blinded with happiness, I felt the sweetness of her lips yield itself, unshrinkingly, to mine. Then my arms folded themselves about her waist, her hands clasped my neck, my cheek caressed the silken, rippled gold of her temples, and I sighed, from the depth of a grateful soul, — "Oh, thank God! thank God!"

She felt the touch of the tear that sparkled on her hair. Once more I pressed my lips to her pure brow, and whispered, — "Tell me, is it true, Isabel?"

She lifted her head and smiled, as we tried to see each other's hearts in the dim mirror of either's eyes.

"I knew it," she repeated, "but I also knew something more. Oh, it is blessed to find rest at last!"

Then she slipped from my arms, and sank into a chair, covering her face with her hands. I knelt down beside her, caressing her lovely head. "I thought I had lost you," she murmured; "I did not venture to hope that you would forgive me so easily."

"Darling!" I exclaimed, taking her hand in mine, — "I never accused *you*. I knew that something had crept between us, which I could not remove until I should discover its nature. Until to-night I have been ignorant of your reason for my dismissal. Had I suspected, — had you given me a chance" —

"Ah," she interrupted me, "you will understand my abruptness now! It was because I loved you, *then*, John, that I felt outraged and humiliated — that I resolved never to see you again. You, of all the young men I knew, seemed to me earnest and sincere; I trusted in you, from the start, and just as I began to hope — as *you* hoped, John — came this blow to both of us. It could not have cost you more to bear than it cost me to inflict. Are you sure you have pardoned me?"

"Isabel!" was all the reply I could make, except that wonderful speech of the silent, meeting lips.

My bliss was too pure, too perfect to be long enjoyed without disturbance. Her maidenly courage, her frank and fearless confession of reciprocal love, filled me with a double trust and tenderness; but it also recalled, ere long, the shrinking, evasive silence of the false-hearted Amanda. That pitiful episode of my life must be confessed — nor that alone. I would not wrong the noble confidence of my darling by allowing her to think me better than I was, — or, rather, had been; for now the highest virtue, the sternest self-denial, seemed little to pay in return for my blessing. Ah, had I found it but to lose it again? This undercurrent of thought drove nearer and nearer the surface, clouding the golden ether I breathed, infusing its bitter drop into the nectar of my joy.

"Isabel," I said, "I dare not win the fortune of my life so easily. I have been weak and sinful; you must first hear my story, and then decide whether it is fitting that I should stand beside you. I owe it to you to complete your knowledge of myself."

"I expected nothing less from you, John," she said. "It is just: nothing in either's experience should be obscure to the other. You give me the Present, you promise me the Future, and I therefore have a right to the Past."

She spoke so firmly and cheerfully that my heart was reassured. I would postpone the confession until our next meeting, and indulge myself, for this one sacred evening, in the perfect sweetness of my bliss. But another reflection perversely arose to trouble me, — how should my poverty consort with her wealth? How should I convince — not her, but the unbelieving world — of the pure, unselfish quality of my affection? Neither would I speak of this; but she saw the shadow of the thought pass over my face, and archly asked, —

"What else?"

"I will tell you," I said. "Your place in the world is above mine. I cannot make a ladder of my love, and mount to the ease and security which it is a man's duty to create for himself. Whatever your fortune may be, you must allow me to achieve mine. The difference between us is an accident which my heart does not recognize, — would to God there were only this difference! — but I dare not take advantage of the equality of love, to escape a necessity, which it is best, for your sake as well as my own, that I should still accept. You understand me, Isabel?"

"Perfectly," she answered, smiling. "Not for the world's sake, but for your own, I agree to your proposal. An idle life would not make you happy, and I ought to be glad, on my part, that my little fortune has not kept us apart. So far, it has rather been my misfortune. It has drawn to me the false love, and now it shall not be allowed to rob me of the true. Do not let this thing come between our hearts. If it were yours, you would share it with me and I should freely enjoy what it brings; but a man is proud where a woman would be humble, and your pride is a part of yourself, and I love you as you are!"

"God grant that I may deserve you!" was all I could say. A softer and holier spirit of tenderness descended upon my heart. Now, indeed, might my mother rejoice over me, in her place amid the repose of heaven.

Presently there was a gentle knock at the door, and a familiar voice said, — "May I come in?"

It was Mrs. Deering, whose face brightened as she looked from one to the other. She said nothing, but took Isabel in her arms and kissed her tenderly. Then she gave me her hand, and I felt sympathy and congratulation in its touch.

"It is cruel in me to interrupt you," she said, when we were all seated, — "but do you know how long I have left you alone? An hour and three quarters, by my watch, and I was sure, Isabel, that you had long ago finished making your *amende*. Mr. Godfrey, I believe this girl is capable of accepting a challenge. I should think her a man, in her courage and sense of right, if she had not proved herself such a dear, good, faithful woman-friend to me. Then, I was afraid, Mr. Godfrey, that you might slip away before I could tell you that I know the cause of Isabel's misunderstanding, and thank you, as a woman, for what you did. And we have been to see Mary Maloney this afternoon, and have heard your praises without end."

"But Jane Berry!" I exclaimed, to cover my confusion; "where is she? I must see her again."

"I have found a quiet place for her, in Harlem," Isabel replied. "But, before you see her, you must know how I became acquainted with her and her story. Only, not to-night, John, pray; to-morrow, — you will come again to-morrow?"

"To-morrow, and every day, until the day when I shall cease to come, because I shall cease to go."

Mrs. Deering laughed and clapped her hands gleefully. "I see how it is!" she cried; "I shall lose the use of my parlor, from this time forth; but the interviews must be limited to two hours. At the end of that time I shall make my appearance, watch in hand. Now, good-night, Mr. Godfrey, — good-night, and God bless you!"

A quick, warm pressure of the hand, and she stole out of the room.

"She has told me all," said Isabel, turning to me, "and we have played the symphony, and wept over it together. It is a little wild and incoherent, but there is the beat of a breaking heart in it from beginning to end. You were a true friend to *him*, John; how I have wronged you!"

"I have wronged myself," I exclaimed; "but we will talk no more of that now. My dear Isabel — my dear wife, in the sight of Heaven, say once more that you love me, and I will keep the words in my ear and in my heart until we meet again!"

She laid her arms about my neck, she looked full in my face with her brave and lovely eyes, and said, — "I love you, — you only, now and forever." Then, heart to heart, and lip to lip, our beings flowed together, and the man's nature in me received the woman's, and thenceforth was truly man.

"Stay!" she whispered, when I would have left, — "stay, one moment!" She glided from the room, but returned almost immediately, with a slip of crumpled paper in her hand.

"Here," she said, holding it towards me, — "this separated us, this brought us together again. It can do no further harm or service. Let me burn it, and with it the memory — for both of us — of the evening when it was written."

I looked at it, and read, with indescribable astonishment, the words, — "Miss Haworth informs Mr. Godfrey that her acquaintance with him has ceased." It was the very note I had received that evening in Gramercy Park!

"Isabel! what does this mean?" I cried, in amazement.

She smiled, lighted one end of the paper at the gas-burner, watched it slowly consume, and threw its black, shrivelling phantom into the grate.

"It belongs to the story," she said; — "you shall hear everything to-morrow. Now good-night!"

CHAPTER XXXVIII.

OF WHICH JANE BERRY IS THE HEROINE.

On my way home, under stars that sang together, my first thought was of my faithful Bob. It was already a late hour for a man of his habits, but, sleeping or waking, I resolved that he should know Jane Berry was found. I turned out of the Bowery into Stanton Street, hastened onward with winged strides, and reached the door breathless with impatience and joy.

All were in bed except the journeyman's wife, who was at first a little alarmed at my untimely visit. I reassured her, declaring that I brought only good news, borrowed a candle and went up-stairs to Bob's room. The noise of my entrance did not break his healthy, profound sleep. I placed the light on the mantel-piece, took my seat on the edge of the bed, and looked on the plain, rugged face I loved. The unconscious features betrayed no released expression of guile or cruelty: there was honesty on the brow, candor on the full, unwrinkled eyelid, and goodness on the closed lips. Only the trouble of his heart, which he would not show by day, now stole to the light and saddened all his face.

He seemed to feel my steady gaze, even in sleep; he sighed and tossed his arm upon the coverlet. I seized his hand, and held it, crying, "Bob! Bob!"

His eyes were open in an instant. "Eh? John! what 's the matter?" he exclaimed, starting up in bed.

"Nothing wrong, Bob. I would n't rouse you from sleep to hear bad news."

"John, have you found her?"

I felt the pulses in the hand I held leaping strong and fast, and answered, "She is found. I have not seen her, but I know where she is, — under the best protection, with the best help, — far better than mine could be, Bob."

He drew a long breath of relief, and his fingers unconsciously tightened around my hand. "You 're a good friend, John," he said. "Stand by me a little longer. You 're smarter at thinkin' than I am, — I can only think with my hands, you know. Tell me what ought I to do?"

"Do you love her still, Bob?"

"God knows I do. I tried hard not to, after you told me what she 'd done; but I could n't help pityin' her, and, you see, that built up the feelin' on one side as fast as I tore it down on t' other. But then, John, there 's the disgrace. My name 's as good to me as the next man's, and my wife's name is mine. I must look ahead and see what *may* come — if — if she should care for me (which I 'm not sure of), and I should forgive her folly. Could I see her p'inted at, — could I bear to *know* things was said, even though I should n't hear 'em? And then, — that would be the hardest of all, — could I be the father o' children that must be ashamed o' their mother? I tell you, my head 's nigh tired out with tryin' to get the rights o' this matter. I 'm not hard, — that you know, — and I could forgive her for bein' blindly led into sin that a man does with his eyes open, if there was more men that think as I do. But it is n't the men, after all, John; it 's the women that tear each other to pieces without mercy!"

"Not all, Bob!" I cried; "it is a woman who protects her now, — a woman who knows her story, — and oh, Bob, that woman will one day be my wife, if God allows me so much happiness!"

I now told him, for the first time, of the great fortune which had come to me. It seemed hard, indeed, to intrude my pure bliss upon the trouble of his heart; but his nature was too sound for envy, or for any other feeling than the heartiest sympathy. Encouraged by the bright congratulation of his face, I allowed my heart the full use of my tongue, and grew so selfish in my happiness that I might have talked all night, but for the warning sound of a neighboring church-clock striking twelve. Poor Bob had thrust aside his own interests and perplexities, that he might rejoice in the new promise of my life.

I broke off abruptly, and replied to his first question. "Bob," I said, "I believe Jane Berry is still uncorrupted at heart. I believe, also, that the conviction of having lost *you* is her greatest sorrow. But do not ask me to advise you what to do; a man's own heart must decide for him, not another's. See her first; I shall learn to-morrow where she is. I will go to her, and prepare her to meet you, if you are willing, — then act as God shall put it in your mind to do. Now, I must go, — good-night, you good old Trojan!"

I gave him a slap over the broad shoulders, and, before I knew it, I was drawn up and held in iron muscles, until I felt a man's heart hammering like a closed fist against my breast. Then he released me, and I went down-stairs to find the journeyman's wife sitting on the lowest step, fast asleep, with her head against the railing, and a tallow dip, sputtering in its socket, at her side.

The next day was only less eventful in my history than its predecessor. I saw Isabel, and adhered to my self-imposed duty. What passed between us belongs to those sanctities of the heart which each man and woman holds as his or her exclusive possession. She knew my life at last, — nothing weak, or dark, or disgraceful in its past was withheld. I felt that I dared not accept the bounty of her love, if it rested on a single misconception of my nature. Had I known her then as I now know her, I should have understood that nothing was risked by the confession, — that her pardon already existed in her love.

But alas! I had looked on married life, and seen — as I still see — concealment and cowardice — honest affection striving to accommodate itself to imperfect confidence! Women are stronger than you think them to be, my brother-men! and by so much as you trust them with the full knowledge of yourselves, by so much more will they be qualified, not only to comfort, but to guard you!

During that interview I learned, also, the wonderful chance — the Providence I prefer to call it — which brought Isabel and myself together again. Some particulars, lacking in her narrative, were supplied afterwards by Jane Berry, but I give them now complete as they exist in my mind. In fact, so vivid and distinct is the story that it almost seems to be a part of my own experience.

Jane Berry's first determination, after my last interview with her, was to find other quarters, commensurate with her slender means, and as far as possible from Gooseberry Alley. One of the needle-women employed by the Bowery establishment had found better work and wages at a fashionable dress-maker's in Twenty-ninth Street, and, with her help, Jane succeeded, the next morning, in engaging a humble room in Tenth Avenue, with the prospect of occasional jobs from the same mistress. She was impelled to this step by her desire to save Mary Maloney from the trouble of malicious tongues, and by a vague instinct which counselled her to avoid me. Thus it was that she only remained long enough to finish the Christmas-gift, which she would leave for me as a token of her gratitude.

The evening after my visit, however, she made a discovery. In repairing the buttons of the waistcoat which Mary Maloney had retained as a pattern for the new one, she found a crumpled paper in one of the pockets. It seemed to be a stray fragment of no consequence, and she was about to throw it away, when her eye caught sight of my name in one of the two written lines. She read them, and her mind, simple as it was, detected a partial connection between them and the reckless words I had addressed to her. I had said — she well remembered it — that I loved one who was lost to me through no fault of mine; that one was probably this Miss Haworth. It was natural that her fancy, brooding always over her own shame, should suggest that *she* might be the innocent cause of my disappointment; my name was disgracefully coupled with hers by the tenants of Gooseberry Alley, and judging New York by Hackettstown, it seemed probable to her that all my acquaintances might be familiar with the report. It was a suspicion which occasioned her bitter grief, and she resolved to clear my reputation at the expense of her own.

Thus, her very ignorance of the world helped her to the true explanation of Miss Haworth's repulse, while the circumstance which actually led to it was so accidental as to be beyond my own guessing. To discover and undeceive Miss Haworth was the determination which at once took possession of her mind. She said to herself, — "What a lucky name! I never heard it before. If she were Miss Smith, or Miss Brown, I might as well give up; but, big as New York is, I am sure I can find Miss Haworth!"

Poor girl, I fancy her search was sufficiently long and discouraging. She may possibly have tried the "Directory," but it could give her no help. Installed in the working-room of the dress-maker, she kept her ears open to the talk of the fashionable visitors, in the hope of hearing the name mentioned. Once it came, as she thought, and with much trouble, much anxiety of heart, and many cunning little expedients, she discovered the residence of the lady who bore it, only to find "Hayward" on the door-plate! It was wonderful that, with her poor, simple, insufficient plan of search, she ever accomplished anything, and this is my reason for accepting her success as due to the guidance of Providence. One species of help, at least, she was shrewd enough to perceive and take hold of; she learned the names and addresses of other conspicuous *modistes* in the upper part of the city, and visited them, one by one, to ascertain whether they numbered a Miss Haworth among their patronesses. It was truly a woman's device, and being patiently followed, brought at last its reward.

The manner of the discovery was curious, and I have no doubt but that I understand how it came about better than Jane herself. Her unsophisticated air very probably created suspicion in the minds of some of the sharp women of business upon whom she called; she may have been suspected of being the crafty agent, or drummer, of a rival establishment, for her question was ungraciously received, and she was often keenly questioned in turn. Her patience had been severely tried, and the possibility of failure was beginning to present itself to her mind, when one day, at the close of March, she was attracted by the sign of "Madame Boisé, from Paris," and timidly entered, to repeat her inquiry. Madame Boisé, who spoke English with a New-England accent, listened with an air of suspicion, asked a question or two, and finally said, —

"I don't know any Miss *Hay*worth."

While saying this, she turned a large, light parcel upside down, so that the address would be concealed. The movement did not escape Jane Berry's eye; the idea came into her head, and would not be banished, that Madame *did* know Miss Haworth, and that the parcel in question was meant for her. She left the house and waited patiently at the corner of the block until she saw a messenger-girl issue from the door. Noting the direction the latter took, she slipped rapidly around the block and met her. It was easy enough to ascertain from the girl whither her errand led, and Jane's suspicion was right. She not only learned Miss Haworth's address, but, for greater certainty, accompanied the girl to the house.

The next morning she stole away from her work, filled with the sense of the responsibility hanging over her, and went to seek an interview with Isabel. If she had stopped to reflect upon what she was about to do, she might have hesitated and drawn back from the difficult task; but the singleness and unthinking earnestness of her purpose drove her straightforward to its accomplishment.

The servant who answered the door endeavored to learn her business, and seemed disinclined to carry her message, but finally left her standing in the hall and summoned Miss Haworth. When Jane saw the latter descending the stairs, she felt sure she had found the right lady, from the color of her eyes; this was the naïve reason she gave.

Isabel said, "You wished to see me?"

"Yes, Miss Haworth, nobody but you. Must I tell you, here, what I 've got to say? Are you sure I won't be overheard?"

"Come in here, then," Isabel answered, opening the door of the drawing-room, "if your message is so important. But I do not recollect that I have ever seen you before."

"No, miss, you never saw me, and I don't come on my own account, but on his. You 'll pardon me for speaking of him to you, but I must try to set you right about him. Oh, miss, he 's good and true, — he saved me from ruin, and it 's the least I can do to clear up his character!"

"Him? Who?" Isabel exclaimed, in great astonishment.

"Mr. Godfrey."

Isabel turned pale with the shock of the unexpected name; but the next instant a resentful, suspicious feeling shot through her heart, and she asked, with a cold, stern face, —

"Did he send you to me?"

"Oh, no, miss!" Jane cried, in distress, the tears coming into her eyes; "he don't know where I am. I went away because the people talked, and the more he helped me the more his name was disgraced on account of it. Please don't look so angry, miss; don't go away, until you 've heard all! I 'll tell you everything. Perhaps you 've heard it already, and know what I 've been; I 'll bear your blame, — I 'll bear anything, if you 'll only wait and hear the truth!"

She dropped on her knees, and clasped her hands imploringly. Her passionate earnestness bound Isabel to listen, but the latter's suspicion was not yet allayed.

"Who told you to come to me?" she asked. "How did you learn that I once knew Mr. Godfrey?"

"Not him, miss, oh, not him! I found it out without his knowledge. When I saw that he was n't his right self, — he was desperate, and said that he was parted from one he loved, and through no fault of his, and he did n't care what would become of him, — and then when I found this," — here she produced the note, — "and saw your name, I guessed you were the one. And then I made up my mind to come to you and clear him from the wicked reports, — for indeed, miss, they 're not true!"

Jane's imperfect, broken revelations, — the sight of the note, — the evident truth of the girl's manner, — strangely agitated Isabel's heart. She lifted her from the floor, led her to a seat, seated herself near her and said, —

"I will hear all you have to say. Try and compose yourself to speak plainly, for you must bear in mind that I know nothing. Tell me first who you are."

"I am Jane Berry, the girl he saved the night of the fire."

"Were you with him one evening in Washington Square?"

"Yes!" Jane eagerly exclaimed. "That was the time I told him all about myself, and how I came to be where I was. And now I must tell you the same, miss. If it does n't seem becoming for you to hear, you 'll forgive me when you think what it is to me to say it."

"Tell me."

Whereupon Jane, with many breaks and outbursts of shame and self-accusation, repeated her sad story. Of course she withheld so much of my last interview with her as might reflect an unfavorable light upon myself. Isabel saw in me only the virtuous protector whom she had so cruelly misjudged. Jane's narrative was so straightforward and circumstantial that it was impossible to doubt its truth. Pity for the unfortunate girl, and condemnation of her own rash judgment were mingled in her heart with the dawning of a sweet, maidenly hope.

"Jane Berry," she said, when at last all the circumstances were clearly explained, "you have done both a good and a heroic thing in coming to me. I promise you that I will make atonement to Mr. Godfrey for my injustice. You must let me be your friend; you must allow me to assist and protect you, in your struggles to redeem yourself. I will take Mr. Godfrey's place: it belongs to a woman."

Jane melted into grateful tears. Isabel, feeling that she deserved the joy of being the messenger of justice to me, wrote a note similar to that which called me back to her, and intrusted Jane with its delivery. The message failed, because I was at that time dishonorably banished from Mrs. De Peyster's boarding-house, and my den in Crosby Street was known to no one.

The fateful interview was over, and Jane, with the precious note in her hands, was leaving the drawing-room, when the street-door opened, and Mr. Tracy Floyd entered the hall. Isabel, following Jane, heard the latter utter a wild, startled scream, and saw her turn, with a pale, frightened face and trembling limbs, and fall upon the floor, almost swooning.

"Damnation! here 's a devil of a muss!" exclaimed Mr. Floyd, with a petrified look on his vapid face. Perceiving Isabel, he ran up-stairs, muttering curses as he went.

"Oh, miss!" Jane breathlessly cried, clutching a chair and dragging herself to her feet, — "dear, good Miss Haworth, don't let that man come into your house! Tell me that you 're not thinking of marrying him! He 's the one I was talking of! I 've never mentioned his name yet to a living soul, but *you* must know, for your own sake. Perhaps he'll deny it, — for he lied to me and he 'd lie to you, — but see here! I call on God to strike me dead this minute, if I 've told you a false word about him!"

She held up her right hand as she pronounced the awful words, but Isabel did not need this solemn invocation. Her pure, proud nature shrank from the ignominy of her relation to that man, and a keener pang of reproach entered her heart as she remembered that his insinuations in regard to myself — doubly infamous now — had made her mind so rapid to condemn me. It was impossible for her, thenceforth, to meet her step-brother, — impossible to dwell in the same house with him.

I have reason to believe, now, that Mr. Tracy Floyd was one of the band of genteel rowdies whom I encountered in Houston Street on the evening of the fire, — that he recognized me and watched me conducting Jane Berry to Gooseberry Alley. Perhaps he may have lain in wait for my visits afterwards. Whether he also recognized Jane Berry, it is impossible to say. Let us seek to diminish rather than increase the infamy of his class, and give him the benefit of the uncertainty.

Isabel only remained long enough to find a safe place of refuge for Jane Berry. The fears of the latter were so excited by her encounter with her betrayer that she begged to be allowed to go as far as possible from the crowded heart of the city, and gladly embraced the proposition of boarding with a humble, honest family in Harlem. When this duty was performed, Isabel, impulsive in all things which concerned her feelings, left immediately for Boston, resolved never to return to her step-father's house while his son remained one of its inmates.

I lost no time in visiting Jane Berry. She, of course, had learned nothing, as yet, of what had taken place, and her surprise at my sudden appearance was extreme. I knew, from the eager, delighted expression of her face, what thoughts were in her mind, what words would soon find their way to her lips, and could not resist the temptation to forestall her by a still happier message.

"Jane," I cried, taking her hands, "it is *you* who have saved *me!* I have seen Isabel Haworth, and she has burned the note you took out of my waistcoat-pocket! — burned it before my eyes, Jane, and she has promised to write another, some day, and sign it 'Isabel Godfrey!'"

"Oh, is it so, Mr. Godfrey? Then I can be happy again, — I have done some good at last!"

"You *are* good, Jane. We shall be your friends, always. Show the same patience in leading an honest life that you have shown in helping me, and you may not only redeem your fault but outlive its pain."

"No — no!" she said, sighing. "I 've heard it said that a moment's folly may spoil a lifetime, and it 's true. I 've been trying to think for myself, — I never did it before, — and though I may n't be able to put everything into words as you do, it 's here," (touching her heart,) "and I understand it."

I thought of Bob, and felt that I was forced to probe her sorest wound, with no certainty of healing it. But for Bob's sake it must be done.

"Jane," I said, gravely, "I have found some one whom you know, — who loved, and still loves you. Jane, he is my dearest friend, my old schoolmate and playfellow, who picked me up the other day, when I was a miserable vagabond, and set me on my feet. He followed you when you left Hackettstown, and has been trying to find you ever since. Will you see him?"

I saw, by her changing color, and the unconscious, convulsive movement of her hands, that the first surprise of my news was succeeded by a painful conflict of feeling.

"Does he know?" — she whispered.

"He knows all, and it is the sorrow of his life, as of

yours. But I am to tell you, from him, that he will not force himself upon you. You must decide, for yourself, whether or not he shall come."

"Not now — not now!" she cried. "If I could look through the blinds of a window and see him passing by, I think it would be a comfort, — but I ought n't to wish even for that. Don't think me hard, Mr. Godfrey, or ungrateful for his remembrance of me when I 've no right to it; but, indeed, I dare n't meet him now. Perhaps a time may come, — I don't know, — it 's better not to promise anything. I may work and get myself a good name: people may forget, if they 've heard evil reports of me; but *he* can't forget. Tell him I thank him from my heart, and will pray for him on my knees every night. Tell him I know now, when it 's too late, how good and true he is, and I 'll give back his love for me in the only way I dare, — by saving him from his own generous heart!"

I sighed when I saw how the better nature of the woman had been developed out of the ruins of her life, and that she was really worthy of an honest man's love through the struggle which bade her relinquish the hope of ever attaining it. But I could not attempt to combat her feelings without weakening that sense of guilt which was the basis of her awakened conscience, the vital principle of her returning virtue. It was best, for the present, at least, to leave her to herself.

To my surprise — and also to my relief — Bob acquiesced very quietly in her decision.

"It 's about what I expected," he said, "and I can't help thinkin' better of her for it. Between you and me, John, if she 'd ha' been over-anxious to see me, 't would n't ha' been a good sign, and I might ha' drawed back. You know what I asked you about, — I 've turned it over ag'in, and this time it comes out clearer. I 've got to wait and be patient, the Lord knows how long, but His ways won't be hurried. I must be satisfied with knowin' she 's in good hands, where I can always hear of her; and maybe a day 'll come when the sight o' me will give her less trouble than 't would now, and when it 'll be easier for me to forgit what 's past."

Bob bent his neck to his fate like a strong ox to the yoke. Nothing in his life was changed: he was still the steady, sober, industrious foreman, with a chance of becoming "boss" in a year or two, respected by his workmen, trusted by his employer, and loved with a brotherly affection by at least one fellow-man. His hands might hew out for him a more insignificant path in the world than my head achieved for me, but they beat down snares and bridged pitfalls which my head could only escape by long and weary moral circuits. Our lives were not so disproportionately endowed as they seemed to my boyish eyes.

CHAPTER XXXIX.

IN WHICH I RECEIVE AN UNEXPECTED LETTER FROM UNCLE WOOLLEY.

Did ever such a summer shine upon the earth? Did the shadow-broidery of trees ever deepen into the perfect canopy of shade, the bud open into the blossom, May ripen to June, with such a sweet, glowing, unbroken transition? Never, at least, had I seen the same diamond sparkle on the waves of the harbor, in my morning walks on the Battery, or the same mellow glory of sunset over Union Square, in returning from interviews which grew dearer and happier with every repetition. Even the coming separation could not rob the season of its splendor: day after day the sun shone, and the breezes blew, and the fresh leaves whispered to one burden, — joy, joy, joy!

And day by day there came to me a truer and holier knowledge of Isabel's nature. It seemed, indeed, that I had never known a woman before, in the beautiful harmony which binds and reconciles her apparent inconsistencies, so that courage may dwell side by side with timidity, exaction with bounty, purity with knowledge. The moral enigmas which had perplexed me found in her their natural solution, and she became at once my protecting and forgiving conscience. I thought, then, that she surpassed me in everything, but her truer instinct prefigured my own maturer development. Love can seldom exist without a balance of compensations, and I have lived to know — and to be grateful for the knowledge — that I am her help and stay, as she is mine.

Fortunately for myself, she was not a woman of genius, to overpower my proper ambition, or bend it to her will. Such may consort with the gentle, yielding, contented persons of our sex who supply that repose which is the coveted complement of the restless quality. Genius is always hermaphroditic, adding a male element to the woman and a female to the man. In Isabel, the strong sentiment of justice and the noble fearlessness with which she obeyed its promptings, were also the sterling attributes of her own sex, and they but made her womanly softness rarer and lovelier. Her admirable cultivation gave her an apparent poise of character and ripeness of judgment, which protected, not obscured, the fresh, virgin purity of her feelings. My sentimental phantom of inconstancy vanished when I compared my shallow emotion for Amanda with this perfect passion in which I lived and moved and had my being. Now, for the first time, I knew what it was to love.

I have said that a separation was approaching. Her summer was to be spent, as usual, in the country, — the greater part of it with Mrs. Deering, at Sachem's Head, — which gave me the promise of an occasional brief visit. Isabel's mother, in her will, had expressed the desire — it was not worded as a command — that she would not marry before her twenty-first birthday. Her fortune, until then, was in the hands of trustees, of whom Mr. Floyd was one, and from her eighteenth year she was allowed the use of the annual income. Until now, her step-father had drawn it in her name, and she had allowed him to use the greater portion of it in his private speculations. Of course his consent to her marriage was not to be expected, and she decided not to mention her betrothal until she should come into the possession of her property, in the following October.

We were discussing these prosaic matters, — not during the second interview, be it understood, nor even the tenth, — and I had confessed the trouble of mind which her fortune had caused me, when she playfully asked, —

"What were the dimensions of this terrible bugbear? Taking your misgivings, John, and the eagerness of certain others, one would suppose it to be a question of millions. Tell me, candidly, what is presumed to be my market value?"

"I don't know, precisely," I answered; "Penrose said — some hundreds of thousands!"

"Penrose!" She paused, and an expression of disappointment passed over her face. "I would rather *he* had not said it. I did not think him selfish, — in that way. There is a mocking spirit in him which repels me, but I detected noble qualities under it, at the last. I could have accepted and honored him as a friend, if he had permitted me. But to come back to the important subject, — he was wrong, and your trouble might have been diminished by two thirds, or three fourths, if you had known it. I am not the heiress of romance."

"So much the better!" I cried. "Neither are you the lady of romance, 'in gloss of satin and glimmer of pearls.'"

"You must hear the fact, John. My whole fortune is but eighty thousand dollars, which, in New York, I believe, is only considered to be a decent escape from poverty. Having never enjoyed the possession of it, I feel that it scarcely yet exists for me. I should value a tithe of it far more, if it were earned by my own exertions, and this is one reason why I yield so readily to your scornful independence of me. I can enter into your feeling, for it is also mine."

I was really relieved that the disproportion between our fortunes was reduced by so much, — though, for that matter, eighty thousand seemed as unattainable as eight hundred thousand. All I could aim at was the system of steady, moderately remunerative labor upon which I had entered, and the prospect of gradual improvement which it held forth. I would, at least, not be an idle pensioner upon Isabel's means. This resolution gave me new vigor, infused life into my performance of mechanical duties, and made my services, as I soon discovered, of increased value, — for the increased reward followed.

Our parting was the beginning of a correspondence in which we still drew closer to each other, in the knowledge of reciprocal want, and the expression of the deeper sympathies born of absence. Our letters were long and frequent, and then came, to interrupt them, the brief, delicious visits, when I stole away for a Sabbath beside the blue water, and Mrs. Deering managed that we should be left alone to the extreme limit which Conventionality permitted. Thus the bright summer wore away, nor once betrayed the promise of its joyous opening.

It was the 9th of September, I recollect, — for in one month, to a day, Isabel would become sole mistress of her fortune, — that, on going down to the *Wonder* office at the usual hour, I found a large, awkward-looking letter upon my desk. The postmark was Reading, and I thought I recognized my uncle's cramped, heavy hand in the configuration of the words, — "Mr. John Godfrey." I opened it with some curiosity to know the occasion of this unexpected missive, and read as follows: —

"Reading, Berks Co. Penn'a.
September the 7th, 185—.

"Respd. Nephew, — I take my Pen in hand to inform you that Me and your aunt Peggy are injoying good Health and Those Blessings which the Lord Vouchsafes to us. It is a long Time since we have heard anything of you, but suppose you are still ingaged in the same Occupation as at first, and hence direct accordingly, hoping these few Lines may come Safely to hand.

"It has been a fine Summer, for the crops. The grass has grown for the Cattle and the herb for the Service of man (Psalms 104, 14,) and the Butter market is well supplied. Prices will be coming down, but I trust you have Found that wealth is not increased by price (Ditto 44, 12,) and that Riches profit not in the day of wrath (Proverbs 11, 4). My business has Expanded, and I have reason to be Thankful that I have so far escaped the Snares which were laid for me as in a Trap (Job 18). Although I was Compassed about, Praise be to the Lord, I have escaped.

"And this is the Reason why I write to you these few lines. I might say to you Judge not that ye be not Judged (Matthew 7, 1) if I was sure that your ears are not closed in Stubbornness. I might Charge you as being one that looketh on outward Appearance (Samuel 16, 7) but I will not imitate your Behaviour to a man of your own Kin. Sufficient unto the day is the Evil thereof, and as there is a time for all things, (Eccl. 3) I hope your time for Acknowledgement has come. I have waited for my Justification. A long Time, it may seem to you, because you were rash to suspect evil, but it has Been longer to me, because I had to Bear your suspicion. With great wrestlings have I wrestled, and I have Prevailed (Genesis 30, 8). It is not good to be Rash, or to speak out of the Stirrings up of the sinful Heart. It has been a sore Tribulation to your aunt Peggy, though not rightfully to be laid at My door.

"Their Snares have failed and I am at last Able to realize — which, since the Road has changed, as I suppose you have seen by the Newspapers, is a proper punishment, showing that the Counsels of the wicked is Deceit (Proverbs 12, 5). And you will See, much as you would not Believe it at the time, that Sixhundredfold was below the Mark, which was all I Promised, but will Act upright, and it shall be even Shares to the Uttermost farthing. I prayed to the Lord on my Bended knees that night, that He would make my word Good, and let me not be Humbled, but it is more than 2 years before He would allow it to come to Pass, which I did not Count upon, and it is all the Better for waiting. The new Survey was Made more than a year ago, but Purchasers did not depend on the second change until there was some Cuttings and Bridges. Besides, the others went about Crying it down, for Disappointment and Spite, which had an effect on the Market, and so I would not Realize until the thing was sure. You see now that it was not Necessary to suspicion me of acting dishonest, and to Breed up strife in the household. Where Strife is, there is confusion (James 3, 16), and you Magnified your own opinions at the time, but Blessed is the man that maketh the Lord his trust and respecteth not the Proud (Proverbs 40, 4).

"I write these few Lines to inform you that Things are now fixed, as I said before, and may be Put into your own hands whenever you like. I Remind you that a Recpt. in full is necessary for the Justification of my name, though not aware of Evil reports, which might have been Expected after the manner in which you Went away from my doors. Your aunt bids me say that things may be Taken back between Relations, and This should not be a matter too hard for judgement, between blood and blood (Deuteronomy 17, 8). Therefore it Rests with yourself on what footing we should stand. I will not bear Malice for past injustice, but hope that you will acknowledge the lesser Truth, and yet be Led to accept the Greater.

"If you come soon, Let me know the day beforehand that all things may be Prepared. Your aunt says the spare bedroom on the second story, if he will Take it, which I repeat also for my own part — though the House is sold, by reason of Retiring from business, we have not Moved away. Our Congregation has been blessed with a great Awakening and increase of members, and we expect to build a Large Church in the spring. The town is growing, houses go up wonderful fast, and Business improves all the time. Himpel has prospered, being known as an upright God-fearing Man, and the talents I leave in his hands, Remaining Silent Pardner, will not be tied up in a Napkin.

"Hoping these few Lines may reach you Safely, and

find you injoying good Health, and waiting for an answer whether you will come, no more at Present from

" Your uncle to command,

" AMOS WOOLLEY."

Two things were evident from this somewhat incoherent epistle, — that my uncle had finally " realized " his venture in the coal-land speculation, and was ready to pay my share of the investment; and secondly, that he had keenly felt the force of my accusations and desired a reconciliation. The matter had almost passed out of my mind during the eventful two years which had elapsed since my last visit to Reading. I had given up my little inheritance as lost, and never dreamed that it might yet be restored to me. My own experience, in the mean time, disposed me to judge more leniently of my uncle's unauthorized use of the money, — especially now that his scheme had succeeded. Success has a wonderful moral efficacy. I could also imagine how his pride of righteousness had been wounded by my words, — how they would come back to his mind and pull him down when he would fain have exalted himself, and thus become a perpetual thorn to his conscience.

Moreover, in looking back to the days of my life in Reading, I was able to read his character more intelligently. I saw that he was sincere, and that his apparent hypocrisy was simply the result of narrowness and ignorance. He had not sufficient intellect to be liberal, nor sufficient moral force to be consistent. In most of the acts of his life, he doubtless supposed himself to be right, and if, in this one instance, he had yielded to a strong temptation, his ultimate intention was honest. I was willing to concede that he never meant to defraud me, — nay, that he was even unaware of the fraudulent construction which might be put upon his act.

The same day I dispatched the following answer: —

"Dear Uncle, —

"The news contained in your letter of the 7th was quite unexpected, but none the less welcome, for your sake as well as my own. While I still think that the disposal of my little property ought to have been left to myself, I cheerfully acquit you of any intention to do me wrong, and to show that I not only bear no malice, but am willing to retract my hasty insinuations against your character, I will accept your proffered hospitality when I visit Reading. You may expect me within the next four or five days.

"Reserving all further information concerning my own fortunes until we meet, I subscribe myself, with an affectionate greeting for Aunt Peggy, your nephew,

"John Godfrey."

Mr. Clarendon, whose fatherly interest in my career was renewed, and to whom I had confided much of my early history, promptly and generously seconded my wishes. I remained only long enough to write to Isabel, and to find Bob Simmons and tell him that he must spend his next Sunday evening elsewhere than in my attic in Hester Street. Then I set out for Reading, by way of Philadelphia.

There was an accident on the road, which so delayed the evening train that it was between nine and ten o'clock before I arrived. Knowing that my uncle was already in bed, I went to the Mansion House and engaged quarters for the night. The host conducted me to a narrow room, which was only fitted for repose and privacy when the adjoining chambers happened to be vacant. One of these communicated with mine by a door in the partition, which, though locked, was so shrunk at the top and bottom that it no more kept out sound than a sieve. I was both fatigued from the journey and excited by my visit to the old place; so I threw myself at once into bed, and lay there, unable to sleep, meditating on the changes of the past two or three years.

Perhaps half an hour had gone by, when footsteps and rustling noises passed my door, a key was turned, and the same noises entered the adjoining chamber.

"Open the window — I won't have my dresses smoked!" exclaimed a voice which sent a nervous shock through my body.

"You did n't used to be so damned particular," was the brutal answer. And now I recognized the pair.

"Well, — never mind about this. I sha'n't wear it again," said she, in a bitter, compressed voice. "I 've told you already, Mr. Rand, that I 've always been used to having money when I want it, — and I want it now. You 've cheated Pa out of enough to keep me in dresses for a lifetime, and you must make it up to *me*."

"How the devil am I to get it?" he exclaimed, with a short, savage laugh.

"I don't know and I don't care. You and Mulford were very free to put everything into Old Woolley's pocket. If you *will* be a fool, don't think that *I* am going to suffer for it!"

"I wish that soft-headed Godfrey had run away with you, before I ever set eyes on your confounded face. You damned cat! Who 'd think, to hear you purring before folks, and rubbing your back affectionately against everybody's feet, that you could hiss, and spit, and scratch?"

"I wish he had!" she exclaimed. "Godfrey will be Old Woolley's heir."

I was first made aware that I had burst into a loud, malicious laugh, by the sudden, alarmed silence, followed by low whispers, in the next room. They were themselves my avengers. Now, indeed, I saw from what a fate I had been mercifully saved, and blessed the Providence which had dealt the blow. There was no more audible conversation between my neighbors that night. They must have discovered afterwards, from my name on the hotel register, who it was that overheard their amiable expressions. I saw them, next morning, from the gentlemen's end of the breakfast-table, as they came down together, serene and smiling, she leaning affectionately on his arm. Let them go! The world, no doubt, considers them a happy and devoted pair.

Nothing in the old grocery was changed except Bolty, who now wore a clean shirt and a pen at his ear, and kept his mouth mostly shut. He had two younger assistants in the business, but still reserved to himself the service of favorite customers. When he saw me entering the door, he jumped over the counter with great alacrity.

"Why, Mr. Godfrey!" he cried, "this *is* a surprise. Not but what I had a hint of it, when your letter came, — by yisterday mornin's mail. Glad to see you in My Establishment, — one o' my fust customers, — ha, ha! Did you notice the sign? I guess not, — you was n't lookin' up."

I was obliged, perforce, to follow Bolty out upon the pavement, and notice the important fact that "WOOLLEY &" was painted out, and "LEOPOLD" painted in; so that now the sign read, — and, I was sure would continue to read, for a great many years to come, — "LEOPOLD HIMPEL'S GROCERY STORE."

I determined that no trace of what had passed between us should be visible in my manner towards my uncle and aunt. I even gave the latter a kiss when we met, which brought forth a gush of genuine tears. There was, of course, a mutual sense of embarrassment at first, but as both parties did their best to overcome it, we were soon sitting together and talking as pleasantly and familiarly as if our relations had never been disturbed.

When Aunt Peggy had withdrawn to the kitchen to look after her preparations for dinner, Uncle Amos gave me a long and very circumstantial history of his speculation. There was a great deal which I could not clearly understand at the time, but which has since then been elucidated by my own experience in matters of business.

The original scheme had indeed offered a very tempting prospect of success. Several large tracts of coal-land had been purchased for a comparatively insignificant sum, on account of their remoteness from lines of transportation. The plan of the new railroad which was to give them a sudden and immense increase of value, had not yet been made public, but the engineering scout employed by the capitalists had made his report. He was an acquaintance of Mulford, who had formerly been concerned with my uncle in some minor transactions. This, however, was to be a grand strike, promising a sure fortune to each.

After the charter for the road had been obtained, and the preliminary surveys were made, the aforesaid tracts of land might have been sold at triple or quadruple their cost. This, however, did not satisfy the speculators, whose appetites were only whetted by their partial success. Then a period of financial disturbance ensued: some of the capitalists interested in the road became embarrassed, and the work stopped. The coal-lands fell again in value, and the prospective fortunes dwindled in proportion. Up to this time the lands had been held as a joint-stock investment, my uncle's share being one fifth; but now there was a nominal dissolution of partnership, at the instance of Mulford, Bratton, and the Rands, each receiving his share of the property, to be held thenceforth in his own name, and disposed of at his own individual pleasure. My uncle was no match for his wily associates. After a series of manœuvres which I will not undertake to explain, they succeeded in foisting upon him a tract lying considerably aside from the proposed line of the road, and divided from it (a fact of which he was not aware) by a lofty spur of the mountains.

When he discovered the swindle, he gave himself up for lost. The others held, it seemed, the only tracts likely to be profitable at some future day, while his, though it might be packed with anthracite, was valueless, because inaccessible. He visited the spot, however, toiled over his two square miles of mountain and forest, and learned one or two circumstances which gave him a slight degree of comfort and encouraged him to wait. In eighteen months from that time the first projected road was still in abeyance, while the trains of the Delaware and Lackawanna were running within a mile of his property! There were facilities for building, at little cost, a short connecting branch: a golden radiance shone over the useless wilderness, and he had finally "realized," for something more than tenfold his investment.

"Now," said Uncle Amos, wiping his fat forehead with a bandanna handkerchief, — for the narrative was long, intricate, and exciting, — "now, you can easy calculate what your share amounts to. I 've allowed you interest every year, and interest on that again, as if it had been regularly put out, and you 'll find that it comes, altogether, to within a fraction of twenty thousand dollars. I 'll say square twenty thousand, because you can then invest it in a lump: there 's less temptation to split and spend. The money 's in the Bank, and you can have a check for 't this minute. If you 've felt sore and distrustful about it all this while, don't forget what *I 've* gone through with, that had all the risk and responsibility."

"We will think no more of what has gone by, uncle," I said. "I will take your advice. The money shall be invested as it is: I look on it still as the legacy of my father and mother, and to diminish it would seem to diminish the blessing that comes with it."

"That 's right, John! I 'm glad that you have grown to be a man, and can see things in the true light. Ah, if you would but see *all* the Truth!"

"I do," said I. "I know what you mean, Uncle. I have learned my own weakness and foolishness, and the strength, wisdom, and mercy of God."

He seemed comforted by these words, if not wholly convinced that my feet were in the safe path. At dinner his prayer was not against "them which walk in darkness," but a grateful acknowledgment for undeserved bounties, in which I joined with a devout heart.

I completely won Aunt Peggy by confiding to her my betrothal and approaching marriage. The next day, before leaving for my return to new York, she brought me a parcel wrapped in tissue-paper, saying, —

"I want to send something to *her*, but I can't find anything nice except this, which Aunt Christina gave me for my weddin'. It 's not the fashion, now, I know, but folks says the same things come round every twenty-five or thirty years, and so I expect this will turn up again soon. I hope she 'll like it."

She unfolded the paper and produced a tortoise-shell comb, the top of which was a true-lover's-knot, in open filigree, rising nearly six inches above the teeth. I smothered my amusement, as best I could, under profuse thanks, and went away leaving Aunt Peggy proud of her nephew.

CHAPTER XL.

CONCLUSION.

The story of my fortunes draws to an end, — not because the years that have since elapsed furnish no important revelation of life, no riper lessons for brain or heart, but chiefly because the records of repose interest us less than those of struggle. I have not enjoyed, nor did I anticipate the enjoyment of, pure, uninterrupted happiness, but my nature rests at last on a firm basis of love and faith, secure from any serious aberrations of the soul or the senses. I know how to endure trial without impatient protest, — to encounter deceit without condemning my race, — to see, evermore, the arm of Eternal Justice, reaching through time and meting out, in advance, the fitting equivalent for every deed. It is the vibration of the string which gives forth the sound, and that of my life now hums but a soft, domestic monotone, audible to a few ears.

Yet there are still some explanations to be made, before closing this narrative of the seven years which renewed my frame, changing gristle into bone, and adding the iron of the man to the soft blood of the boy.

The unexpected restoration of my inheritance, so marvellously expanded, necessarily changed my plans for the future. After returning to New York, I lost no time in visiting Isabel, and in consulting with my honored friend, Mr. Clarendon. The latter, although assuring me that my labors had become of real value to his paper, nevertheless advised me to give up my situation, since I should be now in the receipt of a better income, and could devote a year or two to rest and study. I knew my own deficiencies, and was anxious to supply them for the sake of the new life which was opening. A spark of ambition still burned among the ashes of my early dreams. While recognizing that I had mistaken enthusiasm for power, and sentiment for genius, — that my poetic sympathy was not sufficient to constitute the genuine poetic faculty, — I had nevertheless acquired a facility of expression, a tolerable skill in description, and a knowledge of the resources of author-craft, which, in less ambitious ways, might serve me, and enable me to serve my fellow-men. The appetite was upon me, never to be cured. There is more hope for the man who tastes wine than for him who has once tasted type and printer's ink. Though but one in fifty feels the airy intoxication of fame, while the others drink themselves into stupidity, and then into fatuity, who is deterred by the example ?

My inheritance did me good service in another way. The reason for my withdrawal from the *Wonder* became known, and my friend, the reporter of the *Avenger*, put it into the "Personal" column of that paper, stating that I had fallen heir to an immense fortune. The article was headed "*An Author in Luck*," and, of course, went the rounds of the other papers. I was congratulated by everybody whom I had ever met, and even Messrs. Renwick and Blossom, overlooking the ignominy of my flight from Mrs. De Peyster's boarding-house, left their cards at Mrs. Very's door. I gave the black boy who scoured the knives two shillings to carry my cards to them in return, and went up to Stanton Street, to pass the evening with Bob Simmons.

With October Isabel came back to the city. She had already written to her step-father and the two associate trustees, and on the day when she completed her twenty-first year the papers representing her property were placed in her hands. Mr. Floyd, who had always treated her kindly, and who had found his house very lonely since her departure, begged her to return, even going to the length of offering to banish his son. Then Isabel quietly said, —

"I shall be married to Mr. Godfrey in two months, and will not dispossess Mr. Tracy Floyd for so short a time."

The old man sighed wearily. The announcement, of course, was not unexpected. There was a little affection somewhere among the stock-jobbing interests which filled his heart; he had once imagined that his step-daughter might become his daughter-in-law, and keep a warm home for his old days. His intercourse with his son consisted principally of impudent demands for money on one side, and angry remonstrances on the other. What could he expect? He gave his life to Wall Street, and that stony divinity does not say, "Train up your children." On the contrary, one of her commandments is, "Thou shalt give thy sons cigars and thy daughters silks, and let them run, that the care of them may not take thy mind from stocks."

As for Mr. Tracy Floyd, his fate was already decided, though we did not know it at the time. For one so selfish and shallow-hearted, his only plan of life — to be the idle, elegant husband of an heiress — failed most singularly and lamentably. Miss Levi employed the magnetism of her powerful Oriental eyes to some purpose, for she trod his plans under foot and married him before the summer was over. I would give much to know the successive saps and mines, the stealthy approaches, and the final onset by which she gained possession of the empty citadel; it would be a more intricate romance than my own. She was a Jewess, with very little money in her own right, but wealthy connections. The latter were desirous of rising in society, and it was believed that they allowed a moderate annuity to Mrs. Floyd, on condition that the match should be used to further their plans in this respect, and that the possible future children should be educated in their faith. I will not vouch for the truth of this report, but the gossips of

Gramercy Park that winter declared that the Floyd mansion was frequented by numbers of persons with large noses and narrow stripes of forehead.

We were married in December. Isabel wore the sapphires I loved, but their sparkle could not dim the sweet, tremulous lustre of her kindred eyes. It was a very quiet and unostentatious wedding, followed by a reception in Mrs. Deering's rooms. When evening came, my wife and I left our friends, and went together, — not on a tour from hotel to hotel, with a succession of flashy "Bridal Chambers" at our disposal, — but to the dear little house in Irving Place which was now to be our home. Yet we did not go alone. Three radiant genii, with linked hands, walked before us, — Peace to kindle the fire on our domestic hearth, and Confidence and Love to light the lamps beside our nuptial couch.

Some weeks afterwards, I received, one morning, the following letter from San Francisco: —

"My Dear John, — I know why you have not written to me. In fact I knew, months ago, (through Deering,) what was coming, and had conquered whatever soreness was left in my heart. Fortunately my will is also strong in a reflective sense, and I am, moreover, no child to lament over an irretrievable loss. I dare say the future will make it up to me, in some way, if I wait long enough. At any rate, you won't object, my dear old fellow, to have me say — not that I wish you happiness, for you have it, but — that you deserve your double fortune. The other item I picked up from a newspaper; you might have written me *that*.

"With this steamer there will come a trifle, which I hope may be accepted in token of forgetfulness and forgiveness, — though it is Fate, not myself, that should be forgiven. There may also come a time — nay, I swear it *shall* come, — when I may sit by your fireside and warm my bald head, and nurse my gouty leg, and drink my glass of Port. Pray that it may be sooner for the sake of your (and hers, now) "Affectionate cousin,

"ALEXANDER PENROSE."

The "trifle" was a superb India shawl, and I am glad that Isabel likes to wear it. We have not yet seen our cousin, for we were absent from New York when he came to the Atlantic side, two years afterwards; but we believe in the day when he shall be an honored and beloved guest under our roof. Till then, one side-rill of bliss is wanting to the full stream of our lives.

Within a year after our marriage, Mr. Floyd met the usual fate of men of his class. Paralysis and softening of the brain took him away from the hard pavements and the granite steps he had trodden so long. The mind, absent from his vacant eyes, no doubt still flitted about on 'Change, holding ghostly scrip and restlessly seeking phantom quotations. It was not with us; but we took his body and cared for it a little while, until the mechanical life ceased. Then reverence forbade us to wonder what occupation the soul could find in the world beyond stock.

When spring came, I took Isabel to the Cross-Keys, and gave her the first bud from the little rose-tree on my mother's grave. Kindly hands had kept away the weeds, and the letters on the head-stone were no less carefully cleaned from moss and rust than those which contained my boyish promise of immortality, — the epitaph on Becky Jane Niles. Our visit was a white day in the good Neighbor's life. She tried to call me "Mr. Godfrey," but the familiar "Johnny" *would* come into her mouth, confusing her and bringing the unwonted color into her good old face, until she hit upon the satisfactory expedient of addressing me as "Sir." I don't believe any garment since her wedding-dress gave her as much pleasure as the black silk we left behind us.

Thence we went to Reading, where Isabel speedily won the hearts of Uncle and Aunt Woolley, and so homeward by way of Upper Samaria. Our visit was a great surprise to Dan Yule, who had not heard a word about me since I burned "Leonora's Dream" under the willows. Mother Yule was dead, but Dan and his "Lavina" kept the plain, cheerful spirit of the old home intact, and it was a happy day we passed under their roof. A messenger was sent to Susan, who came over the hills with Ben and their lusty baby to tea, and the lively gossip around the fire in the great kitchen chimney-place scarcely came to an end. I was glad to hear that Verbena Cuff was married. Then first I dared tell the story of the lime-kiln.

And now, having carefully disposed of so many of the personages of my history, after the manner of an English novelist of the last century, my readers may demand that I should be equally considerate of the remainder. But the Rands and the Brattons have passed out of the circle of my knowledge. The same may be said of the Mortimers and Miss Tatting. Mears has married a wealthy widow, and given up art for artistic literature. (I betray no secret when I state that he is the well-known "Anti-Ruskin," whose papers appear in "The Beaten Path.") Brandagee, has, perhaps, undergone the greatest transformation of all; and yet, now that I know mankind better, I can see that it is in reality no transformation, but a logical development of his nature. Having scraped together a little capital, — probably obtained by following Fiorentino's method, — he ventured into Wall Street one day, was lucky, followed his luck, rapidly became a shrewd and daring operator, and is supposed to be in prosperous if not brilliant circumstances. He lives at the Brevoort House, and spends his money liberally — upon himself. He is never known to lend to a needy Bohemian. "Gold," he now says, "is the only positive substance." I frequently meet him, and as the remembrance of my vagabond association with him has left no very deep sting, we exchange salutations and remarks, — but there is no intimacy between us, and there never will be.

"But what of Bob Simmons? And of Jane Berry?" the curious reader may ask. Shall I again lift the veil which I have dropped upon two unfortunate hearts? — Rather let it hang, that each one may work out in his own way the problem I have indicated. Whether the folly of a day is to be the misery of a life, or, on the other hand, a too easy rehabilitation of woman's priceless purity shall be allowed to lessen the honor of the sex, are the questions which my poor friends were called upon to solve. Whichever side we may take, let us not deny human pity to the struggle through which they must pass, before peace, in either form, can rest upon their lives.

If there is any lesson in my story, I think it is not necessary that I should distinctly enunciate it. In turning over these pages, wherein a portion of my life is faithfully recorded, I see, not only that I am no model hero, but that my narrative is no model romance. The tragic element, in externals, at least, is lacking, — but then mine has been no exceptional life. It only runs, with different undulations, between the limits in which many other lives are inclosed. Why, then, should I write it? Because the honest confession of a young man's fluctuating faith, his vanity and impatience, his struggle with temptations of the intellect and the senses, and the workings of that Providence which humbles, sobers, and instructs him, can never be without interest and profit to his fellow-men. If another reason is wanted I will give it, and with it a final, fleeting tableau of my present life.

Time, nearly a year ago. Scene, the little lawn in front of our cottage on Staten Island. I am sitting on the veranda, in an arm-chair of Indian-cane, with Jean Paul's "Titan" — a very literary *nebula*, by the way, the fluid essence of a hundred stars — in my hand. Isabel, fuller and rounder in her form, but with the same fresh, clear beauty in her features, (how often I think of Penrose's exclamation, — "She is my Eos — my Aurora!") sits near me, but her work rests on her lap, and her eyes follow the gambols of Charles Swansford Godfrey, whose locks of golden auburn shine out from the rift in a clump of box, where he is seeking to hide from his little sister Barbara. It is a charming picture, but I am too restless to enjoy it as a husband and father ought.

I throw down "Titan" and pace up and down the veranda with rapid strides. Isabel looks towards me, and a shade (think not that another eye than mine would notice it!) passes over her face. I stop before her chair.

"Bell," I say, "what shall I do? I have tried hard to give up my literary ambition, and enjoy this lazy, happy life of ours, but the taint sticks in my blood. I am restless because my mind is unemployed: these occasional sketches and stories don't fill the void. I want a task which shall require a volume. Can't you give me a subject?"

"I have been feeling the same thing all along, John," says she, "and only waited for you to speak of it. Don't aim too high in your first essay: take that which is nearest and most familiar. Why not tell the story of your own life?"

"I will!" I exclaim, giving her a kiss as a reward for this easy solution of the difficulty.

And I have done it.

THE END.

www.ingramcontent.com/pod-product-compliance
Lightning Source LLC
LaVergne TN
LVHW021312110826
845150LV00003B/550

* 9 7 8 1 4 2 5 5 5 8 0 5 5 *